THE INJUSTICE OF VALOR

Gary Corbin

Double Diamond

P U B L I S H I N G

This book is a work of fiction. Names, characters, businesses, incidents, and dialogue are either drawn from the author's imagination or are used fictitiously, and are not to be construed as real. Any resemblance to actual events or persons, living or dead, is entirely coincidental.

ISBN: 1-7346152-9-X
ISBN-13: 978-1734615296

To my beautiful wife, Renee,

without whose support and inspiration

I could not write a word

Part One

The Redeemer

Chapter One

The Wolf Moon ducked behind the clouds seconds after the power grid failed, plunging the small Berkshires town of Greenville, Connecticut into unexpected darkness. No home lights pierced the gloom. The seasoned veterans of year-round rural living, many of whom had already gone to bed, hadn't yet switched over to their generators. The few still awake knew that these outages, so common in the mountains in winter, rarely lasted longer than a few minutes. Fewer still drove anywhere that late, so the winding roads like Torrington River Highway and Valley Park Drive remained unlit by glaring headlights.

It was the perfect time and place to dump a body.

The corpse splashed into the Torrington River's swift current almost exactly midway between sunset and sunrise on the 14th of January, in the year 2020. Stirred up by stiff winds and threatening rain, the river swallowed the body into its black depths within seconds, each crash of whitecaps against the surface an exclamation point to its haughty declaration: You are mine. Nothing but food for the fishes, more bones to litter its cluttered floor.

So it happened, anyway, in the imagination of The Redeemer, who dumped the body down the rocky embankment into the frothy cascades below. No time to wait around to see the fish devour the victim's flesh. Unfortunate. To have seen the muscle and skin torn from bone would have been the evening's crowning achievement. Ridding the planet of another sex offender who'd escaped justice, freed on some bullshit technicality argued by unethical lawyers, was a sight to be witnessed. Savored, even. Hell, the lawyers responsible for the perv's freedom should join the fray.

Perhaps someday they would. In a perfect world, the event would be televised.

But not tonight. Tonight the world became a better place, with one less sicko to prey upon the innocent. One fewer person—or perhaps several—would risk the painful, humiliating experience of that almost unimaginable violation of their body.

Almost unimaginable. To the unlucky few, they were all too imaginable.

Unforgettable, even.

Chapter Two

Five minutes before noon, on the first Tuesday of March, 2020, the phone rang on the desk of second-year Clayton police officer Valorie Dawes. The jangling noise echoed off the pale walls and government-issue metal desks of the Women's Anti-Violence Emergency (WAVE) Squad office, a long, rectangular room shared by four other officers and detectives. The ringing phone shattered Val's concentration on the case file open on her computer screen: Isaiah Dinker, a suspected sex offender trafficking in child pornography. With reported cases of violent crime against women on the decline—a temporary phenomenon, Val believed—the Clayton police chief had sent some so-called "crossover" cases. Cases like prostitution rings, illegal gambling shops, and indecent exposure, of all things.

Val hated the "crossovers." They diverted resources and effort away from the critical need of protecting women from rapists and domestic abusers. The department had plenty of people better suited to chasing down so-called "victimless" perverts. A misnomer, in her mind—anything that contributed to the culture of lawlessness or exploited women and children had "victims." However, those crimes often proved impossible to solve and almost never resulted in a conviction. Worse, it wasn't even her case—fellow WAVE Squad detective and mentor, Shannon O'Reilly, had asked her to help. Which she did, because her own cases were even more boring.

So, anything that distracted Val from her current task was a welcome diversion.

The phone rang again, and this time she noticed it was the main WAVE Squad line, and it also rang on all the other desks in the office. Desks that, for the lunch hour, remained unoccupied.

"Dawes, WAVE Squad," she said, answering on the third ring.

"Hey Val, it's Gil." Her boyfriend, Gil Kryzinski, headed the Dispatch unit, two floors down in the Clayton Police Department Headquarters building. "We've got something for you."

Val sat up at attention, a broad smile creasing her face. "Hello to you, too, Sergeant—I mean, *darling*," she said in a teasing tone. Almost without thinking, she brushed a stray lock of her jaw-length, light brown hair away from her face, a gesture that Gil would find attractive—if he were there to see it.

"Sorry," he said, his tone warmer. "I expected Petroni or Grimes to pick up. How's your day going?"

"Tedious," she said. "The suspect I'm investigating has no priors, no friends or family, and is a self-employed bike mechanic. In short, nothing even remotely interesting—and my other cases are even more dull."

"Glad to break up the monotony, then. Got a pen?"

"Please tell me you have something good," she said. "Dinner reservations, perhaps. Or, you know, a fresh case. Something in WAVE's actual mandate."

Gil laughed. "You *want* me to tell you there's been another horrible act of violence against a woman in Clayton? My sweet Valorie, I dare say you're getting jaded."

"Did you not hear the part about dinner reservations?"

"Touché. Unfortunately, this might prevent you from getting dinner at all this evening." Gil's voice lowered an octave. "Greenville PD found a body in the river. They think it's one of ours."

"One of our what? Female residents?"

"Suspects," he said. "A cold case you guys worked a few months ago. Guy by the name of Jason Larkin. Ring any bells?"

"Sure," Val said. "Grimes led on that case, and I helped him with it. Teen predator, got picked up soliciting high school girls with drugs and alcohol. I thought he was in jail."

"Larkin's case went to trial a week or two ago, and he walked on a technicality," Gil said. "Some irregularity about his confession, I think."

"Bobby never mentioned that." Val groaned. Grimes, her partner, enjoyed a stellar reputation as a master interrogator, getting confessions from suspects no one else could break. But he could get too aggressive at times. Especially lately. Doctors had been treating his nine-year-old son with radiation for a brain tumor for the past six months. The ordeal left him short on sleep and shorter on patience.

"Anyway," Gil said, "Greenville wants to meet with you guys, compare notes, see if you can share any leads on who might've offed him. Today, if possible."

"That's over an hour away," Val said. "And upriver from us. How would one of our bodies float up to them?"

"It wouldn't," Gil said. "Which is why they're keeping jurisdiction. Anyway, they need our help. I promised someone would call this afternoon."

"I guess that means me," Val said. "Crap. This is what I get for volunteering to answer phones while everyone else gets Chinese food."

"I'll make it up to you. Meet me at one out front? I'll make reservations at Girardo's."

"Ah, wish*es do* come true," she said with a grin. "I can taste the cioppino already."

Val's smile persisted long after she'd hung up the phone and dug into the Larkin file. She and Gil hadn't gone out for lunch together in months. She'd blamed the tough winter weather and the alarming news about this so-called COVID-19 outbreak that closed so many restaurants out of panic and short staffing.

She also wondered if some of the spark between them had faded. An impromptu lunch might provide just the right antidote to their relationship doldrums.

***

Val got up to speed on the Larkin case and briefed Grimes on the news when he returned. She sloughed the task of calling Greenville onto him, though. "I have a lunch date, and anyway, it's your case," she said.

"I can't drive out there today," he complained, rubbing his balding pate and slumping in his chair. "Bobby Junior's got a follow-up appointment at the doctor's, and I promised Audrey I wouldn't miss this one."

"Try to handle it by phone, then." Val's stomach growled. She paused at the door, noting the worry on his face. The ordeal had aged and exhausted her partner. "If there's no other way, I'll go, okay?"

"Thanks, Dawes. You're the best." Grimes stared at his hands, folded on his desk, and appeared on the verge of tears.

Val exited to the hallway, pulling the office door shut behind her. Poor Grimes. She crossed her fingers, hoping the doctor's news later that day would bring him fresh hope.

The news at the restaurant, though, brought only distress.

"Closed due to COVID," read the hand-written sign on the front entrance of Girardo's.

"I take it you didn't make reservations," Val said, turning toward Gil.

Gil's dark brown eyes showed disappointment, and his muscular, six-two frame shrank into a dispirited slump. "They didn't answer. I assumed it was because they were too busy," he said. "Crap. Well, what else is open?"

They found an open hoagie shop nearby, but a sign on the door informed them they could only enter if they wore masks. "I left mine back in the office," Gil said. "Since when do restaurants require masks? I thought that was only hospitals and doctors' offices."

"It's getting more common, according to CNN." Val searched her coat pockets and found a spare—a used one. "I'll pop into Rite-Aid and buy a box of them."

Gil stopped her and took the used mask from her. "We're

fine reusing each other's masks," he said. "Hell, we're swapping spit and God-knows-what-else on a regular basis. If we haven't infected each other, we ain't got it."

"If you say so," Val said, dubious.

They ordered—turkey club for Val, meatball sub for Gil—and took a booth in the corner, away from other patrons.

"I can't wait for this COVID thing to pass," Val said. She tasted her sandwich. Bland. She should have asked for extra mayo. The sacrifices she made to stay slender.

"Some people say it'll be over by Easter," Gil said around a mouthful of meatball sub. "Let's hope so." He swallowed and took another bite of his delicious-looking sub, the aromas of tomato and garlic wafting over them. He never, ever worried about his weight. Somehow he stayed fit anyway.

"Nobody who knows what they're talking about says that," Val said. "Have you seen the news reports? Hospital emergency rooms are getting overwhelmed, and doctors have no idea of how to treat it. It's pretty scary."

Gil shrugged. "I keep hearing it's like a bad case of the flu."

"People die of the flu every year," Val said. "Besides, Mr. I-Never-Get-Sick, when's the last time you've gotten a flu shot?"

He waved her off. "In sixth grade. Which is also the last year I got the flu. So there's that."

Val started to argue, then held off. He could be so damned stubborn, and, besides, she didn't know any more about it than he did.

They nibbled at their lunch in silence for a while, their appetites dulled by the tension rippling through their conversation. After several minutes, Gil sipped his lemonade and asked, "So, are you heading to Greenville this afternoon?"

She shrugged. "Grimes is calling them to see what's up. He can't go, though, so I told him I would."

"So you won't be home for dinner?" His tone

seemed...agitated.

"I...don't know. Why? You made plans?"

Gil rolled half of his sandwich up in its wrapper and closed his bag of chips. "I guess I'm having leftovers."

"Gil, come on. What's eating you? Something seems...wrong."

He looked away. "I'm fine."

She rested a hand on his arm and spoke in a soft voice. "Did I do something wrong? What did I say?"

"Nothing. You've done nothing wrong, Val. I told you, I'm fine."

She waited. Nothing more came. "You seem upset. If I—"

"I'm *not* upset, okay?" He glanced at his watch. "Are you almost done? I gotta get back soon."

She glanced at her sandwich, half-eaten on her tray. "I'll finish it at my desk."

"Let's go, then."

They held hands while walking back, but left their masks on until they returned to headquarters, neither one talking until they reached the door.

"Let me know about Greenville," he said, giving her a perfunctory hug.

"Are you sure nothing's—"

"I'm sure. Val, I'm sorry, I just..." He frowned. "There's something on my mind, and I need time to work through it."

"Let me help you."

He shook his head. "Don't worry, okay?"

She waited until his eyes met hers. "And we're okay? You and me?"

Gil smiled, pulled off his mask, and kissed her. "We're better than okay. We're amazing."

Val held him for a long moment.

She worried.

***

The desk officer at Greenville Police Headquarters showed Val to a meeting room, and a pair of detectives joined her moments later.

A tall, lanky African American man with short-cropped hair graying at the temples offered a handshake. "Phil Gramercy, Homicide," he said, shaking Val's hand with a firm grip. "This is my partner, Martina Torres."

Val shook the younger partner's hand, a petite Latina with large, dark eyes, olive skin, and black hair tied up in a bun.

"We appreciate you making the trip," Torres said. She slid Val a disposable cup full of black coffee. "Your partner couldn't make it?"

"Family issues. He sends his apologies." Val sipped the coffee. Acrid and lukewarm. Typical police-issue. "So, one of our suspects floated in unannounced last night?"

Gramercy chuckled. "I appreciate your humor, Detective."

"Officer."

"Beg pardon?" Gramercy hesitated.

"I haven't made detective yet. So it's just Officer Dawes."

"Huh." Gramercy and Torres exchanged knowing glances. "You're authorized to share case information on behalf of your department, though, right?"

"I am." Val hadn't checked on that with her boss, Sergeant Brenda Petroni, but she didn't see any reason why not.

"Right, then. Down to business." Gramercy slid a folder toward her and continued talking while Val perused its contents. "Larkin floated in, as you put it, around 4:00 a.m. this morning. Prints matched your suspect. Autopsy's not done, but there was evidence of narcotics in the system. He didn't die of natural causes."

"Massive bruising on the head and neck area, no bloating, no water in the lungs...he didn't drown, either." Val scanned the photos of the body, a pudgy white man with black hair and a two-day beard. "Looks like strangulation, and the strangler was in no hurry."

"That's our guess." Torres pointed to a thick red line

around the man's throat. "We're thinking a rope or cable of some kind, a few hours or more before he hit the water." To Val's questioning look, she added, "Most recent call on his cell phone was early evening March first—last Sunday. The ME's initial guess is he's been dead at least a few days, maybe a week."

Val scanned the rest of the file, which wasn't much. She glanced at the two detectives, who both seemed nervous. Wanting to speak, but holding back. "What else should I know?"

"Victim was weighed down...we're guessing rope or twine tied to a heavy object." Gramercy cleared his throat. "We're, ah, scanning the river to see if we can find any cement blocks."

"Okay." From his hesitance, Val sensed he still had more to tell. "And?"

Torres shot Gramercy a pleading look, her eyes widening. She cleared her throat, glaring at Gramercy.

"Detective?" Val said to him.

Gramercy expelled a noisy breath, drummed his fingers on the table. "There is something else."

"I'm all ears." Val closed the file.

Gramercy glanced at Torres again, made up his mind. "The body was found naked..." His voice trailed off, as if searching for words.

"Not uncommon in these cases," Val said. To his quizzical look, she went on, "I've pulled a body or two from the river in Clayton."

"Huh." He regarded her a moment. "Well...because of that, we discovered some unusual...markings, I guess you'd call it."

Val waited, recalling the markings on the body she'd found. "Like, tattoos, or stab wounds, or something?"

"Markings may not be the right word here." Torres's impatience with Gramercy showed in her exasperated voice.

"So, what is?" Val glanced from one detective to the other, wondering which one would ever get to the point. If any.

"Hairlessness." Torres cleared her throat again. "The body's chest and pubic regions were shaved clean. With some fresh cuts and scrapes, so we're thinking it was hurried, and...not done by the victim."

"By the perp, then?"

"Or a very sadistic lover," Gramercy said with a smirk.

"And...there's one more thing," Torres added, nudging Gramercy's arm.

Gramercy sighed and lowered his voice. "The body was castrated. Also recently."

"His testicles were cut off?" Val said.

"The entire scrotum," Gramercy said. "But not the penis."

"Not the *entire* penis," Torres corrected him. "Just the tip."

"Also fresh?" Val's stomach got a little queasy.

Gramercy and Torres nodded.

"And not just the foreskin," Gramercy said. "This was no circumcision."

"Brutal." Val chewed on her upper lip for a moment. "Well, those are some interesting clues."

"There's something else." Torres lowered her eyes and pushed a plastic evidence bag toward Val, containing an off-brand cell phone.

"The victim possessed a burner?" Val shook her head. "How, if you found him naked?"

Torres coughed. "It was inserted in the, ah, rectal cavity. Don't worry, forensics cleaned it after analyzing it." She slid it closer to Val. "There's a video on there you should see. We can't let it out of the building, which is why you needed to come here."

"You couldn't email it?"

Torres shook her head.

Gramercy cleared his throat. "We haven't figured out how to download it off the phone. There's some weird copy protection software on there...anyway, take a look."

Val donned a pair of latex gloves Gramercy provided and

removed the phone from the bag. It powered on without a password and a single icon appeared on the home screen. Val tapped it and the video played, displaying the victim's naked and unmutilated body lying on a table. She squirmed a bit. Naked bodies, even her own, made her uncomfortable sometimes. Something she had to get over.

"How do I turn on the sound?" Val asked.

Gramercy shrugged. "There doesn't seem to be any. Just watch."

The video showed a gloved hand placing a piece of paper over the dead man's groin. The page contained Larkin's name, then the word "Pervert!" in large letters and a date: January 14, 2020. About two months ago. The date, Val recalled, of Larkin's alleged crime.

"Interesting," Val said.

"We've only just begun," Torres said.

The video continued. The page disappeared and a new one appeared: "He will pay." Same large font.

"How prescient," Val said.

The gloved hand reappeared, this time with a straight razor, which the gloved hand used to shave the victim's pubic area. More squirming on Val's part. Then the hand appeared again with a surgeon's scalpel.

"Is this going to show—"

The cutting began before Val could finish.

"Oh my God." Val held her stomach. "This is sick. Holy cow, the bleeding! Wait...doesn't that mean...the victim's..."

"Still alive," Torres finished for her.

Val stopped the video. "I don't need to see more. Um, you really could've told me that on the phone."

"It carries a lot more impact if you see it, don't you think?" Torres said.

Val sipped her water, eager for her stomach to settle. They sat in silence for a minute or two.

"So, we were hoping you might enlighten us on the victim's past, his case, anything that connects those clues to a perp," Gramercy said. "Larkin was an accused sex offender, correct?"

Val nodded, still taking shallow breaths through her mouth. "Picked up for soliciting sex with underage girls, plying them with drugs and alcohol. His confession got tossed on procedural grounds." No need to elaborate that the mistake had been Grimes's.

"Since that evidence got tossed, we can't access it in the system," Gramercy said. "So we were hoping you'd provide some names."

"Not the victims," Torres said, "since they're underage and protected. Maybe their family or boyfriends, say. People with possible motive."

"And who might be mad enough to chop his balls and dick off," Gramercy said.

"Well, just the tip," Torres said, grinning.

Val hesitated. "I...don't know the legalities of that." Her gut grew even more queasy. "I might need to check with our lawyers."

"I thought you said you can help us," Gramercy said, his voice growing tense. "That you had the authority."

"I do," Val said. "Still, even the lead detective would need a lawyer's sign-off. Victims' rights and confidentiality and all that."

"We're not going to arrest them," Torres said. "We only want to talk to them."

"If you do, they'll ask how you found them, and it'd pretty obviously be me." Val shook her head. "I want to help—really I do. But we need to go by the book. For so many reasons."

"How long will that take?" Gramercy asked, his voice calmer.

"I'll get on it as soon as I get back. Sooner, even." She picked up her cell phone and speed dialed. "Hey, Gil. Can you text me the number for Legal?"

"You in trouble?" Gil asked. "What's up?"

"Nothing. I need some advice on evidence-sharing with Greenville. It's a little delicate."

"So, you did go?"

Shit. She'd forgotten to email him she'd gotten stuck with this duty. "Yep. Heading back soon. Probably not by dinnertime, though, as you suspected."

"Right. Okay. I'll send you that number." His voice, clipped and tense. Upset that she hadn't done as she'd promised.

"Thanks. And Gil? I'm sorry I forgot to tell you. I just–"

"Not a problem. This job sucks sometimes. I'll see you when you get home."

He hung up without saying goodbye.

Chapter Three

Sitting in an unmarked squad car the following afternoon, Val squinted through department-issue field glasses at the home of suspected child porn dealer Isaiah Dinker. The small Cape Cod-style house on Clayton's low-income inner Eastside had seen better days. Bare spots on the roof showed where storms had torn off several shingles. Two broken basement windows let in the chilly March breeze, and soon rain, judging by the dark clouds and the smell of moisture in the air. Broken glass reflected the afternoon's dim light where the gravel driveway met the narrow side street, littered with potholes.

"Anything?" Her partner, Detective Bobby Grimes, had spent the last hour complaining about this stakeout. He occupied the driver's side, toward the traffic lane, with Val on the passenger's side, toward the curb. Another team, Shannon O'Reilly and her partner, third-year Patrol Officer Damari Price, staked out the rear of the house. O'Reilly had requested a warrant for a search of Dinker's home for hard evidence of child pornography, as well as stalking and harassing several women. It also included a request for a DNA sample to link him to a handful of rape and pedophilia cases.

Rape. Pedophilia. It all struck too close to home. Val wanted this guy as bad as Shannon did, for reasons far more personal.

But the judge hadn't yet issued the warrant. So they needed to wait. For now.

"Nothing," Val said, pulling the binoculars away from her face. "No lights, movement, or sound. I don't think he's home." She shaded her eyes, despite the gray skies. Her clear, light-hazel eyes were sensitive to the light on even the cloudiest of days.

"Come on, Judge," Grimes said, folding his hands in prayer and lifting his eyes heavenward. "Give us that damned warrant."

Val sighed. She'd expressed her doubts to O'Reilly about the strength of their evidence against Dinker, but Shannon waved her off. "All we need is probable cause," she'd said. "We've got that in spades."

Maybe Shannon was right. An experienced cop with fifteen-plus years of service, Shannon had obtained more than her share of doubtful warrants. She also enjoyed a way-above-average success rate of getting suspects locked up because of them. Seventy-five percent, according to O'Reilly. Almost unheard-of. Val, only in her second year of police work, had requested a grand total of one warrant. Sergeant Petroni "gifted" her the assignment three months before, on Val's 24th birthday. The judge denied the damned thing by lunchtime.

"Someone's coming," Grimes said in a hushed whisper. He pointed down the street, where a beige van with a bicycle-and-wrench logo headed toward them. "It's him," Grimes said. "He's a bike mechanic, right?"

"According to the file." Val trained the binoculars on the van, following its progress as it slowed and pulled into the driveway. Moments later, a wiry, bearded man in his late thirties got out of the van. Several inches short of six feet tall, his long, greasy hair hung around the shoulders of grease-spotted, orange-brown overalls. "Yup," she said. "Definitely our man. Should we grab him?"

"Not until the warrant comes in," Grimes said. "If we spook him, he could escape inside and hide or destroy evidence. We gotta wait."

Val agreed. Mistakes in gathering evidence could mean the difference between Dinker spending his life in prison—or never seeing the inside of a jail cell.

Their radio, turned down low for security's sake, crackled with O'Reilly's voice. "What's he doing out there?" she asked. "Does he show any signs of knowing we're watching him?"

Grimes grabbed the mic. "Nope. He's just going about his business."

The radio went silent, and Dinker unloaded an expensive-looking bike from the rear doors of his van. With a thick frame and lots of cables and chrome everywhere, it looked like it weighed a ton. However, despite his diminutive size, Dinker hefted it one-handed over his shoulder with ease. He kicked the van doors closed and carried the bike around the side of the house. A door slammed shut, presumably the side entry. Lights flickered on inside the garage, then in several other rooms of the house.

"See anything interesting?" O'Reilly asked over the radio.

"Negative," Grimes said.

"He dashed inside awfully fast," O'Reilly replied. "What's up with all the lights?"

"Maybe he hates living like a bat," Grimes said with a grin. "Lots of people turn on lights. So what?"

"I don't like it," O'Reilly said. "I want to get a closer look."

"Don't screw up this search," Grimes said. "You go in without a warrant, there'd better be gunfire."

"I can arrange that," O'Reilly said, laughing.

Val's breath caught. "Please tell me Shannon isn't suggesting firing on him first to justify some sort of 'immediate threat' excuse."

Grimes shook his head, disgust written all over his face. The radio quieted again.

"Shouldn't we provide backup?" Val asked, concern rising. She'd gone into a house once without backup and nearly gotten killed.

"For what? A glimpse into the windows? Nah." Grimes popped an M&M into his mouth and chewed. "And if they're doing anything more than that, well, they shouldn't be."

Val heaved a deep breath, but said nothing. Grimes outranked her, as did Shannon. She hoped they knew what they were doing.

A long, quiet minute passed. Val wanted to ask for an update, but any radio noise would alert the suspect to what

Shannon and Price were up to. They waited a bit longer.

Minutes later, O'Reilly appeared around the front of the garage, her bright blond locks tied up under her police hat. Shannon rarely took to the streets in uniform, but they provided advantages in dangerous situations. They provided a place for everything one might need: weapons, radios, cell phones, and more. Perhaps more important, they did a great job of hiding Kevlar worn underneath for protection.

Shannon, sidearm held upright in both hands, peered into the window of the garage door. After several seconds, she squatted down fast on her heels, gazing back at Val and Grimes, a look of alarm on her face. She grabbed her mic with her left hand. A second later, her voice crackled over the radio in a hoarse whisper. "Okay, guys, time to move in." She disappeared around the corner—returning to the rear entrance, Val guessed.

"What's up?" Grimes asked.

"He's on to us," Shannon replied. "Destroying evidence. Let's go!"

"What evidence? How?" Val asked.

"You heard the woman," Grimes said, pushing open the car door. "Move it!"

Val jumped out the passenger's side and drew her weapon as she ran. Though Grimes had a head start and stood six inches taller, her natural athleticism and regular exercise regimens—daily running, weekly jiu jitsu, gym workouts—kept her in far better shape. She passed him ten yards out and reached the house's front door in a matter of seconds. Grimes huffed up behind her, out of breath. He stood to one side of the entry and motioned to Val, then to the door handle.

She tried it. Locked, of course, with a dead bolt. The door itself, though, was cheap-looking, and showed signs of previous damage and dry rot. Easy peasy. She retreated a step, jumped up, whirled, and karate-kicked the door between the handle and the deadbolt's key cylinder. It gave a bit, a loud *Crack,* indicating its weakened state. A second kick and the door flew open, splinters flying, the deadbolt still suspended in the frame.

"Remind me to never piss you off," Grimes said. "Let's roll."

Val entered and scanned the living room, crouched, weapon ready. A quick glance around revealed worn, mismatched furniture, grimy parquet floors, and a large, wall-mounted TV—the only newish-looking item in the place. Grimes followed her through the home's modest kitchen, a 1960s throwback with undersized, rounded appliances, floral wallpaper, and built-in wooden cabinets. It all looked like it was last cleaned during the Cold War.

Per protocol, Grimes covered Val while she crossed the kitchen toward the garage. Then they swapped again: she crouched, gun ready, while he tried the door. It opened without resistance. Grimes shoved the nose of his weapon through the doorway, then relaxed.

"You two got here fast," he said, then turned and waved Val through.

She followed him into the garage, where Damari Price knelt on the suspect's back, the man's hands already cuffed. Price read him his rights while O'Reilly donned latex gloves and picked up a blowtorch, lit and blazing, and turned off the fuel valve, extinguishing the flame. "He was about to destroy his hard drive," she said, pointing to a laptop perched upon a workspace counter. The computer's screen displayed a picture of a scantily clad pin-up girl and a prompt reading, "Password?"

"You're sure about that?" Val walked over to a metal bike repair stand, holding the expensive 21-speed Trek e-bike Dinker took from his truck. "Looks to me like he was getting ready to do some work."

"Mm! Mmm-mmm!" the man said from the floor, nodding his head and wiggling under the weight of Price's knee. A wide strip of duct tape sealed his mouth shut.

"Wait a minute," Grimes said. "Why the hell is this man gagged?"

"He tried to bite me," Price said. "When I arrested him."

"Well, Damari, you are one tasty-looking man," Grimes said, grinning. "Or so I've been told." Shannon, stowing the torch in an evidence bag, stared at Grimes, wide-eyed.

Price set his lips on a line and looked away. Val knew him well enough to recognize his angry face, and she couldn't blame him. Though he had a long-time girlfriend, rumors circulated about Damari being gay or bisexual. In the testosterone-laden community of the Clayton Police Department, that resulted in harsh, inappropriate, relentless hazing. Clearly he'd had enough, but didn't dare bark back at his superiors.

Val, though, wouldn't stand for it. "That's fucked up, Bobby," she said. "You know better."

Her partner glared at her a moment, then shrugged. "Sorry, Damari," Grimes said. "You know I love you, man."

"Bobby," Val began.

Price cut her off. "Just leave it." He pulled the suspect to his feet and marched him outside.

"Way to kill the buzz, Dawes," Shannon said, still searching the room. "This was fun until you opened your damned mouth."

"Yeah, it's a real damned party," Val said. "We arrested a guy for doing his job, fixing bikes. The judge is going to love this."

"He held that torch right next to this laptop!" Shannon said. "Which, by the way, is evidence. Bag that damned thing, and bring the power cord. And the external hard drive. I bet that machine's loaded with illegal child porn."

Val hesitated. She was the lowest-ranking officer on the scene, but none of this felt right. She turned to her partner for guidance. "Bobby?"

"Do what you're told," he said. "If this goes south, don't worry. It's not on you." He spun to face Shannon. "If this guy walks because you jumped the gun—"

"He won't," Shannon said. "Mark my words. He's going to prison for a long, *long* time."

Chapter Four

What do you mean, he's gonna walk?"

Shannon's shouts echoed off the walls of the WAVE Squad bullpen area, causing actual pain in Val's ears. She covered them, too late, and ended up poking Shannon in the hip with her elbow when the detective jumped up from her chair at the meeting table.

O'Reilly leaned over the table, bumping Val's elbow again, and pushed the papers in front of her away with a flourish. "This is beyond stupid! We had that guy dead to rights!"

Their boss, Sergeant Brenda Petroni, also stood, her stocky frame a solid, stable counterpoint to Shannon's wiry energy. She patted the air with her hands to calm Shannon down. "The District Attorney's office doesn't feel the charges will stick," Petroni said. "The man's lawyer is arguing that you lacked probable cause for entry—"

"He lit a damned blow torch!" Shannon yelled, wadding up the papers and tossing them on the floor.

"Wait. Are you talking about Dinker? The child-porn perv we busted two days ago?" Damari Price asked, incredulous.

Val glanced at her copy of the pages O'Reilly—and apparently Price—refused to read. Though Petroni's report explained everything, Shannon hadn't made it past the first paragraph before exploding in rage. Understandable, perhaps, but still. Grimes, sitting next to Petroni, threw his copy into the garbage. Only Val bothered to read it to the end. Which, she guessed, made her a charter member of the Young, Naive Cop Club.

"To repair his customer's broken bike frame," Petroni said. "It's his job." She ran her fingers through her short brown curls, showing streaks of silver in recent months.

"And it's my job to get creeps like that off the street," Shannon said. "The DA is making that impossible."

"What about the laptop?" Grimes asked. "Did anything come of that?"

Petroni grimaced. "Can't use it. 'Fruit of the poisonous tree.' If the search is no good, the evidence you grab is no good."

"What about the warrant?" Val asked. "Did that ever come through?"

Petroni shook her head. "The judge denied it. Same reason: insufficient evidence to justify probable cause."

"We had plenty of evidence," Shannon said, plopping back down into her chair. The defeat in her voice betrayed her lack of conviction. "The neighbor's twenty-four-year-old son said Dinker bragged about—"

"Hearsay," Petroni said. "Not very compelling. The DA says none of this would stand up in court."

"He's not even willing to try?" Price asked.

Petroni's head wagged again. "He called it a lost cause."

"This sucks," Grimes said. "That perp's gonna victimize another kid, maybe dozens, and there's nothing we can do."

"Regardless," Petroni said, "it's out of our hands. For now." Her lips curled into a catlike smile. "All this means is, we have to get more and better evidence. If he's guilty, no problem, right?"

"If *who's* guilty?" The unexpected male voice startled them all. Val recognized it, but it seemed wrong and out of place. It couldn't be...

It was.

In the open doorway stood the balding, rotund figure of a man who, six months before, was suspended from the Clayton Police Department pending investigation. A man accused of conspiring with urban terrorists who'd shot almost a dozen women entering and leaving family planning clinics.

Detective Ed "Tackle Box" Simpson—complete with

badge and gun.

***

Val recoiled in disgust at the sight of the gray-suited figure filling the entrance of the WAVE Squad office. The once-disgraced and ridiculed "Tackle Box" Simpson, badge and weapon on full display, appeared fully empowered to resume his duties as a senior detective in the Clayton Police Department.

Even more disturbing was that he'd shown up in WAVE Squad headquarters.

"What in hell are you doing here?" Val blurted out before she could stop herself. Her colleagues, and even her boss, shot her admiring glances.

"Reporting for duty," Simpson said with a haughty grin. He stepped into the room and held out a folded page of letter-sized paper toward Petroni, who stood and accepted it in a limp palm. "Your newest, senior-most team member. Here are my orders, compliments of Chief Mahoney."

Petroni scanned the document as at least two gasps sounded around the table. Val wasn't sure if one of them had come from her or not. Petroni cursed under her breath and refolded the orders, then addressed the others. "It all seems in order," she said in a low voice. "Well folks, welcome the newest member of our team." She glowered at Simpson. "Seniority, we'll work out later."

"If you'll notice, paragraph three makes me lead detective on the Isaiah Dinker case," Simpson said, far too pleased with himself. "I hope that doesn't ruffle too many feathers around here."

O'Reilly laughed out loud, and Val nearly joined her. "All yours, Detective," Shannon said. "I don't think it'll keep you up too late at night."

Simpson glanced from one face to the other, his smug grin fading. "What's up? Come on, brief me on the latest. I want this sonofabitch's ass nailed to the wall and I mean right now."

"Go wait by the exit door at county lockup," O'Reilly said. "I'm sure his lawyer will be happy to explain."

"Explain what?" He glared at her, then realization swept over his sweaty, ruddy face. "They're letting him walk? Why?"

"Some bullshit technicality," Grimes said. "Ask your pals in the DA's office."

Val opened her mouth to provide details, but Shannon caught her eye and gave her head a tiny shake. Val read that look: *Don't sell me out here.* Val kept quiet.

A short, slender woman with broad shoulders and dark hair cut into an uneven, collar-length shag entered the office behind Simpson. Dressed in black pants, a white blouse, and an orange casual blazer, IT Security Analyst Shelby Clearwater held in both hands the laptop they'd confiscated from Isaiah Dinker's house. The gleam in her eye communicated excitement, at least to Val, who'd nurtured a close friendship with Shelby in recent months.

"Detective," Shelby said, holding the laptop aloft toward O'Reilly, "did you want to see what I found on this guy's machine?" She glanced toward Val, as if to offer her a peek as well.

Dammit. Val wanted to know what she'd found, but given the DA's decision, that couldn't happen.

"That needs to return to Evidence Control," Petroni said. "He's hitting the street any minute now."

"That doesn't mean we can't take a quick peek at what our techies uncovered," Simpson said, reaching for the laptop. He got a hand on it, but Shelby yanked it away.

"We can't use it?" Shelby asked, crestfallen.

"That depends on what you mean by 'use,'" Simpson said, stepping around Shelby and shutting the office door. "I've heard computers are excellent tools for, ah, *educational* purposes."

"You heard me, Simpson," Petroni said. "It's not evidence. None of it, no matter how compelling."

"Not for our current set of charges," Simpson said,

grabbing for the laptop again. For the second time, Shelby was too quick for him. "However, there's no law against us learning what type of creep he is for future reference."

"Are you sure about that?" Val inserted herself between Simpson and Shelby. "Seems to me it's at least an invasion of privacy, if not an unlawful search."

"He's already done the search," Simpson said, indicating Shelby. "What's the harm if we look?"

"*She*," Shelby said, heading toward Shannon. "*She* did the search."

"Who's *she*?" Simpson said, his face curled up into a puzzled frown. He pointed at Shelby. "I thought he did it."

"I did," Shelby said. "I prefer the pronoun 'She.' Please use it."

"I prefer to arrest perverts, not work with them, but I don't always get my way, either," Simpson said with a sneer. "Now give me that fucking laptop."

Shelby hustled around the table behind Grimes and Price, hiding the laptop behind her back. "Sorry," she said. "I'm not breaking the law to satisfy your lascivious curiosity."

"What bullshit!" Simpson pushed toward Shelby. Val and Shannon blocked his path. "Come on, work with me here," he said in a more reasonable tone. "There's a big difference between bending a few evidence rules and doing what this perv is up to. You can see that, can't you?"

"Forget it, Simpson." Petroni folded her arms across her chest. "Stand down. *Now.*"

Simpson fumed, then threw up his hands in disgust. "No wonder the streets are crawling with child molesters and rapists. You guys give up before you even get started."

"Officer Price, would you please escort Ms. Clearwater to Evidence Control?" Petroni said. "Simpson, in my office. The rest of you—back to work." She turned on her heel and strode into her private office.

Val caught her partner's eye, who shook his head in disgust. "Nice first day on the team, Tackle Box," Grimes muttered to Simpson. "What'll you do for an encore? Plant some drugs on a teenaged prostitute?"

Simpson stiffened at the reference to his hated nickname, but didn't answer. Instead, he followed Price and Shelby with his eyes as they shuffled toward the door. As they passed him, he blocked their path and pointed a finger at Shelby.

"You, young *man*," he said, spittle flying, "better keep your damned nose clean. One step out of line, and I'll nail your ugly little ass. You got me?"

Shelby glared up at him. "I guess you'd know all about stepping out of line and getting caught." She swallowed hard. "Welcome back from suspension, *Tackle Box.*"

He lunged at her. Price intercepted the shorter man's attack and pushed him with unexpected force. Simpson stumbled backward and would have fallen had he not backed into a desk with his oversized rear end. He waited until the threesome reached the door, then called out his final warning.

"Just remember, Clearwater," he said, his voice hoarse. "Watch yourself. Because I'll be watching you, too."

Val and Grimes exchanged glances again. What a joy this guy was going to be.

Chapter Five

After a week of mutilated corpse videos, the botched stakeout, and her unpleasant afternoon with Simpson, Val figured the next work week couldn't be any worse than the prior one.

Wrong.

Gil texted her around 4:30 the following Wednesday, informing her he wasn't feeling well.

> Took an Uber home early. Nothing serious, probably a bad cold. See you at home.

Val's spine chilled. She messaged back:

> Not COVID, I hope?

A long minute later, he responded.

> No, I can still taste food, etc. Sleep should help.

Val worked past 7:00 p.m., running down leads on the Jason Larkin case while hoping to hear from Shelby about what she discovered on Dinker's laptop. Nothing on both fronts. Finally, she gave up and made it home in record time. She found Gil in his bathrobe, eating cereal on the couch and watching *Jeopardy!*

"How's my guy?" she said, heading over to sit next to him.

Gil held up his hand, stopping her. "In case I'm contagious, best if you don't come too close. I figured I'd sleep on the sofa tonight, to be safe."

"Ugh. Okay." Val made a tuna sandwich and sat on the recliner opposite him. "Do you have a fever or anything?"

He shrugged. "A slight temperature—one-oh-one. But no sore throat or headache. Mostly an upset stomach, coughing, some aches and pains." He coughed as if on cue, a hoarse, raspy sound full of phlegm.

"Let me get you some cough medicine or aspirin."

"I'm fine." He coughed again, this time for several seconds.

"You don't sound good." Five feet away, Val wondered if she should stay even that close.

"Yeah, well, being sick sucks. What the fuck do you expect me to sound like?"

Val froze, mid-bite of her sandwich. "Jeez. Sorry I offended you."

Gil set down his bowl, too fast. The spoon splattered raisin bran and milk onto the coffee table. "Dammit!"

"I'll get a towel—"

"Stay put and eat. I'm not lame." He grunted to his feet and pounded out to the kitchen, returning with a paper towel. He wiped up his mess and tossed the soggy paper on top of his half-eaten cereal.

The silence percolated for a moment. Then Val could stand it no longer. "Gil, have I done something wrong?"

"No."

"Hurt your feelings in some—"

"Goddammit, I said no!"

Val froze again, then set her sandwich down and folded her hands. "Please don't shout. What did I do to upset you?"

Gil glanced at her, and his face fell. He rubbed his face, rested his chin on his palms, elbows planted on his knees. "I'm sorry, Val. I'm an asshole when I'm sick. You've done nothing wrong."

"Okay. I appreciate knowing that." She forced a smile to lighten the mood. "I've never seen you sick before."

"You think that's funny?"

Val's mouth hung open. No matter what she said, he seemed determined to bite her head off. "Look, you seem to want to be alone, and I'm okay with that. Let me know if you need anything." Grabbing her plate, she escaped to the bedroom, closing the door behind her.

She lay on the bed, munching her sandwich without enthusiasm. Gil's tantrum had sent her mood into a dark place, too, and she needed a distraction or else she'd dwell on it. She picked up a book she'd started over Christmas, but she couldn't remember what she'd read before, and it frustrated her more. She returned to page one to start over—

"Val." Gil stood in the open doorway, looking haggard. Moisture glistened in his eyes. "We need to talk," he continued, his voice hoarse.

Dread washed over her. Here it comes.

Taking heavy, slow steps, he stumbled to her makeup table and sat in the chair, without making eye contact.

Val set down her plate on the bedside table, her appetite nonexistent. Possibilities, all terrible, flew through her mind. He'd gotten fired. He had cancer. Or, worse, he would tell her what he hated about her, why their relationship wasn't working, and how it was all her fault. She stared at him, mute, worrying her fingers into knots on her lap.

Gil heaved a long, dramatic sigh, and she knew, dammit, he was dumping her. A lump rose in her throat and she gripped her hands together to keep them from shaking.

"I got a call yesterday," he said, "from someone I...well, hell. You know all about her. Why am I being so obtuse?" He shook his head and fixed her with an unsteady gaze. "From Jessica."

Gil's ex-fiancée from a decade before. Beautiful, dynamic, and much closer to him in age. Shit!

Val found her voice, thin and quiet, after far too long of a pause. "What...did she want?"

Stupid question. Val knew damned well. Jessica wanted Gil back. And he wanted it, too. Dammit all to hell! Fuck, fuck, fuck!

He heaved another deep breath. "She had bad news."

A heavy burden settled on Val's shoulders. Guilt, for being so selfish. Gil almost never talked about Jessica. So far as she knew, they hadn't spoken in over a year. For her to call, the news must be terrible. "Is...is she sick?"

Gil glanced away. "Not her." Another deep sigh. "Her dad. He and I...used to be close. Jessica sometimes complained that I loved him more than I loved her, and...well, she wasn't always wrong." A grim smile, and another pause. "He was like a father to me. I was the son he never had. When she and I split up, he was so upset...we haven't spoken since."

"I'm sorry." Val scooted to the foot of the bed and reached across to him, offering a hug.

He waved her hands away. "I don't want to infect you. But, thanks."

Val sat back, stung by Gil's abrupt response. Tried to keep the hurt out of her tone. "What's the prognosis?"

He licked his lips and locked eyes with her again. "Pancreatic cancer, stage four. Or five, whatever it is when you're about to die." He swallowed. "He has days, maybe hours."

Val nodded. She didn't want to say this, but her conscience forced it out. "You should go to him—wait." Realization dawned. "You can't. You're sick."

Gil grimaced. "He's dying. I can't make him worse."

"You can make other people sick. They won't even let you inside the hospital like this. Not with this COVID thing going on."

He shrugged. "They already sent him home from the hospital. All the COVID patients are crowding everyone else out, particularly people they can't save anyway."

"That's horrible."

"Yeah." He wiped his face and coughed again. "I think you're right about this COVID thing after all. It's worse than we all thought."

Another long pause. Val fretted, not knowing what to say. "So, when will you go?"

"Tomorrow, early. Hopefully I'll feel better."

"I can drive you."

"No." The word darted out of his mouth, urgent and fearful. "The pandemic down there is even worse. It's spilling over from New York and a lot of towns have declared emergencies. They probably will here, too. In the meantime, though, you should avoid going. I'll come back right away, I promise," he said, his words rushing out over her objections.

Val chewed on her lip, wishing she could touch him, hold him, make him feel better. Hell, make herself feel better.

"Get some rest," she said. "I'll see you in the morning."

***

Val rose early Thursday morning, dressed, and washed up in silence, careful not to wake Gil still snoring away on the couch. She headed into the kitchen to make coffee and found a note in Gil's handwriting on the counter.

> *Val,*
>
> *Sorry I was such a grouch last night. Guess it's true what my mom always said—I'm the world's biggest brat when I get sick.*
>
> *The plan is to drive to New Haven around noon today. I'll be back tomorrow at the latest, unless things go south with her dad's condition. I will miss you every minute I'm gone.*
>
> *I love you. — Gil*

Val reread the message twice, taking in its implications. Gil might spend the night in New Haven. With Jessica. His gorgeous ex-fiancée.

He didn't disclose that the night before. Probably because he knew she'd get insanely jealous.

She started the coffee maker and sat at the kitchen table, calming herself. Gil wouldn't cheat. He sure as hell wouldn't tell Val in advance about it, wouldn't walk into an obvious cheating opportunity without putting up mental and emotional defenses. And other than his recent grumpiness stemming from the news of Jessica's father, and from being sick, he'd shown no signs of unhappiness with Val. No indications that he might stray.

Still.

Val glanced at him, snoozing on the sofa, and her stomach grew queasy. She imagined him entangled in Jessica's long, lean body, her red hair flowing over his shoulders in a passionate embrace—

She poured coffee into a travel mug and hurried out the door.

***

Val sleepwalked through her morning at work, every task and boring meeting a dreadful slog. Simpson interrupted Sergeant Petroni multiple times during the WAVE Squad staff meeting, inserting his insufferable opinions on matters with which he had no familiarity or expertise. Afterward, Val made what seemed like dozens of calls to leads on cold cases Petroni assigned her, all leading to nothing. Then came a pair of announcements that put her into a funk.

"Quick heads-up." Sergeant Petroni spoke to the room from the doorway to her office. "That guy Dinker you guys arrested last week? The one who walked?" She paused, her expression grim. "He's disappeared."

"Already?" Grimes said. "Didn't we keep eyes on him after booting his ass to the curb?"

Petroni smirked, then grew serious again. "Yup. Hilton and Rowse from Vice. Somehow Dinker got wind of it and snuck out without detection. His house is empty, he's not at his bike shop, and nobody knows how he did it."

Simpson rolled his eyes and faked a loud snore. Grimes, Price, and O'Reilly laughed out loud. Val had to admit, it was pretty comical, and too close to what often happened with stakeouts.

A heavy weight fell into the pit of Val's stomach. Not only did he escape arrest. Now he would set up his slimy operations outside their jurisdiction. Crap. "When did they last see him?" she asked.

Petroni grimaced. "Friday."

"The *same damn day* we let him go?" Simpson shouted. "And we're just hearing about this now? Why?"

"My guess is poor technique," Grimes said, and added with a sneer, "Didn't you train Hilton when he came on board?"

"That was over ten years ago, you stupid—"

"Enough!" Petroni glared at both of them. "No more of this bickering. Next one who utters so much as a discouraging word gets written up. Am I clear?"

The room went silent. Simpson hummed "Home, Home on the Range," and Val couldn't decide whether to laugh or hit him, so she did neither.

Clearly Petroni didn't hear it, because her expression and tone softened. "We also have some good news. Shannon?"

O'Reilly stood at her desk, as did her partner, Damari Price, at the adjacent desk. "Last night, Damari and I arrested and booked the Sorority Row Rapist. Damari, you broke this case, so you should tell it."

"The perp confessed to raping three women between September and December on the Clayton State campus," Price said, beaming with pride. "We acted on a tip from a women's safety hotline we set up after the second incident. Thanks to the hotline, we arrived in time to prevent a fourth rape."

"Damari's being too modest," O'Reilly said. "He kicked the crap out of the guy when the suspect tried to run. I mean, bad. This guy won't be able to molest anyone ever again." She punctuated her remarks by miming a knee to a man's groin.

Val imagined the beating and, despite her appreciation

for Price removing a rapist from the streets, the description made her wince.

"That ought to help you in the detective exam coming up," Simpson said, shaking Price's hand. "Congratulations, son."

The reference to the exam—the city's term for written job applications—dampened Val's spirits further. Simpson's return to active duty reduced the number of open detective positions from two to one. With dozens of likely applicants, everyone expected fierce competition for the available slot. Val prided herself on closing multiple high-profile cases in her first eighteen months on the job. But Gil and O'Reilly often told her that the hiring process favored recent success—something she couldn't claim much of.

"We should celebrate," Petroni said. "This is a big deal."

"Drinks at the Blue Line at five?" Shannon said. "First round's on me."

"Hear, hear!" Grimes said. "Dawes? You in?"

"On a school night?" Val said. "Don't we all work tomorrow...?"

The disapproving stares around the room told her she'd get no support for that sentiment.

"We're not talking about an all-night bender," Shannon said. "Just a quick salute to success."

Val sighed. "Sure, I can join for a quick one." Without Gil, dammit.

"I'll be there," Simpson said. "And I hope to make an announcement there, too. Right, Sarge?"

Petroni winced. "We'll see. Oh, by the way. Tonight at the bar, we all need to wear masks. New COVID rules. Starting Monday, we gotta wear them here at the office, too."

"How the hell are we going to drink with masks on?" Simpson said. "How asinine."

"Wear them any time you're standing," Petroni said. "Seated at a table with your drink, you can take them off."

"Sit? At a bar? How are we supposed to mingle?" Simpson shook his head. "Fucking politicians ruin everything."

Val turned away so Simpson couldn't see the disgust on her face. Maybe before 5:00 p.m. rolled around, she'd come up with a reason to miss the event. At that moment, even catching COVID sounded like a better prospect than spending an hour with Tackle Box Simpson.

Chapter Six

Connor Cox crouched behind the budding wild blueberry bush on the sloping bank of Clearwater Creek, listening. By straining and keeping extra quiet, he detected the high-pitched chirp that sounded almost like the one his mom played on her computer that morning. She'd shown him a picture, too. The bird was called a "Purple Martin," though he hadn't spotted any purple birds yet. Only brown or black, with maybe a little blue. They were good hiders, these Martins.

Maybe he needed to use his binoculars.

He opened the case holding the ultra-cool "field glasses," as his dad called them when Connor unwrapped them on Christmas morning, trying hard not to make any noise. But when he unsnapped the case, it made a sound, and the bird chirping went quiet all of a sudden. Then they started up again, so he guessed he'd remained hidden well enough not to scare them away. Even at nine years old—officially, not "going on nine" anymore, as of two weeks ago—he could be a really awesome scout. A spy, even. He was, his dad bragged once, "stealthy," a word he looked up which meant super-duper good at keeping secrets and staying invisible. Even without a magic cloak like Harry Potter.

Connor lifted the binoculars (a cooler word than "field glasses," he decided) up to his eyes, then remembered his dad's instructions. Always, he said, put the strap around his neck first, in case he dropped them. Which he would never, ever do. But anyway, Dad said, so he did. Then he used the adjuster knob on top so that it wasn't fuzzy when he looked through. Sharp as a knife, like his dad said. Like he'd practiced in the weeks since Christmas, waiting for the snow to melt and for his ninth birthday to come. At age nine, Mom and Dad allowed him to play outside the property lines by himself for an hour at a time. An hour, no longer. With his spy gear.

Connor gazed through the binoculars. All he saw at first was a bunch of sticks and branches. He swept left, right, up, and down, like the guy in the instruction video on mom's computer, until he spotted the bird.

Holy cow! To his naked eye, the bird seemed tiny, like it would fit in his shirt pocket. In the "binocs"—an even cooler word the video guy used to show what an expert he was—the bird filled his "field of view," cool term number two. It seemed purpler up close, and rougher, as if someone had rubbed the bird's belly like a dog's, and made the feathers stand up. The Martin's head turned and its black eyes stared back at him, shiny and beady, unblinking, so alert. Kind of mean-looking, even. Then its short, curved beak opened and it chirped again, and yes, it was definitely his bird chirping! He'd done it. He'd found a Purple Martin, like his mom said he would!

Mom had challenged him with finding the bird as part of his science homework, his favorite subject. Not birds so much as rocks and outer space, but a good scientist had to know something about all the sciences. Anyway, this bird was pretty cool.

Connor stared at his subject so intently that he didn't hear any footsteps or breathing or anything before someone tapped him on the shoulder.

"Anything interesting in that spyglass of yours?" a man behind him asked.

Connor lowered the binoculars and spun around to see who'd spoken. Although he should have known by the voice, he also recognized the man's face. Similar to his father's, with lighter-colored hair, like Connor's, and a beard. Same long nose and small teeth like Dad's. He also wore nicer clothes than anyone should wear in the woods.

Brand-new khaki pants, chinos, and a crisp white shirt, with a maroon sweater tied around him like a scarf instead of wearing it like a normal person. Mom would kill him if he wore his good pants out here.

"Hey, Uncle Am." Connor stood, even though that would scare away the Purple Martin, and it did, darn it. "Just looking at birds."

Connor hoped he wasn't in trouble. Dad told him to stay away from Uncle Ambrose, that he was dangerous and mean, although he'd always treated Connor nicely.

"Hello, Connor. I hope I didn't disturb your mission." Uncle Am always seemed ready to laugh when he talked, like everything in the world was funny. The opposite of his parents, who were always serious.

"No. I finished my homework, so I guess I ought to go home."

"Come on, Con-Man. Don't interrupt your play on my account. I was just taking a quick walk and…well, I've never seen you out here before."

"I'm nine now." Connor stood up straighter, taller. He'd topped four-foot-three on his birthday, and almost 70 pounds, which Mom said made him a big boy. "Dad says you shouldn't call me Con-Man. It's der…dour…de-rigor—"

"Derogatory? Nonsense. Anyway, I don't mean it like that. But I'm sorry. I'll always call you Connor now, okay?"

Connor nodded, then that queasy feeling came up in his stomach, the one he got whenever he'd accidentally done something bad. "Kind-of it doesn't matter because I'm not supposed to play with you."

"I see." Uncle Ambrose's face lost its almost-ready-to-laugh expression. He looked kind of sad, even. "Well, I don't want to get you in trouble with Mr. Connor Theobald Cox III. We all know what that would mean."

"I'd get grounded. And I'm sorry, Uncle Am, but I really want to keep exploring my science out here. There's not much nature on The Grounds." The Grounds is how Mom and Dad always called the property inside the walls of their fifty-acre estate. Connor didn't know how big fifty acres was, although it had to be a lot, because it included a horse stable, with two horses. And he'd hardly ever been outside The Grounds before. In fact, he'd never even seen the "far side," the part where Uncle Am lived in "The Cottage."

"Okay. I'll leave you to it then." Uncle Ambrose made a face, like he wanted to say more. Then he shook his head and walked away. He didn't seem to care how much mud got on his new khaki pants.

Connor waited until Uncle Am made it over the hillside. Then he spied on him through his binoculars to make sure he kept going. Which he did, all the way back to The Grounds, where the woods stopped and where there were no Purple Martins to find.

***

Val always made it a point to arrive late to after-work celebrations. People called her anti-social, and not always without justification. Her real reason, though, was simpler: she didn't drink as much as her colleagues. The old guard like Simpson and Petroni seemed to prefer harder liquor, and more of it, and faster than the younger ones like her and Price. Even some of the younger cops drank like frat boys on nights of celebration. As it turned out, Damari Price, the man of honor at tonight's happy hour, had gotten a bit of a head start already, too.

Once inside, Val noticed that almost no one at the Blue Line Tavern, a cop-friendly watering hole a few blocks from headquarters, followed the new rules requiring masks and six feet of distancing. She slipped on a blue surgical mask and made her way toward the crowded bar.

"Dawes!" Price, though he knew better, wrapped a long, clumsy arm around Val's shoulder. "For a minute, I thought you weren't gonna make it!" He yanked her in close for an uncomfortable hug and pressed his lips onto the top of her head for a sloppy kiss. On her hair. Ew.

"Wouldn't miss it, Damari." Val wiggled out of the

embrace and searched for a napkin to dry the wet spot on her head. "Congratulations on the big collar. It's good to have that guy off the streets."

"He's an animal!" Price gulped a half-shot of whiskey and slammed the empty glass on the bar. He gestured to the busy bartender already serving O'Reilly and Petroni ten feet away. "Another one, please, Ronnie!"

Val glanced around at the crowd, mostly men and women in blue packing the tavern to near-capacity. Her old bosses from Liberty Heights precinct, Lieutenant Lawrence Gibson and Sergeant Travis Blake, waved from across the room, inviting her over. Both wore masks, two of the few who did. She mimed getting a drink and bellied up to the bar to wait her turn, slipping ahead of a tall guy she didn't recognize.

"Hey, Dawes, whatcha drinking?" The rotund, balding man next to her grinned and high-fived her before she recognized him behind his mask. She'd met forensics specialist Dalton Fletcher on the abortion shooter case they'd worked with Ed Simpson. "I owe you at least a drink or two. Let me buy you one." He lifted his mask, a cloth one bearing a Red Sox logo, to sip amber liquid from a highball glass.

"I'm the one who owes you," Val said. "Isn't the first one on Shannon, anyway?"

"Hell yeah, girl!" O'Reilly toasted her from the other end of the bar and clinked glasses with Petroni. Neither wore masks. "Put your first one on my tab. After that, it's up to the good-looking guys to get you drunk. Hey, Fletch, you sure your wife's okay with you buying drinks for a pretty woman half your age? She's got a boyfriend, you know. Big guy." She laughed and took a swig of something red in a cocktail glass.

"Just as long as he doesn't grab her ass," said the male voice behind Val, who—right on cue—placed a slinky hand on her hip. She elbowed him in the ribs, hard, then turned to see his face.

All the blood in her body rushed to her feet.

"Ben *fucking* Peterson?" Val said, in what could have been a whisper or a shout. The guy she'd shimmied in front of to get to the bar. "What are you doing here?"

"Good to see you too, Dawes." A maskless Peterson smirked down at her, his lanky frame hovering over her like a creepy wet blanket. His brown hair had grown shaggy since she'd last seen him, over a year before when she enlisted the help of the Hartford Police Department on her first big case. "I see you've kept in good shape, despite the year on donut patrol."

She rolled her eyes at the disparaging term for her desk job and turned away from him. "Yeah, you look good, too— for you. You're a little out of your jurisdiction, aren't you?"

He laughed. "I don't work for Hartford anymore." He leaned in a little too close and murmured into her ear, "You might say I've moved on to greener pastures."

"Green pastures is the perfect spot for a bullshit artist like you." She wiggled away and tried in vain to attract the bartender's attention.

"You guys know each other?" Fletcher asked.

"Dawes and I were Academy sweethearts," Peterson said. "Even worked a case together. Remember Richard Harkins?"

"Oh, yeah. He was a bad one." Fletcher raised his glass in salute. "Congratulations, you two. You made a good team, eh?"

"Hell ya," Peterson said.

"No," Val said louder and, rising onto her tiptoes, leaned over the bar. That got the bartender's attention. "Red wine?"

The bartender nodded and held up a single digit. One minute.

Again a hand pressed onto Val's body, this time firmly on her ass. Without looking, she grabbed the hand's thumb and twisted it backward. Hard.

"Ow! Jeez, Dawes, I was trying to help you up so Ronnie can see you." Peterson winced, rubbing his right hand with his left.

"Try it again and I'll break it off. And I don't mean your finger."

Fletcher guffawed, slapping the bar, and knocked over his drink glass. He wiped it up with a soggy bar napkin and signaled for a refill.

"That's no way to talk to your new teammate." A voice she recognized, but not Peterson's or Fletcher's. Worse, though. Far, far worse. Ed "Tackle Box" Simpson.

"What do you mean, 'teammate'?" Val's drink appeared, and the bartender slid her a coaster.

"That's my big announcement," Simpson said. "Ben here is joining Clayton PD as my partner on the WAVE Squad."

Val, taking a sip of wine, nearly spit it out.

"Good pinot?" Fletcher said with a grin.

Val waved Petroni over. "Is this true? Is this guy part of the team?"

Petroni, pushing into their little circle next to Simpson, grimaced and nodded. "He starts tomorrow. Sorry, Val, I couldn't loop you in on this in advance. HR rules and all."

"Brenda, for God's sake! He—he—" She couldn't finish. This couldn't be happening.

"I thought you'd be thrilled," Simpson said with more than a little sarcasm. "Didn't you guys used to date or something?"

"*No!*"

"Kind of," Peterson said with another evil smirk.

"Socializing in a group setting does *not* constitute dating. Jesus!" She sipped her wine. Terrible. "Simpson, didn't you check his references?"

"Of course," Simpson said. "All glowing."

"That can't be even remotely true." Val took another sip of her awful wine and gave up on it, abandoning the drink and the group at the bar. She shot Peterson a final, withering glare, making sure it registered. Then she stalked out the back of the tavern onto the outdoor patio, not caring about the slow, chilly drizzle that coated her hair and face. She had the patio to herself. Good. She whipped out her phone, found the name she needed in her contacts, and dialed.

"Hartford Homicide. Marshall."

"Jalen. Val Dawes."

"Valorie! Long time no see. How are you? How's my boy Gil doing?"

"Good, and...good. We're still dating."

"Ah, shucks. So much for my chances of recruiting my old pal up to Hartford. What's up? Got another case I can help you with?"

Val sighed. "In a way. I need to ask about one of your former partners. My old academy classmate, Ben Peterson."

"That asshole? I mean, that fine, upstanding officer of the law? Wait, no, I stand by my original comment. Fucking waste of oxygen, that boy. Why? Is he applying down your way?"

"Worse." Val rubbed her aching forehead. "We already freaking hired him, apparently."

"Are you guys crazy? For what? Hopefully nothing more responsible than crossing guard. Useless sack of muscle, that guy. Couldn't tie his shoes without watching a YouTube video first."

"To make matters worse, they're assigning him to my team."

"Ha! You guys must be desperate."

"You know Ed Simpson? He *requested* him."

"Old Tackle Box? He must hate you."

"That's the only rational explanation." Val's gut boiled in frustration as she realized the truth of Jalen's conclusion.

"Well, silver lining, Dawes. Ben's so incompetent, he'll get himself fired there, too. Hopefully, before getting anyone killed."

That upset Val's stomach even more. She needed food, and not the pub grub from this greasy spoon.

"Listen, Val, I gotta go. You give Gil a punch in the nose for me, will you?"

"Thanks, Jalen." She put her phone away and wrapped her arms around her midsection, hugging herself hard. Damn. This was bad. Worse than bad. She couldn't have dreamed a worse scenario.

"Valorie! Are you sure? What about your boyfriend?"

Peterson's voice startled her, not only for what he said, but for how loud and close it was. As in, right by her ear. She turned to face him.

A moment later, she couldn't breathe. Not with his arms enveloping her in a crushing embrace, his mouth plastered over hers, the taste and smell of whiskey overwhelming. His hands found her ass and squeezed, and he pressed his full weight against her, backing her against the half-wall inside of a server's prep station. She fought against him, pushing him, but her arms got trapped between their bodies, her legs bent back, her weight falling backward. Finally, she pulled her mouth away and thrashed her face side to side to evade his gross, pervasive tongue. She tried to yell "Stop!" But his mouth covered hers again, his teeth crushing against her lips, his hands grabbing tighter on her butt. She bucked against him, creating a few inches of separation, then drew back her head, and landed a vicious head-butt on his forehead.

He howled and let go, stumbling back. She swung at him, but only grazed his cheek, and dodged his hand, swinging back at her. She kicked him, aiming for the crotch, instead finding purchase on his shin, and a second kick landed hard on his kneecap. He screamed again and collapsed onto the ground. She followed up with two more quick jabs of her heel into his spleen, and he curled into a ball on the wet stone patio.

"Don't. You. *Ever*. Touch. Me. Again!" Another full-strength blow to the ribs, harder than she'd ever kicked a soccer ball, and he howled in pain on the ground.

"Jesus, Dawes, what the hell are you doing?" Simpson

stood in the doorway leading back into the bar, mouth agape.

"Defending myself." She stood over Peterson, breathing hard. A crowd gathered behind Simpson, all men. All older. Many of them, according to rumor, competing with her for promotion to detective.

"Crazy bitch!" Peterson screamed, still curled up on the wet stone of the patio. "She came on to me, started making out, then all of a sudden she starts throwing punches. This chick's insane!"

"That's ridiculous," Val said. "I never—"

"Ben's telling the truth," Simpson said. "I saw the whole thing." He cast an evil glance at Val, complete with a cruel grin. "Dawes, you're going down for this."

The men standing behind Simpson stared at her, shaking their heads in disbelief, some in utter dismay...and some with smug expressions of sheer joy.

"Your police career," Simpson said, pointing a finger at her, "is over."

Chapter Seven

Val arrived home in a state of shock, rage, humiliation, and loneliness. She'd left the bar a few minutes after pleading her side of the story about the confrontation with Ben Peterson to Lt. Gibson, Travis, and anyone else who would listen. Her few friends and allies seemed to believe and side with her. Simpson and his cronies sided with Ben and claimed she'd started it all, even though none of them were there when it happened. The others...she couldn't tell. Which, by itself, upset her.

Val sat in her car for a minute or two, hands gripping the wheel, still shaken. A cool drizzle coated the windshield, blurring the rays of light from Gil's front porch into a harsh, yellow glare. She should go inside. With no Gil there, though, the place seemed...uninviting. Foreboding, even. Probably cold—he liked to turn down the thermostat when they left for the day. She never complained—he owned the house, and her monthly contribution to help pay the bills amounted to far less than half, at his insistence. But it meant the house would greet her with a chilly reception.

Which, she mused sourly, would still be the case if Gil were home.

Val shook off that thought. She had no reason to believe that. Right?

She sat for several more minutes, mired in a funk. Then her stomach growled, a reminder that she'd skipped dinner, and she couldn't think of anything good and quick in the fridge.

She needed Gil. He'd promised to call on his way back from New Haven, but nothing yet. Impatient with waiting, she speed dialed him.

"Hey." His voice sounded rough and tired. "I was about to call you. Good day?"

"No. Terrible day, and a worse evening. Ben Peterson got hired onto the WAVE Squad, grabbed my ass at the bar—"

"I'll kick his ass!" Gil said, and though he sounded like he couldn't hurt a fly in that moment, it warmed her heart.

"And," she went on, "I may get suspended for kicking the shit out of him. How was your day?"

He took a few moments to respond. "That's awful. Suspended, seriously? How bad did you beat him?"

"He'll live. However, a few so-called witnesses—well, Peterson and Old Tackle Box—claimed I started it, which is bullshit."

"That asshole. I *will* kick his ass."

Val laughed, but her mirth died away quickly. "Gil...I'm in trouble. I wish you were here."

"Oh, honey." A long exhalation followed, and his voice grew even rougher. "I wish I were there, too, except then I'd be giving you this flu or cold or whatever I've got. Damn thing is knocking me on my ass. I can hardly stay awake."

She sat up, on full alert. "Are you sure it's not COVID? Have you gotten tested?"

"Not yet. Pretty much all I've done since I got here is sleep. I saw Hank, though, from a distance."

Val guessed Hank was Jessica's dad. He'd never mentioned the man's name. "How's he doing?"

"Not good." Gil coughed, then again, erupted into a coughing fit that lasted twenty or thirty seconds. When he regained his ability to speak, he continued, "Jessica's preparing for the worst."

Val took a deep breath, willed herself to ask the polite question. "How's she doing?"

"She's a wreck. She's no Stoic, and they were so close." He paused. "She's going to need some help."

"I see." Val did the math. With Gil sick, Jessica falling apart, Hank dying... "I take it you won't be coming home tonight, then."

He sighed. "The way I'm feeling, I doubt I could make the two-hour drive anyway. And, I hate to say it..." He lowered his voice. "I think we'll be holding a funeral here in the next few days."

"We?"

Gil cleared his throat. "Jess asked if I could help, and...you don't mind, do you?"

Val's throat tightened. She hated playing the role of needy girlfriend, but if there was ever a time...

"No. Of course. Have you said goodbye yet?"

"I'm hoping to in the morning."

"Okay. Well, feel better. I love you."

"You, too. I mean...you know what I mean."

"Of course." Val hung up, hoping like hell he meant what she thought he meant—what she *wanted* him to mean.

But he didn't say it. Why not?

Because Jessica was too close by, maybe?

Right then, Val hated everything about her life.

***

Val got up early after another restless night and went for a three-mile run to shake off her doldrums. She showered, changed, and arrived at work a half-hour early, hoping to have the office to herself for a bit. To her surprise, she wasn't the first to arrive.

"What are you doing here at seven-thirty in the morning?" Grimes asked.

"I could ask the same of you. Doesn't Bobby Junior have treatment today?"

"Later. I came in early to get a head start. What's your excuse?"

"Can't sleep. Might as well work." Val poured a cup of coffee and the two sat at their front-to-front adjacent desks.

"I heard about the scuffle at the Blue Line." Grimes slurped his coffee. "The rumor-mill version, anyway, which

I don't believe for a minute. What really happened?"

"The new guy, Peterson—"

"Who you knew from before, right?"

"Right. First, he got all handsy in the bar. Then he assaulted me on the patio, all groping hands and sloppy kisses. I fought him off, took him down kind of hard, and the next thing I know, Tackle Box accuses *me* of assaulting Peterson."

"Okay, that's not far off of what I heard," Grimes said. "You're sure you didn't do anything that could be mistaken for coming on to him?"

"What? No. Of course not." Val shot him an irritable glare and noticed Sergeant Petroni listening in from the doorway to her office.

"You didn't see anything?" Petroni asked Grimes.

"I hadn't made it there yet," Grimes said. "I ran to the pharmacy after work to get some meds for my son. By the time I got to the tavern, Simpson and Peterson were gone. But Sarge," he said, turning to Petroni. "Rumor is this Peterson character is joining the team?"

Petroni nodded, a glum expression on her face. "Dawes, bad news. Simpson and Peterson are filing formal complaints. Sexual harassment and assault. There's going to be an Internal Affairs inquiry, and they're demanding you get suspended in the interim."

"That's ridiculous!" Val jumped to her feet, splashing coffee onto her desk. "It's the exact opposite of what happened, and Simpson knows it. Why is *he* party to this complaint, anyway? Neither of us touched him."

"Tackle Box says you flirted with him in the bar and pushed him 'violently' when he tried to separate you from Peterson."

"Flirted with *him*? Of all the—! Both claims are lies. *All* of this is a lie. What the hell is going on?"

"Sounds like Simpson's going all-out for revenge for getting him suspended, and he found a willing accomplice," Grimes said. "If it helps, Val, I'll stand up for you. You wouldn't do anything like that."

"It won't help much," Petroni said. "However, it won't hurt, either. For now, try to keep your distance from Simpson and Peterson until we can sort this out."

"How?" Val said. "They work here!"

"Peterson won't start until Monday, and Tackle Box is using his old office for the time being," Petroni said. "So, stay off the second floor, and I've told him to stay the hell out of here."

Val settled into a grumpy funk at her desk. The funk deepened after she repeated the story for Shannon O'Reilly and Damari Price when they showed up, ten minutes apart, around 8:00 a.m. Both expressed support for her, though, like Grimes, neither had seen anything, except both recalled Val and Peterson "chatting" at the bar before the dust-up.

"We weren't chatting," Val said. "He grabbed my ass, and I was trying to stop him."

They left her alone until Grimes left at 10:00 a.m. for his son's doctor visit.

A few minutes before noon, Shannon hung up from a phone call with an ashen expression and called everyone together around the meeting table.

"I just got word that Isaiah Dinker's body washed up on the riverbank this morning," Shannon said. "Strangled and mutilated."

"Mutilated how?" Price asked.

"Let me guess," Val said. "Pubic region shaved? Scrotum removed, penis decapitated?"

Shannon stared at her, mouth agape. "How did you—"

"Same thing happened to Larkin, up in Greenville." Val frowned. "Did they find a burner phone up his butt?"

Shannon's jaw dropped further. "They did," she said. "Holy crap. Sarge, do you know what this means?"

Petroni frowned, a loud rush of breath escaping before she spoke. "Yes, Shannon, I do." She hung her head and shook it in disgust.

"What?" Price said. "Someone explain it to me?"

"It means," Val said with a growing sense of dread, "we have a serial killer in our midst—one who targets accused sex offenders that have been set free."

"Murders," Petroni said, "that we will investigate like any others."

"Not frigging likely," Shannon said. "Half the detectives in the department would rather give this killer an award."

The statement rang true to Val, and she wondered whether the killer might be someone who wore a Clayton uniform—and if so, if the crimes would be investigated at all.

***

Val met Shelby for lunch at Hoagie Heaven, a nearby sandwich shop. Both women arrived in a mood as lousy as the cold, rainy weather drenching everything that moved or stood still in downtown Clayton.

"Figures," Shelby said after unwrapping her meatball sub. "I've looked forward to this weekend for months. We're going to drown out there!"

"Where are you going?" Val took a bite of her turkey club. "You and Sanjit, I presume?"

Shelby nodded. "We're going camping near Greenville State Park. The original plan was to sleep in a tent, but with this weather, Sanjit ponied up to rent a small cabin for a week. We might never leave the house if the rain keeps up."

"And that's a problem, why?" Val said, laughing. "Assuming it has a comfy bed, I mean."

"I *enjoy* hiking and getting out into the forest," Shelby said. "Don't you?"

"As long as there's a soft mattress and central heating to go back to, sure."

"It's a two-bedroom place. You and Gil should join us."

"That would be lovely, if only Gil were here." Val chewed a bit of sandwich, which suddenly lost its flavor. "Plus, he's sick. I'm worried he might have COVID, but he refuses to get checked. I've never known a man more afraid of seeing a doctor."

"Reminds me of my brother," Shelby said. "Austin hates science of all kinds, medical and otherwise. Calls it 'White Man's Voodoo.' This from a guy who shuns all association with the tribe and makes his living developing websites."

Val laughed again. "Sorry to make light of it, but you have a way of putting things, Ms. Clearwater. Oh, speaking of computer stuff...any update on that laptop?"

Shelby's expression soured. "From Dinker? Nope. Before I got anywhere, his lawyers forced us to release it back to him. He's dead now anyway, so what's the use?"

Val shrugged. "It might contain clues as to who might've killed him."

Shelby nodded, chewing and wiping red sauce from her chin. "I suppose we haven't seen the last of it, then." She sobered and set down her sandwich. "Rumors are flying about the Blue Line incident last night. It sounded bad."

"It was worse than bad," Val said, "and now it's downright tragic. Internal Affairs is investigating *me* for sexual harassment and assault on that cave dweller Peterson, when all I did was defend myself."

Shelby grinned. "Pretty well, too, from all accounts."

Val surrendered an embarrassed smile. "Fourteen years of jiu jitsu lessons did not go to waste."

"You might need those mad self-defense skills again if Simpson gets his way." Shelby glanced around and lowered her voice. "Word is, he's on the warpath, to use a term often mis-attributed to my race." She snickered. "You white folks and your cultural appropriations. Anyway, and you didn't hear this from me..." Shelby lowered her voice even further. "Let's just say I have ways of tracking what he does on our computer systems. He's poking around your personnel file for dirt."

"Thanks for the warning." Val stared at her sandwich, wishing she had an appetite. "Unfortunately, my file's not as clean as I'd like. This isn't the first time I've brought pain to a member of the male population...and to Ben Peterson in particular."

"Wish I could stick around to help more, but we're leaving as soon as—oops, wait." Shelby's cell phone buzzed and she checked it.

Val nearly laughed out loud when she saw the back of the phone case, a large sticker of a clam shell with a "B" in the middle. Shell-B. She smiled at the pun.

"I stand corrected—we're out of here right now," Shelby said. "Look, the day I get back, I'll pull everything on Simpson from every system we've got. You'll know more about him than his wife does." She gave Val a quick side-hug. "You hang tough, girl. We'll get you through this."

"Thanks, Shelby." Val wrapped up her sandwich and gazed after her friend exiting into the rain. Shelby's support reassured her...until Val realized that she, like Gil, would be away while Val's ordeal only got worse.

Chapter Eight

When Val arrived back at the WAVE Squad a short while later, two fiftyish men in black suits and crew cuts greeted her, their expressions grim. One stood at least six-five, with a lanky build, and both looked like they enjoyed eating puppies for breakfast. Because, Val recalled from their previous meeting about a year before, they probably did.

"Inspectors Finley and Blanchard," she said to the two Internal Affairs investigators. "If you've come to treat me to lunch, I'll have to disappoint you—I've already eaten." She tried her best to appear casual, and hid her hands behind her back so they couldn't see them shaking. Their presence unnerved her, and the fact that they showed up without an appointment was downright intimidating.

Blanchard, the taller and more senior of the two, pointed to the small private conference room next to Petroni's office. "We'd like a word with you about what happened at the Blue Line last night. If you'll join us?"

Finley, shorter and heavier with a six-foot, 250-plus-pound frame bursting out of his cheap suit, led the way into the meeting room. Blanchard waited for Val to follow, then closed the door behind them. Someone had turned up the heat to about 80 degrees, so Val shed her uniform jacket and draped it over a chair at the head of the table. She took that seat on purpose. Petroni coached her a year before on how to take control of IA interviews in case the circumstance should ever again arise. She hoped this one went better than her prior meetings had.

"I understand you and Officer Peterson have a bit of a history," Finley said with a crooked smile. He sat halfway down the table to Val's right and leaned back in his chair, still sporting that shit-eating grin. "Care to share your side of the story?"

"Sure, once my union rep shows up," Val said. "You know as well as I do, that's department policy for IA investigations." Another Petroni coaching point.

"Did we say this was an investigation?" Blanchard ran a hand through his short-cropped salt-and-pepper hair. He sat across from Finley, wiping sweat from his forehead with a handkerchief. Both investigators kept their jackets on, despite the room's muggy heat. "I don't recall labeling it as such, do you, Finley?"

Finley smiled at her and rolled his eyes again, this time at his partner. His ruddy face gleamed with a sheen of perspiration. "Of course, you're entitled to having anyone you want in the room with us," he said. "It might take a lot more time to run them down, though, and—"

"That's okay," Val said. "I'm more than willing to wait. It's important." And hot, especially for the two men in their heavy black suits. Fine with her. She pulled out her cell phone and texted the person who'd recently taken on the union rep role:

Need you at WAVE HQ as my union rep—IA inquiry.

"While we're waiting," Finley said, loosening his tie an inch, "why don't we cover some deep background? Not the events of last night, but stuff that sets the context. Sound reasonable?"

"No," Val said. "It doesn't sound reasonable. My union rep might offer some advice for me on—oh, wait." Her phone buzzed with a text message:

On the 3rd floor—I'll be there in 2 mins.

"They'll be right up," she said.

"They?" Blanchard shook his head. "How many people are you bringing in here?"

"One for now," Val said. "I am allowed to include legal representation as well as—"

"Don't get all legalistic on us, for Christ's sake," Blanchard said, his voice loud and irritated. "That's the problem with you millennials. You won't just have a conversation. Everything's a goddamned federal case. In our day—"

A series of sharp raps on the door interrupted them, and the door swung open. In walked the hefty, bear-like frame of Sergeant Travis Blake, one of Val's best friends on the Clayton police force. Travis carried his uniform jacket draped over one arm, meaning, Val guessed, Petroni had warned him about the room's temperature setting. Which means she probably jacked up the thermostat herself. Val made a mental note to thank her later.

"Hey, Tony. Steve." Travis nodded to Blanchard and Finley. "I see I made it just in time."

"We were just getting started," Finley said, extending a handshake.

Travis crushed Finley's hand in his massive paw, eliciting a wince from the Inspector. He offered a handshake to Blanchard next, who pretended not to notice. Then he hung his jacket over the back of a chair and sat between Val and Blanchard. The two men shared the same height, but Travis's hefty frame dwarfed Blanchard's, almost hiding him from Val's view, and vice versa. Which, Val guessed, was Travis's intent.

"So where were we?" Travis said. "Let me guess. You were reminiscing about the good old days when we first got on the force. How internal investigations trampled over the rights and dignity of patrol officers. So glad we've adopted rules since then that leveled the playing field, eh, Tony?"

Blanchard's expression soured even more, somehow. "Never mind all that. Let's get to the meat of the matter. Officer Peterson filed a complaint, alleging you assaulted him at the Blue Line—"

"Peterson sexually assaulted *me*," Val said, seething. "I

defended myself. Period."

Travis rested a hand on her arm. "Let's listen to the allegations in full before we respond," he said, his voice calm. "Please continue, Inspector."

"Witnesses corroborated Officer Peterson's account," Finley cut in. "Story goes, you and Peterson were flirting inside the bar, talking real close and lots of touchy-feely. Then you invited him to follow you out to the patio area and, you know, one thing led to another."

"No, we don't know," Travis said, cutting Val off. "Please elaborate. Who is this witness?"

"That needs to stay confidential for now," Blanchard said, his tone curt. "The last thing we want is to raise the potential for retribution or witness intimidation—"

"Like I could intimidate Tackle Box Simpson?" Val said, incredulous. "He's twice my size with thirty years seniority, not to mention rank and political pull for God-knows-what reason. *Simpson's* the one trying to intimidate *me* and exact revenge for getting his ass suspended last fall. Rightfully so, by the way."

"Nobody mentioned any names," Finley began, but Val cut him off.

"Come on, it's no secret he's behind all this crap. And stop calling Ben Peterson 'Officer.' He hasn't even clocked in here yet."

Blanchard blew out a noisy breath and leaned around Travis to glare at Val. "The point is, you don't deny assaulting Peterson—"

"Of *course* I deny it!"

"And as my colleague mentioned a few minutes ago," Blanchard said, talking over Val's objection, "you two have a rather sordid history of romantic entanglements intermixed with hostility—"

"There was never a 'romantic entanglement' of any kind between us!" Val stood and slapped the table. "If he's claiming that, he's lying. Hell, everything he's alleged is a damned lie. Every word!"

"Val," Travis said, again in a calm tone. "Please. Sit. Listen." He waited for her to sit, then leaned closer and lowered his voice. "Try not to respond, okay? That only plays into their hands. We need to learn everything they know before volunteering any information. Got it?"

Val nodded, heat flushing her face and neck.

"So, Steve." Travis turned toward Finley, almost turning his back on Blanchard. "Can you provide the details of this alleged 'sordid history'? What is Peterson claiming went on between them that led up to this?"

Finley cleared his throat and cast a quick glance at his senior partner, who fluttered his fingers as if to say, *Go ahead.* "It's, ah, not a real detailed account. Peterson says he and Dawes socialized in a romantic capacity back at the academy—"

"Psht!" Val couldn't hold back her objection, despite Travis's warning. "Ben asked me out, and I—"

Travis held up his hand in front of Val's face to quiet her, nodding at Finley.

"And it didn't end well," Finley finished for her. "Dawes took out her anger on Peterson in a self-defense workshop."

"I executed the self-defense technique being taught—"

"Shh!" Travis's eyes widened, his face growing red with impatience.

Val closed her mouth, swallowed, and nodded.

"A little over a year ago, both were assigned to an inter-city task force. Dawes took every opportunity to humiliate Officer Peterson, who was then an officer with the Hartford force," Finley said. "When the two met up in the Blue Line last night, Dawes engaged in good-natured banter and initiated intimate contact with Peterson. Squeezed right up next to him at the bar, despite the COVID distancing guidelines. He says she dropped strong hints that Peterson should follow her outside into a private space for a more, ah, *private* rendezvous, so to speak."

"That. Is. All. Utter. Bullshit!" Val ignored Travis's consternation and raised hand. "I did no such thing." She thought her blood might boil right out of her skin.

"Then," Blanchard interrupted, his tone impatient, "when Dawes noticed they had company—witnesses to their little make-out session—she panicked, grew violent, and assaulted Peterson. *Allegedly,*" he added when Travis seemed ready to interrupt. "The assault, which Ms. Dawes does not deny and instead claims is 'self-defense,' resulted in serious injuries to Mr. Peterson, requiring treatment by medical professionals. That part is fact, not allegation."

"Really?" Travis said, his tone gleeful. "She put him in the hospital?"

Val suppressed a smirk. She hoped.

"Peterson checked in to urgent care, yes," Finley said. "It seems Ms. Dawes got a few good licks in." He, too, seemed amused.

Not Blanchard. His tone grew even sharper. "Ms. Dawes, you're trained in martial arts, are you not?"

"Jiu jitsu," Val said before Travis could stop her. He flushed red, and she thought he might explode. Chastened, she declined to elaborate further on her training.

"Did you employ those techniques in your, ahem, 'self-defense' maneuvers against Ben Peterson?"

"Ms. Dawes prefers not to answer," Travis said, quicker than Val this time, "until we've heard the entirety of the allegations against her."

Finley and Blanchard exchanged weary glances. "That's pretty much it," Finley said. "Now we'd like to hear what Dawes has to say. Her side of the story, so to speak."

This time Val waited and let Travis respond. "Give us a few minutes alone to confer, would you?" He pointed toward the door.

Blanchard signaled to Finley with a raised hand: *Stay put.* "That's not how this works," he said. "You're not her lawyer, Blake. You're here to observe, to make sure we follow the process. We get to ask questions and Dawes answers them. If she's honest and forthright, things go a lot smoother for everyone. If she lies or stonewalls us like you're advising her to do…things don't go so smooth." His tone grew menacing.

"I understand," Travis said. "What I want to do is help Val understand the situation and inform her of the process. I'm *not* saying she should withhold anything. I just want the conversation to be…productive. We all want that, right?"

Blanchard scowled, but Finley put on his friendly-smiley face again that struck Val as utter fake bullshit. "Sure, sure," he said. "We're okay with that, aren't we, Tony?"

Blanchard stood and stomped out of the room, muttering under his breath.

"I guess we're taking a quick break, then," Finley said. "See you in five." He followed his partner out, closing the door behind him.

"Now," Travis said, turning to Val. "Tell me what *really* happened."

***

The rain stopped after lunch, which, on Fridays, was always Connor's favorite: mac and cheese with extra cheese on top, sliced apples, and chocolate milk. So much better than what Mom ate: kale salad with beets and some sort of rice-like thing, *king-wa* or something. It looked yucky, and he said so. But Mom said that's what kept her skinny and healthy. Dad came in and said she could stand to chow down on some mac and cheese once in a while. That made her sad, and even though he said "Only kidding," Mom cried and locked herself in her downstairs bedroom again. Which she called her "workout studio," although she kept a bed in there next to her Pilates machine. Most mornings that's where she'd come out, wearing PJs and rubbing the sand out of her eyes. So it had to be her bedroom, right? Dad slept upstairs in the largest bedroom, next to his office, a room Connor never, ever went in. *Ever.*

With no Mom to tell him he couldn't, Connor put on his warm jacket and hat and ran outside to play. He returned to his favorite spot on the banks of Clearwater Creek, his mom's science lesson from that morning fresh in his mind. Today they'd studied a fascinating new subject: rocks. The building blocks of geography...no, that wasn't quite right. Geo-log-raphy, or something like that. Darn. He'd already forgotten the most important thing—the name of his new-favoritest science. Flunk!

Anyway. Connor's camp-out spot on the creek, which he wanted to call his secret hideout except that Uncle Ambrose had already discovered it, had lots of cool rocks. Today's homework from Mom: find at least five new kinds and figure out their names. Mom hadn't taught him all the names, though, so he might need to come up with some on his own.

He found three super-fast. First, slate, a shiny, black kind that formed in flat layers and poked its sharp edges out of the dirt pretty much everywhere. When he picked up a piece, it broke in his hands, even though it felt super hard. Mom called it "brittle." Which must mean "breaks easy," because it did. He'd discovered a long time ago that "slate" skipped really well on the surface of the stream if he flicked his wrist right. In Connor's mind, he called those kinds of rocks "skippers."

Almost as abundant (a word that Mom said meant "lots and lots of it") were the brownish-gray speckly rocks that covered the bottom of the creek. She called those "sandstone," a word that made him laugh. How could it be sand *and* stone at the same time? Connor called them "potato rocks" because they looked like unpeeled potatoes, except without the little eyes that grew into new potatoes. Or rocks, in their case.

He searched all afternoon and saw all kinds of rocks. He picked up samples of each, hoping that Mom would feel better and give him an extra lesson to help identify them. If she stopped being sad. Maybe if he found some pretty ones, it would help cheer her up.

While reaching for an extra-sparkly one that looked like

a robin's egg, voices rose up nearby. Grown-up voices, but not voices he recognized, like Mom or Dad or Uncle Ambrose. Or even Miss Embley, who cleaned the house on Mondays and sometimes helped Dad in his office on days when Mom went out somewhere. He couldn't tell if they were men or women or one of each. One of them talked with a funny accent, sort of like the Apu character in Dad's favorite cartoon, *The Simpsons*. It sounded like they were coming toward him from downstream. Not in the stream itself—probably up on the hiking trail. The one that followed the brook from the state park to the cabins that his parents owned and sometimes rented out to tourists in the summer.

Not usually in March, though.

Stranger danger!

He crept up the bank of the creek, secret and quiet like a spy, careful not to step on sticks or anything that would make a noise. The rain made everything pretty soft, so that helped. When he reached the top, he peeked out over the bushes toward the trail.

Sure enough, two people, not far away, maybe the distance of running from home plate to first and second base in baseball. Much closer than he'd guessed. A small man with brown skin, dark hair, and bright white teeth. Big teeth! Not like Dad's or Uncle Ambrose's or Connor's. Even larger than Mom's normal-sized teeth. And a woman with broad shoulders and a man-like face, dark eyebrows, short black hair, and a big chin. And the Adams-Apple thing in her neck that usually only men had. But holy mackerel, what big boobs! Way bigger than Mom's, even bigger than Miss Embley's. Which Mom said were fake, so probably this lady had fake ones, too. Her skin was kind of dark, although not as dark as the man. She looked twice as strong as him, too. She even carried a big basket of stuff, like one of those pick-a-nick baskets he'd seen on TV. The man carried only a walking stick.

The man said something that made the woman laugh, probably one of those things grown-ups think is funny but really isn't. They got all giggly and she hugged and kissed him, *ew*, even as they walked. Connor was glad it wasn't funny to him—he didn't want to laugh and give away his secret position. But to keep it secret, he'd have to move, or they'd see him soon. The trail would cross the brook upstream a ways and they might look back and see him easy-peasy, with him wearing a red jacket and hat, plus white shoes. He didn't look like a rock or a plant or even a deer.

He beat a "hasty retreat" as Dad liked to say, scampering down the bank to the side of the stream. There he waited for them to pass by, which they did without looking down at him at all. While they continued upstream toward the footbridge, he crept downstream to where he could climb back up the bank unseen.

Connor hadn't finished his rock-finding homework, but he had all weekend to do that. He'd encountered strangers. He had to tell someone. A grown-up who could keep him safe.

He hoped Mom had gotten over her sadness and would come out of her "studio" soon.

***

Val stared at her folded hands on the table in front of her, her mood as gloomy as the gray, rainy weather outside. "I screwed up, didn't I?" she said to Travis Blake, who paced the small meeting room in silence.

Travis glanced at her, his body turned sideways at the opposite end of the table, hands clasped behind his back. He sighed and shook his head in dismay. "How many times did I tell you to shut up and listen? More than once, right?"

"I couldn't sit there and listen to them repeat lies about me and what happened—"

"That's exactly what you should have done." Travis whirled to face her and leaned his massive frame over the table, supporting his weight with both hands. His face flushed red again, a bright contrast to the short salt-and-pepper curls lining his forehead. "The first rule of investigation is to listen and learn. You did neither."

Val scoffed, throwing her hands wide. "Sorry, I thought *they* were investigating *me*, not—"

"That's what they want you to think," Travis said. "And sure, they are, but you're also investigating them. The best defense is what, again?"

"A good offense. Which is what—"

"Which is what you didn't do," he said, his tone grim. "You let them make the rules, and ignored the advice you asked me to give. Which is your prerogative, of course, but in that case, why involve me?"

Val had no answer for that.

"What you need to do, going forward, is listen to what they've got. The questions they ask reveal a lot about what they think they know." Travis straightened and ambled closer to her, sitting on the table and half-facing her at a 45-degree angle. "Listen first. Then we figure out the information you've got and what you're willing to share."

"Then they'll accuse me of withholding information pertinent to the investigation. They'll paint me as an uncooperative witness."

"They will anyway." He surrendered a wry smile. "Look, I know these guys. Blanchard and I came in together as rookies, Finley not long after—a legacy hire. Neither one is very smart. However, they're tenacious and manipulative, especially Finley. He'll pretend to be your friend, only to soften you up for Blanchard to stab you in the throat. Don't fall for it."

Val reflected on that. Of course Travis was right, and she felt grateful to him now that the pressure was off—for a moment. "Okay, so how do I regain the advantage?"

"The trick," Travis said, slumping into a chair and facing Val head-on, "is to answer not the question they asked, but the one you want answered. For example." He paused. "When they ask about your 'dating history' with Peterson, you say something like 'There is none,' and then you tell them what a creep he is. Technically, you've answered their question. In reality, you've redirected their inquiry into him, not you."

"I tried that. It didn't work."

"You jumped in before they finished asking," Travis said. "Don't do that. It not only pisses them off—it lets them know you have information you can't wait to share. Plus, the more time they spend talking, the less you have to. Understood?"

Val nodded. She drew in a deep breath and let it out in a shuddering staccato, slouching in her seat. "This sucks. IA has investigated me five times now in twenty months— three for shootings and these guys twice for alleged wrongdoing. You'd think I'd know better by now."

"Yeah, you'd think." He chuckled. "They do seem obsessed with you. Another fact we can use to our advantage."

Val straightened to attention. "How?"

"It means they've got files on you, and you have a right to see them," Travis said. "That'll reveal some angles on why they're busting your ass and what they're trying to find. Not on this case, per se, but in general."

Val's jaw dropped. "That's awesome. I hadn't thought of that."

"I know," Travis said with a triumphant grin. "That's why you brought me in, right?"

Over the next half-hour, Val filled Travis in on the details of the events at the Blue Line, and Travis shared what he had seen and heard as well. Then they strategized over how to deal with the next round of questions from Blanchard and Finley.

"It's been almost an hour since we kicked them out," he said, checking the clock. "I thought they'd bust the door down after five minutes. What's going on with those two?"

Travis ducked his head out the door into the WAVE Squad bullpen, then strode out, disappearing from Val's view. She followed him out a moment later and found him standing next to Petroni near her office, arms folded, an angry expression on his face.

"They left," Petroni said to Val's questioning stare. "They said they were, quote, 'done wasting their time with this prima donna bitch,' unquote." She frowned and shoved her hands into her pockets.

"They said they had more questions," Val protested.

"They will," Petroni said, "and not friendly ones. Their last words to me were, 'Your pretty young woman-cop is in trouble.'" She flashed a Cheshire-cat smile. "Don't worry, I will inform Human Resources about their sexist bullshit when the time comes."

"So, now what?" Val asked at the same time as Travis Blake.

"If I were you, I'd get busy putting pen to paper," Petroni said. "Write down everything you can about what happened last night, and every encounter you've ever had with Peterson and Simpson in the past. And not on the computer," Petroni said when Val headed toward her workstation. "At least, not on a departmental computer. Keep your notes private and wrap your head around how you want to present your side of this story. Because they'll be back, and you need to be ready, and you need to be consistent."

Val took Petroni's advice, filling several pages of a spiral-bound notebook with scribblings under various topics. She started with Ben Peterson's sexual harassment of her at the tavern. Then she documented his history of hitting on her at the police academy despite her rejecting every overture and invitation. She included her own version of their brief time working together on the Richard Harkins task force. She even located and printed every word Peterson's cousin Paul ever wrote about her in his anti-police blog, *Clayton Copwatch*. Almost all of it was negative, and she suspected Ben fed him most of the lies Paul printed.

At five o'clock, when she was wrapping up for the day,

exhausted, an email popped into her inbox from Inspector Blanchard. He'd addressed it to the downtown precinct commander and cc'ed Val, Finley, and Petroni. Not Travis, she noted. Its subject line: "Internal Investigation of Officer B. Peterson complaint vs. Officer V. Dawes."

Val skimmed the email, which summarized their meeting from the slanted perspective of an Internal Affairs hell-bent on finding dirt on her. Certain phrases popped out at her. "Dawes was uncooperative, refusing to answer even the most benign questions about the facts of the case. She showed violent tendencies, frequently interrupting and yelling and getting physically aggressive...Dawes contradicted herself on numerous issues of fact."

Her blood boiled, but she couldn't *not* read it all. The email concluded with a pair of recommendations about her:

1. Pursue formal investigation into the conduct of Officer Dawes and her fitness for continued service to CPD.

2. Suspend Officer Dawes without pay pending conclusion of the investigation.

The suspension would take effect upon approval of the Chief. Which, Val guessed, might happen as soon as Monday morning.

Val collapsed back in her seat, energy draining from her body. What a way to end a work week—and, possibly, her career in law enforcement.

Chapter Nine

Val tried calling Gil before leaving work and also when she got home. Both calls went straight to voicemail. Either he'd once again forgotten to charge his phone, or...

The other explanations were all worse, and she didn't want to think about them.

Val took a long shower, scrubbing the day's memories away. Maybe she scrubbed *too* hard, trying to expunge the stench of Ben Peterson and Ed Simpson from her entire life. She shook off those thoughts and adjusted the nozzle head to Gil's favorite setting—pulsing massage. She stood under the hot spray, wishing he was standing in there with her, holding her, kissing her—

Afterward, she dried her hair, pulled on her most comfortable jeans and sweater, and checked her phone. Still no word from Gil. A third call to him landed in voicemail hell. This time, she left a quick message of "Call me, I'd like to hear your voice," hoping it didn't sound too pitiful. Checked the clock—she'd be a few minutes late to dinner at Dad's. She grabbed a half-gallon of rocky road ice cream out of the freezer and broke a few speed limits on the short drive to her father's house.

She realized when she pulled up it had been almost three months—since Christmas—since she'd visited Dad at home. The two-story 1930s-era Cape Cod had seen better days. He still hadn't painted the siding where the old blue paint peeled away and splotches of gray showed through. Clumps of moss spread across the roof. At least the winter had killed most of the weeds on the front lawn.

Chad's BMW sat behind her dad's SUV in the driveway,

which meant she had to park in the street. She touched the BMW's hood—already cool. They'd arrived early, of course.

"Auntie Val is here! Auntie Val is here!" The happy cheer of her seven-year-old niece, Ali, accomplished what no shower massage or dead-end phone call could: lifted Val's mood right out of the doldrums into joy land. Ali's skinny frame appeared a moment later, dashing out the front door, arms wide. She captured Val in a tight hug around the waist that almost knocked her down onto the soggy lawn.

"Hey, girl," Val said, holding her niece's face in her free hand. "You're getting so big! You're almost as tall as me."

"I'm four feet, two and a half inches," Ali said with obvious pride. "Second tallest in my class."

"I'm taller!" Val's ten-year-old half-brother Sammy barreled out of the house, tugging on his jacket. He stumbled on the lowest step and landed face-first in the wet grass, arms still tangled up inside the sleeves of his coat. "Ow!" he yelled, rolling onto his back. He freed his hands and dabbed his finger at each nostril, as if checking for a nosebleed.

"Oh my God, are you all right?" Val peeled away from her laughing niece and rushed to Sammy's side. She helped him up, amazed the boy wasn't crying his eyes out.

"Yeah," Sammy said with surprising dignity. "I fall all the time." He wiped blood from his lip and hugged Val, burying his face in her chest. With a little too much enthusiasm. "I've missed you, Auntie Val."

Val smiled and bit back a correction. Though they were siblings, she almost preferred it when Sammy called her "Auntie," like Ali did. The boy adored their niece and copied everything she did. Val found it endearing, anyway. She maneuvered to his side, allowing Ali to sneak under her other arm so they could return to the house together.

"How's school?" Val asked as they walked.

"I love second grade," Ali said. "I'm getting straight A's!"

"Second grade is a lot easier than third," Sammy said, his tone dour. Val recalled Chad saying Sammy was struggling to adjust to his new school in Danbury, and his prior homeschooling from Mom left a lot to be desired. Even though he was at least a year older than his classmates, he required extra tutoring to earn passing grades.

"Right on time for dinner!" Dad held the door open for them and reminded the kids to remove their muddy shoes. Val kicked hers off, knowing he'd directed the remark at her as well. "Your favorite," Dad said to no one in particular. "Chili and cornbread."

"Yay! I love chili and cornbread!" Ali said.

"Me too!" Sammy added. "Let's go wash our hands up to our elbows!" He and Ali disappeared up the stairs.

"Use the downstairs bathroom!" Val's brother Chad said, entering the spacious living-slash-dining room. Dressed in a white dress shirt and navy slacks, he looked like he'd come straight from work. Val expected to find his suit jacket and tie hanging in the coat closet.

"Aw, I want to use mine," Sammy called back from upstairs.

Val, arms opened to embrace her brother, halted in surprise. "He has his own bathroom here now?"

Chad gave her a quick, clumsy hug, his black-rimmed glasses scraping against her forehead. He'd gotten his hair cut since she'd last seen him, his usual unruly brown mop replaced by a conservative, over-the-ears 1950s style. He'd gained a few pounds since Christmas, too. "Long story," he said. "We'll talk after dinner."

"Always putting off the difficult, inevitable conversations," a female voice said in a teasing tone. Val pulled out of her brother's hug to accept a warmer, longer one from Chad's wife. "Don't let him get away with that," Kendra murmured in Val's ear before breaking the embrace. Then, louder: "You look terrific, Val. Happier than I've seen you in a long time. Gil must be treating you well."

"Thanks. You look amazing, as always," Val said. Kendra's tall, slender frame dazzled in an aquamarine sheath dress, one she'd once worn during a solo violin performance in New York. Compared to Kendra and Chad, Val felt underdressed. "Get away with what?" she asked.

Kendra's answer needed to wait, though, because Dad returned from the kitchen carrying a pot of chili. Chad followed him in with a plate piled high with cubes of steaming cornbread. "Let's eat!" Dad said. "Where are the kids?"

"I've already fed Dar," Kendra said. "Hopefully he'll stay down for his nap. Sorry, Val, your visit with him will have to wait a bit."

"A rested baby is a good baby," Val said with a wistful smile.

Sammy and Ali pounded down the stairs, drying their hands on their shirts. "Mommy, can we eat in the TV room?" Ali said. "Daddy said we can if it's okay with you."

Kendra rolled her eyes at Chad, then smiled at the children. "Sure. The grown-ups need to talk about adult things, anyway."

Chad cast her an imploring glance, then blew a blast of air out of his pursed lips. "Fine. Go on out and I'll fill your plates."

The kids cheered and scrambled to the sofa, clicking on the TV way too loud.

The "TV room" was the far end of the living room, appointed with an old leather recliner, ripped in a few unlikely places, and a matching sofa in similar condition. Both faced an oversized flat-screen TV mounted to the wall. At least Dad had cleared away his usual collection of old *New York Times* newspapers and *True Crime* magazines. He might even have vacuumed the floor.

Val took a seat at the table, bewildered by the flurry of activity and loud voices. The kids would still be in earshot of the "adult conversation" if they got bored with the TV. She wondered what the "grown-up talk" would be about.

"No Gil tonight?" Dad said after they'd all filled their bowls and plates.

"He needed to go out of town," Val said, her head bowed.

"Visiting a friend who's ill. He sends his regrets. Yummy as always, Dad." She washed down a mouthful of the spicy chili with a gulp of ice-cold milk. The family tradition of chili, cornbread, and milk for Friday night dinner dated back to her childhood. Chad preferred beer nowadays, but everyone knew not to bring alcohol to an alcoholic's house.

"Nothing serious, I hope?" Dad said. "With this COVID thing going around..."

"I'm afraid so," Val said. "Cancer. It's a guy he knew before we met." She kept her eyes pointing down, not wanting to reveal any emotion.

"No way I'm watching that stupid girly-girl show!" Sammy yelled from the sofa. "I want to watch SpongeBob!"

"But you *like* DC Super Hero Girls," Ali shouted back. "We always watch it at home!"

"Kids!" Kendra turned and pointed a finger at them. "Take turns. Do rock-paper-scissors to see who goes first. I don't want any more shouting."

"Sorry, Mom," Ali said.

Sammy blew Kendra a raspberry and sulked into the sofa. Kendra sighed and turned back to Val, shaking her head with a heavy weariness.

"Speaking of COVID," Chad said. "That's part of the 'grown-up' conversation we mentioned." He lowered his voice. "Sammy's father's got it. With his liver condition, they don't expect him to make it."

Val's throat tightened, making it hard to swallow her chili. "So, Milt McCloskey will die in jail. How appropriate." She'd tried to keep the bitterness out of her voice, and failed. Over a decade before, a few weeks before Val's thirteenth birthday, a very drunk Milt raped her in her own bed. A little over a year later, her mother left them all and bore a child—Sammy—with Val's rapist. Val had always envisioned a much more violent death for Milt, but dying alone in a prison cell would have to do.

She glanced at Sammy, engrossed in his TV viewing, and felt some remorse for her little brother, who seemed oblivious to his father's imminent demise. "Does Mom know?" Val asked.

"*She* told *me*." Chad shook his head and glanced at Kendra, who glared at him.

"There's something else, isn't there?" Val said. "About Mom?"

Chad took a huge mouthful of chili, chewed it much longer than necessary, and washed it down with a sip of milk. They all waited, despite Chad's imploring gazes at his wife to bail him out.

"You could say that," he said, finally.

"Jesus, Chad." Kendra's annoyance boiled over, and her spoon fell to her bread plate with a clatter. "Would you just tell her?"

Val's internal alarm bells rang. Mild-mannered Kendra never snapped at Chad in front of people.

Chad cleared his throat, his face reddening. "Milt changed his story about the July Fourth incident, a kind of deathbed confession," he said. Val had to strain to hear over the television. "He's taking the position that the whole thing was his doing and that he forced Mom into cooperating, under threat of bodily harm."

"That's bullshit!" Val said, too loud. Ali and Sammy gasped, covering their mouths and giggling. The other adults in the room cast disapproving glances at her. "Sorry about the language. Plenty of other witnesses testified…look, this can't work, can it?"

Chad shrugged. "There's a good chance she'll plead down to simple conspiracy, or aiding and abetting," he said. "With her age and health, it wouldn't surprise me if they gave her no more than a year."

"One year? For plotting and attempting the murder of hundreds of people? You're shitting—er, kidding me," Val fumed.

Chad looked away. "It's not up to me. I'm not her lawyer."

"Your firm—"

"Passed her case on to another practice. We're not involved. Didn't I tell you that at Christmas?"

Val frowned. He might've told her. She pushed her bowl of chili away, her appetite ruined. She sipped her milk, but it tasted sour now. The idea of her mother getting off with such a light sentence for a violent crime seemed like a terrible injustice—one she couldn't swallow.

"Let's change the subject," Dad said. "What's new with you, Kendra?"

"I'm going back to work full time," Kendra said, taking a dainty bite of cornbread. "I auditioned for and earned second chair at the Long Island Philharmonic."

"That's fantastic!" Val said, grateful for any bit of good news. "When do you start?"

"Next week," Kendra said. "Although I won't perform with them for at least a month. I have a lot of new pieces to learn."

"I want to attend your first performance," Val said. "I wouldn't miss it."

"Me, too," Dad said. "So exciting! Wait, who will watch the kids? Are you hiring someone?"

Kendra rested her hand on Chad's shoulder and gave him her sweetest smile. "Back to you, honey."

"Ah, yeah. That brings me to our next 'grown-up conversation' topic." Chad crumbled the remaining half of his chunk of cornbread on top of his chili and stirred them together. "Last summer, when Mom went to jail, we agreed to bring Sammy back to Danbury...temporarily. Our understanding was that once you guys got situated, we'd all share the responsibility for his care. He'd spend half his time here at Dad's, with Val and Gil helping out. Right?"

A heavy weight settled on Val's shoulders. "Right. And he's spent *some* time here..."

"Far less than we discussed," Kendra said. "A weekend here and there, and a week over the holidays. And he spent the bulk of his time with your father rather than you. Wouldn't you agree?"

Val, after a moment's thought, nodded. She and Gil had not helped much, even on those few brief visits.

"So? I loved having him," Dad said. "I welcome every opportunity I get to spend with Sammy. I've done what I can to make him feel at home. He has his own room—"

"My old room," Chad said. "The best!"

"And his own bathroom, apparently," Val said with a wry grin.

"Going forward, though," Chad continued, "we think it's best if he spends more time here in Clayton. Perhaps even full time."

The dinner table conversation paused for an awkward minute, the cacophonous noise of the TV filling the void.

"Best for whom?" Val asked to break the silence. "For Sammy, for Ali, for you...?"

"For everyone," Chad said.

"And," Kendra said, "we think it would be best for Sammy, and for your father, if you and Gil could engage more in his care. He is, after all, your brother. While your father has been gracious enough to devote considerable time to Sammy, he's not actually related. He bears no legal obligation—"

"I consider him my grandson, like Ali and Dar," Dad said.

Val and Chad exchanged wary glances. Though young, Sammy was their sibling—technically, Dad's stepson, not grandson. Was senility already setting in, as Chad sometimes argued? Was he in denial about who Sammy's mother and father were? Or was his alcoholism taking its toll?

No. Innocent mistake, she insisted to herself.

Another thought struck her. Even to Val and Chad, their father was at best inattentive—absent in most ways other than physical. He paid the bills, but had little to do with their upbringing, even after Mom left. He possessed neither the skills nor the inclination to take care of a rambunctious ten-year-old boy with special needs like

Sammy.

Right on cue, Ali and Sammy started arguing over the TV remote again, their complaints reaching high volume in seconds.

"Kids!" Kendra glared at them. "Must I come in there and turn the TV off?"

"Sammy keeps changing the channel—"

"No, you did!" Sammy said.

"On the count of three," Kendra said. "One, two—"

"Fine," Sammy said. "DC Super Hero Girls, then." He bowed his head, pouting. Ali clicked the remote, and the living room went quiet, other than the TV.

"Well, Val?" Chad leaned forward on his elbows, his gaze fixed on hers. "Are you willing to step up a little more?"

Val glanced from face to face around the table. They all stared at her with hopeful, if not expectant, expressions.

"You agreed, after all," Dad said, his voice unsteady. Val surmised that his prior episodes of caring for Sammy had shaken his parenting self-confidence.

"I should talk to Gil—"

"I thought Gil bought in last summer," Chad said, "when we first agreed to all this."

"Well, yes, but—"

"Has he changed his mind?" Dad said.

"Gosh, guys, back off for a second," Kendra cut in. "You're going to twist her arm off at this rate." She smiled and rested a hand on Val's. "It's a big ask. Please talk to Gil. I don't want this to be a problem for you two."

"No, that's okay," Val said. "Chad's right. We agreed, and we won't renege now."

"Thank you," Kendra said.

"Yes, thanks, Val," Dad said. "And no one's asking you to board him at Gil's. He'd live here, as we planned. But I'd love your help when he's here. Maybe you can stay here during his visits?"

"To be clear," Kendra said, "we're hoping he'll transition to living here full-time...sooner rather than later. Although not necessarily right away."

"You mean, permanently." Val took a bite of her chili, now cold. She pushed it aside.

"At some point," Chad said. "This summer, perhaps?"

Val exchanged glances with her father, who, after a brief pause, nodded. "Okay," she said. "That will give us time to prepare."

"Although," Chad cut in, "this week is their spring break, and we'd arranged with Dad for Sammy to stay through next weekend."

Her father nodded. "Then he'd go back to Danbury...right?"

"Correct," Kendra said. "For a bit."

Val ran all of this over in her mind. "So you want me to start now."

"Consider it sort of a trial run," Chad said.

Val stole a glance over at the kids—scratch that. One kid. Sammy remained on the couch—alone. "Sammy," she said, "where did Ali go?"

"She got mad and ran upstairs," Sammy said.

"Got mad, why?" Kendra asked.

"I don't know."

"Did you change the channel again?" Chad asked.

Sammy shrugged. "Just for a minute when the commercial came on."

Kendra leaned her forehead onto two clenched fists. "God, give me strength," she said in a whisper.

Chad, meanwhile, crossed the room and snagged the remote off the coffee table. A moment later, the TV faded to black. "To your room, young man," Chad said.

"What? It's not even seven o'clock!"

"I don't care. Go!"

Sammy curled up into a ball on the sofa. "What about ice cream?"

"Crap, I left the ice cream in the car!" Val jumped up and dashed to the coat closet, pulling on her jacket and checking for her car keys. "It's probably all melted. Crap,

crap, crap!"

"Crap, crap, crap!" Sammy yelled and broke into laughter.

Val hurried out to her Honda, fuming. Her brother had sandbagged her with this surprise request-slash-demand for help, leaving unspoken the now-obvious friction developing between Sammy and Ali. She also detected a fair amount of tension between Chad and Kendra, too, though—no doubt in part because of Sammy. She wondered how much additional stress it would bring into her relationship with Gil—already at an all-time high.

Still, she and Gil *had* agreed to help. They'd have to make the best of the situation...apparently, before he returned from his trip to New Haven.

She opened the car and retrieved the ice cream, which had, as predicted, melted into soft goo. Just like her stomach.

Chapter Ten

Most disturbing.

The Redeemer, a man who despised perverts above all else, had taken what some might consider extreme measures to protect his community from their wretched, insidious influence. Yet somehow he'd failed to notice when two—*Two!*—new offenders waltzed right into his orbit. So close they could touch him—

He retched, holding his stomach until the sharp pain passed, doubled over in his rolling desk chair. He wiped sweat from his brow and reached for the glass of water perched a safe distance from his keyboard and trio of 36-inch displays. He took a sip, wondering if he should go out there, intervene, kick them off his property.

However, technically, they weren't on his property. Yet.

He rewound the recording to where the so-called woman entered the picture. Native American, judging by the facial structure. Her blocky body, with no feminine curvature other than big tits, should have given her away right there.

The "woman" appeared alone at first, moments before her diminutive, brown-skinned boyfriend—he retched again—joined her at the water's edge. "She" dipped a bare toe into the frigid rushing water of Clearwater Creek, then leaped back, as if shocked by the cold. Idiot.

She—or he? No, *It*—exclaimed something. Probably said "It's freezing!" or some such—sound quality suffered at that distance—to the man standing offscreen. Then she—*it*—laughed and pulled off her—*its*—sweater, revealing those large, gravity-defying tits. No bra. Pants followed a shirt onto a blanket already spread on the ground, and the odd, misshapen creature stood there in boxy briefs, waving the man closer. Said something like "Don't chicken out," or words to that effect.

The man entered the picture, half-naked, holding pants, a shirt, and shoes tight against his shallow chest, shivering in the cold and giggling like a girl.

The big-titted one said something encouraging. Then the boxers came off, and the perversion became all too real. Despite disfiguring itself with enhanced mammaries, the creature's genitalia betrayed its genetic truth. Its tiny penis and scrotum shriveled from the cold, peeking through a bushy thicket of black fur. Then it ran into the icy current, hiding all of its full-frontal perversity from his camera, with only its toned brown ass on flagrant display. And then it dove into the water, shrieking and splashing and urging the little man to join it.

Which he did. Thank God his body had not endured the synthetic mutations of his companion, his gender's equipment intact on his slender, man-shaped body.

However, the man proved himself as perverted as the Native American creature when he caught up to it and wrapped his arms around its body. He planted his lips on its face, then engaged in sexual foreplay, right there in the goddamn river. They endured the cold less than a minute, then splashed to the shore, rolling into a heap on the blanket, and the sick, twisted creatures resumed their obscene depravity. Especially the man, performing oral stimulation of the creature's manufactured breasts and mismatched genitals. As if no one would ever see—not the man, not his drone, not the all-seeing God above.

And not the nine-year-old lad who had adopted the riverbank as his playground of sorts. An innocent boy didn't need to see *that*—hell, he didn't need to witness *normal* sex at his tender age, much less this disgusting display of deviant debauchery.

He shut off the recording and sat for several minutes, considering his options. He needed to find out where they'd come from, and when they'd leave. If they were newcomers to town, or tourists from the city, perhaps they would leave on their own accord.

Otherwise, he'd drive them away by force.

He closed his eyes and meditated on that. Would that be enough? Or must he again resort to more extreme measures?

Might these perverts be scouting for a young boy? What if they encountered him? What disgusting acts would they try to tempt him into?

He drew deep breaths, calming himself. It took a while to get there.

He tapped a few keys on the keyboard, reactivating the live camera. They'd left the clearing and brought all their belongings with them. He elevated the drone above the treetops, steering it upriver until he spotted a cluster of cabins near the state park. Three of the four huts remained empty. On the front porch of the fourth, the brown man sat, removing his shoes. His companion stood in the doorway, wearing only a robe. When the little man stood, it opened the robe, drawing him into an intimate embrace—

Sure enough, the two degenerates were staying there. The cabin was vacant the day before, which meant the pervs wouldn't be going anywhere, at least for a few days.

Of their own accord, anyway.

He pondered that further. He could keep them away— from the boy, anyway—for a day or two. However, he would not abide these two perverts remaining in the boy's orbit beyond that.

If they remained past Sunday morning, he'd take action. Swift and severe.

Which reminded him.

He fired up his secure browser and searched for reports that would prove whether his efforts earlier that week had rippled through the news media.

Sure enough, authorities had discovered the body, identified the perv, and revealed his criminal past— "*alleged*," the woke media asserted to cover their asses. A sexual deviant who preyed on children. Dead, and brought to justice in a way the cops and the courts could not bring themselves to accomplish. Though with all the hand-wringing by local politicians in the press, a person might conclude one of society's leading lights had been extinguished.

Not so. Some—a very few—knew the truth. One man alone took action.

And would continue to do so as long as the perpetrators of perversion and obscenity threatened the people of this community.

He closed the browser and began making plans for Sunday.

***

Val called Gil again once she got back to his place. This time, he picked up.

"H'lo?" His gravelly voice resembled a cement mixer.

"Gil, are you all right?" Val said. "You sound…terrible." She paced the living room, gripping the phone hard against her ear.

"I feel worse than I sound." The raspiness in his voice grew worse with each syllable. He coughed, a phlegmy blast that sounded wet and painful. "It's good that I'm not with you right now. I'd just make you sick."

"Is it…is it COVID?"

Gil sighed, coughed again. "I tested positive today," he admitted. "I'm supposed to quarantine for anywhere from five to fourteen days, depending on who you ask. You should get tested—I probably caught it before I left."

"Crap. Okay, I will." She sank onto the sofa. "Shouldn't I show symptoms, though? I heard you lose your sense of taste and it's hard to breathe."

"A lot of people experience that. I did, plus low energy…so low. I've slept most of the day today, and everything tastes like sawdust." His vocal volume fell to a whisper. He cleared his throat, coughed again. Another few moments of silence followed. "So, what's new in your world?"

Our world, Val corrected him in her mind, but refrained from saying out loud. "Internal Affairs busted my chops about the Blue Line Tavern incident. They're siding with Simpson and Peterson. Hell, they've already recommended suspension, maybe even termination. It's a mess."

"They can't fire you for that," Gil said. "Not after decades of guys getting slapped on the wrist for much worse." He lapsed into a paroxysm of coughing that lasted well over a minute.

"They're claiming I initiated the whole thing, even flirted with that asshole." Val curled her feet up under her on the couch and wrapped her free arm around her knees.

"It's all bluster and bullshit," Gil said. "Don't waste a minute more thinking about it."

Val's temper flared, and she took a moment to calm herself. "Gil, did you hear me? They want me fired. At minimum, it shot to hell my hopes of moving up to detective anytime soon. This sucks!"

"It does suck. But it's nothing, trust me. It'll all blow–"

"It's not going to blow over, dammit!" The tensions of the day and evening boiled over, her patience with Gil's "don't worry" message at its end. "They're coming for me, Gil, and I have no defense. No witnesses, no advocates—"

"They've got nothing—"

"Dammit, listen to me!" Val jumped up off the couch again and resumed her frantic pacing. "Don't be so dismissive of this. I'm in serious trouble, Gil. I wish you'd treat this situation with a little more *respect*."

A long pause, followed by a cough on Gil's end. "I'm sorry," he said. "I'm not myself tonight."

"You sure aren't." Not with gorgeous Jessica nearby and her father dying, anyway.

Gil cleared his throat again. "You kind of aren't yourself, either, my love."

Val sighed and leaned back against the wall, rubbing

her temples. "Fair enough. It was a rough night."

"Oh?"

"Dinner at Dad's, remember?"

"Ah." He paused. He hadn't remembered. "Family night didn't go so well?"

She heaved a deep breath. "Chad brought up our promise to help raise Sammy, and he came to collect on it."

Gil wheezed a moment or two. "Meaning what, specifically?"

"He wants to leave Sammy at Dad's this coming week. Which means I need to spend more time there. Dad's really not capable of handling Sammy. He wasn't the most efficacious parent, even for Chad and me."

He chuckled, coughed, caught his breath again. "You're trying to claim you were easy to raise?"

"I was a perfect little angel," Val said, then laughed, her tension easing a touch. "Trust me, Sammy's a handful."

A beat passed. "As soon as I'm cleared to be around people..."

"So, not this week, then."

Gil sighed. "Probably not."

Val let the silence linger a moment. She got that he'd landed in a tough spot, but so had she. Val wanted him by her side, helping, but that couldn't be. She'd have to make the best of it.

"How's Hank doing?" she asked.

Gil's turn to sigh. "In and out of consciousness. He doesn't have long."

She fought to get her next question out. "And Jessica? How's she doing?"

"Falling apart half the time, in denial the rest," Gil said. "She's a wreck."

"I see." Val pushed away from the wall. "You know this despite being asleep all day?"

"She calls and texts a lot."

"Uh-huh. You're talking to her several times a day, yet you can't take a single one of my calls. Got it."

"Val. Please don't be jealous. It's not like you."

"Gil. Please don't be an insensitive clod. It's not like *you*."

A long, *long* silence followed.

"You know I'm not able to see her in person," he said.

"You're staying with her, aren't you?"

"No. I'm in a motel. Have been from the start."

"Oh." She felt ashamed now. "Sorry. I just assumed..."

"Val, I wouldn't. And with COVID, I *can't*. Again—quarantine. I can't see anybody."

Fear rose inside her. "How will you eat? Do you need to see a doctor? Should I come—"

"I'm getting meals delivered," he said. "The motel is in the middle of fast-food heaven. If I get worse, there are hospitals and doctors everywhere. In the meantime, I need to stay away from people, take aspirin, and rest until the cough and fever subside. Which they are..." He belied the statement by lapsing into another coughing fit.

"I'm coming down there in the morning," Val said.

"Don't," Gil said. "Look. I miss you. But I can't see you and I don't want to give this crap to you."

"So, that's it, then? No matter what, we can't be together? Don't I get a say in this?"

He heaved a loud breath. "I don't get a say, either. It's a public health crisis, Val, and I'm caught in it. And so are you. It's awful, but that's the way it is."

She stewed for a moment. "What if you don't get better? Then what?"

"I will," he said, insistent. "Listen, this will pass. All of it—COVID, your work crisis, the family, everything. In the meantime, please—take care of yourself, and Sammy, and I'll come back and help you as soon as I can. Okay?"

Gil coughed again, and again, and after a long pause, he coughed without stopping. It sounded painful and frustrating, and Val felt helpless. Finally, he stopped long enough to say, "I gotta go," and hung up before she could tell him goodbye.

Val lay down on the couch, clutching the phone to her chest, hoping he'd call back soon.

She woke up in the same position several hours later, and no calls appeared in her call history.

She worried.

***

Val stumbled into Gil's kitchen, the empty house yawning a cold unfamiliarity at her in the dim light of early morning. Like almost everyone else, she hated the transition to daylight saving time. Even six days after the switch, the "extra" hour of daylight in the evening never made up for the late sunrise and dark mornings. For a morning person like her, it made the start of the day more foreboding and unforgiving.

For example, where the hell were the English muffins? She swore she'd put them in the cupboard next to the fridge—

No. She ate the last one on Friday. Today, Saturday, she'd be stuck with wheat toast for breakfast.

Or...

Val recalled a breakfast Gil made for her one Saturday. Excited, she raided the fridge for its ingredients: two eggs, a chunk of sweet onion, feta cheese, sun-dried tomatoes, and spinach. She heated oil in a skillet while mincing the onion and tomatoes, then started the sauté on low heat. Gil always made a big point of the next step: once the onions softened, add the spinach, and sauté only for a minute, until they began to wilt. Then she added the scrambled eggs and feta, covered the skillet, and simmered it for a few minutes until the eggs bubbled, and oh, my God, it came out just like Gil's.

Better, even, because she added more feta.

Today, she vowed, would be a good day.

Her fortunes continued to improve after breakfast when the rain held off long enough for a brisk four-mile run. Even better, not a single creepy dude hit on her the entire route.

Score one for daylight saving time, keeping the douchebags home an extra hour.

After a long, hot shower, she checked her messages. Nothing from Gil or family. However, a welcome note from Shelby appeared:

> The cabin is spectacular! Beautiful & comfy but remote. No TV and sucky cell/internet…pure bliss. Sanjit hasn't used his laptop once.

Val laughed. That sounded perfect. She continued to get dressed, wishing she could get away from it all like Shelby, when her phone pinged again:

> Two bedrooms. You and Gil should join us.

Val responded:

> Sounds divine. But Gil's out of town & has COVID. Besides, we wouldn't want to crowd you guys.

It took a few minutes, but Shelby wrote back:

> Wouldn't crowd us at all. Offer's open. Please come.

Val smiled. Shelby had become one of her closest friends in recent months. Val loved her matter-of-fact straightforwardness, her quirky humor, and her inclusive nature. Shelby often invited Val to partake of new adventures she would dream up. She sometimes startled Val with her candor about the most personal of confidences. More than once, she'd divulged details of her sexual exploits with Sanjit, discussions that made Val a little uncomfortable. Still, her fondness for Shelby combined with curiosity about trans sex prevented her from shutting those conversations down.

Besides, she never knew when something Shelby

shared might turn out useful with Gil.

Her phone rang, startling her—she'd expected it to chime with another message from Shelby. She checked caller ID and answered. "Shannon? What's up?"

Shannon O'Reilly sounded as chipper as ever, despite the early hour on a Saturday. "Work, if that's okay," she said. "I was going to wait until you got here, but you surprised me by not showing up."

"It's my day off," Val said. "Besides, I might get the rest of my life off if Simpson gets his way."

"Sorry," Shannon said. "If you want me to hold off until Monday—"

"No, no," Val said. "I have no plans for today, so maybe I should work while I can. You have news on a case I should know about?"

"Yeah, the Dinker autopsy came in," she said. "Not a drowning—a strangling. Similar to that Larkin guy they fished out of the river in Greenville."

"The guy who'd also been mutilated," Val said. "As I suspected."

"We're discussing with the Greenville PD whether Clayton will send our case to them or vice versa, or coordinate our separate investigations," Shannon said. "Since you have a relationship with the detectives up there, I hoped you could weigh in. The lead there—Gramercy—is waiting on you to provide some of Larkin's local victim info."

"Oh, shit," Val said. "I started pulling that together before all this other crap happened. I'll come in and get that to him."

"Or," Shannon said, "see if they're willing to transfer the case. Petroni wants us to own both, for some reason."

"Really?" Val pondered that a moment. "Seems odd. Grimes has taken so many days off lately with his son's treatment demanding his attention, and combined with my IA bullshit, we're a little short-handed, so..."

"That IA thing *is* bullshit," Shannon said. "You'll beat that rap and make them eat their words. Trust me, with

Simpson's reputation, and Peterson's, you're going to come out of this smelling like a rose."

"Gil thinks so, too," Val said. "It feels the opposite to me. They seem to want to burn my ass, and I can't figure out why."

"Because you're a woman," Shannon said. "And you're smart, and great at what you do. That makes you a threat to the dinosaurs like Simpson and Blanchard. Listen, we'll get you through this. Brenda and I have both been through it and kicked their asses. We're on your side. So's Price, Grimes, Travis Blake, and a host of other well-respected cops in this department. Everybody knows Simpson blows bullshit out both nostrils, and he has a bug up his ass about you because you showed him up last year. But they can't do anything without evidence—and they've got none. You're good. Trust me."

"Wow, what a great pep talk," Val said. "Makes me miss having you as a partner. Speaking of which...is Grimes in, too? I should bring him up to speed on this crap."

Shannon's voice turned despondent. "Nope. I'm surprised he hasn't called you. The scan found another spot on Bobby Junior's brain. He's going back in for treatment."

"Aw, shit." Val slumped onto the recliner in Gil's living room. "That's awful."

"Yeah, worse than awful," Shannon said. "You should call him. Sorry, I thought you knew. Um...this is a little awkward, but until Grimes returns, Petroni plans to put you on my team with Damari. We'll all work our cases together for a bit."

"A three-person team? That's unusual."

"Unusual times call for unusual strategies, I guess."

"So, I guess I do get to partner with you again, then," Val said. "In a way."

"I don't want this to be weird," Shannon said. "With both you and Damari both going for detective...I want you to know, I won't play favorites. We've got to work as a team. We can't let competition for a promotion get in the way.

Okay?"

"Of course," Val said.

But deep down, she harbored doubts.

Chapter Eleven

Of all the days in the week, Connor loved Saturdays best. No homeschooling, yay. Also, Miss Embley often made pancakes and link sausages for breakfast, and then he got to watch two whole hours of TV. Sometimes Mom got up in time for breakfast, although she never ate any pancakes. Weird, because she liked them, but she said they went "straight to her butt." Connor imagined her having pancakes stuck in her butt, and it always made him laugh. Not out loud, though, because then Mom would get mad or sad and go back to her studio for the rest of the day.

Anyway, she didn't join them for breakfast this morning. So at least he didn't have to worry about upsetting her today.

That meant he could watch an extra episode of *Fast and Furious Spy Racers* on Netflix with nobody caring. *Plus,* he watched a whole hour of *Archibald's Next Big Thing*—including one of his favorite episodes, too. In this one, Archibald traveled way, way far from home, so far that Connor always made-believe he wouldn't even make it back this time. He'd seen it before, so he knew Arch would find home again. Anyway, it was fun to pretend he'd go off and explore the entire world this once and make cool scientific discoveries or something.

That would be so awesome.

He wanted to watch Pokémon, too, but he heard noises coming from upstairs, which meant someone might come and catch him watching extra. So, he real-fast turned off the TV and pretended to read his picture book for almost ten whole minutes, just in case.

Some Saturdays, but not today, Dad would watch *The Simpsons* with him. Connor liked Bart. A lot of Homer's jokes that Dad liked, Connor didn't get. Sometimes he laughed anyway, though, because it made Dad smile even more.

After TV and reading, he went to his bedroom and changed into his explorer clothes. He put on his blue jeans with scuff marks on the knees, his thick, warm socks, a comfy shirt with pockets on both sides for storing cool stuff. Most important, he remembered his floppy hat, like Indiana Jones wore—Dad liked him, too. He also put on his Explorer Belt, one with all the stuff he needed for discovering unknown places. He'd gotten it for Christmas, and Mom said nobody else his age had one. So cool.

Connor walked by Dad's office, and his door was open. He peeked in and saw Dad at his desk. He waited until Dad looked away from his computer screens before saying anything—he didn't want to startle him. Dad hated being startled.

"I'm going outside to play," he said when it seemed like a safe time to talk.

Dad glanced up at him and appeared surprised for a moment. Connor almost ran away or peed his pants, but Dad smiled at him, so he knew it was okay. Even though he hadn't shaved yet this morning, which often meant he'd just gotten out of bed, even though it was almost ten o'clock. "Okay, buddy," Dad said. "Don't wander too far today, okay? We're having pizza for lunch. I wouldn't want you to miss out."

"Pizza's my *favorite!*" Connor ran into the room, his arms wide, and his father laughed and gave him a big hug. "Thank you, Dad! Thank you, thank you!"

"All right, all right," Dad said, "that's enough. Go play and let me get my work done so I can finish in time for pizza, too."

Connor ran out into the hall, whooping with excitement and nearly bumping into Miss Embley, carrying a tray full of coffee and stuff toward Dad's office. He almost leaped down the whole set of stairs in one big jump, but he remembered Dad saying that was dangerous. Instead, he ran *fast fast fast* to the bottom. Then he kept running out the door and across the yard of The Grounds, through the gate at the end of the driveway, and into the woods.

Then he slowed to a walk, because it was hard to run between trees and over bushes. He could've used a trail if he wanted to. But not today. Today was Exploring Day.

He used his compass, one of the many cool tools on his belt, and his explorer's map, making careful notes of new things he encountered: a huge huckleberry bush next to a giant rock, a fallen oak tree that still grew leaves, and an abandoned well with no bucket to draw water up with. Connor marked all of it on the map. And then, what he found no matter how hard he tried to go the other way, Clearwater Creek.

At least it was a part he'd never explored before. Way further upstream, where the banks were closer together and the current splashed over big boulders rising up from the bottom. On the bank of the creek, he found all kinds of new rocks, way more than the two he needed to finish his homework. One was gray and kind of shiny and looked like it contained chunks of white soap. His mom told him about this one, called soapstone. Another kind was sort of clear and yellowish with cool patterns in it. He hoped it was an agate, but it might only be quartz. Either way, he'd never found one before.

While he cataloged his findings in his Explorer Notebook, something splashed in the water nearby. He wondered if a cat or squirrel needed rescuing from drowning. Probably neither one was a good swimmer. If he saved it, maybe Dad and Mom would let him keep it. They wouldn't let him have a puppy yet, but a rescued kitten? They'd *have* to let him bring it home.

His heart pounding, he followed the course of the water upstream, keeping his eye on the current to see if anything furry was floating or thrashing about. He hoped it hadn't already drowned. Since he didn't hear any more splashing he got worried that he was too late, and he feared the worst—

Ker-plunk!

He not only heard another splash—he saw it. And not just one. Five! *Splish-splash-skippity-sploosh-kerplunk.*

He froze, and then it happened again: *splash-splash-plunk.* Only three this time. And definitely not a squirrel. It was a black, flat stone, the size of a potato chip.

Someone was throwing rocks at him.

Not just someone. The two creepy grown-ups he'd seen the day before.

Escape or attack?

He picked up a rock. If they came closer, he'd be ready.

***

Val made it into work by 10:30 a.m., pleased to find a fresh pot of coffee waiting. She hadn't expected that on a Saturday.

Damari Price poured her a cup and raised his mug in a toast. "Glad to see you, Dawes," he said. "After all the crap that happened yesterday, I wasn't sure if the sharks got to you or not."

"There was chum in the water all around me," she said with a smile, "but I wouldn't cash in on any bets yet regarding my survival."

"Safe money's on you, Val," Shannon O'Reilly said, strolling up behind them with an empty mug. "Thanks for coming in on your day off. Hopefully, you won't need to stay long. The Greenville team is expecting your call."

"Getting right on it." Val sipped her coffee on the way to her desk. Her phone blipped, and she checked it. A text from her old partner, Rico Lopez, with a link and a quick note:

> FYI. BTW, I am NOT the "former partner" mentioned in the article.

The link went to her least favorite place on the internet: the CopWatch blog, authored by Ben Peterson's equally slimy cousin.

Dust-up Cover-up?

Clayton PD Protects Its Favorite Daughter—Again
by Paul Peterson

Clayton Police are investigating allegations of sexual misconduct and assault by one of its most celebrated young officers.

Or are they?

Information obtained from sources inside Clayton PD indicates second-year patrolwoman Valorie Dawes attacked a fellow officer—a newcomer to the force—at an after-hours celebration Thursday evening at the Blue Line Tavern, a popular hangout for off-duty cops.

Sources indicate Internal Affairs opted not to pursue the sexual harassment charges—without an explanation as to why this serious offense was dropped. However, IA recommended suspension of Officer Dawes for her acts of violence.

"What the—? Oh, for God's sake!" Val fumed and set her coffee down a little too hard, spilling a few ounces onto her desk.

"More bad news?" Price strolled over with his steaming mug.

Val showed him the article on her phone.

"Wait, isn't he Ben Peterson's brother or something?" Price said.

"Cousin. Still, this is beyond unethical and complete horseshit."

"Well, at least they've dropped the sexual assault thing," Price said, reading over her shoulder.

"News to me," Val said. "And who knows if this idiot has any of his facts straight?"

"That *would* be a first," Price said with a chuckle.

Val scanned the article, searching for nuggets of actual information rather than the pure innuendo that characterized most of Peterson's blogs. Halfway down, she found a beaut.

> Sources say this is not the first Internal Affairs inquiry into Dawes's behavior. In addition to her three officer-involved shootings, the department investigated Dawes on at least two other occasions in her brief career. Each involved disputes with now-former partners, which may have turned violent.
>
> We say "may have" because the details surrounding those cases, like this one, are suspiciously sealed from public view.
>
> Dawes, who has served since September, 2018—a span of about 20 months—has already burned through six partners—an unusually high number in such a short period.
>
> One department insider noted, "She's a hazard. Nobody wants to partner with her anymore—it's practically a death sentence, either literally, or to your career."

"You beat up your partners?" Price said, laughing. "Who have you partnered with, besides Grimes? O'Reilly?"

"I didn't beat up any of them. I started with Gil Kryzinski." Val's insides warmed at the memory. How she wished they could have remained partners!

"They split you two up?" Price asked. "Because you started dating?"

"No. He…" A lump formed in her throat. "He got shot. So they assigned me to Alex Papadopoulos."

"He retired, right?" Price said.

"Medical disability," O'Reilly said, ambling over to join the fray. "Then me, right?"

"Rico Lopez, briefly," Val said, "then you. Then Grimes, and when he took leave to deal with his son's cancer, Jan Morgenstern filled in for a few weeks."

"Damn, girl," Price said, grinning. "You *are* a bit of a menace."

"There's an awful lot left out of that narrative," O'Reilly said. "Like, I'd be happy to partner with you again. So would Jan."

"Grimes refuses to give you up," Price added. "He brags about you all the time." His expression soured a bit.

"Kryz got shot because he was trying to play the hero," O'Reilly said. "Can't blame that on you, either."

Val said nothing. She blamed herself for that all the time.

"And Alex wasn't her partner anymore when *he* got shot," O'Reilly told Price. "Rico got pulled from patrol because of PTSD from an event that happened before they were assigned—"

"Is that what this paragraph is about?" Price pointed to a section a few paragraphs down.

> One former partner was removed from patrol, suffering from post-traumatic stress disorder after an incident in which Dawes's behavior was described as "reckless."

"Again, a partial truth at best," Val said. "But yes, that refers to Rico."

"So then, who's this about?" Price asked. He pointed to another section a half-page down.

> Tellingly, a second former partner alleged Dawes made sexual advances on them while on duty. But guess who took the rap?
> Three guesses, and don't bother with the name Valorie Dawes.

"Who would that be?" Price said. "It sure ain't Kryz, right?"

"Nor me," O'Reilly said, "and I think we can safely eliminate Jan. Unless you're switching teams on us, Dawes." She chuckled. Val found no humor in the situation.

"Rico already said it wasn't him," Val said. "That leaves either Grimes or Pops—and Bobby wouldn't make up a story like that, much less blab it to CopWatch."

"So it's Papadopoulos," O'Reilly said. "That asshole. And since he's retired, we can't touch him."

"The story itself must've originated from Ben Peterson, right?" Price asked. "I mean, if they're family..."

"They both claim they don't get along," Val said. "At least, they used to. Although you're right, that's the only thing that makes sense."

"Or someone on the inside planted it," O'Reilly said. "Someone with access to confidential IA files. Like Blanchard or Finley."

Or...Val recalled Shelby's warning about Simpson digging into her record.

"Couldn't they get fired for that?" Price asked.

"Let's hope so," Val said. "Whoever it is, he better hope he's not the one I kick in the balls next. Get me started and I might never stop."

Price's eyes widened, and he made a comical show of protecting his crotch and sliding away from Val's desk.

"I'll poke around and see what I can find out," O'Reilly said. "Best if you stay away." She lowered her voice. "Try not to mention kicking more of our colleagues in the balls for now, okay? It won't serve you well in the internal investigation of your case."

Val reddened. "It was a joke, but...point taken. Anyway, I need to get some research done and then get on the horn with Greenville." She closed the blog and opened the Larkin file and a web browser on her desktop. Before she got very far, her cell phone rang—a call, not a text, this time. From her father.

"What time should I expect you today?" Dad said after a quick exchange of hellos.

"Um...did I say I was coming over?" Val said. A pang of guilt stabbed her in the gut.

"You promised you'd help me look after Sammy," Dad said, his voice betraying disappointment. "He's dying to see you. He wants to go back to the dinosaur theme park in Rocky Hill. Did you promise to take him there?"

"No," Val said, frustration with her father rising. "I have no idea where that's coming from. Anyway, I had to come into the office for a few hours."

"Ah. I see. Work trumps all *again*. Just like your mother."

Heat rose up Val's neck to her face. Dad sure knew how to push her buttons. "I won't be too long. Maybe we can take him to the zoo or something later this afternoon?"

"It's raining again." Disappointment clouded her father's voice.

Val rolled her eyes. Why they could run around an outdoor theme park in the rain, and not the zoo, she didn't understand. "How about we meet for lunch? McDonald's, say? My treat."

He laughed. "Last of the big-time spenders. Okay, he'll like that. Then the dinosaurs tomorrow?"

She agreed and ended the call. She spent a half-hour pulling together the information on Larkin's alleged victims and their families, then emailed it to the Greenville cops. After a refill on her coffee and a bathroom break, she followed up with a phone call.

"Thanks for the info," Detective Torres said once they'd exchanged hellos. "I noticed the names of his friends and family are all local to you, though, in Clayton."

Val chuckled at the 'friends and family" reference. Travis Blake had a similar style of gallows humor and it never got old. "That's what we know of—and those are 'alleged' victims, remember? There might be others outside our orbit, but I wouldn't have access to that."

"Can you help us out with running them down and talking to them?" Torres said. "Since you're local and all. We've got a much smaller department here with a massive caseload, and..." Her voice trailed off.

Torres left her a huge opening there, and Val picked up on the cue. "I talked to my boss, and we're willing to take the lead on the case—take it right off your hands if you want," she said. "We'd still share our findings as we go, and all the credit when we find the perp, of course."

"I like the idea, but I don't know if the higher-ups would go for it," Torres said. "Any chance you can meet with Gramercy and me and our boss in person?"

"You mean, in Greenville?" Val said.

"I doubt I could get him to Clayton. Looks like his calendar is free first thing Monday morning. Say, 8:00 a.m.?"

Yikes. Val would have to wake up at 5:30 to get showered, fed, and on the road in time.

Unless...

Recalling Shelby's invitation and her father's plea to rescue him from Sammy, an idea formed in her brain.

"Let me place a few phone calls," Val said. "I might find a way to make that happen."

Chapter Twelve

Connor hid behind a wide-trunked tree and peeked downriver, toward a sandy spot at a bend in the creek. The little brown man stood at the creek's edge, rock in hand. A short ways away sat the black-haired woman with the big boobs. She sat right there on the sand, as if it wouldn't get her butt soaking wet.

At least she wasn't holding a rock.

"Hey, there." The man smiled at Connor and skipped the rock across the water. Two skips, then it sank. "Come on out. You don't need to hide."

Connor froze. How did they see him? They must have X-ray vision.

"Don't worry," the woman said, "we're friendly." She smiled and stood, walking toward him. "Do you live around here?"

No point in hiding anymore—they'd spotted him.

Connor stepped out from behind the tree and glanced from the woman's face to the man's. He recalled what Mom always said: *Don't talk to strangers.*

But they didn't throw rocks at him, after all. In fact, both seemed friendly, smiling at him. Nothing creepy or dangerous, like inviting him into their car or offering candy. Just skipping rocks in the stream, as Connor liked to do. A fun thing, not a bad thing.

Besides, he'd seen them yesterday. Did they still count as strangers if he'd sort of met them before?

"We're staying in the cabins over there." The man pointed toward the little huts Mom often rented out in the summer. He didn't know she also rented them out in the spring. "My name's Sanjit. This is Shelby. We're here on vacation. Are you visiting, too?"

"No," Connor said before he remembered not to answer questions. That counted as talking.

"You live here, then? Lucky you," the woman said. "It's so beautiful. What is this little river called?"

"Clearwater Creek," Connor said. It seemed okay to answer a question about geography.

To his surprise, his reply made the two grown-ups laugh. "No way!" Sanjit said.

"Yeah, *way*," Connor said. No-talking rules also don't keep you from stopping people from calling you a liar. "That's its name. I can prove it." He unfolded his Explorer Map and spread it out for them to see.

Both Sanjit and Shelby edged closer, peering at the map with squinty eyes. "Well, I'll be damned," Shelby said. "It's my stream!"

"No, it's my dad's and mom's," Connor said, *again* just correcting their mistake. "Okay, not all of it, but it runs onto our land, and we own that. This part is public property."

"I see," Shelby said. "Well, guess what? My last name is also Clearwater. Isn't that cool? And I didn't mean I really owned it. I was making a joke."

Connor folded his map back up, not knowing what to say. Sanjit and Shelby glanced at each other like they didn't know what to say, either.

"Hey, are you good at skipping rocks?" Sanjit said.

"Uh...I'm okay." Mom always said not to brag, although Dad did it anyway sometimes.

"Just okay?" Sanjit laughed. "I bet you're an expert."

Connor shrugged. "Not as good as you. You made it skip five times. I've never gotten it to skip more than three."

"Want me to teach you?" Sanjit smiled and held out a flat, brown stone. Nice and smooth. "Here. Show me your technique and I'll give you a few tips on how to do it better."

"Okay." Connor shuffled closer to the bank and curled his index finger around the stone's sharp edge. He cocked his arm back and whipped it into the stream. It knifed into the water...and sank.

"Ah, too bad. I think you were nervous," Sanjit said. "Here's a better rock. Try it again."

Connor took the rock and flicked it across the surface. It hit, skipped once, then sank.

"Good, good," Sanjit said. "Much better. Now watch me." He flicked a rock into the water. It *splish-splash-whooshed-dut-dut-dut-dutted* across before thunking into the bank on the other side.

"Wow!" Connor forgot everything about how not to talk to strangers and, mouth wide, faced Sanjit again. "That was awesome. How did you do that?"

Sanjit grinned. "First trick of great rock-skipping: pick the flattest, smoothest stone," he said. "Not too heavy, or it'll sink anyway. Not too light, or the wind will blow it sideways and it won't skip. Here's another good one." He snagged a rock off the ground and handed it to Connor. Then he showed him how to hold it, using the gap between his index and middle fingers—"stronger and more stable than one finger," he explained. Then he flicked it, using what he called "a sidearm motion" like pro baseball pitchers sometimes use, to keep the rock flat as it skimmed the surface. How to choose a nice calm spot on the water, into the current or across it, not downstream. So many little details.

On his third try, Connor's rock *skip-scoop-splish-splashed* across the stream.

"Holy smokes!" Connor grinned. "I did it!"

"You sure did!" Shelby said, coming up behind them. "Four skips!"

"Nope," Connor said. "Three. The one where it sinks at the end doesn't count as a skip."

Sanjit nodded. "Technically correct. You know your stuff, kid-with-no-name."

"I do *too* have a name. Connor Theobald Cox the Fourth. I live at The Grounds." He smiled and pointed downstream. "It's our family estate. My great-grandpa built the house we live in."

"Wow," Sanjit said. "Pleased to meet you, Connor Cox. I am Sanjit Patwari—the First."

"You have a funny accent," Connor said. "Are you from England?"

"I was born in Pakistan," Sanjit said. "Do you know where that is?"

Connor shook his head. The woman, Shelby, seemed upset for a moment. Maybe he shouldn't have asked about the accent.

"Have you heard of India?"

Connor nodded. "It's in Asia. Over a billion people live there."

"That's right," Sanjit said. "Pakistan is next to India. It's a beautiful country—"

A song played in Sanjit's pocket. He pulled a cell phone out and frowned. "Sorry, I must take this call." He stepped aside and spoke into the phone in a low voice.

Connor took the time to practice his rock-skipping. Shelby helped him find rocks and skipped a few as well. She was almost as good as Connor, even though Sanjit didn't give her any lessons. She seemed strong and her body shape resembled his dad's and uncle's more than his mom's, except for the big boobs. And she had kind of a mustache, and that thing in her throat that men have but not many women. It made him curious, and Mom taught him to ask questions when you want to learn something, so…

"Are you a boy or a girl?" he asked after she managed a three-skipper across the stream.

Shelby cast him the nasty side-eye like his uncle did when Connor asked where he went on weekend nights in his fancy sports car. Oops.

"That's not a very appropriate question," she said. "It's often considered rude, at least when grown-ups ask that way. Didn't your parents teach you that?"

Connor bowed his head, his ears growing warm. "Sorry.

I just like to know stuff."

"Do you know what 'non-binary' means? Do they ever talk about that in school?"

He shook his head. "My mom homeschools me."

Shelby folded her arms across her chest. "Okay. Well, I'm a girl."

"Cool." Connor picked up another rock and almost skipped it, but he liked its red streaks that ran through the black part. "What kind of rock is this?"

Shelby glanced at it and shrugged. "I don't know. Why?"

"I'm investigating," he said. "I'm a scientist. We like facts and if we can't explain something, we make up theories and test them with data and experiments."

"That's a smart way to learn," Shelby said. "That's how I learn, too."

"Are you a scientist?"

She laughed. "I'm a computer scientist, so yeah, I guess," she said. "So is Sanjit."

"My dad owns a bunch of computers," Connor said. "He's on them all the time."

"He sounds smart, too," Shelby said.

Connor nodded. These grown-ups were really cool and friendly. Not stranger-dangers at all.

"So sorry," Sanjit said, hanging up his phone, his face sad. He faced Shelby, not Connor, as he spoke. "That was work. They're having system problems—more hackers. They need me to go in early tomorrow."

"We rented the cabin through Friday!" Shelby said, upset again. "You took vacation time! They can't—"

"They wanted me back right now," Sanjit said. "I talked them out of that. But tomorrow is the latest. I am so sorry." He turned to Connor. "The place where I work is having computer problems. I must go fix them."

"Do you want me to ask my dad to help?" Connor asked. "He's wicked smart with computers."

Sanjit laughed. "No, thank you, I'm sure I can handle it. However, it means our friendship must take a brief hiatus."

Connor searched his vocabulary and came up empty. "What's a *high-ate-us*? Is that like going on a trip?"

Sanjit grinned. "In a way. It means we will not see each other again for a while. I am disappointed—I was enjoying your company. You're an excellent student at rock-skipping."

Connor frowned, then shrugged. Mom always said, make lemonade. "It's okay. I think I can perfect my technique on my own."

Sanjit laughed again, and this time, Shelby did too, despite the sour expression on her face. They said goodbye and hiked up the hill toward their cabin.

Connor, walking back home, grew sad that his new acquaintances needed to leave. He didn't have many friends, much less people from Pakistan or people who changed their minds about being boys or girls. They were a lot more interesting than the boys and girls his parents had him meet for playdates—kids of their friends who knew nothing about rock-skipping or foreign countries.

Maybe next time he went exploring, he'd discover a place like Pakistan.

***

Val had no problem convincing her father to let her take Sammy off his hands. A quick phone call and a promise to bring the boy to the 4:00 p.m. showing of *Dolittle* at the second-release theater in Clayton did the trick. She also committed to picking him up early on Sunday so Dad could make his 8:15 a.m. tee time.

That meant getting her work done, pronto. And checking with Shelby and Sanjit to confirm it was okay to bring him along to Greenville. She called Shelby, who picked up on the first ring.

"Val, I was about to call you," she said. "Bad news. Sanjit needs to go back to Clayton tomorrow morning. Instead of extending our stay, we've got to cut our vacation short. And I was so looking forward to hanging out with you!"

Val's stomach fell to her feet. "Oh, man," she said. "What a shame—wait. Did you say he's leaving Sunday morning?"

"That's right. Why?"

Val's heartbeat quickened. "I have a meeting in Greenville early Monday, and I was hoping I could come out early Sunday and hang out with you..."

"That would be awesome!"

"One catch," Val said. "I also committed to taking care of my ten-year-old brother for a few days. I hope I can bring him along...if that's not too much trouble."

"Actually," Shelby said, "that might work out. There's a kid here about his age who seems a bit lonely. Maybe they can play together while you and I spend some quality girl time?"

"Are you sure? It wouldn't mess up your plans too much?"

"I insist. Besides, I'm interested to see what a mini-Dawes would be like. Even if it is a boy."

At that moment, Shannon reappeared at Val's desk. "Okay, then," Val said. "Gotta go. Text me the details. We're there!"

Only after Val hung up did it occur to her she hadn't worked out who would look after Sammy during her Monday meeting. Crap. Well, she'd burn that bridge when she got to it, as Gil liked to say.

She opened the case files for Jason Larkin, the guy who washed up on the riverbank in Greenville, and for Isaiah Dinker, the guy with similar mutilations found in Clayton. Both alleged sex offenders. Both sported long rap sheets—always for arrests, no convictions. Another similarity she didn't notice before: for both men, their whereabouts for the evening prior to their death remained unknown.

Yet another interesting fact came to light in reviewing their financial records: both used their credit cards in

Greenville a day or two before their murders.

Val called one of Larkin's local contacts, a guy named Vinny, who'd vouched for him as an alibi on a theft charge for which Larkin got released without indictment.

"I'm calling to investigate the murder of your former associate, Jason Larkin," Val said after introducing herself.

"About time," Vinny said. "I been waiting for you guys to call me back all week."

"Evidence has come to light which may help us find Jason's killer," Val said. "We were hoping you might help us track down where he was the day before his death."

"I don't know," Vinny said. "I wasn't with him."

"When did you last see him?"

"About two weeks ago. We had…a business thing out of town."

"In Greenville, by chance?"

Vinny took a moment before answering. "Yeah. How'd you know?"

"Do you recall the names of places you visited in Greenville while you were there?" Val asked. "Restaurants, bars, retail establishments, anything."

"We met at the home of…an associate," Vinny said. "Did our business there. Then we all grabbed a bite to eat. Stayed at the Greenville Motor Inn and returned home early Sunday. Separate cars. His car was still there when I left. That help?"

"Name of the restaurant on Saturday?"

"Some Italian place. I had lasagna, Jase ordered, lessee…I don't remember."

"Were you together the entire time?" Val asked.

Another pause. "Nah. I was tired, hit the sack straight away after dinner. Jase went out for drinks and got in pretty late…I don't know what time. Separate rooms and all."

"Which bar did he go to?"

"He said the name…Step Out, I think? I never been there."

Val thanked him and hung up. She searched Step Out

on the internet and discovered it was a gay-friendly dance club. Interesting.

She tried more of Dinker's contacts, but none would talk to her. Another review of his financials revealed he'd visited another underage dance club in Clayton a few days before his murder. For a guy well into his forties, that didn't make sense…except that he was accused of dealing in child porn. Dinker might've been scouting for talent.

She shared her findings with Shannon.

"Don't hate me for saying this," Shannon said when she'd finished. "That's going to make your meeting in Greenville tougher. They won't want to give up Larkin's case if it was local."

"They're already convinced it was local," Val said. "I'm more concerned about the gay bar thing."

"So, he swings from both sides of the plate," Shannon said. "So what? How does that change things?"

"It expands the universe of probable suspects, for starters," Val said. "In addition to his alleged victims, now we have spurned hookups in the mix. It also strengthens the case for a hate crime. Anti-gay crusaders, or, given his record, someone who's out for vigilante justice against what they view as a pervy lifestyle."

"It also makes it less likely they'll see it as related to the Dinker case," Shannon said.

"True." Val's head grew weary. This might give Detective Torres cold feet about their Monday meeting, and she'd already committed—to Dad and to Shelby—to bring Sammy camping. "Thanks. I'll…figure something out."

"Keep me posted," Shannon said. "Oh, and tread lightly. Old Tackle Box has friends in Greenville, too, apparently. He still wants this case, and if he believes you're treading on his turf, God knows what he'll try next."

Val tried composing a preemptive email to Detective Torres, pleading her case for allowing the Larkin investigation to transfer to Clayton. But everything she came up with seemed to support keeping it in Greenville. In the end, she decided to proceed with the meeting and hope for the best.

She texted Shelby:

> One thing I forgot to mention…that Monday a.m. meeting? Sammy, my little bro, might need some supervision.

Shelby didn't hesitate:

> No prob. I'm great with kids. Besides, I want to pick his brain and learn all your secrets! LOL

Val laughed and replied:

> Most of my secrets are safe, then. I've only known him less than a year. Long story…

Shelby replied after a long pause:

> Yup. That was during our first case together, remember?

Val slapped her forehead. Of course. How could that have slipped her mind?

Shelby's text continued:

> Speaking of brothers and secrets…apparently my brother Austin is in town and is looking for me. PLEASE PLEASE PLEASE do not tell anyone—especially him—where I am! (He may come sniffing around police HQ. He knows I work there.)

Val grimaced. Shelby's brother disapproved of her "lifestyle choices"—his term for her gender transition—and they hadn't spoken in years. As messed up as her own family was, at least she didn't have battles like that to fight.

She replied:

> I'll guard the knowledge of your whereabouts with my life.

Val put her phone away and, for the first time in days, relaxed at her desk. It felt good to have a plan and be in control of her situation again.

***

Unbelievable.

The gall of those two, stalking that young boy and working their degenerate wiles to gain his confidence. Pretending to make "friends" with a nine-year-old. Advancing their sick agenda in the most insidious of ways.

Who were they kidding? Everyone knew their tactics. They find a vulnerable, innocent kid, one who doesn't know the ways of the world. Pretend to be a normal, kind person who wouldn't hurt anyone. Show generosity at first—in this case, teaching him little tricks that a young boy would consider cool. Gain his trust.

Then they reel him in. Show him other things that aren't so innocent. Make their victim believe the perverted lives they live are normal. Trick him into believing it can even be a better, happier way to live. Then, turn him against everything he's known before: his family, his religion, his way of life. Turn him into of their own—indoctrinate him with their immoral, illegal bacchanalian ways—and meanwhile, the legal system turns a blind eye to their depravity.

The Redeemer had to stop it. Now.

Bad enough that he'd looked the other way when his own brother ventured down the path of promiscuity—and, according to salacious rumors, unspeakably kinky nastiness. His affairs besmirched the family's proud name, flaunting his turpitude in public, no longer exercising even a modicum of discretion. So disgusting!

He'd let it go on too long. It was time to act. To rid the family, and his community, of these degenerates. All of them.

Especially these two.

This time, he'd send a clear message to the authorities. The last few deviants he'd cleansed from the gene pool hadn't generated the appropriate response. The cops and judges were still all too willing to let these miscreants walk the streets, free to foist their twisted sexuality onto an unsuspecting community. This time, he'd make sure they'd hear his message: take action, or allow the more valorous members of society exact justice in a more direct, permanent way.

But not before these obscene creatures saw the error of their ways. Saw it, admitted it, vowed to cleanse their souls of their debauchery.

He shivered with anticipation. He *loved* that part.

And, as soon as they acknowledged and committed to the path of righteousness, he would see that they never again strayed—by keeping their passage on this mortal coil short. Ending that journey by delivering them, purified, to their creator—immediately, before they succumbed once more to temptation and revert to their evil ways.

Part Two

The Grounds

Chapter Thirteen

Val woke early on Sunday and packed a cooler full of groceries that would span the gap between her health-oriented diet and what ten-year-old Sammy might prefer. That meant lean roasted turkey as well as Kraft slices, hamburgers and salmon steaks, fresh veggies along with boxed mac and cheese. She loaded it along with her suitcase into the Honda and hoped she'd brought warm enough clothes. March weather in the Berkshires could range from bitter cold to balmy, and change without notice. At the last moment, she grabbed some entertainment options for Sammy—games, videos, an old football she found in Gil's garage—and a few books for herself.

Before she finished loading, a silver Chevy Blazer parked at the end of Gil's driveway. Brenda Petroni hopped out, her expression grim. A moment later, a Clayton police cruiser pulled up with Ed Simpson at the wheel. He stayed in the car and lowered the driver's side window, fixing Val with a steely gaze and a smug smile. A plainclothes cop who looked a lot like Inspector Tony Blanchard sat shrouded in the gray morning's dim light in the passenger seat.

"This can't be good," Val said to Brenda when she drew near. Her body weighed a hundred extra pounds.

Petroni waited until she got within a few feet of Val, speaking in a low voice. "Do you want the good news first, or the bad news?"

"Is there good news?" Val asked.

Petroni, after a brief pause, shrugged. "The good news is, it's me doing this instead of them." She wagged her head back toward Simpson and Blanchard.

Val let the dread wash over her and heaved a calming breath before replying. "Should I get my gun and badge?" Her voice sounded tinny and shaky in her ear.

Petroni nodded.

Val swallowed an elephant-sized lump in her throat and pointed at the backseat. "It's in my suitcase."

"Bring it inside. I'll come with."

Val grabbed the bag, and Petroni followed her into the living room and stopped there while Val retrieved her gun, ID, and badge from her suitcase.

Val handed them over, sadness and anger competing for dominance in her psyche, even as she maintained a calm demeanor on the outside—she hoped.

"I wanted to get out of earshot of those two idiots for a minute," Petroni said, her face as sad as Val's heart. "This whole thing is stupid and a complete travesty. I expect the whole thing to get thrown out within five minutes of your hearing. When it's all done, I'll ensure the department expunges it from your record and issues an apology. By the way, everyone on the team agrees with me."

"Good to know," Val said, though she expected as much. "When is this hearing, then?"

"Wednesday morning. The review board will send you an official summons, probably tomorrow. Keep your phone handy, and bring an attorney if you've got one."

"Should I cancel my trip?" Val nudged her suitcase with her toe and wondered if Chad might refer a lawyer to her.

Petroni shook her head. "Getting out of town may be the best thing for you. And since you're suspended, best if you hold off on meeting with the Greenville detectives. We might forego taking the case from them, anyway." She lowered her voice further. "As it stands, higher-ups are pressuring me to give the Larkin and Dinker cases to Simpson. If he catches wind of you snooping around while you're out there, he could use it to get you fired outright."

Val cursed under her breath. Petroni heard her

anyway, if her coy smile was any indication.

"Val," Petroni said, "I'm serious about getting away. Use this time to clear your head. You've been under a lot of stress, and it'd be best if you showed up on Wednesday refreshed, rested, and calm—in appearance, if not reality." She grimaced. "I know you can't put it out of your mind entirely. Do the best you can."

"Wouldn't it be better to use the time to prepare my defense?" Val said.

Petroni considered that. "Like I told you before, get your story straight and commit it to memory. Get a lawyer and talk to him or her. Above all, don't show up angry. That'll only feed the narrative that you're too unstable to return to duty. Okay?"

Val nodded and escorted her boss outside. Petroni showed the gun, badge, and ID to Simpson and Blanchard before getting into her car. The two men gave Val sneering, ugly grins before following Petroni down the street. Assholes.

Val returned to the house to grab her suitcase and took a deep breath. She hated the idea of giving up on linking the Larkin and Dinker cases, particularly since Simpson seemed content to let the vigilante killers walk—similarly to how he treated the abortion clinic shooters six months before. As long as the victims were people he didn't like, he showed no interest in finding the perps. But how could she continue if he took over the case?

She tried not to care. If Simpson got her kicked off the force, she'd have no say in this or any future case. Still, she couldn't shed her commitment to finding the culprit, and couldn't imagine not being a cop anymore. It would kill her.

While zipping up her bag, Val discovered a business card tucked inside. Petroni's. She flipped it over and found a web address in her boss's handwriting, one of those generated by URL-shortening sites.

What was Petroni telling her? Was it related to Val's

suspension? To the two cases? Or something else?

Whatever it was, it would have to wait. Val was late getting over to Dad's to pick up Sammy.

***

Sammy more or less behaved on the drive to Greenville State Park, thanks to a slavish devotion to his game tablet. It stopped driving Val crazy once he volunteered to wear his earbuds. That, at least, eliminated the constant stream of buzzing, bell-ringing, cartoon animal-howling, and car-crashing noises produced by his infinite supply of entertainment apps. It also meant they didn't talk much. No big deal. Val figured they had plenty of opportunity for that in coming days.

They arrived at the '80s-vintage cedar-shake cabin around 11:00 a.m., a full hour after her target time, amid a cold, misty rain shower. The parking spot in front remained empty, as she'd expected—Sanjit had planned to leave no later than 9:00 a.m.—and the house appeared vacant, locked, and with no lights on inside. However, the code Shelby sent for the lockbox worked, and they unloaded the car in minutes, with Sammy's enthusiastic help. He ran from room to room, exclaiming things like "Cool!" and "Hey, look!" while Val read the note her friend left behind:

> *Went for a hike, should be back in time for a late lunch. Help yourself to whatever's in the fridge.*

"Stay out of Shelby's room!" Val called to Sammy.

"Which one is hers?"

"The one with her stuff in it, silly," Val said.

Sammy emerged a moment later from one of the bedrooms, a sheepish smile on his face. "They took the best room. Which one is mine?"

Val checked the second bedroom, a tiny space with

bunk beds, a wooden dresser, and a small closet. "We'll share this one," she said, and wondered if Shelby had really expected her and Gil to fit in that tiny space.

"Dibs on top bunk!" Sammy clambered up with his gaming tablet.

Val sighed and returned to the living room. Shelby's absence disappointed her, but she understood. Who wants to wait around for people who arrive an hour late? She took stock of the cabin, a rustic two-bedroom with a tiny kitchen-dining room-living room combo and a full bath. She looked forward to relaxing in the tub later that evening after Sammy went to bed. The cabin had no TV or internet service, but she found a weak yet serviceable cell signal, and Shelby had set the electric heat at a toasty 72 degrees. Sweltering. Val turned it down to 68 and planned to beg forgiveness when her friend returned.

With no other real agenda, she relaxed while checking email and scrolling Instagram until that bored her. She called Gil—no answer. Then she tried Shelby—same. She sent them both texts and settled down on the sofa, waiting. It felt good to rest after the long drive.

After a few minutes, she closed her eyes, just for a minute.

***

A pinging sound awakened Val from a restless slumber. She sat up on the couch and checked her phone. A message from Gil:

> Sorry I missed your call. Talk tonight? Things changing fast here. BTW, I feel a little better.

Val replied, asking if he'd be home soon. No answer. She checked the time: almost 1:00 p.m.

"Auntie Val?" Sammy called from the bedroom. "I'm hungry. Can we have lunch?"

Val considered asking him to wait for Shelby to

return—no sign of her yet—and thought better of it. She made them both peanut butter and jelly sandwiches, sliced an apple into wedges, and poured them both a tall glass of milk.

"I want chocolate milk," Sammy said around a mouthful of PBJ.

"Sorry," Val said. "The rain's letting up outside. Want to go exploring?"

"Yeah! Let's go discover some stuff!" Sammy jumped up and ran in circles around the cabin, his half-eaten sandwich in one hand, raising the other in a strange sort of salute to God-knows-what. The Explorers Guild, she guessed.

Val snapped a photo of a decades-old framed topographic map hanging on the wall by the door and hoped that the dotted lines representing trails and bridges remained more or less accurate. They donned sweatshirts and raincoats and followed a gravel path down to a broad creek with rushing water splashing over rapids. She scooped a handful—ice cold—and tasted it. Pure and delicious.

"Ew!" Sammy said, watching her. "Aren't you afraid of catching germs?"

"Cleanest water you'll ever find," Val said. "Try it."

Wide-eyed, he crept toward the edge of the bank and scooped some up to his mouth. His eyes lit up. "That's even better than Orange Julius!"

Val laughed. "And better for you. Come on, let's find this place on the map called The Grounds. I wonder what it is?"

"A fort?" Sammy guessed. "Or a castle!"

"I bet you're right," Val said. "Let's see. First one to find it gets an extra dessert."

Sammy dashed off down the trail ahead of her. "Me! I'm gonna find it first! I will, I will!" In moments, he disappeared over a hill, out of sight, though not out of earshot.

In mid-exclamation, his shouting stopped.

"Hi," he said to someone. "I'm Sammy. Who are you?"

Val hurried to catch up. While she hoped he'd encountered a kid his age, Sammy's social skills and danger awareness were more than a little lacking. She crested the hill, ready to call his name.

What greeted her allayed all of her concerns. A young blond-haired boy, more or less Sammy's age, stood by the creek, holding binoculars.

"I'm Connor T. Cox the Fourth," he said. "My family owns this place. Well, not all of it. That part over there." He pointed behind him, up another hill. "Are you new around here?"

Val smiled. "Sort of. I'm Valorie. Sammy and I are staying in a cabin near the state park." She stepped closer and extended her hand.

"You too?" Connor backed away and his face curled into a puzzled frown. "Are you friends of Shelby and San-jee?"

"Yes, although his name is Sanjit, with a T," Val said. Relief washed over her. Finally, some sign of Shelby still being here. "Have you seen Shelby today?"

Connor's face clouded. "Yeah, a long time ago. Maybe an hour or even longer." He brightened. "You're prettier than Shelby. Although she has bigger boobs."

Val choked in surprise, trying not to laugh. "Yes, she does," Val said, "although we don't talk about that in polite conversation."

"Sorry," he said. "Do you know my mom? She's pretty, too, and skinny like you. Wait, is that rude too?"

"It's okay." Val laughed in spite of herself. "Why don't you boys play? What are you finding in those binoculars of yours?"

"Birds and stuff," Connor said. "Want to look?"

"Can I?" Sammy said. "I want to see."

Connor glanced at him, skepticism all over his face.

"How old are you?"

"Ten and a half," Sammy said. "I'm in third grade. You?"

"Nine," Sammy said. "I just had a birthday."

"What grade are you in?"

Connor shrugged. "Kind of third or fourth. My mom homeschools me."

"My mom used to homeschool me, too!" Sammy said. "Before she—"

"Why don't you two see what species of birds you can find?" Val said before Sammy said too much. All she needed was for him to blab about their mother being in prison, and God knows how this kid would react.

"I'm done finding birds," Connor said. "Go ahead and look if you like. I need to find some cool rocks."

"I'll help! I'll help!" Sammy said. "I love rocks. And dinosaurs. I want to be a scientist when I grow up."

"Me too." Connor smiled and handed the binoculars to Val. "Here. You can find birds if you want. Us guys are going to explore."

Val chuckled and took the glasses from him, but kept her focus on the boys. They chatted about their favorite dinosaurs and types of rocks while she rested on a flat boulder on the side of the creek bank. After several minutes, Sammy challenged Connor to a rock-skipping contest. "Auntie Val, will you be our referee?" he asked.

"Valorie's your aunt? I thought she was your mom," Connor said.

"She's really my big sister," Sammy said. "I just call her that."

"I wish I had a sister," Connor said. "Or a brother. Okay, most skips wins. Three rocks each. You go first."

Sammy picked up a long, flat rock about the length of Val's hand and flicked it across the water. It skipped once, then plunked beneath the swift, splashing current.

"That wasn't a very good rock," Connor said.

"What's a good rock?" Sammy said.

Connor picked up a flat black stone a few inches in diameter. "This is slate. It's a good skipping rock." He proved it with an impressive triple-skip across the stream.

"Whoa!" Sammy found a similar rock and managed a double-skip on his next try. "Those are good skipper rocks." He picked up another, this one long and tubular with rounded-off ends. "Not this one. This one's a see-gar." He held it up to his lips and pretended to puff it like a cigar. Val wondered if his disgusting piece-of-shit father, Milt, taught him that.

Connor, for his part, found the mime hilarious, and he picked up a similar rock. "Look! I got me a see-gar too!" He puffed it for a moment, then skipped it. Only one skip before it sank.

They sampled dozens of other rocks, their competition forgotten as they made up names for the different shapes they found.

"This one's a potato!" Sammy held up a lumpy stone that, Val had to agree, looked like a fresh-picked tuber. She found their rock-naming game hilarious.

"These are tossers," Connor said. "They don't skip and they don't jump. Rejects."

"This one's cool." Sammy showed Val and Connor a yellow-and-red rock with spots and wavy stripes. "Those are girl rocks," he said. "Pretty, like Auntie Val, but they're not really useful."

"Hey!" Val said. "Who says I'm not useful?"

They ignored her, finding more rocks and categorizing them. Val made a mental note to talk to Sammy sometime about stereotypes and sexism. In the meantime, she picked up the binoculars and scanned the trees for interesting birds and any sign of Shelby. She didn't find anything other than crows. Probably the rest got scared away by all the noise.

"This is a button rock," Sammy said, holding up a

smooth, shiny pebble. "You can use it to make buttons."

Connor flicked another stone into the stream, which flipped and flopped as it skipped over the water. He held up a second one with a similar shape. "These are flippers," he said. "They flip when you skip 'em."

"These are jumpers," Sammy said, showing him a stone more or less flat with some curvature. "They jump out of the water!" He demonstrated, and sure enough, the stone bounced high off the surface before landing with a big splash.

"Airborne!" Connor said, tossing another one. "Like the 82nd Army Airborne Division. My great-grandpa was in that brigade in the war." He sang: "I want to be an Air Force Ranger, I want to live a life of danger. Sound off, one, two. Sound off, three, four. One, two, three, four. One-two. Three-four!"

Sammy's mouth hung open and then he burst out laughing, rolling on the wet ground, holding his sides. "That's amazing!" He got back to his feet and joined Connor in a lock-step march along the bank of the creek, belting out the song together.

Val, watching them from her now-sunny vantage point on the flat creekside rock, caught herself humming along, and realized how fortuitous it was that they'd met Connor so soon. Sammy had a playmate, as Shelby predicted, a boy his age with similar interests. She couldn't have asked for a better situation. Except, of course, having Shelby around.

Or Gil.

She heard a buzzing sound—kind of like a hummingbird. Val scanned the area with her naked eye, then with the binoculars, but didn't see—

Wait. She saw something. It looked like one of those robotic drones used by hobbyists...and by some law enforcement agencies to investigate unsafe spaces. Why would someone want to spy on her here? And who?

As if startled by her, the drone pointed right at her,

then buzzed away.

Val shivered. She didn't like it. And it reminded her they ought to get back and see if Shelby had returned. They hadn't left her a note, although Shelby would see that they'd arrived with all their stuff there. It still bothered Val that she hadn't answered her text or tried to call, though.

She wondered why the drone, and why no word from Shelby, and came up with no answer to either question. None she liked, anyway.

Chapter Fourteen

The man-girl creature stirred awake. With its eyes blindfolded and ankles and wrists zip-tied, The Redeemer couldn't confirm the man-girl's return to full consciousness. The creature's movement appeared deliberate, though, its head no longer lolling to one side and the muscles in its legs straining against the bindings around the ankles.

Then the creature made a noise through the gag, confirming it was awake. Goosebumps rose on its skin, even though he'd turned up the thermostat. However, stripped to boxers and that ridiculous tank top, he-she might shiver for any number of reasons.

Humiliation, he hoped, topped the list.

"Welcome to my safe house, Shelby," the man typed into his laptop, and the computer's robotic voice pronounced the words in the British accent he'd chosen. The cramped, dank room's concrete floors and walls, broken up only by a single shag throw rug and a four-foot geometric-pattern quilt, echoed his machine's words with a chilling sharpness.

He typed on. "Despite what your fears may be telling you, you are, for now, safe here."

The creature strained against its bindings again, groaning through the gag.

"I'd love to remove the gag, and perhaps even the leg restraints," he typed, and the laptop did the talking for him. "First I need assurances you won't scream or try to run. Both would be futile. Nobody can hear you and there's nowhere to go."

More grunts, though not as loud. Then a nod of the head, and a noise that sounded like a muffled "Okay."

"Give me your word. No screaming or running." The words sounded so elegant in that British accent.

Another nod.

"Very well, then. We'll start with the gag, so we can talk...*man to man*." He let that phrasing sink in. Then he reached across and tugged the gag down to Shelby's chin and returned to the laptop. "Is that better?"

"Yes," Shelby said, its voice strained. "H-how do you know my name?"

"Tut-tut. I'll ask the questions." He loved how that sounded in the computer's high-society, almost royal voice. He thought of how a prince or duke might word things, and typed on. "Suffice to say, I'm quite familiar with who you are...or at least, who you were, and who you try to be in your...present configuration." He even loved how the machine paused over the ellipses. Beautiful program, this.

"Where am I?" Shelby asked.

"That's irrelevant," The Redeemer typed. "What is important is knowing that you'll never leave here under your own power—at least until you've repented. Until then, consider this space...home."

Tears spilled from the blindfold down Shelby's cheeks. "What did I ever do to you to deserve this?"

"What haven't you done?" the man said out loud before he could stop himself. Hopefully, his voice sounded raspy and angry enough to mask his identity. He did not want Shelby to know who he was. Yet.

He resumed typing: "Our task here is to remind you of whom you really are. To guide you back to embracing your original self, and to repudiate the abomination that you've chosen to become. Do you understand?"

"Please don't do this," Shelby said, its voice rushed and thin with terror. "You don't understand—"

He wanted to shout, but he'd committed to the

computer voice approach, so instead he silenced Shelby the old-fashioned way. With a sharp slap across the face.

"Do not tell me I don't understand," the computer said under his command. "I do understand. I understand you are an abomination. A perversion of nature, self-inflicted, and that now you seek to foist your evil upon the young and innocent, the unsuspecting youth—"

"Do you mean Connor? I would never—"

Another slap, harder than the first, enough to knock Shelby's face sideways and leave a red welt.

The man regretted the move, hating himself for it. He'd not wanted to go this route, for so many reasons. Skin-to-skin touching, even violent touch, created an intimacy he'd rather not develop. Shelby was getting to him in ways he'd never anticipated.

"Remain silent," he typed into the laptop. Then he strode into the washroom, prepared a soft washcloth with soap and a bowl of warm water, and set it down next to Shelby's bare legs. Shaven, like a woman's, though the tiny bulge in Shelby's boxer shorts revealed what he already knew about this creature's true gender.

And now, because of his earlier lapse, he needed to touch Shelby again. It repulsed him, but he had no choice.

He dipped the washcloth into the water and washed his DNA off Shelby's red face with a gentle hand—the way he intended his touches to land, even when they weren't premeditated. Always with respect for the humanity he strived so hard to heal. He wrung out the cloth and dipped it again, another set of gentle strokes to rinse off the soap.

Back to the laptop. "Better?"

Shelby nodded. "I...I need to pee."

The man frowned and typed. He couldn't untie her, even for this. "There's a blanket underneath you. It will absorb whatever issues from your body."

"That's...disgusting."

Flashing anger, he typed, "How appropriate for you."

He waited for a reaction and, seeing none, continued. "I will leave you to your ablutions. In the meantime, think about what you've become and what your return to normal will look like. Because that is your path back to freedom. I trust you can do this, Shelby. After all, you got yourself into this mess, didn't you?"

Shelby's only response: more tears.

Fuck. Maybe Shelby really *had* become a damned girl.

He pulled the gag back over Shelby's mouth and put the laptop into password-protected slumber mode. Then he exited the space, locking the door behind him.

Trudging up the stairs to ground level, he checked his phone and clicked the icon showing new footage from the security system. He paused halfway up to watch.

More people in the area. Dammit!

And they'd met the boy.

God help them if they, too, were queer like this one.

***

Val and Sammy returned to the cabin as the sun sank into the budding treetops, a brisk wind chilling the late afternoon air. Val expected Shelby to be waiting for her and had crafted a heartfelt apology for being out so long. She'd hoped to return well before 3:00 p.m., but didn't want to short-circuit the boys' fun and instant friendship. None of that would enter into her apology, though. She'd lost track of time, glad for the distractions nature provided from the grind and pressures of her job.

However, a dark, empty cabin greeted them. No messages on her phone. No note. No sign of Shelby.

Val's worry meter spiked. Where did she go?

She considered calling or texting Sanjit to see if Shelby had returned to Clayton, but she couldn't get cell service. Which, she realized, might explain why Shelby hadn't called or texted. Val's worry eased a little.

Inside the cabin, she found contact information for the owner—Kayleigh Cox, with a phone number. Fat lot of good that would do with no phone service. The address, though, was for The Grounds. She recalled Connor saying something about living at The Grounds. Was Kayleigh his mother? Perhaps she'd have some idea of where Shelby might've gone. But she hated to bug them unnecessarily.

Val glanced over at Sammy...fast asleep on the sofa. The afternoon had worn him out. Not her, though—she needed exercise. She wrote a quick note for him to stay put until she returned, pulled on her running shirt and pants, and headed out for a quick run. Val relished the unexpected opportunity for exercise, limited as it was, and reached a quick six-minute-mile pace within the first few hundred yards. The cool breeze dried the sweat from her forehead as soon as it appeared. Her legs lost their stiffness, and she fell into a steady rhythm. She followed the winding paved road for about a mile through a mix of meadows, forest, and pasture, drinking in the fresh country air. Running, as always, cleared her head, and she realized she should check in with the Coxes about Shelby— to ease her mind, if nothing else.

Then she turned around, kicked into high gear, and raced back, graining speed with every step, imagining the trouble Sammy got into during her absence.

Val need not have worried. He hadn't budged from the sofa during her fifteen-minute run, so far as she could tell, and she roused him from his slumber with a gentle shake of his shoulder.

"Is it dinnertime?" he asked, rubbing sleepy-sand out of his eyes.

"Almost," Val said. "First, we need to run a quick errand."

They climbed into her Honda and, ten minutes later, she spied a high stone wall and drove along it for several hundred feet before reaching the gated entrance. A faded engraved-brass sign announced she'd reached The Grounds. She lowered her window and pressed the buzzer to one side of the locked iron gate.

A muffled woman's voice answered. "Who is it?"

"Valorie Dawes," she said. "I'm staying at the cabin with Shelby Clearwater. She went for a hike this morning and hasn't returned. Can I chat with you for a minute?"

After a few seconds, the woman replied, "Yes, of course. Come in." Something buzzed, and the iron gate creaked open.

Val drove up a long, curved driveway that cut through acres of golf-green-perfect grass. Occasional clumps of topiary and flower gardens lined the drive, boasting a rash of crocus, budding forsythia, and a few tips of bulb flowers poked through the surface. At the end of the path, a three-story brick-and-fieldstone mansion with thick white columns arose from the turf as if it had grown there, along with the mature flora surrounding it—rose vines, lilac bushes, arborvitae, and what looked like miniature spruce. An oversized black door with gold inlays and a giant brass knocker dominated the front patio. She wondered why they'd need a knocker, given the walls and gated entrance. Then again, it appeared older than everything else. Maybe the stone perimeter walls came later.

"Stay in the car—I'll just be a minute," she said to Sammy. When he didn't reply, she glanced back at him and smiled. He'd fallen asleep again during the short drive over. She locked the Honda and approached the front of the mansion.

The giant door opened, and a slender waif of a woman in a linen dress and blue sandals appeared in the doorway. She appeared to be in her thirties, with deep-set eyes that seemed sad, despite the smile creasing her delicate face.

"Come in, Miss Dawes," the woman said. "I'm Kayleigh Cox. I believe you've met my son Connor?" Kayleigh stepped aside and waved Val in. "And," she said, "this is my husband, Theo."

A fortyish man about six feet tall with a trim, athletic

build entered the room, wearing slacks and a crisp dress shirt. He smiled at her, with straight, white teeth that seemed too small for his mouth. He wore his dirty-blond hair cut in a conservative "High and Tight" style like a lot of her colleagues on the police force, reinforcing an aura of personal power that emanated from his confident smile. "Connor's told us about you," he said, offering a firm handshake. Theo glanced around Val. "No Sammy? Connor *loves* his new rock-skipping buddy."

"No, Sammy's taking a quick nap." Val suppressed a pang of guilt for not bringing him in, but she wanted the visit to focus on Shelby. She followed Kayleigh into a small adjacent sitting room and sat on a white leather loveseat, and the Coxes sat together on the matching sofa opposite her. The aroma of roasting meat and fresh bread wafted into the room. "I won't stay long," she said. "Sorry to interrupt your dinner. I should come back later."

"Oh, I hope you'll stay and dine with us," Kayleigh said. "Though I suppose you'd need to retrieve Sammy. Or we can send a car—Theo, is Miss Embley still on the premises?"

Theo's smile faded into a tight grimace and his eyes turned glassy. "No," he said, his voice terse. "She's gone for the day. Of course, Ms. Dawes and her son are welcome anytime."

"Sammy's my brother," she said, "and thank you, but tonight I'll have to take a rain check." Val also wanted to get back to the cabin soon in case Shelby returned. "As I was explaining to your wife, Mr. Cox, my—"

"Theo, please." His pleasant smile returned.

"Theo. Thank you. My friend Shelby, who rented the cabin from you, has been missing all day. I wondered if you'd heard from her or might know where she could've gone?"

Theo squinted at Val, as if perturbed by her question. He turned to his wife. "You rented the cabins?" He shook his head. "Off-season? News to me."

"I...wasn't going to allow it," Kayleigh said. "Sanjit seemed so nice, though, and... well, he mentioned her last name—Clearwater—and that sold me. Can you imagine, Theo? Like the creek. It seemed so fitting to allow them to vacation in a place named for her."

"She and her boyfriend, you say? Well, that explains it, doesn't it?" Theo laughed, a sudden joviality that startled Val a bit. She saw where Connor got some of his social awkwardness. "Let me guess. He's also 'missing' this evening?"

"Sanjit returned to Clayton this morning. Shelby and I planned to spend some girl time for the next few days...although my brother joining us sort of complicates that...and, anyway, she's been gone all day." Val didn't know why she got so flustered. Something about the intense stares from both Kayleigh and Theo unnerved her. Her desire to keep the visit brief intensified.

"Well, I haven't seen her," Theo said. "I didn't even know she was here. Kayleigh? Since you arranged this behind my back, perhaps the two of you had something going, a secret gathering of some kind?" His smile, directed at his wife, contained no mirth, and his voice was edged in steel.

"No, of course not. Why would you say such a thing?" Kayleigh sprinkled a light laugh in among her words, delivered in an almost frivolous tone. Such an odd couple.

"Kayleigh, why don't you ask Connor if he's seen Shelby—that's the name, right? Shelby?"

"Good idea, Theo," Kayleigh said, and she leaned toward him, lips pursed to kiss his cheek.

Theo pulled away before the kiss landed. He ignored the hurt expression on Kayleigh's face and waited for her to disappear into the next room before sidling closer to Val.

"I didn't want to offer this while my wife was present," Theo said in a low voice. "It's probably worth our while to check with my brother, Ambrose, to see if he's, ah, *encountered* your friend today." He cleared his throat. "My brother lives in a cottage on the opposite end of the property, and he's been lurking around the creek in recent days."

"That would be great," Val said. "How can I reach him?"

"I'll call him," Theo said. "Better yet, I'll go confront him in person. Ambrose has a nasty habit of ignoring my calls when he's, uh...on the prowl, so to speak?" He rolled his eyes. "Am is a bit of a playboy. Another reason to keep him away from a pretty young lady like you."

Pretty? Still sweaty and dressed in running clothes, Val felt anything but. Theo's compliment seemed calculated and disingenuous. "I can take care of myself, but I appreciate the help," she said. "Whatever you think is best."

"Leave me your number," Theo said. "I'll call once I know something."

"Connor hasn't seen her, either," Kayleigh said, re-entering the room, although this time she remained standing. "I'm sorry. If she calls, how can we reach you?"

"Here you go," Val said, handing Kayleigh—not Theo—a business card. "My cell number is in the bottom right. Although cell service here is pretty spotty, to say the least."

"It often is," Kayleigh said. "Oh, you're a police officer, Miss Dawes?"

"Off-duty at the moment," Val said.

Theo's eyes narrowed, and he gave her that icy smile again. "Your investigative skills should far outpace ours, then."

"I ought to get back before Sammy wakes up," Val said. "Thank you both so much."

"Are you sure you won't stay for dinner?" Kayleigh said. "We'd love to get to know you—"

"Miss Dawes already made her intentions clear," Theo said, irritation in his voice. "Won't you respect her wishes, *darling*?"

Kayleigh dropped her gaze, holding the tips of the fingers of one hand in the other. "Yes, dear. Of course. I was just—"

"Connor is waiting for us at the dinner table," Theo said. "We should rejoin him. I'll show you out, Miss Dawes."

He ushered Val to the exit, practically pushing her outside, and the door eased shut behind her.

Sammy woke up when Val started the car. "Where are we?" he asked.

The pang of guilt returned. "I...had a meeting," she said. "We're heading back now." The gate opened in front of her and closed moments after she drove through it. The Coxes—father, mother, son—were a strange bunch. Beyond that, though, something was amiss. Theo seemed ready to explode at a moment's notice, especially at Kayleigh, who seemed cowed, even frightened, in his presence. While she welcomed their help in searching for Shelby, she worried about what else she might learn about this strange, wealthy family.

***

Connor curled up on his bed, his dinner growing cold and untouched on his desk. Dad sent him to his room without supper for "interrupting" his boring stories about the land he wanted to buy or sell or build something on. But Mom came by to "check on him," and snuck him some macaroni and cheese with hot dogs, his favorite. Way better than the slimy scalloped potatoes and strange-smelling meat they were eating. And asparagus, gag. Who would eat that on purpose?

He stared at the underside of the upper bunk, a bed no one ever used except sometimes Connor played Action Figure Fighting up there. Someday he'd make a friend his own age who'd use it on a sleepover. Like Sammy, maybe. He'd hoped that, when the Valorie lady showed up, she was bringing Sammy over for dinner and then he might stay the night. But Sammy didn't come with her. Not even that

Shelby lady came with her. Miss Valorie seemed upset that she couldn't find her friend. Hey, at least she had one.

The reason Connor interrupted his parents at dinner was, he remembered seeing Shelby earlier that day, hiking the trail along the creek all by herself. She'd looked sad and Connor wondered where Sanjit was. Maybe she missed him and that's why she was sad—or maybe they'd argued, like Mom and Dad do sometimes. That always made him sad.

Before dinner, Connor overheard his parents saying to Valorie they hadn't seen Shelby all day, which was probably true because they never went outdoors, at least not outside The Grounds. He thought he should tell them he'd seen her so they could tell Miss Valorie. But not if they were going to punish him for it.

He'd also spotted Uncle Am down there, hiking the same trail in the same direction, ten or fifteen minutes before Shelby. Mom and Dad always warned him to stay away from his uncle. Sometimes Am found Connor, though, and they would talk for a minute or two. That wasn't Connor's fault. He didn't go knocking on his uncle's front door asking him to be friends. Uncle Ambrose always started it. Always.

The thing is, Uncle Am always treated Connor like a pal. Friendly, never mean, asking him about his adventures and exploring and stuff he'd learned in homeschool. Mom sometimes called him "creepy" when she didn't think Connor could hear, and he wondered why. Creepy meant doing gross things that monsters or swamp critters did—drooling or smiling weird or taking their kills back to their lairs. Ambrose never did anything like that to Connor. He didn't even own a real "lair." Just a little cottage across the property.

Where he was supposed to stay, Dad said. That was "their deal."

Still. Maybe he should say something about seeing Uncle Am? That might help the Valorie lady find her friend and make Shelby less sad.

But then Mom would blame Uncle Am for Shelby going away, and Dad would yell and slam things, and Uncle Am might get in trouble. If Uncle Am had seen Connor, he'd realize that Connor was the snitch, and then he really might do something creepy or horrible. Or Mom and Dad might yell at him for being a tattle-tale. He hated getting in trouble almost as much as the creepy stuff he imagined his uncle might do. Plus, it probably had nothing to do with Shelby going away or being sad.

Nope. Connor would not be a snitch. No way.

He sat up and grabbed his plate off his desk, took a bite of cheesy-mac-and-hot-dog. Not too cold, and still good.

He loved his mom. And Dad, even if he didn't sneak him supper after punishing him. But especially Mom.

Chapter Fifteen

Minutes later, Val parked her Honda back at the cabin, still unnerved by the encounter with the Coxes. Something about Kayleigh and Theo left her uneasy. One or both seemed to hold back something important from her. Something about Connor, perhaps? She wondered if she should discourage Sammy from hanging out with him.

Then again, knowing him, an adult telling Sammy "No" would only make him more determined than ever to befriend the boy.

Once inside, she checked messages. Still no word from Gil and no sign of Shelby. Her worry intensified. She needed to step up her search.

"I'm hungry," Sammy said, rubbing his tummy. "What's for dinner?"

After a long day, cooking seemed a daunting task. Val half-wished she'd accepted the Coxes' invitation to dine with them.

"How about we go out?" Val said.

"I want hamburgers!" Sammy said, brightening. "McDonald's!"

"I'll take that as a yes," Val said. "We'll go right after I shower."

"Hurry, I'm starving. Wait, I gotta pee!" Sammy ran into the bathroom ahead of her, not even closing the door before dropping his pants to the floor.

Val shut the door for him and chose a pair of jeans, a warm pull-over, and comfy flats from her suitcase. Once Sammy emerged from the bathroom—after a return trip to wash his hands—she showered in record time. She took a few extra minutes to dry her hair and apply a quick dab of lipstick. Val wondered why—she didn't even always do that for dinners out with Gil. But in a strange town, it felt necessary.

Greenville had no McDonald's, and the Italian place that Larkin's pal Vinnie mentioned was closed. She found a family-style restaurant in the tiny downtown area, a dusty old joint with a broad menu and placemats with games and coloring for kids. After the server brought their drinks—soda for Sammy, lemonade for Val—Sammy ordered a burger and Val a chicken Caesar salad. When Sammy excused himself to pee yet again, she signaled the server, a twenty-something white dude with nose piercings and bright red hair cut into a fluffy crop.

"Refill on your drinks?" He reached for their tall, red plastic cups.

"Sure. But first," she added when he seemed eager to peel away, "have you seen this woman in the last day or so?" Val showed him a picture on her phone, an old headshot of Shelby she'd found on Instagram.

"Nope. You a cop?" the server asked.

"I'm not investigating her," Val said. "She's a friend of mine and we were supposed to meet at her cabin today. She hasn't shown her face all day. I wondered if she'd gotten sidetracked downtown or something."

"Girl," he said with a drawl, "there ain't enough to do in Greenville, downtown or otherwise, to sidetrack someone for that long. Have you checked the bars?"

"That's next," Val said. "Which ones would you recommend?"

"All of them," the server said. "Trust me, it won't take long."

Val Googled "Greenville bars" and found six—only four of which were open on Sundays. Two of them were gay- and trans-friendly bars. That helped narrow it down.

Sammy returned a moment later, and their food came soon after, so she focused on keeping Sammy from tossing his French fries onto the floor.

"They let us throw peanut shells on the floor," he complained. "Why not fries? They're too hard, anyway."

"Just don't. What do you want to do after dinner?"

"Play games," Sammy said.

"There's a video arcade up the street," Val said. "If you finish your hamburger, I'll bring you."

"Awesome sauce!" Sammy chowed down with renewed gusto.

Meanwhile, Val picked at her soggy Caesar salad, pushing aside the four strips of chicken that, though charred on the outside, remained ice cold in the middle. When Sammy gave up on finishing his burger and dipped his third French fry into his mostly-ice Coke, she gave up and settled the bill.

They walked to the arcade and she bought Sammy ten bucks worth of game credits, hoping it would last at least a half-hour. He ran straight to an immersive shoot-em-up spaceship adventure, one that took several minutes to finish. Meanwhile, Val tried Shelby's phone again— voicemail. Then she searched local news sites for stories of car crashes, missing persons, and anything else she could think of that might provide a clue as to her friend's whereabouts. Nothing.

"That was fun!" Sammy said when the game ended.

"What's next?" she asked.

"I want to beat my score!" He stuck his card in the slot and the bright lights and loud explosions started all over again.

Val sighed. "My turn to pee. Don't leave until I get back."

"'Kay," he said without looking up.

Val used the restroom, then spied Sammy, still immersed in his game. He'd probably spend all of his credits there. Fine by her. One game was as mind-numbing as the next. He'd stay put for at least a few minutes.

Stepping outside for a breath of fresh air, she spotted a bouncer at a bar two doors down. She glanced back at Sammy, already starting round three of his game. She approached the bouncer and showed him Shelby's picture.

"Nope. Ain't seen her. Try the gay bar across the street. She looks the type."

Step Out, the gay bar, was the same place Larkin visited on his last night in town. No bouncer guarded Step Out's door, so she'd have to go inside. Sammy remained immersed in his shoot-em-up space game. He still had at least half of his credits left. She could risk one minute inside the club.

Val entered and sauntered up to the bar, almost empty at this early hour on a Sunday, and waved down the bartender, his mouth and nose covered by a light blue surgical mask. "I wondered if you might've seen—"

"You a cop?" the bartender asked, a forty-something Latino man whose cropped-sleeve shirt revealed bulging muscles and lots of tattoos.

Why did everyone ask her that? "Off-duty." she said, "Right now I'm inquiring about a friend." She showed him the picture.

"You gotta buy something," the bartender said, "or I ain't answering nothing."

"Fine. A light beer, please." Val slapped a five on the bar.

He scowled at the bills and filled a half-pint glass with a pale, fizzy lager. "Eight bucks."

Val dropped another fiver on the first and took a sip. Awful, as usual. She wished they had that one dark, sweet beer she'd tried with Gil and liked. She pointed at the picture again.

The bartender glanced at it and shook his head. "Nope. Ain't seen her. When was she in?"

"Not sure...today or yesterday?"

He frowned. "Ask Angie. She'll be out in a minute." He whisked himself away to the end of the bar.

Val tried another sip of the bitter, thin brew, then pushed it aside. A waste of money in so many respects.

She sat on a barstool, its uncomfortable wooden seat swiveling her around until she faced the tables and booths lining the long, dark space. Most were vacant. On a few, empty drink glasses and rolled-up napkins littered the tops. Occasional neon signs displayed logos of industrial lagers like the one in her glass, and the place smelled of sweat and disinfectant.

Way in the back, a man in a gray quarter-zip sweater smiled at her. For a moment she thought it was Theo Cox, as he shared the same slim-athletic build and undersized teeth. His dirty-blond hair was longer, styled into a contemporary French crop, and he wore a trim beard. Theo's brother, perhaps?

As Val started toward him, a short brunette, somewhere in her twenties or thirties, called to her from behind the bar. "Martin said you wanted to ask me something?"

Val turned back to her. "Angie? I'm looking for a friend." She showed the photo to the tiny barkeep. "She's been missing all day."

Angie leaned in for a closer look. "Nope. I don't know, actually, maybe. I see a lot of trannies in here. Do they ever dress like a man? Kind of looks like a guy who came in a few days ago."

"What makes you think she's trans?" Val asked.

"That's a man if I ever saw one," Angie said. "Hey, no judgment here, though. It's a free country. You say she's missing?" She shook her head. "That's rough. I feel for ya."

Val nodded. "If you see her, would you call me?"

"Sure, happy to help," she said to Val's surprise. She'd half-expected Angie to laugh at her request. "My friend went missing once. Turned out some creeper dude kept her tied up in his double-wide for a week. I hate to see stuff like this happen."

Val thanked her and scribbled her number on a paper coaster. She turned back toward the guy in the booth—

Who was no longer there. And his beer glass was empty.

She thought about looking for him, but she didn't dare delay another moment before getting back to Sammy. She thanked Angie again, scanned the bar one more time, and left.

***

Val found Sammy near tears at the entrance to the arcade, standing next to a slender man with greasy, stringy hair and a straggly beard, wearing a "Greenville Games" T-shirt.

"This kid yours?" the man said in a surly tone.

"Sorry, I got distracted—"

"Yeah, getting wasted in the fucking gay bar," the man said, his tone even nastier. "Take care of your damn kid. I ain't your fucking babysitter."

"Thanks, sorry," Val said, heat and shame rising in her face. "Come on, Sammy. Time to go."

"I want to play more!" he said. "But I'm out of money. Where'd you go?"

"Looking for my friend Shelby," Val said. "Sorry it took so long."

"That's okay," Sammy said. "I knew you'd come back. Just like Mom always did."

Stung by the comparison to her mother, Val paid dearly for her guilt. Sammy talked her into adding twenty bucks to his game card and buying him another soda. "I need to step out again for a minute," she said. "Stay here, no matter what, okay?"

He shrugged and slurped his drink, then pressed "New Game" on the space-war machine.

Val snuck out without the greasy-haired guy spotting her and ducked into both of the remaining nearly-empty bars on the strip. She got the same results: nobody recognized Shelby, nobody had seen her, and neither would tell her even that much unless she bought something. More pricey, untouched drinks. Her fruitless search had turned into an expensive night out with nothing to show for it.

On her way back to the arcade, Gil called. She paused outside the arcade's exit to take the call, despite the stomach-turning aroma of stale fried food that emanated from the takeout window next door. At least she could keep an eye on Sammy from there.

"Hello, darling," she said with as much enthusiasm as she could muster. "Are you feeling better?"

"Definitely." Gil's voice sounded almost normal. "My fever's back under a hundred. How's Clayton?"

She brightened. Hearing his voice, healthier and stronger, cheered her up a bit. "I'm out in Greenville already. Shelby extended her cabin rental for the week and invited me out. I brought Sammy—he's loving it."

"Sammy? Why?" Gil said. "What am I missing?"

"Long story," Val said. Dammit, it had been way too long since they talked. "Lots to catch up on. Be prepared to put on your daddy-slash-favorite-uncle hat when you get back. Which is when, by the way?" His chipper mood and back-to-normal voice gave her hope it might happen soon.

Gil sighed. "Bad news on that front. Hank died this morning. Funeral services are Friday. And with this COVID thing, I can't travel before then anyway."

Her heart sank. "So, you can go to a funeral, but can't come home to your own house?" Dammit! She didn't mean for that to come out quite so edgy and wished she could take it back.

"Right now, I can't go anywhere or see anyone," Gil said, his tone almost as churlish as Val's. "Yes, if I trusted myself to stay awake for the two-hour drive back to my house, I could stay there, but then you couldn't. We still wouldn't see each other, and I'd have to come back to New Haven for the funeral in a few days anyway. So what's the point?"

Val let the silence linger on the line for a moment. Something didn't add up here. She wanted to lash back at him, but what good would that do? Plus, she'd snapped at him first. "No point, I guess," she said, subdued. "I just wanted you closer, that's all."

"Me too." His voice calmed too, and he sounded tired. "I hate this virus. Not only for how I feel and how it's separating us, although that's bad enough. People are panicking—grocery stores can't keep food and toilet paper on the shelves, everyone's wearing masks, and New Haven looks like Europe during the Black Plague. Streets are empty and the hospitals are overrun. Everybody spouts a different theory for how it spreads and how to stop it, yet nothing's working. It's a mess."

"And you learned all this how?" Val said. "Aren't you confined to your motel room?"

Another long pause before he answered. "I'm watching a lot of local news on TV and browsing the internet. Can we change the subject? How's Shelby, by the way?"

Val sighed. "That's the other problem. I don't know where she is." She explained how the day had gone, including the nearly-empty bars and main drag in downtown Greenville. "I guess it makes sense now, if everyone's freaking out about COVID."

"Is that what happened with Shelby?" Gil said. "Maybe she checked into a hospital. It would explain why she hasn't answered her phone."

"I hadn't thought of that," Val said. Good old Gil. Even in the middle of a crappy argument, he found ways to be helpful. "I'll call around. She left a note, saying she was going hiking. That was almost ten hours ago, and no word from her since."

"I wish I was there to help look for her," Gil said, his voice tender and a little raspy again. "And to beat up Ben Peterson. How's all that going, by the way?"

"Oh, crap, I can't believe I haven't told you," Val said. "I got suspended this morning. My hearing is on Wednesday. Petroni thinks they've got nothing, but Simpson is working this thing hard, for some reason. Which reminds me—I need to check out something while I have a decent cell signal. A link Petroni shared with me. She thinks it might help me with my case. If I can find a moment to focus. Sammy can be a handful."

"Send the link to me," Gil said. "I've got nothing else to do except surf the net and watch TV. At least I can be useful to you."

"Oh, I would love that. Thank you, Gil. That's sweet of you."

"I love you," he said.

"Love you more."

"I doubt that, but I hope you're right."

Val laughed and they hung up a few moments later. She sent him a picture of the link Petroni had given her.

Then she called Sanjit. She explained the situation and asked, "Have you heard from her?"

"Not since I left the cabin," he replied, worry lining his voice. "Every time I call, it goes straight to voicemail. Maybe she's coming back to Clayton and is in a dead zone?"

"In what car? Didn't you drive?"

"Oh, right, of course. Oh, God. Val, she wouldn't disappear like this. Should I come back?"

"I'd love some help finding her. How soon can you get here?"

Sanjit paused. "Monday evening, the earliest. The system breach at VeroniCare is bad. I doubt I'll get any sleep before then. Plus, my car died on me and it's in the shop. Something wrong with the fuel line, they said."

"Get here as soon as you can," she said. "Any ideas

where else she might've gone? Anyone she might have gone to see?"

"As far as I'm aware, she doesn't know anyone out there."

Val pondered a moment. "Shelby mentioned her brother might be looking for her in Clayton. If he'd gotten in touch and followed her here—"

"She'd run the other direction, fast," Sanjit said. "If he found her...God knows where she might be or what he would do to her. He's bad, Val. Lots of hate in him—and she's very afraid of him. Terrified."

"Good to know." They promised to keep each other posted. She located two hospitals in the area online and called both. Neither would reveal any information about patients except to family members, citing federal regulations. Another strikeout.

Darkness fell on the drive back to the cabin. While Sammy brushed his teeth and changed into his pajamas, Val searched the immediate vicinity to see if Shelby fell into a ditch somewhere. But she didn't dare venture far, and her flashlight's rechargeable battery faded within minutes, so with a heavy heart, she returned to the cabin.

Still no call or text from her.

Val's worry grew.

***

The Redeemer returned to the main room of the Safe House and confirmed what he'd expected to see. The half-male, half-female pervert sat against the wall, hands tied behind its back, face contorted. The recording he'd put on loop hours before droned on, currently in the midst of some righteous doctrine. Which meant that several minutes of grotesque, perverted erotica would soon follow, violent in the extreme. The mix had proven effective in penetrating even the most callous of consciences, breaking their spirit, propelling them to repent.

The discomfort on Shelby's face told him it disturbed

him-her as much as he expected. Maybe even more. Good. A few more hours of this and Shelby would crack and confess.

He strode to the laptop, paused the recording, and typed, "How did that make you feel?"

Shelby spat onto the floor. "You're disgusting. I'm not answering questions until I hear your real voice. No more robots doing your dirty work for you."

The man's breath caught in his throat. He'd expected more crying and pleading. But he liked this better. Such spirit. Impressive, really. The others broke long before this.

"Perhaps you need to listen to a bit more," he typed, and the machine turned his words into more of the stilted, staccato pronunciations.

"If you're going to play porn for me, at least get some good stuff," Shelby said. "None of this rape-and-torture bullshit. Only a true creep like you would get off on that shit."

The man grabbed the leather belt off the desk he'd brought for this purpose and whipped it across Shelby's face. She yelped in pain, tears flowing from her blindfold, dripping from the red welt now lining her cheek.

"Speak to me with respect," he typed, but the laptop's metallic British monotone did not generate the level of authority he intended. Instead of cowering under his threat, Shelby *laughed*.

"You expect me to respect that tinny piece of crap?" Shelby laughed again, louder, haughty. "It's as thin and weak as your puny, limp cock."

"You've never seen my genitals," he typed, fingers shaking with rage. The squawky voice that repeated his taunt reflected about as much of his anger as a robocaller selling life insurance. "Nor will you ever, you perverted monster."

"I don't need to see it to know you're overcompensating for your pitiful male endowment," Shelby replied. "Leather straps, high-tech voice generation, tying me up so I can't defend myself—all marks of a weak, spineless coward."

He whipped Shelby's face with the belt again, this time with the buckle end, drawing blood from a split lip.

"Want more?" the machine squawked.

"No matter what you do," Shelby said, "I won't say what you want."

Another slap. "You know how to stop all this," he typed. "Do it."

Shelby remained silent. Stoic, even.

"You're fooling no one," the machine said. "Not even yourself."

"Apparently I'm fooling you, if you think this is working."

He snarled and slapped Shelby a third time.

Nothing.

The Redeemer raised the belt to hit the creature again, then stopped. Perhaps Shelby was telling the truth. Perhaps physical pain had no effect on its resolve—or worse, strengthened it. He'd encountered one like that before.

On the other hand, the mental game always worked.

He pushed Play on the next audio file. More sounds of obvious rape and torture flew out of the speakers—men defiling men, men dominating women, screams of pain and humiliation filling the air.

Shelby seemed unaffected. Even nodded now and again, as if in approval.

"Hey, got any popcorn?" Shelby said after a few minutes. "I'm starved, and I love me some movie snacks."

The man slipped on his noise-canceling wireless headphones. He didn't need to hear her idiot jokes, nor any of this carnage. He wasn't the one that needed to cleanse his mind and soul of this depravity, to listen until it sickened the heart inside and demanded that it stop. He set it to play again on an endless loop.

It pleased him that Shelby wanted food. That he would provide. He prepared Shelby's rations—stale bread submerged into a bowl of water, laced with Rohypnol. Shelby would sleep for hours, with the recording still playing, and wake much more compliant in the morning.

"Dinnertime," he typed. He stuffed the wet bread into the creature's mouth and forced it shut. Shelby sputtered a bit. He held firm until the food had been chewed and swallowed. Then shoved another chunk in, repeated the process until it was gone.

He paused the recording and placed the headphones on Shelby's head. "Sleep well, my friend," he typed. Then he restarted the filthy playback and departed into the chilly darkness outside.

Chapter Sixteen

Val woke several times through the night, thinking—or wishing—she'd heard Shelby entering or moving around the cabin. Each time she found something different. A few times the wind and rain woke her. Once a flushing toilet startled her and she glimpsed Sammy heading back from the bathroom. The final time the grinding gears and roaring engine of a diesel truck on the highway stirred her awake. At that point—around 6:00 a.m.—she ventured out to the kitchen to make coffee.

While it brewed, she checked her messages for the umpteenth time. Nothing from Shelby, the Coxes, Gil, anyone. With only one bar of cell service at best—often none—she figured she shouldn't expect anything so long as they stayed in the cabin.

Which meant she needed to head into town again. Petroni had ordered her not to meet with Gramercy and Torres of Greenville PD, but she ought to report Shelby missing, so...

She discovered Sammy had woken up for good when his tablet beeped a few times and played the startup music for his favorite chase-the-animal-around game. She waited for the series of notes that signaled Game Over and stopped him before he began a new round.

"How about we head into town for breakfast?" Val asked.

"Yay! Do they have a Pancake House?" Sammy asked, bouncing on the sofa.

She Googled it. "Looks like it. Let's go," Val said, and drained her coffee.

After dressing in warm clothes—the temperature had

dropped to near-freezing overnight—they headed out, and reached the edge of town by 7:00 a.m. The Pancake House was closed because of COVID, it turned out. They circled around for twenty minutes before choosing a family-style diner that, to her relief, offered several variations of the basic pancake breakfast for kids. Val nibbled at her rubbery scrambled eggs, a dry biscuit, and overcooked sausage, washing it down with weak coffee, too worried about Shelby anyway to eat.

Still no messages. From anyone.

"Can we go to the arcade?" Sammy asked when they got back to the car.

"Maybe later," Val said. "I need to run an errand first."

"*Another* one?" His face filled with disgust. "Some vacation."

"You'll like it, I promise," Val said. "It's cool." She doubted he'd agree, but what else could she do?

She pulled into the Greenville police station as a torrent of icy rain began to fall. "Okay, we need to run super fast to get inside," Val said, helping Sammy zip his coat. "Whoever gets wettest, buys lunch."

"No fair!" Sammy said. "I didn't bring any money."

"Run extra fast, then," Val said.

She let him reach the double glass doors of the old brick building a few steps ahead of her, laughing when he celebrated his win by dancing the Griddy in the lobby. "Now, I need you to be patient while I talk to the nice police officers," she said. "Did you bring your game tablet?"

"It's in the car," Sammy said, pouting. "Can I go back and get it?"

"Sorry, it's raining too hard," Val said. "Just try to be good, okay?"

He crossed his heart. Val's confidence in him keeping his promise was about as high as her faith in a politician promising not to lie, but she had no choice. She turned to lead him over to the front desk. A sign in the lobby stopped her.

Effective immediately: Masks required for entry.

Val pulled two blue KN95 masks from the dispenser and helped Sammy put his on.

"I can't breathe!" Sammy complained, tugging it down over his chin.

"Yes, you can," Val said, though she found the mask uncomfortable too. "Everyone else is wearing them. It's the new cool thing."

"I hate it," Sammy said.

She sighed and tugged the mask back over his nose and mouth, then dragged him to the reception desk.

"I'd like to report a missing person," Val said to the uniformed officer staffing the desk, a bored-looking white guy in his late twenties. Hard to tell with the mask. His nameplate read "J. Wallingford."

"Family member?" Wallingford studied Val for a long moment while he pulled up a form on his computer screen.

"Friend," Val said. "Her name is Shelby Clearwater. We were supposed to meet—"

"Like the creek?"

"The creek?"

"Clearwater Creek. Cuts through the state park a few miles outside of town."

"Exactly. That's where our cabin is. She rented it for the weekend with her boyfriend, then invited me to come when he needed to leave. However, she wasn't there when we arrived."

"Great for rock-skipping!" Sammy interjected.

Wallingford chuckled for a moment, then grew serious again. "So, you can't verify she was ever there."

Val fought the urge to roll her eyes. "Her stuff was there, and she left a note, saying she'd be back. That was yesterday morning, and we've been unable to reach her or find her since."

Wallingford pecked a few words into his form, cursing and backspacing a few times. No way he'd recorded even half of what Val told him. "Did you try contacting her next of kin, or that boyfriend you mentioned?"

"The boyfriend hasn't heard from her either. I don't know how to reach her family."

"Your name?" He continued typing, one letter at a time, it seemed, while waiting for Val's answer.

"Valorie Dawes. Val-LOR-ee, with an O. I'm a police officer, too, in Clayton."

He looked at her again, recognition dawning in his eyes. "Weren't you here last week?"

Val nodded, wary of him now. "I met with Detectives Gramercy and Torres on another matter."

"Want me to get them?" He leaned closer, his voice low. "Sometimes it helps to know someone on the inside. I'm sure it's that way in Clayton, too. Am I right?"

"Yeah, sure," Val said.

Sammy tugged at Val's jacket. "Can we leave now? I'm bored."

"In a minute," Val said. "Patience, please. I need to take care of this, okay?"

Sammy huffed, crossed his arms, and turned away from her.

Wallingford pecked out something else on his screen. "Oh, damn. Says they're about to go into a meeting...wait. The meeting is with you." He raised his eyebrows and shot Val a puzzled glance. "What the hell?"

"I was supposed to meet with them," Val said. "I thought it was canceled. However, if it's still on the calendar...is there a place I can park my little brother while we meet? He's a well-behaved kid. He won't be any problem."

Wallingford leveled a doubtful stare at her. "Sorry, the

baby-sitting squad called in sick today. Okay, then, I'll need your ID, a phone number, and your badge to check you in for your meeting. And for this missing persons report." He extended his hand, palm-up.

"Uh...I didn't bring my badge," Val said. "I'm off-duty, so..." She dug into her purse. "Here's my driver's license. All my info should already be in your system from last week."

"Sorry," Wallingford said. "Can't let you into the secure area without a badge. Regulations. Let me set you up in one of our public meeting spaces here in the lobby instead. I'll send the detectives down in a few minutes."

Val turned away to hide her frustration. She walked Sammy to the room, where they waited in the space for about fifteen minutes before Wallingford returned.

"Sorry," he said. "Bad news. Gramercy's out today—COVID, probably. Torres is out on a call. Looks like your meeting got canceled after all."

"Yay!" Sammy danced around his chair. "Can we go now? I told Connor I'd be there for the Clearwater Creek Rock-Skipping Championships!"

Wallingford signaled for Val to huddle in the corner opposite Sammy. "Those cabins you're staying in...are they the ones near the Cox family compound?"

Val nodded. "Why?"

A pained expression overtook Wallingford's face. "Have you or your friend had any run-ins with them?"

"If you mean meeting them, yes," Val said. "Nothing contentious, though. At least not us. I can't speak for Shelby...wait, yes I can. I spoke with Theo and Kayleigh Cox. They say they haven't met her, other than renting the unit to her online."

"What about the brother?" Wallingford asked.

That startled Val. He knew about Shelby's brother somehow? "Austin?"

Then it was Wallingford's turn to look surprised. "I

mean Ambrose Cox. Theo's younger brother."

Okay, that made sense. "No, why?"

Wallingford took a deep breath. "Stay clear of that guy, okay? He's...dangerous."

"In what way?" Val asked. "Does he have a rap sheet, or—"

"He's a creepy dude," Wallingford said. "He prowls the night clubs around here, looking for young girls—and boys, so I hear. He's never been caught, but...best if you stay away from him."

"What does he look like?"

"Kind of like Theo, with lighter hair and often grows a beard," Wallingford said. "You'll know he's a Cox as long as he's not wearing a mask."

"Why's that?"

Wallingford lowered his voice. "All the Cox men have ridiculously small teeth," he said. "Like a kid's."

That squared with Val's mental image of Theo. Then she recalled the man in the booth in the gay bar the night before. He matched that description perfectly.

Including the creepy part.

***

Back at the cabin, Val discovered a welcome surprise: a decent cell signal, probably thanks to a break in the rainstorm. Two bars' worth. She ordered Sammy into the bathtub after learning he hadn't bathed since Friday— something his rank body odor confirmed—and checked her messages. A long one, from Gil, revealing what he'd found via the link she'd shared from Petroni: a series of links to articles dating back over two years, and a cryptic note.

You're going to love this. Hope it helps.

At first, the stories didn't seem relevant to anything. Nothing related to police suspensions, missing persons, Greenville, or Clayton, for that matter. Then a headline caught her eye:

Clayton Detective 'Safeguards' Contested
Arlington High Homecoming Ballot

That piqued her curiosity. Why would a Clayton detective get involved in a high school popularity contest? Who would do such a thing? She opened the article and scanned until she spotted a familiar and unwelcome name.

Edward Simpson. *Tackle Box!*

She read from the top. A young woman, Ava Simpson, won the honor of Homecoming Queen in the tiny Connecticut town near New London. Ava used her coronation ceremony as an opportunity to come out of the closet as a lesbian, much to the dismay of her conservative family and church members. After a brief uproar that consumed the community for about a week, the school administration stripped her of her title. Students rebelled and re-elected her by a landslide in a hastily called second election. The school attempted to hide the results, even stealing and destroying the paper ballots, but not before the final vote tally leaked to the press.

The odd twist was, the local police brought in the girl's uncle, Detective Simpson, all the way from Clayton—over an hour's drive away. His role: act as a "security consultant" to "safeguard"—i.e., destroy—the stolen ballots.

Val sat back, her jaw dropping in awe. Ed "Tackle Box" Simpson tried to deny his own niece's election as Homecoming Queen—because of his outrage over her being a lesbian. A "pervert," he was quoted as describing her.

Val shook her head in dismay. Things made a little more sense now. Simpson demanded ownership of the investigation against the vigilante killers of Larkin and Dinker, then slow-walked them. He did that not out of indifference, but out of his hatred of anything he considered "deviant."

It also explained his hostility toward Shelby.

She texted Gil a quick "Thank you, darling—it helps a lot!" Then she pondered the implications of this revelation.

How far would Simpson go, she wondered, to punish people like Shelby to pursue his anti-gay agenda?

***

Once Sammy emerged from the bathroom, more or less clean and wearing fresh jeans and a flannel shirt, they headed down to the creek to where they'd encountered Connor the day before. Sure enough, they found him in the same place, this time with a stash of flat, skippable rocks already collected and ready to fire into the stream.

"Finally!" Connor said. "Let the championships begin!"

"Why don't you two practice your skipping for a few minutes before the competition begins?" Val said. "I need to stretch my legs a bit more."

"We need you to referee," Sammy said.

"And keep score," Connor added.

"I will," Val said. "I won't be long, I promise."

The two boys fell upon the rock pile with relish, zipping the rocks across the water and cheering each other on. "Good one!" Sammy said. "Awesome!" Connor replied. "Whoa! Airborne!" they said in unison.

Val trudged up the trail, noticing for the first time the slight upward incline as she proceeded downstream. In under a quarter-mile, the bank of the creek rose a good ten to twelve feet over the surface of the water. Rounding one bend, she found a clearing tucked back in the trees that overlooked a deep pool in the stream. A thick downed tree trunk provided an inviting spot to sit and rest, for those so inclined. From there she could keep an eye on the boys, too.

"I see you've discovered my secret swimming hole."

The male voice behind Val startled her. She whirled to face the man and recognized him. Theo Cox.

"*Your* swimming hole?" Val shook off her surprise, yet couldn't shrug off the chill that ran down her spine. "I would expect a man of your means to prefer a private, Olympic-sized pool."

"Oh, I do," Theo said with a smile. He strolled closer, and Val realized he'd approached the spot from the opposite direction—heading upstream from The Grounds. "This is where my brother and I came as boys when we wanted to escape adult supervision."

"It's idyllic." Val gazed over the rushing stream. Theo's gentler side surprised her as much as his unexpected presence. Contrived, maybe? "I bet that water gets pretty cold, though."

"F-f-f-rigid." Theo laughed. "That was half the fun. Ambrose and I often competed to see who could stay in the longest. I won, of course."

Val couldn't suppress an eye roll. The brag seemed more authentic than his appreciation of nature. "Of course. And today? Are you out for a swim?"

"No, you're right," Theo said. "These days, I prefer my heated pool. Twenty laps every afternoon. Are you a swimmer, Ms. Dawes? You're welcome to join me."

"Oh, shucks," Val said with a hint of sarcasm. "I forgot to bring a swimsuit."

"I'm sure we could provide something...comfortable." Theo flashed a suggestive smile. Yuck.

"You didn't find me here to talk aquatics," Val said. "Do you have an update on Shelby?"

"A bit," Theo said, and the vampish smile vanished. "Not great news, I'm sorry to say. My brother, Ambrose, *claims* he hasn't seen her. *Claims* he didn't even know she was here." His voice betrayed a hearty volume of doubt.

"Claims?" Her suspicion of this mysterious brother grew.

Theo shrugged. "Ambrose doesn't make a habit of revealing whom he associates with. Insists that it's his right to keep it private." He glanced away, pursed his lips as if he might spit.

"Would he open up more to a stranger than to, say, his big brother?" Val said. "If my older brother came asking, I might give him the cold shoulder, too."

Theo shook his head. "Doubtful. If he found out you were a police officer, he'd plead the Fifth and hire a lawyer, even if all you asked was the time of day." He smiled. "Like I said, he's rather private."

"I see. Well, thanks." Val turned back toward the stream. "Don't let me keep you."

A moment passed. "Have I offended you, Ms. Dawes?"

Val glanced at him. His face bore an expression of hurt. "No. Sorry. I'm just worried about my friend. I can get pretty single-minded about something like this."

"Understood. Listen, if there's anything else I can do to help…"

Val faced him again. "There might be. Do you maintain security cameras around your property? Perhaps there's some footage I could watch from yesterday morning."

Theo frowned and shook his head again. "I'm afraid our cameras focus inward on our grounds. If I investigated every pedestrian who strolled down this public path, I'd have no time for anything else."

"What about the footage of your property inside the walls, then?"

Theo laughed. "Would Shelby have scaled the walls or stormed the gates? You've been to my home, Ms. Dawes. Surely you noticed how extensive our defenses are. We're very good at keeping people out. However, if you insist, I'll check our archives, just in case."

"Thanks," Val said. "You never know."

"Perhaps," Theo said, "you'd like to join me in my office for a viewing session? You and Sammy could come to dinner."

"Perhaps," Val said. "Thank you for the offer. I'll have

to get back to you on that."

Perhaps never, she said to herself.

After an awkward silence, Theo offered a handshake. "I'll be on my way, then. Sorry to disturb you."

"No problem. Thanks." Val accepted his clammy hand and pulled hers away a moment later. She waited until he disappeared around the corner, back the way he came, before slumping onto the downed log. For whatever reason, she couldn't relax around Theo. Probably because she got the feeling that he was always hitting on her. She wondered how his wife put up with that—or if she knew.

While resting on the log, Val glanced around. A glint of light reflecting off a flat, glassy surface caught her eye. She leaned closer...

A phone.

She pulled her warm gloves out of her pocket and picked up the phone. Pressed a few buttons. The screen remained black.

She turned the phone over, examined every side. It had a shock-proof case with a clear plastic shield over the screen. Val recalled Shelby had one like that. She'd claimed to be "rough on phones," always dropping them or getting them wet or dirty.

On the back, she found a sticker in the image of a shell. Inside the shell, the letter "B". She recalled Shelby's phone case bore that same sticker. It had to be hers.

Val needed to get back to the cabin, stat, and recharge this thing. After checking the area and finding no further sign of Shelby—including a harrowing glance over the creek bank into the rushing stream below, thankfully coming up empty there—she hurried back up the path.

Chapter Seventeen

When Val returned to the site of the World Rock-Skipping Championships, she found Sammy sitting alone, making languid attempts at tossing rocks into the frigid water.

"Where's Connor?" Val asked when she got within earshot.

"Who cares? Connor's a cheater," Sammy said.

Uh-oh. Val looked for a dry spot on the ground next to Sammy. No dice. She cleared away some soggy leaves and sat within arm's reach. "What happened?"

Sammy made a pouty face and tossed another rock into the current. *Plunk.* No skips. "We were dividing up the rocks and he took all the good ones. He said, since it's his property and he found them, he got to choose."

Val winced. Connor sounded even more spoiled than Sammy. "So, no tournament today?"

"Not until he says sorry and his nose stops bleeding."

"Wait, what?" Val pulled Sammy around by the shoulders until they faced each other. "How did he get a bloody nose?"

"He threw a rock at me, so I threw it back, and on *accident,* it hit him in the face," Sammy said. "So he ran home crying."

"Sammy!" Val heaved a deep breath, striving to remain calm, and not doing the best job at it. "You can't go throwing rocks at people."

"He threw it at me first!"

"Still." Val exhaled a noisy blast of frustration and studied his face. Dried tears marked his cheeks. Not a good morning for him. "We need to go back to the cabin for a while. After that, we're going to the Coxes' house so you can apologize."

"But—"

"No buts. You hurt him—stop and listen to me. Yes, he was *also* wrong. You don't own what he did, but you own your actions, and there will be consequences. Understood?"

Sammy snarled at her. "You're not my mother."

Val bit back her instinctive retort about his mother—their mother—being in prison for even greater violence. Instead she said, "As long as you're in my care, you're going to act like a decent human being, no matter how much it hurts. Now come on."

They walked up the path to the cabin, with Val tugging him along half the time, and struggling to catch up with him the rest. Sammy disappeared into the bedroom as soon as they got inside, the sounds of his gaming tablet filling the silence within moments. She ought to take it away from him and make him...what? Something. Val had no idea what a parent should do in that situation. She lacked examples, even from her own upbringing. Her mother neglected her long before she ran off with Milt the Rapist, and her father disengaged soon after. The fact that she and Chad grew up to become law-abiding citizens defied all odds, no doubt.

Anyway, she had things to do. And she'd be far more effective doing them if she didn't have a troublemaking ten-year-old to care for.

She found Shelby's charger and plugged it in. While she waited for it to recharge, she called her father. After summarizing the Shelby situation, she dove into the question at hand. "Is there any chance I could bring him back to Clayton while I continue to search for her?" she asked.

Silence reigned over the phone for a long moment. "Can

we wait until tomorrow or the next day?" he said. "I mean, you've only had him one day."

"I know, but it would really help my search," she said in a low voice to make sure Sammy couldn't overhear.

"Well...I've got an AA meeting tonight," he said. "I can't bring him along, and I can't leave him home unattended, either."

Val sighed. "What about tomorrow, then? I need to go back anyway for my hearing, so..."

His sigh lasted longer than hers. "I guess I can't argue with that. Okay."

Relieved, she said her goodbyes and sent Gil a text:

Feeling any better? Miss you.

She really wanted to fill him in on the rapidly changing situation...and hear his voice. But several minutes ticked by with no answer.

While waiting for his reply, she checked Shelby's phone. Once its power-up logo appeared, she called Sanjit on her own phone.

"I can't talk," Sanjit said. "I'm dealing with a crisis—"

"You don't have a choice. I need your help," she told him and recapped the day's events.

"I don't understand how I can help from here," he said. "And the sooner I get this system back up on its feet, the sooner I can return to Greenville."

"I'll tell you how," Val said, fuming at his time-wasting excuses. "How do I break into her phone? We need to track where she's been, who she called, all that."

"You found her phone, but not her? Where is she?"

"That's what I'm trying to figure out," Val said. Said, not shouted, like she wanted to. This guy!

"This is bad," Sanjit said. The man possessed a keen sense of the obvious. "Shelby would never leave her phone behind. Something's happened to her—something bad!"

"We don't know that for sure," Val said to calm him,

although her own anxiety was rising as well. "Her phone can give us clues. Do you know her unlock password?"

"Of course." He rattled it off.

Val gasped. "She trusts you with her password? That doesn't sound like her."

"Of course not. I watched her type it in a few times, though."

Val typed in the code. Sure enough, it worked.

Val checked Shelby's call and text history, found mostly outgoing calls and messages to Val and Sanjit. An incoming call from an unknown number with a 314 area code had gone unanswered, then blocked.

"That's a St. Louis, Missouri area code," Sanjit said. "I'm guessing it's her family."

"Her brother Austin?" Val said.

"Could be. I'm not sure."

Val called the number from her own phone. No answer. Then she browsed Shelby's contacts. No entry for Austin or anyone with the last name Clearwater.

"He might be listed under 'Asshole' or 'Nazi' or something," Sanjit said.

Val fast-scrolled through Shelby's contacts again. "I don't see anything, but I'll keep looking after we're done."

With Sanjit still on the line, Val checked Shelby's photos next. The last photo taken was a blurry shot of what looked like leaves on the ground.

"Maybe that got taken when she dropped the phone," Sanjit guessed.

Val brought up the previous photo, taken moments before the blurred-out one. Also a bit out of focus, it included the image of a tall man wearing a warm knit cap, his face obscured by leaves and branches. Bright sunlight behind him cast his face in shadow, but the background resembled the forested area around the cabin and The Grounds.

"Do you recognize him?" Sanjit asked.

"It's too blurry. It could be one of the Cox brothers, but it could be anyone."

"What is he wearing?"

"One of those camel-colored suede jackets with fringe thingies on the sleeves," Val said, "and jeans. Kind of western, cowboy-ish. Not the type of thing I'd expect a rich guy like Theo Cox to wear."

"Austin might wear that," Sanjit said. "How would he have found her?"

"Have you met him? Might you recognize him from a photo?" Val asked.

"No. However, there would be a family resemblance, no?"

Val sighed. "If only we could make out the face." She browsed the other photos, blushing when she encountered one of Sanjit standing naked in front of the fridge in the cabin.

"There's nothing else," she said, clearing her throat. "I'll call this in to the Greenville police."

Sanjit scoffed. "Fat lot of good that will do. Those bozos called me, harassing me, all but accusing me of kidnapping her. I've been expecting them to show up in jackboots and haul me off to jail any minute now."

"I'll steer them in the other direction," Val said. "When can you get here?"

Sanjit sighed. "I'm not sure. My car's still in the shop. The problem with my fuel line? Yeah, some jerk put dirt in the tank. Can you believe it?"

"Borrow or rent a car, then," Val said. "Come on, man. I need you here."

"As soon as I can break away. Look, I need to get back to work." He hung up amid mumbled apologies.

Val set her phone down, frustrated. Sammy's game tablet chirped and warbled from the next room. She felt anchored to one spot so long as she had to supervise him. She needed to get him back in Connor's good graces so she could free herself up to investigate.

First, though, the local police.

***

Several minutes later, Val reached Detective Torres by phone, though the connection cut out a few times during their conversation.

"Okay, we'll list her as missing," Torres said after Val filled her in, "but we're playing catch-up at this point. Not unusual in these cases. If you can locate her brother, that'd be a big help. I still think this Sanjit character needs watching, too. If anything has happened to her, you know as well as I do, it's almost always a family member or a significant other."

"Sanjit's as worried as I am," Val said. "And he's promised to return, as soon as tonight. Besides, if anyone can help us track down Austin Clearwater, it's her boyfriend."

"Can't your people in Clayton assist?" Torres asked.

Val held her breath. "That'd be tricky. A, we don't own the case, and B, if Ed Simpson gets wind of my involvement—"

"Oh, he's aware," Torres said. "Old Tackle Box chewed me out an hour ago for letting you 'meddle', as he called it. What's up with you guys? Bad blood?"

"You could say that."

"He said you're suspended," Torres said. "Under investigation..."

Val growled. "He's the one accusing me, and it's all bullshit. Wait—how did he find out I was even here?"

Torres chuckled. "Everybody knows him. Old Tackle Box taught at the Academy, and God help anyone who learned everything from him. I feel for you, though. Simpson's the number one reason my bosses won't give up the Larkin case to you guys. We actually want it solved."

"Great," Val said, voice full of sarcasm. "Anything new on that front?"

"Nothing solid. All we know is, he hit every gay bar on the strip on the Saturday night, then disappeared. Nobody saw him after about eleven o'clock. It appears he got lucky...then, very unlucky."

Val grimaced. Cops and their morbid humor.

"We're trying to talk to all the bartenders," Torres said. "With COVID, though, we're short-handed. So far, nobody spotted him with anybody, but we're still looking."

Val thanked Torres and spent a fruitless hour scouring Shelby's phone for clues to her brother, other family members, or anyone else with a possible motive for taking her. She had to admit, if she didn't know Sanjit, she also would consider him the prime suspect. Almost all of Shelby's messages, calls, photos, and social media posts mentioned or pictured him.

Toward the end of her search, Sammy grew restless. "Come *on*," he complained in a high-pitched whine. "I'm hungry, and I want to go back to the creek."

"I need to work a little longer," Val said.

Sammy pouted. "This was supposed to be a *vacation*, where we go on lots of adventures."

Val sighed. Fair point. The morning mist had dissolved into sunshine, and she was a little hungry too.

"Okay," Val said, closing her phone. "No more work for today."

"Yay!" Sammy jumped up and down, rotating his body as he clapped. "I hope we make new friends today. This is boring."

Val laughed. "I'll try, I promise." She packed a picnic lunch of sandwiches, sliced apples, and crackers with peanut butter to take with them, along with two bottles of water. They'd just spread their blanket on a dry-ish spot overlooking the creek when a familiar-looking figure approached on the path. The man's quick gait and forward posture indicated he was in a hurry.

He stopped short, though, when his light brown eyes

met Val's. Athletic in build, he resembled Theo Cox, though with a more modern-style hairstyle, more of a French crop than Theo's conservative cut. He also sported a deeper tan and lighter-colored hair. He wore designer hiking clothes that looked straight out of an LL Bean catalog. Except for being wrinkled, as if he'd slept in them.

The man smiled at them, revealing those tiny teeth again, the Cox family trademark. "Good morning, Miss Dawes," he said, his tone friendly, yet guarded.

Val paused a moment before replying. A cold tingle of mistrust and recognition ran down her spine. Definitely the guy from the bar on Sunday night. "You must be Ambrose Cox," she said. "Theo's brother?"

"I prefer to be known as the son of C.T. and Clara Cox. Or Connor's uncle, take your pick," Ambrose said with an affable grin. "Mind if I come aboard? I brought my own lunch." He shifted a backpack Val hadn't noticed off one shoulder and unzipped it partway, revealing the neck of a wine bottle. "I'm happy to share."

"Uncle Am!" Sammy said, clapping. "Connor says you're cool. Can he eat with us, Val? Please? You said we could make friends today."

Crap. Trapped by her promise to a kid. "Sure," Val said, trying to hide her unease. "Grab a corner of the blanket and make yourself at home. No wine for me this early, though, thank you."

Ambrose stepped closer and pulled a blanket out of the backpack, bearing a logo Val recognized from online shopping, one well out of her budget. He spread it next to theirs and set the wine, a block of cheese wrapped in plastic, and a loaf of French bread in the middle. He knelt beside his goodies, produced a corkscrew from his pocket, and set to work on opening the wine. "Theo said you wanted to talk," Ambrose said once he'd pulled and sniffed the cork.

"Have you seen Shelby?" Sammy blurted out around a

mouthful of peanut butter and jelly.

Val glared at him and placed a finger to her lips. Sammy shrugged and sipped on a bottle of lemonade.

"Who's Shelby?" Ambrose said, searching his backpack. "Oh, darn," he said in mock frustration. "I forgot to bring a glass." He smirked and took a long pull from the bottle, wiping a trickle of red wine from the corner of his mouth. "Wow, that's good pinot. You sure you don't want some?"

"I'm sure, thanks. Shelby is a friend of ours who was staying at the cabin this weekend."

"This time of year?" He sipped again from the bottle.

"She disappeared on Sunday and we're worried about her." Val showed him a picture on her phone, watching his eyes. "Look familiar?"

Ambrose leaned closer, squinting at her phone, the smell of wine on his breath. "Nope. Have you tried calling her?" Up close, he looked disheveled. Stubble poked through his tan around the edges of his light brown beard, and dark circles under his eyes gave the impression he hadn't slept in days. His eyes betrayed no sign of recognition of Shelby.

"We found her phone on the trail earlier," Val said. "So far, we haven't discovered anything helpful on it..." She stopped when she recalled the picture of the hiking man on Shelby's phone. It looked a lot like him, other than the clothes. She wished the face hadn't been so shadowed and blurry.

Val's expression must have given her away, because Ambrose peered closer at her, his brows furrowed. "Something wrong?" he asked in a guarded tone.

Val debated whether to show him the photo and opted not to. Cornering him—and letting on that she suspected him—might provoke a violent response, which she wanted to avoid, particularly in front of Sammy.

Instead, she shook her head. "Nothing...other than not

knowing where Shelby is. She went hiking yesterday morning…any chance you spotted her out here? I think she left around nine o'clock." She didn't know what time Shelby disappeared, but she figured naming a specific time would reveal more.

"Ah…where I was this weekend and with whom, I'd rather not say." He unwrapped the plastic from his block of cheese. "But I was nowhere near your friend." He laughed. "So far as I can tell."

"Why do you think this is funny?" Val said, her impatience growing. "A woman is missing, possibly in danger—"

"All I can tell you is, I wasn't with her, or any woman, this weekend," Ambrose said. "Trans or otherwise." He took another swig of wine and tore off a chunk of bread.

"How do you know she's trans?" The question came out sharper than Val intended.

Ambrose stuffed a lump of cheese into his chunk of bread. He took a bite and grunted with pleasure. "Mmm, this is good. You really ought to try it."

"Answer my question, please."

Ambrose chewed, swallowed, and sipped the wine again. "As to why I know she's trans?" He chuckled. "I didn't until you just confirmed it. But the mustache was my first clue, and her Adam's apple is bigger than mine."

"You seem to know a lot about this," Val said.

Ambrose stared at her a moment, mouth agape. "For a cop—yes, I know you're a cop, Theo's got a big mouth—you're not very observant," he said. "Or have you forgotten where we first met, so to speak? Last night?"

Val reddened. She'd hoped he hadn't noticed or recognized her. "So?"

"So," Ambrose said, "suffice to say, I have a little more exposure to the LGBTQ world than, it appears, you do, or Theo. I know my way around the community, so to speak. While I haven't seen your friend in any of the, ah, usual haunts, I'd be willing to keep my eyes open and even ask around a smidge. If I can overlook your obvious suspicion of me."

"I'm not—I don't suspect you," Val said, reddening over the semi-fib. "I'm just worried about my friend."

"Understandable." Ambrose finished his makeshift sandwich, washed it down with another sip of pinot, and offered Val the bottle. When she shook him off, he stuffed the cork back in, packed up his lunch, and stood. "In that case, I should move on." He picked up his blanket and rolled it up into a tight ball, then pointed to Sammy. "By the way, my silent young friend...Connor misses you already." He winked, stuffed the blanket into his backpack, and strode back down the trail.

***

After lunch, Val discovered a sweet spot by the river that registered three bars on her phone. She lay on the blanket and searched for information on the Cox family. Meanwhile Sammy practiced his rock-skipping, exclaiming now and again how much better he was at getting multiple skips and "going airborne" than Connor.

"Don't you think I'd beat him in the championships?" he asked Val after about ten minutes.

"Of course," Val said, having no clue how one would even establish scoring rules for such a contest. "Keep practicing. I'm sure you'll beat him soon."

"Ha!" Sammy said. "Connor's too chicken. He's afraid of losing, the loser." He splashed another stone across the stream's current, laughing in delight when it skipped five times before thudding into the mud on the opposite bank.

What Val first found online about the Cox clan amounted to garden-variety gossip about rich, reclusive families. A Wikipedia page revealed that Connor's great-grandfather, "Teddy" Cox, made the family's fortune around the turn of the 20th century. After inheriting a modest fortune from his own father's dabbling in the railroad industry, Teddy increased the family's wealth tenfold by diversifying into various industries, particularly oil and mining. When he died at the ripe old age of 88, he left millions to Theo's father, "C.T." Cox. Over the next decade, C.T. tripled the family's fortune through a series of shady real estate deals that smacked of insider access, though no charges ever stuck.

She searched federal campaign financing databases and found that C.T. became a big-time donor to a broad array of politicians in both major parties. The recipients, though, shared one common characteristic: all made a show of supporting big business and "economic growth." That made sense, Val concluded—like most wealthy people, C.T. wanted even more money and to pay the least amount possible in taxes.

The surprises began when Val discovered, through assessment and taxation records, that C.T. was still alive, living on another vast estate in California. Val had assumed that Theo inherited The Grounds from his father. In truth, 63-year-old C.T. still owned the property, among many others. That explained, at least to Val, why both brothers lived there, despite their apparent animosity: neither seemed willing to yield their interest in it to the other.

Another surprise: the old man's love life. Celebrity gossip mags revealed C.T. remained active as a philanthropist and political donor. His public appearances always resulted in him being photographed with a woman half his age, the current one a recent *Sports Illustrated* swimsuit model. Prior photos showed he'd run through at least two other "girlfriends" of similar pedigree, despite still being married. Theo's aspersions about his brother, and Ambrose's vagueness about his whereabouts that weekend, hinted that perhaps he emulated his father in that respect.

Those same magazines divulged that C.T.'s wife Clara— Theo's and Ambrose's mother—was a former high-society matron in New York. Early-onset dementia sidelined her in her forties into a care facility not far from The Grounds.

"Val," Sammy said, interrupting her deep dive into the Cox family history, "will you play with me? My arm is getting tired." He threw one last rock across the water, and it plunked below the surface without a single skip.

"Give me a few more minutes," Val said. "Then we'll walk up the trail, okay?"

Sammy made a sour face and picked up a long stick, splashing it into the water from his perch atop a flat rock along the bank. "How many minutes?"

"Five?"

He glared at her, then shrugged. "Okay. I wish I brought my games with me."

Val wished he did, too.

Now feeling rushed, she delved into Theo's life and those of his siblings. Birth and financial disclosure records showed that Theo and Ambrose had a younger brother, James, who died in infancy. An older sister named Rebecca led a quiet life in Palm Springs with her husband of twenty-plus years, one of C.T.'s protégés. Val found no photos or news stories of Theo with his siblings—any of them. From what she could gather, Theo had almost nothing to do—by his choice—with any of his family members, other than Ambrose.

Val hadn't gotten as far as she'd hoped when her phone rang. The number seemed familiar, but she couldn't place it. She answered, "Hello, this is Valorie."

"Miss Dawes?" A woman's voice. "This is Kayleigh Cox. Did I catch you at a bad time?"

Val sat upright. "Mrs. Cox. Did you find out anything about Shelby?"

A long pause ensued. "Um...no, I'm sorry," Kayleigh said. "I was calling about Connor and your little brother. Apparently the two boys quarreled earlier today?"

Val sighed. "I've asked Sammy to apologize to Connor

next time he sees him," Val said. "His behavior was inappropriate and—"

"Oh, that's funny," Kayleigh said. "After Connor told me what happened, I insisted that he apologize to Sammy. It seems both boys share the blame for their little dust-up."

"That sounds about right," Val said, smiling.

"Hey," Sammy said. "Are you talking about me?"

Val ignored him and covered her ear to hear the phone better. "If we could arrange a time for them to shake hands and make up, I think they'd both appreciate the opportunity."

"Is that Connor?" Sammy said, scrambling up the bank toward Val. "Is he calling to say sorry?"

Kayleigh chuckled. "I heard your brother there," she said, "and trust me, Connor is saying similar things on our end. I would love to get the two together for a playdate here at our house. Are you free this afternoon or tomorrow sometime?"

"I'll check." Val covered the phone. "Want to go to Connor's to play?"

Sammy's eyes grew wide. "At his *house*? The ginormous mansion with the pool and horses? Hell, yeah!"

"Sammy! Language." Val suppressed a laugh at the mild curse, though. "Anytime," she said to Kayleigh. "What works best for you?"

"Can you be here in an hour?"

"See you then." Val hung up and faced Sammy, now panting out of breath in front of her. "One condition," she said to Sammy. "You need to apologize for throwing a rock at him."

Sammy dug his toe into the dirt. "I'm sorry."

"Not to me. To Connor."

Sammy glanced up, an embarrassed half-smile on his face. "Okay."

Val stood up and gathered up the blanket and backpack. "All right, then. Let's go to the cabin so you can change into a clean shirt and I can freshen up a bit."

Sammy whooped and raised his arms in a victory salute. "Yay! I always wanted to play at a big ol' mansion house! I want to bring my swimsuit and ride the horses and eat sandwiches and pickles on gold plates. Yahoo!" He ran down the path toward the cabin, not waiting for Val to finish packing up.

Val breathed a sigh of relief. She needed some time to search for Shelby without leaving Sammy unsupervised or putting him in danger. A playdate might give her the right opportunity to get started on that.

Chapter Eighteen

The Redeemer downed his drink, letting the bite of alcohol shock him out of his mental haze, brought on by the long, dull meeting he had endured. The dark tavern, nearly empty at midday on a Monday, exaggerated his ennui. Perhaps not the best choice of venues, but his meeting partner chose the location. When they left, he'd opted to celebrate his victory in their absence...and the absence of other, prying eyes.

He should have canceled, or at the very least, insisted on a remote meeting. They'd become all the rage, with COVID scaring people into seclusion. However, closing deals sometimes required face-to-face conversation, handshakes, and perhaps most important, reading the body language of the opposite party. Finding their vulnerabilities, where they'd give. Where, and what, he could take from them.

Their assistance, for example. Helping him complete his mission with maximum discretion and a minimum amount of interference.

Mission accomplished.

An in-person rendezvous also provided a view of the multiple televisions positioned over the bar, silent but closed-captioned, tuned to local news stations. His proximity to the screens and his excellent eyesight gave him plenty of opportunity to read the important bits. National coverage of the election, the spread of COVID, and the fears of a tanking economy soon gave way to local news. As always, crime topped the list of items to discuss.

Nasty, violent crime, in fact. Crime committed, once

again, by a perverted animal who, according to the announcer, walked free because of a legal technicality, despite the mountain of evidence the police collected against him.

He swore and rapped the table, signaling to the barkeep for a third round. So many of these damned pervs walking the streets, victimizing women, men, and even children at will, suffering no consequences for their actions. The legal system was too preoccupied with process to concern itself with true justice—exacting the punishments that would deter these wretched animals from further depravity upon innocent, law-abiding souls.

His mind raced with thoughts of where this perv was now, whom he might victimize next. What awful acts would he perpetrate on them? How could anyone—a judge, a prosecutor, a cop—let this cretin go free?

If they wouldn't take him off the streets and protect the women and children, who would?

He knew the answer to that.

At the moment, though, his plate was full. He had a project yet to complete—a soul to redeem. One that was taking far too long this time.

He needed to accelerate the process. Much more work must be done.

***

Val pulled her Honda up to the gate at The Grounds and pressed the Call button, expecting Kayleigh Cox to answer. Instead, an unfamiliar female voice surprised her, with a hint of a southern accent. "May I help you?"

"I'm Valorie Dawes, bringing Sammy over for his playdate with Connor," Val said. "Mrs. Cox is expecting me."

"Of course. Please come in." The speaker buzzed and the gate swung open.

Val pulled the car up close to the house. Sammy jumped out as soon as it stopped rolling and dashed up the steps. The front door opened seconds after he knocked, with Val still unbuckling her seat belt.

A curvaceous and pretty blonde woman in her late twenties stepped out and bent over to shake Sammy's hand. She wore full makeup and a form-fitting dress appropriate for a high-powered business meeting. "Welcome to the Cox residence," she said in a soft voice.

Sammy seemed at a loss for words, and Val realized why. By bending over, the woman gave him a close-up and personal glimpse of her generous cleavage. Even at ten, Sammy clearly had developed an interest in that part of a woman's anatomy.

The woman straightened and smiled at Val. "I'm Cedar Embley. You must be Valorie. Welcome." She extended a limp handshake as Val approached.

Val took her hand and gave it a light squeeze. "Pleased to meet you. Do you...work for the Coxes?"

"I'm Mr. Cox's executive assistant," Cedar said, "although my duties extend to...let's just say, I help with certain household affairs as well, including supervising Connor from time to time. Please come in. Connor is waiting for you, Sammy."

Sammy dashed inside, yelling, "Connor! Connor! It's Sammy! I'm here!"

Connor's whoops of excitement told Val all she needed to know about the boys' lack of hard feelings over their morning scuffle.

"May I speak to Kayleigh?" Val said, still standing on the steps. "I'd like to thank her for this generous hospitality."

Cedar averted her eyes. "I'm afraid Mrs. Cox isn't...*available* at the moment."

Val's internal alarms rang, her imagination running straight to what the controlling, quick-to-anger Theo might have done to her. "If this isn't a good time, we can come back—"

"I'm sure it's fine," Cedar said. "Mr. Cox is out on business right now, so I'm free to supervise the boys. It's…not an uncommon situation around here." She flashed Val a knowing glance and smile, as if sharing a secret between girls.

Val's unease grew. "Well, if you're sure…I mean, I expected to stay and help supervise them." Which was true, but the urgent desire to continue to search for Shelby tore at her as well.

"Not necessary. Come in, let me show you." She gestured Val inside and guided her to a small office space off the main hallway. A laptop, large-screen monitor, and printer perched atop a glass, multi-level workstation. Behind her desk, a television screen mounted on the wall showed a sharp image of the two boys sitting on the floor in another room, setting up a board game. "This is my office. As you can see, we monitor Connor's playroom— unbeknownst to him, of course—through motion-activated cameras. If the boys get a bit too rough, I can intervene within seconds."

"I see." Val glanced around the office and realized she'd be in the way if she stayed, and Cedar seemed more than competent. Still, she hated to leave Sammy. "Would it be okay if I remained on The Grounds while they play? Out of your way, of course. I mean, I've never been to a place like this."

Cedar laughed. "Of course. I know what you mean. Before coming to work here, I was stuck on a cubicle farm. The Grounds is a beautiful place. I recommend you explore the gardens. They're brilliant in the afternoon light."

"I noticed lots of blooming flowers out there." Val headed toward the front door, a few steps ahead of Cedar. "How do they manage that so early in the spring?"

Cedar widened her eyes and leaned closer, as if letting Val in on a secret. "See if you can find the greenhouse," she said. "If the gardener is in there, though, I wouldn't go in.

He's kind of a grump, and he once chased me out with a rake."

Val laughed. "Thank you for the heads-up. I'll take a walk and see you in, say, a half-hour?"

Cedar held Val's gaze. "Take as long as you need."

Val, mesmerized by Cedar's crystal blue eyes and soft, Southern accent, found herself tongue-tied for a moment. The woman seemed at once comforting and...off. She hurried outside. Walking along the stone pathway that encircled the house, Val wondered if leaving Sammy in the care of the strange and beautiful Cedar Embley was a mistake.

She shook it off as an overreaction to the unfamiliar surroundings and her preoccupation with Shelby. Her parents left Val and Chad alone at a young age more times than she could count. From what she could tell, Mom had continued the practice with Sammy. He was more accustomed to it than not.

Besides, Kayleigh and Theo entrusted Cedar to take care of Connor all the time. She would never let anything happen to them.

***

Val followed the path around the mansion, and the well-kept gardens gave way to a far less manicured mix of tree stands, rustic outbuildings, and natural meadows. Much more shaded because of the dense foliage and the house's long shadows, the rear of the property seemed mysterious and dark in contrast to the front yard's bright colors and grassy expanse. Sunshine filtered through the trees, their branches sporting the tiniest of buds that would sprout later into broad leaves of oak, maple, and poplar. Evergreens sprinkled throughout provided patches of shade, greenery, and the welcome scent of pine and cedar. From the center of the wooded glen, she lost sight of all evidence of civilization—no buildings, walls, or power lines. It recalled for her a memory of the backwoods of Maine from a childhood camping trip, where she'd long hoped she would return someday with Gil.

Which reminded her: he *still* hadn't replied to her last text, over an hour ago. What was keeping him?

She headed farther upstream, parallel to the stone wall. The pathway turned to gravel, then to bark mulch, and the trees grew more sparse. She investigated a large rectangular building to her left, more modern in construction, which turned out to be the pool, Jacuzzi, and a small gym. A small, foggy rectangle of glass in the door felt warm to the touch, and a faint scent of chlorine leaked out. Locked, but she peeked in the window. No Theo, despite his claim of taking a daily afternoon swim. And no sign of Shelby.

Past the pool came two outdoor tennis courts, caged in wire-mesh fence. Then the path ended, giving way to a grassy meadow about one hundred yards wide and several times that in length, rimmed by a split-rail fence. Across the meadow stood two barns, one with an open door spilling hay onto the ground, and the second, too dark to see inside. Moments later, though, a brown horse with a white splash on its chest and straw-colored mane strolled out the door into view. Moments later, a second, shorter horse appeared, mostly white but spotted with black and gray, its mane and tail as gray as an angry rain cloud. The two horses broke into a trot, then a gallop, racing toward the stone wall at the end of the meadow.

Horses, Olympic indoor pool, tennis courts, an onsite gardener, and an "executive assistant." Serious money, these Coxes.

She turned to her right, following the wooden fence away from the creek, her running shoes getting drenched by the tall, wet grass. Soon she happened back onto another gravel path that led to a cottage. Small by Cox standards, it resembled a log cabin in appearance, with a thin wisp of smoke escaping its brick chimney. A dim light shone inside through a window that must have held glass at least a century old, given its uneven texture. Three cars sat parked outside the cottage. Two bore Connecticut plates—a Range Rover and a late-model Porsche. A third, a Lexus, sported New York tags. Whoever lived there had company.

Approaching the cottage, she noticed a series of miniature video cameras attached to the walls and fascia, and a quarter-sized disk stuck to the corner of the window on the inside. A thin wire gave it away as a security system sensor. A sign on the path reinforced that impression: "Monitored by GBT Systems." A second notice read, "Private—Keep Out." She wondered why they'd bother with signage of that sort within The Grounds, already secured by stone walls, cameras, alarms, and locked gates around its perimeter.

Still, fair warning, right? She stopped at the sign and looked over at the cottage. Movement inside the window caught her eye. The figure of a man, muscular, thick-chested, and wearing no shirt, stood in profile close to the window. His rumpled dark hair and two-day-growth of stubble on his cheek enhanced his rough-and-ready look. He smiled at something, or someone, out of Val's view. Then his body lowered, as if he were kneeling on something—a bed?—until only his head and shoulders remained visible. His eyes focused downward. On what, Val couldn't see. For a moment.

The top of another man's head came into view, one with shorter, lighter-colored hair. The second man wrapped his arms around his dark-haired friend. Val couldn't see the second man's face, but otherwise he bore a striking resemblance to the men of the Cox family. Whether Ambrose or Theo, she couldn't tell.

The dark-haired man pulled the second man down, and they disappeared from view.

Her phone rang, its chimes sounding louder than a

church bell's, and Val nearly jumped out of her skin. She grabbed it out of her jacket pocket and muted it—too late. Alarmed voices inside the cottage told her they'd heard it, too.

She turned and ran back up the path toward the mansion.

***

Connor double-jumped Sammy's last remaining checkers, his piece landing on his friend's home row, and he raised his hands in victory. "I win! That's two out of three. I'm the champion."

"We said the first one to *win* three is champion." Sammy crossed his arms over his chest. "Nobody's champion yet."

Connor heaved a deep breath. He liked Sammy and was glad they'd made up after their fight, but he could be so stupid sometimes. They'd *clearly* agreed best-out-of-three before they started playing. Sammy was just a sore loser.

But if they fought again, he'd be back to having no friends his age nearby.

"Okay," Connor said. "Let's have a snack before we play again, okay?"

"Cool! Do you have root beer?"

Connor grinned. "The best. A&W!"

"Yay! Yeah, let's have that," Sammy said. "And cheesy crackers!"

Connor stood and ran to the intercom by the door and pressed the red "Talk" button. "Can we have some crackers and root beer, please?"

"It'll be right down," Miss Embley responded. "Go ahead and play while you wait."

They set up the checkerboard again and each took a few turns, then Sammy sat back, scratching his head. "Can we play outside after our snack?" he said. "I like it by the creek."

"Sure," Connor said. "If my mom or Miss Embley say

it's okay."

Miss Embley brought the snacks a few moments later, and after setting them up at a small table in the corner of the room, she said, "I'll be leaving soon. If you need anything else, ask your mother. She's in her studio."

"We're fine," Connor said. "Thanks." He nibbled at the cheese crackers and sipped his soda.

Sammy glared at him, mid-cracker-chew. Connor knew what he wanted—to ask permission to go outside. Which might get a "no."

He had a better idea. He waited until Miss Embley left, then whispered, "Once she leaves, we can go outside all we want. My mom never comes out of her study unless there's an earthquake or something."

Sammy's eyes widened. "Are you sure?"

Connor nodded. "Besides, I want to show you something."

Sammy's mouth popped open for a sec. "Like, a secret?"

Connor grinned. "Yup. But only if you pass the test."

Sammy's expression grew guarded. "Like, what kind of test? A school test, or like doing twenty pushups, or eating something gross, or what?"

Connor shook his head. "A loyalty test."

"What's a loyalty test?"

Connor thought for a moment. "It's when you prove to your friend that you'll never rat him out, no matter what. Even if grown-ups say you'll get in trouble unless you confess."

"Confess what?" Sammy asked.

"The secret, dummy."

Sammy ate a few more crackers and drank more soda. "What do I gotta do to pass the test?"

Connor thought and thought. He wanted to come up with something cool, and he should've done that before challenging Sammy. Then he remembered something he'd seen on TV once, where two friends poked their fingers until they bled and mushed them together.

"We should be blood brothers," he said.

Sammy frowned. "Like, bleed on each other? My mom says that's a stupid idea. You can give each other diseases and stuff."

Connor scoffed. "Grown-ups always say stuff like that to scare you. I doubt it's even true."

Sammy still looked troubled, though. "How about," he said, "instead of blood brothers, we become spit brothers?" He hocked up some saliva and spat it into his glass of root beer, then pushed it toward Connor. "You spit in yours. Then we trade."

Connor laughed. "That's gross. We should do it!" He spat into his glass and they traded. Each boy held his glass up to his lips, then stopped.

"On three," Sammy said. "Drink it all. One...two...*three!*" He gulped down Connor's drink.

Connor hesitated a moment, then realized he had no choice. Sammy had drunk all of his root beer. If he wanted any, he'd have to drink Sammy's spit. "Here goes nothing!" he said, and chugged it down.

"Now," Sammy said, finishing off the last of his crackers, "What's this secret you're gonna tell me?"

"Get your coat on," Connor said. "We're going exploring."

Chapter Nineteen

Val ran until she reached the cover of the thick canopy of trees mid-property. Then she glanced back, confirming the cottage was out of view, and nobody had followed her. She leaned over, taking deep breaths, and collected her emotions.

First, guilt. Although she'd come upon the scene by accident, she'd stared transfixed for several seconds, and she felt downright voyeuristic, having invaded their privacy like that.

Second, a bit of shock. Val had seen one naked man in the past year—Gil—and very few before that. Never two together, having sex. It was the last thing she expected to see on a stroll of The Grounds.

Third, a little queasiness from an unexpected source. She'd gotten a good enough view of the dark-haired man to realize he was hairless from the neck down. All the way down. The Ken-doll look turned her off. She couldn't help but compare him to Gil, who had a similar body type, yet presented a more traditional masculinity. A few tufts of chest hair, a thin, dark stripe from his sternum to his waistline, more fur down below...

Thinking about a naked Gil wasn't helping. In fact, it only made her miss him even more.

Val needed to distract herself, then remembered the phone call that interrupted the scene. She checked the number, and didn't recognize it. A 314 area code.

Shit! Austin! The one person who might have a clue as to Shelby's whereabouts. And she'd missed his damned call!

He'd left voicemail, though. She listened.

"Ms. Dawes, this is Austin Clearwater." His flat, Midwestern accent on top of the deep baritone sounded ominous, and it chilled her, as did his next sentence: "I need to see you right away. Call me back at this number."

Austin *needed* to see her? Why?

Because he had Shelby?

Val had no choice. She called back.

No answer.

Tried again. Straight to voicemail. Almost unable to breathe, her voice a tight, nearly inaudible whisper, she kept it to the point: "This is Valorie Dawes returning your call. Call me as soon as you get this message." She repeated her phone number even though he clearly had it.

Val retraced her steps toward the mansion, checking her phone every few moments to no avail. Still, she noticed a few features of the property she'd missed on the way out: an old well, with no rope or bucket for lifting out water. Concrete steps led down to a metal door, probably an old storm cellar. A small pond down the hill fed a stream that bled under the stone wall that marked the property's edge. A few birdhouses sat empty, and a manmade beehive appeared to be no longer in use. She wondered which members of the Cox family were so interested in nature. Theo didn't strike her as the type. Maybe Kayleigh, or previous generations of Coxes. They probably hired people to do it.

She reached the front door of the house and rang the bell. Waiting, she heard loud voices. Theo's and Kayleigh's argument spilled out of an open window overhead.

"I've told you a thousand times not to let the kid roam around unsupervised!" Theo's voice rose from tense and strained to uncontrolled fury.

"*I* didn't *let* him do anything," Kayleigh shot back. "Your little whore did. Then she abandons them! I tell you, Theo, I'm firing that bitch the moment—"

"No, you're not," Theo yelled. "She doesn't work for you. She works for me. I'll decide—"

"Works? Hah! On her back, you mean. Or are you into kinkier positions now?"

The sound of a slap, followed by a woman's scream, punctuated Kayleigh's retort. The slap jolted Val as if she'd received the blow herself. Out of instinct, Val reached for her sidearm and badge—not there. Still, she felt the urge to knock down the door and rush upstairs to intervene. Theo could crush Kayleigh's tiny body without even trying.

The shouting continued. Theo: "Don't you dare *ever* imply—"

"Don't touch me!"

"Touch you? I wouldn't lay another finger on your disgusting so-called body if you begged me."

"Don't worry. I will never beg you. I doubt *she* needs to, though."

Val fretted on the front steps, not knowing what to do. She imagined the trouble she'd invite if she shifted into cop mode—outside her service area, suspended, no gun or badge or authorization of any kind. Regardless, she needed to get Sammy out of there before the violence escalated. She reached out to knock on the door—

"Get out of this house, you cheating cuck!" Kayleigh shouted.

"Oh, that's rich," Theo said, cynical laughter on the edge of his steely voice. "Throw me out of my house, would you?"

"Your daddy's house, you mean!"

"Oh, look who's talking, you little brat. Hey, what the fuck are you—"

A parade of fabric fluttered out the window. Val recognized some items: dress shirts, ties, and men's boxer shorts. A roll of socks landed with a *thump* on the grass. Theo's face poked out a moment later, flushed red.

"Oh. Hi there." His voice calmed and his face grew an

even deeper shade of crimson. "Excuse us...a little husband-wife chat." He flashed a sheepish grin. "We'll be right down."

"Who is it?" Kayleigh's face replaced Theo's in the window. "Oh... Ms. Dawes. The boys went out exploring, apparently. I'm sure they'll return soon." She ducked back inside and shut the window.

Val heaved a sigh of relief. At least Sammy hadn't suffered through hearing all that. How horrific. He'd witnessed more than his share of violence and trauma in his short life, courtesy of his criminal parents.

But now, where the hell was he?

The door opened, and Theo shuffled outside, closing the door behind him. He spoke to Val in a low voice. "I'm sorry you had to witness that. One of our nastier arguments, I'm afraid."

"Sorry to intrude," Val said. "I was hoping to check in on Sammy."

"My wife and my assistant conspired to allow them to roam with the freedom of adults to God-knows-where," Theo said. "I'm sure they're fine—they can't get into too much trouble here on The Grounds."

Alarmed by the revelation, still Val edged away from him, keeping an eye on his right hand—presumably the one that had struck his wife. "Still, I'd, uh, feel better if we knew where they were," she said.

"As would I. Perhaps together we can team up to find them?"

Val cleared her throat. "Uh, sure. If we each searched a separate part of The Grounds—divide and conquer—"

"An excellent idea." Theo showed none of the anger or aggressiveness that he'd unleashed on his wife moments before. "Let me make sure I have your correct number, and you mine, so we can share any discoveries we make." He showed Val his phone, which already displayed her name and number.

"That's right," Val said.

Theo tapped the "Call" button, and it rang on Val's phone once before he tapped "End Call." He smiled, a flirty grin. "And now you have mine. Go on ahead. I, ah, need to pick up a few things on the lawn." He shuffled away onto the grass and gathered up the belongings Kayleigh tossed outside.

Val hustled off, back up the path she'd just taken from the stables and tennis courts. She had no idea where to look. But she needed to find Sammy. And the sooner she put distance between herself and Theo, the better.

***

Val called the boys' names at the top of her lungs as soon as she reached the backyard, though she doubted she'd find them that close. She cursed herself for leaving Sammy in Cedar Embley's care, or anyone's outside of her own, for that matter. So stupid. Far too trusting. She wouldn't make that mistake again.

She guessed the boys took refuge in the wooded area nearest to the creek. Both loved the forest and "exploring," and she'd avoided that detour on her hurried escape from the cottage. She headed straight to that area.

Thinking of the cottage triggered another realization: since Theo was in the house upon her return, the light-haired man in the cottage must have been Ambrose. As for the other man, she had no idea.

A new thought stopped her in her tracks. Might Ambrose be the one behind Shelby's disappearance? Might Shelby have discovered him *in flagrante delicto,* as Val had, and panicked Ambrose into a rash act to protect his reputation?

Then: Could Ambrose have killed Larkin and Dinker as well? Larkin had been spotted weeks before in the same gay bar where she'd first encountered Ambrose. Maybe they met there, he'd brought him home, and killed him after his conquest.

It fit, kind of. She'd studied cases in criminal psychology at UConn where men, ashamed of their own sexual appetites, targeted others they labeled "perverts" to assuage their guilty consciences. Was Shelby, a transitional woman, his latest target?

Or was she jumping to conclusions? Val always considered herself an ally of the LGBTQ community, but she couldn't rule out subconscious bias.

On the other hand, the Greenville police and Ambrose's own brother had made pointed references to his suspicious history...and hinted that it might not all be in his past.

She paused on the trail. Speaking of his brother... Theo always seemed to be trying to hide something. A guy with a violent mean streak, who intimidated and even struck his tiny, frail wife. She didn't trust him out of her sight...or even within it.

Val trudged on, thinking about the couple's fight—a brawl, really. A human hurricane, with fists and clothes flying. So foreign to her experience. The tension between her and Gil felt tame by comparison, and they'd never actually quarreled. Growing up, she witnessed few fights between her parents, and never anything so extreme. Instead, her parents' disputes resembled something closer to an Arctic blast across the tundra: cold, distant, and lonely. For days after, they lived with a punishing silence so forced and heavy, she and her older brother Chad dared not speak—out of fear they, too, might get sucked into the icy, loveless void.

Val shook off that memory and delved deeper into the woods. The boys might have gotten lost in there—by accident or on purpose, knowing Sammy. The land sloped downhill, toward the creek, and she followed the trail down until she encountered the stone wall encircling the Cox property. From there she angled away from the wall until the trees thinned into a clearing and small outbuildings came into view—tiny rectangles of various ages and construction that smelled of fresh-cut wood and something more dank, like fertilizer.

Coming over the crest of a small hill, she spotted the glare reflecting off a glass roof. The greenhouse. Could they be in there? Noticing movement inside, she found the entrance and paused, recalling Cedar Embley's warning about the gardener's ill temper.

She couldn't let that stop her. She swallowed her trepidations and knocked on the door.

No answer.

Val knocked again, waited a moment, then pulled the door open and stepped inside.

"Close the damned door!"

A stooped, slender man with deep wrinkles, a long white beard, and dark age spots on his face yanked an unlit, half-smoked stogie out of his gritted brown teeth. His long gray hair was pulled back into an unruly ponytail, its fringes forming a hazy halo around his leathery face. He wiped dirt from his free hand on black-stained rust-colored overalls and gestured at the door. "I said close it, goddamm it! You're letting all the warm air out! Not to mention the moisture."

Val unfroze and yanked the door shut. "S-sorry. I'm looking for a boy—my little brother. He and Connor—"

"Ain't here. Ain't seen 'em. Hope to fuck I don't, either. Last kid that wandered in here ruined an entire bed of camas lilies." He shook his head and clenched his teeth around the stogie again. "Who the hell are you?"

Val took a step toward him. The room grew warmer and more humid with every inch of ground she covered. "I'm Valorie Dawes. My brother Sammy had a playdate with Connor—"

"Not here, they didn't. This is a workplace, not a fucking playground." The gardener scowled, shoved his hands into a bucket of black soil on his workbench, and tossed some into a large, teal-colored clay planter on the floor.

"So you haven't seen them—"

"No, I ain't fucking seen them, and if they know what's good for 'em, I won't. Now get the hell out of here." He threw another clump of black soil into the pot, then sprinkled some fertilizer from a box into the planter.

Val edged closer. Something told her this guy might be the only person on The Grounds without an agenda—someone she could get answers from. "May I ask you another question? A friend—"

"You just did." The old man laughed, a thin, wheezy sound that devolved into a coughing fit, and he held himself upright with both hands on the workbench. The aroma of sweet liquor and stale tobacco wafted over to her. "Go ahead, then, ask. Last one, though, so make it good."

"Right." Val smiled at the man, partly out of nerves, and in part because of the way his brusque manner reminded her of her late Uncle Val. He, too, could be impatient, but underneath his rough surface beat a soft heart, full of passion. Uncle Val's passion was crime-fighting. This man, this gardener, loved his plants and his workspace...and maybe more. "I wondered if you've seen this woman on The Grounds in the last few days." She showed him a photo of Shelby on her phone.

The gardener glanced at the photo and gave no reaction to it, instead turning back to his work. He pulled a lush, yellow-and-green-leafed hosta from a small pot and set it into the teal planter. He bent over and, with gentle hands, spread another few handfuls of soil around the hosta's base. "Now," he said after a long pause, "what would an ugly fucking girl like that be doing in a place like this?"

"Hiking," Val said, her irritation showing. Why did men always make it about looks? "Have you seen her or not?"

The gardener straightened and brushed the soil off his hands and grabbed the cigar out of his mouth, pointing it at her. "Lady," he said, "I don't see people if I can help it.

Which ain't too often, and it ain't happened in weeks, until you. In my experience, people ain't worth the time." He chortled a bit and gave Val an appreciative once-over stare. "Now you might be worth a minute or two. You ain't bad to look at and you got some spunk. You like coffee?"

Val nearly fell down in surprise, trying to keep up with the man's random utterances. Did he, a man several times her age, believe he could charm her with clumsy compliments?

"Some other time, perhaps. I really need to find my brother. It's a pleasure meeting you, mister, ah...I didn't catch your name?"

The old gardener scowled. "No, you didn't." He sucked on the still-unlit stogie, patted his pockets until he found some matches, then glanced back at her. "Don't let the door hit your cute little ass on the way out. Remember to close it this time." He lit a match, held it close to the tip of his cigar, staring at her. When she didn't move, he lowered the match. "What's the matter? You thought of another goddamn question or something?"

Val stalled a moment. She did have another question. "Is there some place on The Grounds where a woman like my friend Shelby might've stumbled into and gotten hurt, or lost, or—"

The gardener blew out his match and tossed it to the floor, shaking his finger as if he'd burned it. "Lady," he said, "nothing in this place happens by accident. *If* she's here..." His voice trailed off and he lit another match, this time not waiting for her to leave before lighting the cigar. "If she's on these grounds, she didn't get here by accident." He took a deep drag and held the smoke in his lungs for a few seconds, then exhaled a blue cloud into the sky.

Val stumbled out of the greenhouse, shutting the door behind her. The gardener's last statement chilled her more than the late afternoon air and the northerly breeze. He seemed to imply that Shelby was somewhere on The

Grounds, and taken there by force...yet he knew nothing about her.

What the hell was going on?

Movement up ahead captured her attention. Val gazed up the trail to where it crested a small hill. A tall figure, masculine, darted out of view. She caught only a glimpse, and at first assumed it was Theo catching up to her. But why would he hide?

She ran up the trail, out of breath when she reached the top. No man in sight. Nor the boys.

The boys! She called their names again. Her voice disappeared into the wind.

Val closed her eyes a moment to focus on the face she'd just seen. It was familiar and out of place. Not one of the Cox brothers, but one she'd seen a few days before—in Clayton.

It made no sense, but the man she'd seen in that way-too-quick glimpse was her nemesis from the Academy and now the Clayton Police Department: Ben Peterson.

***

Val resumed her search for Sammy and Connor, calling their names every hundred yards or so, until she spotted the horse corral, where her phone rang. Caller ID told her who it was, and she came close to sending the call to voicemail. However, if it led to a clue, somehow, about Shelby's whereabouts...

She drew a deep breath, let it out, and answered. "Dawes here."

"What in the *fuck* do you think you're doing in Greenville?"

Val counted to five, maintaining her calm. "A pleasure to chat with you as well, Detective Simpson. How may I be of service to you today?"

"Stop the fucking meddling in my damned case, that's what!" Simpson's voice hit top volume in Val's ear—eleven on a scale of one to ten. The man knew how to communicate anger.

Still, something seemed off. Contrived, even. The bogus "meddling" accusation, for one thing.

"I'm not 'meddling' in your case, or anyone's." Val kept her tone even, and refrained from adding, somehow, *asshole.* "I'm on vacation—a forced one, thanks to you, remember?"

"Oh, I remember," Simpson said. "And if you keep this bullshit up, it'll be permanent."

"Detective, I'm sure I don't—"

"You think I don't know what's going on out there?" Simpson's maximum-volume voice returned. "I know your every move, Dawes. Every rogue, illegal mistake you make."

Val rolled her eyes. "What are you talking about?"

"Do you deny meeting with the Greenville PD to, quote, *exchange information,* unquote, about the Larkin and Dinker cases?" Volume control dialed down to seven.

"Of course I deny it," Val said. "I met with them to report a missing person."

"Bullshit," Simpson said, volume back to nine. "But I'm glad you're lying. We'll just add that to the list of charges to discuss at your suspension hearing. Now stay the fuck off my case!"

"I'm not on *your case,*" Val said. "I told you, I'm—"

"Reporting a missing person, blah, blah." Volume down to six, but sarcasm meter up to ten. "Guess what? We don't need your help and neither does Greenville. We'll find the killer, and we'll find Shelby Clearwater without your help. So get lost."

Recalling the news articles Gil sent, she doubted he'd even try. "Detective, Shelby's my friend. I refuse to—"

"Final warning, Dawes. Stay clear!" The line went dead.

Only then did Val realize Simpson knew who she meant by "missing person" before she'd even told him.

Chapter Twenty

The conversation with Simpson distracted Val enough that she lost the rough trail, and had to fight through some thick underbrush for a few minutes. She vented her frustration on the knee-high thicket, kicking through and yanking the spindly growth until the exertion left her out of breath. Stupid Simpson! He seemed preoccupied with her, blocking her every attempt to find Shelby.

Almost as if he didn't want her to find her friend at all.

Val shook off that thought. Tackle Box was a cretin, a homophobe, and an incompetent fool. Even so, she couldn't conceive of a sworn officer of the law getting involved in kidnapping Shelby, much less murdering Larkin or Dinker.

After emerging from the trees, Val spotted Theo Cox walking toward her at a brisk pace. He waved to her, signaling she should wait.

"I found the boys," he said, his voice tense and his face grim. He brushed past her. "While I can't speak for Sammy, Connor's in trouble."

Val hurried to keep up with him. "Where are they? Are they okay?"

"You'll see."

Val stumbled over a root in the path and cursed. Her frustration carried into her voice when she called out again to Theo. "Care to fill me in? Or do you have a reason to keep me in suspense?"

Theo slowed his pace, allowing her to catch up. "They're not where they're supposed to be," he said, calmer. "Somewhere I've told Connor a thousand times to stay out of." The trail veered off to their right, toward the small cluster of buildings Val noticed earlier.

"How do you know?" Val's irritation grew. Why the roundabout, evasive language? So much about this guy bugged her. Recalling the scene outside the house earlier, she stayed as far away from him as possible while remaining within earshot, but out of arm's—fist's—reach.

Theo glared at her a moment, then his face relaxed into an amiable smile, turning on the same type of charm Ambrose showed her that morning by the creek. "I'm sorry," he said. "I've suffered a few setbacks today in my personal life...as you know." He cleared his throat, lowering his gaze. "I shouldn't take that out on you. I apologize."

Val studied his face, now serious, and body language, stooped and unthreatening. Theo's contrition appeared genuine. She relaxed and offered a cautious smile. "Apology accepted. So, how'd you find them? The detective in me has to know." She broadened her smile, hoping he'd buy into her I'm-just-curious act.

"Once I...calmed down," he said, "I was able to focus on the problem and resources at hand." He stopped and pointed to a birch tree, trimmed of its branches up to about ten or twelve feet. At a fork in the trunk sat a miniature camera mounted on a brace and pointing toward the tiny cluster of buildings. "We monitor a fair amount of the property. Not all, of course, but the buildings containing valuables and...well, you'll see. Smile, by the way. You're on TV."

Val frowned. "You had time to search all of your recordings since I last saw you?" She'd searched security film archives before and found the process tedious and slow.

"The cameras are motion-activated, which makes review much easier." Theo surrendered a rueful, lopsided grin. "Besides, it's not the first time I've tracked my boy down. He likes to roam, that one." He pulled out his phone, tapped it a few times, and showed the screen to Val. "See? Here they are, sneaking around like they're on some secret spy mission—one of Connor's favorite games."

Sure enough, the footage showed the two boys hustling down the path, crouched over and glancing around them, as if trying to avoid detection. Then they snuck behind the back of one windowless building, about the size of a tool shed, perhaps large enough to house a rider mower. Which is what Val assumed when she spied them earlier.

"Let's join their little spy game, shall we?" Theo grinned at her. "Would you rather be the Russians or an alien invader?"

Val groaned. "My Klingon is a little rusty."

"Russians, then. You can be Catherine the Great." He shot her an exaggerated, lascivious wink. Stories of Catherine's alleged perversions flashed through Val's mind and she wanted to vomit. Or run—

Not without Sammy. Dammit. Okay, she'd play his stupid game.

Theo bent over into a crouch, indicating Val should do the same, and they crept toward the buildings. When they reached the one the boys had disappeared behind, Theo rested his hand on Val's shoulder, stopping her advance. It startled her, and she edged away. His fingers brushed down to her waist, then dropped to his side.

Val shivered. She could excuse his touch as accidental...or not. Either way, she didn't like it.

"What's the plan?" she said in a hoarse whisper. "And what is this place?"

Theo shushed her with a finger to his lips. "Best not startle them too much," he whispered back. "You'll see why in a moment." He raised his voice to normal volume, grinned, and said: "*My okruzhili ikh, kapitan.*"

Val understood no Russian and showed as much with a shrug. Theo mouthed: "We have them surrounded, Captain."

Inside, sounds of frantic scrambling emerged, together with the unmistakable panicky voices of nine- and ten-year-old boys. Moments later, the front door of the building burst open, and Sammy and Connor dashed out onto the path, racing toward the woods. Connor reached the trees and disappeared, but Sammy lost his footing and fell, face-first, into the grass alongside the trail.

"Stop right there!" Val shouted at him when he rose to his feet.

Sammy froze in a ready-to-run position, a comical stance, like a sprinter emerging from the blocks. Val laughed despite herself.

"Connor!" Theo called out. "Get back here, young man. You are in big trouble, sonny boy."

No surprise, Connor did not appear from the woods. His footsteps echoed in the distance, pounding down the gravel path.

"I'll take care of him later," Theo said. "I'd better close up here. And call a locksmith." He pushed the door shut—

Not before Val spied the contents inside. Rack after rack of glass-fronted cabinets—closed and locked—containing a varied assortment of rifles, handguns, and accessories.

The boys had broken into a veritable armory, enough to arm a small militia, on the Cox family property.

***

Val helped Sammy to his feet and glared at him, hands on her hips, while he dusted himself off. He lifted his tearful gaze toward her. "I'm sorry, Val. I didn't know—"

"Save it. I'm in no mood." She stepped toward him and grabbed him by the collar.

"Valorie." Theo's voice cascaded up from behind her.

Val turned, still holding onto Sammy. She glared at Theo, trembling with rage. "Yes, Mr. Cox?"

"It's not his fault. Sammy couldn't have gotten in here without Connor's—"

"Don't even think about blaming your son," Val said, spittle flying. She could have lit a bonfire with her breath in that moment. "You keep a stash of guns on your property, secured only by a combination lock that a child can beat—it invites trouble. We're lucky nobody got hurt!"

Theo started to object, then hung his head, nodding. "You're not wrong. Trust me, I will redouble my security to ensure it never happens again."

"Damn straight it won't," Val said. "At least not to Sammy. He won't be coming back under any circumstances. Damned idiot. What were you thinking?"

Theo seemed to wrestle with his explanation, as if debating what to tell her, then heaved a deep sigh. "Clearly I wasn't. But don't be so hard on Sammy. He followed Connor's lead—and his own curiosity. I guess Connor is growing up faster than I expected."

Val's anger cooled a bit at Theo's calm, conciliatory speech. She had to admit, she'd made some pretty bad choices herself in the area of child supervision recently. People who live in glass houses, she reprimanded herself.

She nodded at Theo. "We'd best be going."

"Miss Dawes." Theo stepped toward her. "I understand your concern about not wanting Sammy around danger such as this. But I hope it doesn't mean the end of the boys' friendship...or of ours." He flashed her a coy smile.

Val's ears burned. Incorrigible, this guy—flirting in the midst of all this. "We'll see," she said. "For now—"

Her phone rang. The 314 area code again.

"Sorry, I must take this. Good day, Mr. Cox." She pushed Sammy up the trail and accepted the call.

"Valorie Dawes?" The male voice on the phone betrayed surprise, as if he hadn't expected her to answer.

"This is she. Who's calling?" Val trailed behind Sammy, heading down the path toward the Cox mansion. A north wind rustled the bare branches of the nearby trees, and the sun cast long shadows on the path before her.

"This is Austin Clearwater. I believe you know Shelby."

Val stopped cold in her tracks, snapping her fingers at Sammy. He either didn't hear or he ignored her, plodding onward toward the curve in the path. "Yes, Mr. Clearwater. Thanks for calling. I'm hoping you have some information as to the whereabouts of your sister."

His voice grew tense. "My brother, you mean. Just because he dresses in women's clothing and bought a pair of boobs—"

"Cut the crap, Austin," Val said. "Do you know where Shelby is?"

A pause. "I was hoping you'd be able to tell me. You're the damned cop, aren't you?"

Val gritted her teeth. Not a good start. She glanced at Sammy, already thirty yards ahead of her. She covered the phone and yelled to her brother, "Sammy! Wait up. Please."

Sammy slowed his pace, but continued on—in the wrong direction, toward the woods. Val hustled to close the gap between them.

"Mr. Clearwater," she said, her voice tense, "I understand you tried to reach Shelby this weekend. Were you successful, and if so, did she—?"

"No, I was not," Austin said. "However, I know Shelby's in Greenville. But not at the cabin he rented. And his *friend* Sanjit is as useless as Shelby's new tits. Weren't you going to meet up with them here?"

Val's head spun, unpacking everything Austin said. "Wait. You said *here*. Are you in Greenville as well?"

"At the cabin itself," Austin said, "sitting on the front porch. Where are you?"

"Nearby," Val said. "I can be there in fifteen minutes, maybe ten. If you'll wait there—"

"Nope," Austin said. "Thanks for your *help*. Such as it is."

The line went dead.

***

The Redeemer double-checked the locks on the door to the safe house. Handle, deadbolt, swing guard, and slider. All secure. No one could get in or out—except him.

He walked past the still-unconscious figure on the floor, glancing down when the scent of urine and feces drifted into his sinuses. Shelby had relieved itself while sleeping. A sign of declining resistance, not to mention the obvious humiliation the creature would endure upon waking. Good. He wanted weakness in his subject. Repentance would soon follow.

He reached the bedroom and unlocked the top drawer of the old maplewood dresser to retrieve his tools. Straight razor blade, shaving soap, tweezers, suture, fresh gag, and blindfold. A small container of smelling salts and, just in case, an inhaler infused with carfentanil, a fentanyl derivative. A last resort, but perfect for his purposes due to its low traceability should the coroner think to check for it. They hadn't the previous times, but one could never be sure.

He tested the razor's sharpness by slicing the leather of Shelby's shoe, his heart racing when it gashed through with almost no resistance. He kept his tools in pristine condition. Grandfather would be proud. For so many reasons.

He grabbed a towel from the bathroom and returned to the living room where Shelby slept, spreading the towel underneath the pitiful creature's legs up to its soiled underwear. The towel absorbed the sticky urine, already drying on the floor. He'd need to clean that up later. But not until he completed the evening's operation. No sense cleaning twice.

He held the smelling salts under the unconscious Shelby's nose. No reaction. He needed to take the risk, then.

With a sigh, he reached for the inhaler, inserted it into Shelby's mouth, and activated it.

The creature suffered a sharp intake of the stuff, making a slight gagging sound, followed by an audible groan. "Go away," Shelby said. Tears spilled down its cheeks.

The man stepped away to his keyboard, the first line of dialog already prepared, and pressed Enter. "Did you sleep well, Sunshine?" the robotic voice said.

"Just fucking kill me already," Shelby said. "I'm done with this shit."

"We have business to conduct," the machine replied. The man wiped the edge of the razor on his slacks and typed again. "You have something to tell me."

"No, I don't," Shelby said. "I won't satisfy your sick agenda with any sort of confession or retraction or whatever. Just cut my damned throat or shoot me or poison me, I don't care how, just end this."

"You can end this right now," the machine said in its reasonable British accent. "Say the words: *I am a deviant, I abhor what I've done, and I am done pretending to be a woman.* Say it."

"No."

The man slammed the keyboard with his fist, and the machine squawked a series of unintelligible syllables. Dammit! What would it take to break this one?

He calmed himself, typed again. "You are only prolonging this ordeal. There is no escaping your fate. You alone can end this. Say the words."

Shelby spit, the wad of saliva and phlegm splashing the floor at the man's feet.

He restrained himself from hitting Shelby again. He sensed that striking the creature only made it more defiant. Instead, he inhaled a deep, calming breath, then typed: "Very well, then. Let's take a little trip to the spa."

He stepped closer, grabbed the waistline of Shelby's underwear, and yanked them down past the knees. Shelby kicked at him, but missed.

Back to the desk. "You won't want to kick while I'm holding the razor near your genitals," he typed, and the machine obliged. "Things could get messy."

Shelby went still, even bent its knees outward to enable clear access.

He grabbed the shaving soap, swirled the brush in the dish to get it good and foamy, and brushed it onto Shelby's genital fur. He'd remove only the hair—for now.

Chapter Twenty-One

Val hurried after Sammy, who'd put fifty yards' distance between them. He took an unexpected turn on a trail Val didn't notice before, more of a semi-trodden path between clumps of underbrush than a trail. It headed more or less toward the creek, though Val expected it would dead-end at the stone wall surrounding the Cox property. She called his name, but he either didn't hear or ignored her, and she soon lost sight of him.

"Sammy!" Val yelled, her voice growing shrill. "Come back! To the *car*, goddammit!"

No sign of him turning back. She could've strangled him. She stomped onward.

The brush grew thicker, the trees clumping closer together, and with darkness falling she became concerned for their safety. They could get lost, or encounter whoever had taken Shelby, or cross the crotchety old gardener, or—

As if summoned, the old man appeared alongside the path, stroking his long, thin beard and cackling with laughter.

"Lost something?" The gardener's eyes sparkled and he cast her a wicked grin.

"Did you see a ten-year-old boy—"

The man waved his omnipresent cigar in the general direction of the creek. "The boy's fine. Healthy young'un. I wouldn't worry. Kid doesn't look like he makes a habit of skipping dinner."

Val swallowed the testy remark on the tip of her tongue. Bees and honey and all that. "Thanks. I hope he didn't disturb you."

"Not a-tall. Did you find your friend?"

Val paused, surprised by the sudden change of topic. "Shelby? Not yet...are you sure my brother's okay?"

"Resting at the foot of a tall oak, last I saw. Reckon it'll take him a minute to catch his breath. Otherwise, yeah, I'm sure."

Val calmed. The old man had a curious style, though a reassuring one. "If you don't mind, then, I have something to ask you. About Shelby."

"Another goddamn question!" He sucked on the unlit stogie and pulled out a book of matches. "Do I look like a tourist information booth to you?"

"Sorry," Val said. "I hoped you might clarify...when you said Shelby wouldn't be here by accident, did you mean you're certain she's here, or—"

"I don't know nothing," the man said, lighting the cigar. "All I'm saying is, Christ, you've seen the security they got here. You think someone stumbled in with nobody knowing?" He laughed. "Anyone comes here that Theo or Kayleigh Cox don't want around, they're liable to go home in a wooden box." He puffed on the cigar and blew out a cloud of pungent blue smoke.

"But you haven't *seen* her—"

"Asked and answered, young lady. Now you best get after your little boy before he stumbles into a bear trap out there. Or worse."

"*Bear* trap?"

The gardener laughed. "Figure of speech. Don't worry. Ain't no bear on The Grounds. Or traps." He ambled past Val on the path toward the mansion.

Val turned and called after him. "Thank you," she said. "Mister...?"

The old man stopped, eyed her sideways, and grinned. "Dupree," he said. "Folks call me Clay."

"Thank you, Clay."

Dupree waved acknowledgment and continued around

the bend in the path, lost moments later in the trees and brush.

Val hurried away in the direction Sammy had gone and found him a few minutes later, sitting on a thick branch of a mature maple tree by the stone wall. "What are you doing up there?" she asked. "Get down. We need to get out of here before it gets dark."

"That's what I'm doing." Sammy scooted out on the branch, which extended over the wall to the outside. "Connor showed me his secret escape route."

"We don't need to escape," Val said, exasperated. "We need to get to the car. Which is out front."

Sammy let out a loud whoop, a battle cry of sorts, and leaped from the branch. His body disappeared behind the stone wall with a thud. "Come on! It's a wicked cool shortcut!"

Val cursed under her breath. She had no choice but to follow him. She could come back for the car later.

Val hated climbing trees, even as a kid. She'd always cut or scraped or twisted something on the way up or down. Plus, Chad and his pals usually climbed higher and dropped acorns or pebbles on her—or worse, spit—adding to the unpleasantness.

Of course, Chad wasn't here, and she had no way of knowing if Sammy knew a way back in. He'd forced her hand, and that made her even grumpier.

"Wait, then." Val shimmied up the tree. She sat on the branch, nervous whether it would hold her weight or if she'd fall or bump her head or otherwise hurt herself as usual.

Then she glanced around, and her mood changed. The view, even from ten feet off the ground, was rugged and beautiful. Pines and firs provided a backdrop of greenery among the budding deciduous trees, framed by a cloudless sky awash in the pinks and blues of sunset. The stream gurgled over some rocky cascades some thirty yards away, slicing through a rock embankment, dampness glittering in the soft light. Down below, Sammy grinned up at her, his joy at seeing his big sister in her unusual perch infectious.

"Yay, Val!" He gripped his hands over his head in a victory salute. "You got this!"

She laughed and did as Sammy had done, scooting out on the branch past the edge of the wall and dropping to the soft earth beside him with a grunt.

"The way-back-in tree is over there." Sammy pointed at an old birch tree whose trunk bent low over the wall. "Cool, huh?"

"So cool. So long as you remember how to get to the front gate of The Grounds from here."

Sammy frowned. "I think we just follow this path." He marched toward the creek, then yelled out in surprise. He squatted and picked up something shiny off the ground.

Catching up to him, Val recognized the object in his hands: a shell-shaped brooch with the letter "B" inscribed inside. Shell-B, her friend's trademark. "Holy crap. That's Shelby's!" She reached for it—

Sammy yanked it away from her. "How do you know it's hers? It might be anybody's. Anyway, I found it, so it's mine."

"Sammy, come on. It's evidence. It might have fingerprints or DNA. Please give it to me."

"No." He skipped away. "Finders keepers."

"Sammy!" Val stepped closer and reached—

Sammy dashed down the path toward the creek. "Mine, mine, mine!"

Val cursed again and pursued him. He reached a fork in the path and continued on the route that brought him to the high banks along the rushing stream. Val followed, trapping him at the end of the trail, with nothing but steep, rocky banks behind him, leading down to the water.

He turned to face her, as if seeking an escape route, and found none. A foot behind him, the steep banks loomed. Nowhere to go.

"Now give me the brooch." Val held out her hand, frustration building.

"No. I found it fair and square. You can't steal it from me."

Val's patience ran out and she grabbed at the brooch. Sammy twisted away from her. She lunged after it, missing, and her feet got tangled in his. She stumbled, waving her hands to grab ahold of something—Sammy, a tree, anything—and she grasped only air.

Val fell, her knee and hip scraping the rocks on the creek bank, and her body teetered over the edge. For a moment she seemed suspended in midair. Then the world spun around her, and gravity did its job, pulling her down into the icy water.

The cold paralyzed her for a few seconds. It must have been close to freezing, the product of mountain snowmelt and underground springs, and it encased her entire body at once. The shock of the cold made her gasp, causing her mouth, throat, and lungs to fill with frigid water, an icy-hot sensation that gripped her in fear. She'd expected her body to slam into the bottom. Somehow, though, she'd landed in a deeper, swirling pool, and her outstretched hands raked the sandy creek bed below.

Val pushed away with both hands, her head bobbing above the surface, but the fast, cold current pulled her under the water, before she'd taken a breath. Her left ankle hurt, and she realized in horror that her foot was caught between two rocks, with her head downstream. She tried to shake it free, but the strong current pushed her ankle back into the jagged trap of stone and yanked her below the whitecaps again. Her lungs burned, demanding air. The foamy water blinded her when she opened her eyes. Her arms flailed, unable to find purchase on anything to yank herself above the surface. She held her breath as long as she could—

Val's body needed air. And warmth. And an end to the pain in her leg.

She couldn't hold out any longer. Her body refused her conscious command and convulsed in an involuntary intake of what should have been air, but was instead, icy, dense water. Pain seared her lungs, and consciousness drifted away—

Rough hands grabbed her, yanking on her hair, and pulled her head out of the water.

***

"There you are."

Connor froze at the sound of his uncle's voice wafting in from somewhere behind him. Nobody knew about his favorite hiding spot, a long-abandoned wooden platform perched in the branches of an aging oak tree overlooking the property's creekside wall. Nobody ever found him here before. Always he'd escaped trouble at home, or whiled away hours pretending to lead a sailing mission like Christopher Columbus, or an outer-space exploration like the Guardians of the Galaxy. It never occurred to him who might've built the platform, or when.

"Come on, don't pretend I can't see you." Uncle Ambrose stood at the base of the tree, smiling up at him, hands on hips. After another moment, he cocked his head. "Mind if I join you?"

Connor shrugged. He didn't want his uncle to invade his space, but Mom and Dad always taught him to respect his elders, which meant going along with whatever they said. So who was he to say no? Especially since, he now realized, the fort was probably Ambrose's and Dad's to begin with.

Ambrose took forever to climb up, despite the perfect layout of sawed-off branches and nubs to place his hands and feet. And Ambrose was ten times stronger than Connor. Finally his long body heaved onto the platform with a loud grunt. Only then did Connor notice the binoculars hanging from his uncle's neck.

Connor's binoculars.

"Anything good out there today?" Ambrose asked, sitting next to Connor.

Connor pointed to the spot along the wall where he'd seen Sammy shimmy up and over. "Sammy's running away."

Ambrose glanced at him with a puzzled frown. "You sure?"

Connor held out his hands in the shape of the binoculars. "Not sure. Maybe if I could look closer..."

Ambrose laughed and lifted the field glasses over his head, placing them in Connor's hands. Connor peered through, and this time a woman appeared in view, shimmying up the tree. Sammy's big sister Val. "I guess he's not really running away," he said. "Looks like him and his sister are sneaking out together."

"Over the wall, using the old maple tree?"

Connor lowered his binoculars and gazed in wonder at his uncle. "You know about the secret escape route?"

Ambrose grinned. "You're not the first kid to grow up on The Grounds with crazy parents."

"Huh." Connor offered the binoculars back to Ambrose, who waved him off. "Why do you suppose they used the escape route?"

"Maybe they were trapped. Have you ever felt trapped?"

Connor thought about that for a moment. "Sometimes my dad makes me stay in my room for a long time."

"Ah. My dad used to do that to your father and I, too. It never seemed fair to me, either."

"Did you have TV or anything in your room back then?"

Ambrose shook his head. "No game tablets, either."

"Aw, that sucks."

Ambrose nodded. "It wasn't as bad as getting whipped, though. Your dad ever do that to you?"

Connor's heart beat super-fast and his ears burned

red. Dad had told him to never, ever tell about that, even to Mom.

"Connor? Has he?"

Connor shook his head real hard a bunch of times. He wouldn't lie out loud, but he could with his head.

"Good, I'm glad." After a pause: "How about your mother?"

"She's never hit me once," he said, the words coming out so fast he couldn't stop them. Because they were true. Mom never, ever spanked him. She never even really yelled too loud.

"Good." Ambrose took a deep breath. "Have you ever seen him hit her?"

Connor froze again. He hadn't *seen* it, although he'd heard things…

"We both know that he does, though, right?" Ambrose went on.

Connor tried to swallow a big lump that formed in his throat. He couldn't. But with that lump there, he couldn't talk, either.

"It's good that you have a place to escape to when things get dangerous at home," Ambrose said in a soft voice. "Now listen to me. Don't go back if you don't feel safe there. Okay?"

Connor shrugged. "Usually things get safe again after a while, once Dad calms down."

"Until he gets mad again. Right?"

Connor said nothing. Right then, it felt like maybe he needed to pee.

"Listen to me, Connor." Ambrose sounded worried. "Your father is dangerous when he gets like that. If he ever raises his hand to you again—"

"He says *you're* dangerous," Connor said. So did his mom, sometimes, but only after his dad said so first.

Ambrose's face grew red as a frozen beet. "Never mind what he says about me. If he ever hits you, or if you see him strike or threaten your mother or even Miss Embley–"

"He never even yells at Miss Embley," Connor said. Uncle Ambrose didn't know *anything.*

He definitely needed to pee.

"Anyone," Ambrose said. "If you see anything at all like that, you tell someone. Me, or Mr. Dupree, or…someone. An adult. Okay?"

Connor thought for a moment. "Should I tell Miss Valorie? She's a police officer and—"

"No. Not Miss Dawes. She's not to be trusted, either."

That confused Connor. Mom always taught him that the police were on the side of good people.

Maybe Uncle Ambrose was the one he shouldn't trust.

"I think I'll go back home now," he said. "I need to go to the bathroom."

"Only if it's safe," Uncle Ambrose said.

Connor scooted around him and climbed down the tree trunk fast-fast-fast. He might not make it back to the house in time to pee. He might have to go in the woods.

When he reached the ground, screams echoed through the forest. He imagined his father and his mother fighting, his father raising his fist to strike her—

Connor ran through the woods, not even following the path. He had to get home to see if it was safe. For Mom.

Chapter Twenty-Two

Val's lids fluttered open, bright light stabbing her eyes. Sunlight sifted through the trees. Heavy cloth pinned her to the ground. A damp cold enveloped her.

She couldn't move.

A face hovered over her, blocking the sun. A man's face. She expected to see Gil's smile shining down on her, but no. Another, unexpected face. One she knew, but not one she loved. One she could. Not. Stand.

Ben fucking Peterson!

"Well, hello there, sunshine." Ben smiled down at her. "Welcome back to the land of the living."

Val forced herself into a sitting position, a damp blanket and overcoat falling from her wet clothes. Sammy squatted a few feet away, his tear-streaked face laced with fear and wonder. She glanced over at Ben, his arm on her shoulder, down on one knee. "H-how the hell...w-what happened?"

"You fell into the creek," Ben said in a gentle voice. Not mocking, the way he always spoke to her. Not leering, either. No malice at all. Just...genuine concern. So alien, coming from him.

"H-how d-did I g-get out?" Val's teeth chattered. Her arms, torso, and legs kept shaking too. So. Fucking. Cold.

"Your friend here saved the day," Ben said, nodding at Sammy. "He's quite the hero."

"S-Sammy p-p-pulled me out of th-the water?"

Ben tossed his head this way, then that. "Okay, I freed your leg from the rapids and pulled you ashore. Still, if not for his cries for help, I never would have gotten to you in time. He's got quite the set of lungs, that one."

"I shouted super loud," Sammy said, grinning.

Val glanced at each of them. Sammy's pants were wet up to his waist, Ben's above his knees. Ben wore only a flannel shirt on top—no jacket. Which explained the one around her shoulders. But the blanket?

"You just happened to bring an extra blanket on a hike?" she asked.

"Let's just say it was a lovely day for a picnic on company time." Ben chuckled. "You feeling up to walking? We should get indoors before we all freeze to death."

Ben helped her up, holding Val steady and supporting her weight, and only then did she realize she'd lost a shoe. Ben seemed to read her thoughts because he added, "Sorry about that. Casualty of the rapids. Here, put your arm on my shoulder. We can three-leg-race it back to your cabin."

"Nah, I'm fine—ouch! Dammit!" Pain jolted up her leg from her shoeless left ankle when she tried putting weight on it. Her elbow hurt, too—probably bruised—and her backside felt like someone had scrubbed it with sandpaper.

With reluctance, she accepted Ben's help down the path, Sammy in the lead. At a fork, he tugged her toward the path leading to the cabin. Val tugged the other direction, toward The Grounds. "My car is this way," she said.

"The cabin is a shorter walk," he said. "Let's get you there and I'll run back and pick up your car later."

Val wanted to argue, but the pain in her ankle flared, and she had to agree that the shorter walk sounded better.

"How'd you fall in, anyway?" he asked. "You're not what I'd call clumsy or careless."

"I tried to grab something from Sammy and slipped— which reminds me. Sammy, do you still have Shelby's brooch?"

Sammy spun around and held it up for Val to see. She

grimaced. No way any fingerprints or predator DNA survived him carrying it this long. However, it confirmed that Shelby had been close to, if not on, The Grounds. And it seemed unlikely that something pinned to her clothing would fall off without a struggle of some kind.

"That explains it," Ben said with a smirk, startling her back to their conversation. "I thought you'd opted for an impromptu swim lesson."

Val rolled her eyes, then grew serious. "Ben, thank you. I'm grateful for your help. I...I would've drowned."

Ben shrugged. "Thank your buddy here. Is he your nephew or something?"

"Sammy's my brother."

Surprise filled his face. "I thought your brother was, like, three or four years older than you."

"Chad is. This is Sammy. Long story, but the short version is, when you and I met at the Academy...I didn't know about Sammy then."

"Ah." They walked on for another few minutes in silence, her brain in a fog. She'd come so close to drowning. Somehow, Ben showed up at the exact right time and saved her. The man with whom she'd shared a mutual dislike, if not hate, for over two years now.

"Can I ask you something?" Val said when the cabin came into view.

"Sure."

Val paused. "Not to sound ungrateful or anything, but what the hell are you doing here?"

Ben drew in a deep breath and exhaled it. "My job."

"We're a long way from Clayton."

He chuckled. "Nothing gets by you, Dawes."

Another few steps in silence. "Come on, Peterson, answer my question."

"I did. I'm doing police work."

"Spying on me?"

Ben started to deny it, then shook his head. "Okay, a

little. Simpson assigned me the task of coordinating our efforts with Greenville on the Dinker and Larkin cases. And, while I'm at it, make sure you didn't, as he put it, interfere."

"So you're the one who told him I'm 'meddling' in the case. Thanks a lot."

"Well, you were."

They reached the porch of the cabin and she shook free of him, sitting on the steps to rest her sore ankle. "I've got it from here."

Ben blew out another gust of air. "You sure? You can barely stand up. Here, let me help." He reached out his hand.

Val batted it away. "Why? So you can search the inside of my cabin and report back to Simpson? No thanks. Sammy, open the door."

"That's not fair, Dawes."

Sammy ran to the door and yanked on it. It didn't budge. "Locked," he said.

"Don't you remember the combination?" Val said.

Sammy shook his head.

"3-1-8-7," Peterson said.

Val stared at him, open-mouthed. "How did you know?"

"It's the combination to everything around here," he said. "It's also the birthday of Kayleigh Cox—March 1, 1987. Two weeks ago. Heh, you should send her a card."

Sammy opened the lockbox and pulled out the key. "It worked!"

"How many times have you used the combination to snoop around in here?" Val asked Peterson, alarmed.

"None that I can recall." Ben grinned, then his expression soured in response to Val's scowl. "Kidding. I wouldn't do that."

Yeah, right. Val made a mental note to ask Kayleigh to change the combination. The last thing she needed was for Ben Peterson to access her private space. "Okay, then.

We're good from here. Thanks again." She wobbled to her feet. Pain shot up her leg, and she collapsed back onto the steps, cursing.

"Let me help you." Peterson held out his hands.

She tried one more time to get up on her own and realized it wasn't going to happen. "Okay, fine. Just until I get inside." Val let him pull her up. She leaned on his shoulder and he slid a long arm around her, supporting her weight...and reached a little too far, his fingers pressing into the soft flesh of her breast. Val yanked his hand down and glared at him. "Watch your paws," she said with a snarl.

"Sorry, sorry," he said. "Accident."

Right.

Ben behaved himself for the rest of the way in, easing her down onto to sofa and helped prop her leg onto a pillow.

"Sammy, can you fill a plastic bag with some ice, please?" Val said, and the boy complied. "Now go change into dry clothes, and bring a robe or something for Mr. Peterson."

"I'll be fine." Ben pressed his fingers against her ankle.

Val yelped in pain. "What the hell?"

He frowned, almost a scowl. "I'm trying to see if it's broken or whatever."

"Not so damned hard!"

Ben removed Val's wet sock and tested her ankle, much gentler this time. Val winced and sucked in a quick breath. "Does *that* hurt?" he asked.

"Not as much as a moment ago," Val said. "I think I twisted it in the rapids."

He nodded and wrapped the ice pack around her ankle. "You should see a doctor. And get out of these wet clothes."

"I'll manage that on my own, thanks."

Ben laughed. "I wouldn't presume to undress you."

Val scoffed. "Bullshit. You spent twelve weeks at the Academy trying to undress me."

He reddened, stood, and held up his hands in surrender. "Okay, so I might have entertained thoughts of that sort in the past. After this weekend, though, forget it. My shins may never recover."

Val cocked her head. "So you admit that you came after me in that bar, not the other way around."

Ben backed away and stumbled over the coffee table. "On the advice of my attorney, I admit nothing."

"I'm hungry," Sammy said, emerging from the bedroom in dry clothes. "When are we having dinner?"

Val glanced at the clock. Almost 7:00 p.m. No way she'd be able to stand long enough to cook anything...

"Make yourself a sandwich," Val said.

"I don't know how," Sammy said, whining. "I want a hamburger."

Val sighed. What kid didn't know how to make a sandwich? "Ben, would you mind...?"

"Sure," Ben said. "And if it's okay, one for me? I haven't eaten either."

"Fine." Val got up and leaned on various pieces of furniture to support her weight on her path to the bedroom. She changed into a pair of sweatpants and a warm sweater and returned to the sofa.

Ben exited the bathroom a moment later, wearing Shelby's terrycloth robe, which draped almost to mid-thigh. He looked ridiculous, but didn't seem self-conscious about it. He hung all of their wet clothes near the heating vents to dry. Then he emptied the fridge of sandwich ingredients—meat, cheese, tomatoes, and mustard. "Ooh, Dijon. Fancy."

"Yellow mustard and mayonnaise for me!" Sammy said, perched on the floor with his game tablet.

"You got it, kid."

Val settled onto the sofa and lay her head back on a pillow. "Why are you being so nice, Peterson? It's not like you."

"What are you talking about? I'm always nice." He shot her a sideways grin, the oily, creepy one she knew so well.

She barked out a laugh, but stopped when his face registered genuine hurt. "Come on, Ben. This isn't how we normally interact."

"That's as much your fault as mine." Ben sliced some meat and cheese and spread condiments on several slices of bread laid out on the counter. He glanced at Val and added, "You need to trust me more."

"People who say 'trust me' are always the ones least worthy of it," Val said. Typical of him, though—always in denial, admitting no wrongdoing.

She sat up so she could watch him. Ben seemed right at home, slicing and piling up ingredients with efficiency. Standing there in Shelby's bathrobe, he appeared as comfortable in the kitchen as Gil did on Saturday mornings, preparing breakfast.

Ouch. She suppressed that thought.

"Since we're trusting each other now," Val said with a sly smile when he delivered their sandwiches, "tell me something you've learned from Greenville about Dinker and Larkin."

Ben chewed on his sandwich, staring at her. "Simpson would kill me," he said after swallowing.

"Welcome to the club," Val said. "Come on. We're on the same team, aren't we?" She paused and nibbled at her own sandwich. Not too bad, considering. "Or are we? Or are you here to spy on me after all?"

"Valorie." Ben set down his sandwich. "Come on. You're putting me in a tough spot here."

"No one's in a tougher spot than me, thanks to you. Or have you forgotten about our hearing in two days?"

He frowned, chewing another bite. "Promise you won't rat me out to Old Tackle Box?"

Val crossed her heart and pinkie-swore.

"Okay." Ben drew in a long breath. "It's the main reason

I'm here. A witness recalled seeing Jason Larkin hanging around one of Greenville's gay bars a night or two before he was killed. He left with a man meeting this description." Ben brought up a picture on his cell phone and passed it over to Val. "Nobody in town was willing or able to ID this guy, but you have fresh eyes. By any chance, do you recognize him?"

The picture, an artist's rendering, showed the slender face of a man of about forty with wide-spaced dark eyes, short hair, a three-day growth of beard...and tiny teeth.

A chill ran down her spine.

The eyes were wrong, but the teeth were a dead giveaway. The man in the photo was one of the Cox brothers.

And given that it was a gay bar, she had to guess it was Ambrose.

***

With a few bites left of her sandwich, Val's phone chimed, and Gil's number and picture displayed on her screen. Peterson's eyes met hers. He surrendered a tiny, mischievous smile and carried his empty plate into the kitchen.

"Darling," Val said into the phone. "I've missed you."

"You too," Gil said, his voice all gravel and almost a whisper. "How goes the search for Shelby?"

Val sighed. "No luck yet. Still looking, though I'm running out of ideas." She shifted her weight on the sofa and a sharp pain ran up her leg. She sucked in a tight, audible breath.

"What's wrong?" Gil's tone grew concerned, his volume a little louder. "Are you okay?"

"I...suffered a minor mishap today at the creek," she said. "My foot got twisted in the rapids and I, uh, swallowed a mouthful or two of water."

"Yikes. How'd you get back to the cabin? God, I'm so sorry I'm not there."

"I'm safe now." Val lowered her voice. "Of all people, Ben Peterson helped me."

"Peterson? What the hell is he doing in Greenville?"

Val cast a long look at Peterson, who chose that moment to run water in the sink, ostensibly to wash the dishes. She turned away from him. "Simpson sent him to, quote, coordinate work, unquote, on the Larkin and Dinker cases. And to spy on me." She glanced over at Ben, who clanked the dishes louder than necessary.

"What's going on there? It sounds like you're breaking some china or something." Gil chuckled, his voice growing hoarse again.

Val bit her lip, considering how to explain the situation without making Gil jealous. "Ben half-carried me back here, and I thanked him by letting him make us all dinner. Wasn't that nice of me?"

A long silence ensued. Then: "He's...still there?"

"He's leaving soon. Please don't be angry, Gil. Without him, I'd be toast."

Another long beat passed. "Okay." A snort of sorts. "You're telling me the guy who is trying to get you fired, who attacked you sexually four days ago in a bar and claimed you started it—"

"Saved my life. Yes, and it's weird to me, too. I bet he'd also admit to a high state of shock over the whole thing." Val faced Peterson again, who made a big show of nodding, his eyes wide.

"I see. Well, thank him for me." Gil's tone betrayed a strong sense of displeasure and frustration, then softened. "I wish I'd have been there for you."

"Me, too. When might that happen?" Val said. "How are you feeling?"

"A little better." Gil's voice faded into a throaty rasp. "The chills-and-fever cycle seems to be letting up."

Val signaled to Peterson to stop making so much noise in the kitchen so she could hear. He turned off the running water and dried a plate with a towel.

"That sounds bad," she said. "Are you taking anything?"

"For what?" He sounded bewildered.

"For the chills and fever. And your cough. You sound like you have a sore throat."

"Uh...yeah. How'd you know about my fever?"

Val stared at her phone for a moment. "You just told me. Don't you remember?"

"Huh. Yeah, I guess...Hey, I was wondering, too, how the search for a lawyer is going," Gil said. "And, uh, what approach they'll take in your defense." It sounded like he was reading from notes.

"Shit. In all the fuss over Shelby, I spaced out the whole attorney thing. I'll call my brother right after we hang up."

"When is your hearing?"

"Wednesday morning." Val fretted. Not much time to get ready.

"That's what, three days from now?" he said. "Four?"

"Thirty-six hours, more or less. Today's Monday." Was he losing track of days? Her concern over Gil's health rose to all-out worry.

"Is it? Crap, Val. Don't tell me you haven't even begun to prepare?"

"Don't scold me!" That came out sharper than intended. "I said I'll get on it. *Thank* you for the reminder." Again, too sarcastic.

Five seconds passed with neither of them talking. Ten. Then he uttered a simple, tense, "You're welcome."

Val let out a tension-relieving breath. She wanted to thank him for the articles on Simpson, but didn't dare with his lackey within earshot. Ben's frequent glances in her direction convinced her he was eavesdropping. Bad enough he knew she hadn't prepared yet.

"What about postponing?" Gil asked, his tone shifting into friendlier territory. "I'm not sure what the rules are, but I've heard of cases where a hearing gets pushed back if the accused needs more time."

"Hmm." Val considered that. "I'll ask about that."

After another few seconds of silence, Val changed the subject. "Any news on your end? How's the funeral planning going?"

"Not good," he said. "Jessica's got COVID, too. And no funeral home wants to have anything to do with services. Everything's shutting down."

"What will they do with her dad's body, then?" Val asked, horrified.

"No idea. I saw on TV, some hospitals are bringing in refrigerated trailers to store bodies. They don't know what else to do with them."

"That's horrible."

"Everything's horrible right now." The disgust in his voice was palpable, and Val guessed that at least some of that was directed at her.

Val glanced back at Ben, and her guilt, misplaced or not, intensified. "Well, I'd better call Chad, then."

"Yeah. Or go see him."

"In Danbury? That's two hours away. I need to find Shelby before I go, or at least get some sort of idea of what's happened to her."

Gil paused. "You don't suppose she might've had an accident like yours? But with no white knight like Paul Peterson there to save her?"

Val gritted her teeth over the "white knight" reference and opted to let it pass. "You mean Ben?"

"Ben. Not Paul. Right. Sorry."

"I never considered it, no. I guess I should."

Another uncomfortable silence. "I'm sorry," Gil said. "For not being there to help you. And for being such a jerk."

"I'm sorry, too," she said. "I miss you."

Val hung up with an aching heart and fresh fear over what might have happened to her missing friend.

***

Limping all the way, Val pushed Peterson out the door minutes later, angry at herself for not doing so sooner. He returned her car about an hour later. She sighed with relief when he left again, hopefully for good, to return to his own car, parked only a few minutes' walk away.

Val made sure Sammy was occupied with his gaming tablet, ears covered with noise-canceling headphones, then called her older brother.

"I've been meaning to call you," Chad said after a quick hello. "How's it going with Sammy?"

"Complicated." She described everything that happened since she last spoke with him on Friday night. "I've been so focused on finding Shelby, I prepared a defense for my suspension hearing on Wednesday...and, well, I need a lawyer."

"HR isn't my specialty, of course," he said, "unless it somehow involves contracts and intellectual property. However, I'm sure someone at our firm could help. I'll set something up for tomorrow. Any chance you can make it down here, or at least to Clayton? It'd go much smoother in person."

"I don't want to leave here until I find Shelby," Val said. "She's been gone a full day-plus, and I'm getting worried."

"I hate to say it, since I was the one that insisted you spend more time with Sammy," Chad said. "But it sounds like you'd make better progress if he wasn't tagging along. Can you take him back to Dad's? Then you can get that ankle checked, and—"

"All right, all right," she said. "You're right. Sammy will be disappointed, but...well, it sounds like his new friend is off limits for now, so maybe the timing is good all around."

"Great. I'll text you the time and place to meet. Call me when you get back into town."

Val hung up and glanced over at her little brother, happy as a clam with his game, humming along with whatever music played in the background. She hated to spoil his good mood. She decided to wait and tell him in the morning.

Chapter Twenty-Three

Loud, persistent knocking woke Val from an uneasy slumber early Tuesday morning. Way too early. As in, pre-dawn early.

"Miss Dawes?" A woman's voice. Angry, or perhaps afraid. "Please open up at once."

Val pushed herself off of the sofa, where she'd slept to minimize the distance to the bathroom if necessary during the night, and hobbled to the door. Copious doses of ibuprofen had reduced the pain to bearable, and icing it lowered the swelling to almost normal. She peeked out the window and confirmed the woman's voice belonged to Kayleigh Cox.

"What's wrong?" Val asked. Dressed only in shorts and a long-sleeve T-shirt, she hated to open the door to the cold...and to anyone named Cox, at this point.

"Miss Dawes, you need to leave," Kayleigh shouted through the door, her voice muffled. "Immediately."

"What—? Wait a sec." Val pulled her coat down from the peg where it hung by the door and tossed it over her shoulders, then unlocked the door and opened it a crack. Kayleigh stood outside in the gray mist of morning, huddled in a parka, a blue surgical mask covering her mouth and the tip of her nose. Her breath steamed through the thin mask and her cheeks shone red.

"Would you like to come in?" Val asked.

Kayleigh hesitated. "Well...okay. For a moment."

Val waved her inside and shut the door behind her. "Sorry I can't offer you any coffee or anything. I wasn't yet out of bed. Now, what's this about us having to leave?" She hobbled back to the sofa.

"I'm sorry, but you must," Kayleigh said, unzipping her coat. Underneath, she wore a wool cardigan that cost more than Val made in a week. She stayed close to the door, several feet away from Val. "For...safety reasons."

"Are we in danger?" Val imagined a series of horrible possibilities—murders, wild animals, storms—and couldn't resist placing Ambrose and Theo Cox in the middle of each of them.

"Your continued presence here is putting my son at risk, and I cannot have that. So you must go. Now."

"How am I endangering Connor?" Val said.

Sammy chose that moment to poke his sleepy head out of the bedroom, rubbing his eyes and yawning. "Hello, Mrs. Cox," he said. "Is Connor here to play?"

"The two of you won't be playing together anymore," Kayleigh said. "Please, Ms. Dawes. Don't ask questions. I'll refund your rental fees—all of it. Just go."

"I don't understand how I'm putting you or your son in danger by being here," Val said, now getting a little cross. "Please explain."

Kayleigh stared at her for a long moment, arms crossed on her chest. "Because of...COVID. You should all be wearing masks and quarantining. They've closed the schools, the stores, everything. Please. Go, now."

"Closed the schools?" Sammy said. "Lucky ducks!"

"Get dressed and pour yourself some cereal," Val said to him. Sammy scooted back into the bedroom.

Val turned back to Kayleigh, her suspicions about this visit growing. "If you're so afraid of us giving you COVID, why didn't you just call?"

Kayleigh sniffed. "Could I have convinced you to leave over the phone?"

She had a point. "Are you feeling ill? Or Connor, or...anyone else in your home?"

"My family's medical information is not relevant,"

Kayleigh said. "The authorities declared a public health emergency and they are closing down all, uh, hotel-like operations. That's all you need to know."

Val heaved a deep sigh. "If someone we've been in contact with is showing symptoms, it *is* relevant, and very much our business."

Kayleigh glowered at her, saying nothing.

Val shook her head. "Fine. We'll go as soon as we can. I'm a little gimpy, so it might take us a while to pack. I promise we'll be gone by lunchtime."

"Not lunchtime. Now." Kayleigh stepped back and pressed her body against the door, fumbling for the handle behind her. "If you're not gone in an hour, I'm calling the police."

Val hid a bemused smile with one hand. The police would more likely side with her than the Coxes. Whatever. She'd planned to spend at least part of the day back in Clayton to see a doctor, meet her lawyer, and drop Sammy off at Dad's. This just got her going a little earlier than expected. "Fine. However, I won't abandon my search until I find out what happened to Shelby. That means you *will* see me again, Mrs. Cox."

"You'll need a warrant to step foot again on my property," Kayleigh said. "And no matter what you do—stay away from my son. And my husband." She spun around and opened the door.

"If Theo has information about Shelby—"

"He doesn't."

"You're certain this is true? How?"

Kayleigh closed the door partway and sniffed. "Theo wouldn't associate with a woman like that."

"Not his type?" Val instantly regretted the snotty tone.

Kayleigh sneered at her. "I won't defend my husband regarding his infidelity. After what you witnessed yesterday, there's no point. Still, I know one thing about Theo. He prefers real women, not...whatever you call

Shelby Clearwater. Don't get me wrong," she added in a rush, holding up one hand. "I don't judge what Shelby does with her life or her body. However, I know what type of woman catches my husband's wandering eye, and Shelby isn't it."

"How can you be sure?" Val asked. "Please understand. I don't mean to punish you. I'm trying to figure out what's happened to my friend."

Kayleigh studied her fingernails, picking at her flaking polish. "A woman knows what her husband wants. Even when she can't give it to him." Her voice cracked, and she sniffled, wiping away tears. For a moment, Val felt sorry for her.

Kayleigh glanced back at Val. "For a short while, I convinced myself that I pleased him. Now I know better. Sure, I gave him a few things he needed—a son, a proper marriage in society to a well-established family, and a cover story for his dalliances. But in the bedroom...well, Miss Dawes. You've met Cedar Embley. Imagine a long line of Cedar Embleys, each one prettier than the next. Beautiful and boring. She's lasted more than most, but now a new pretty young thing has caught his eye." She glared at Val.

Val gulped. "You mean me? No. I'm nothing like—"

"I know Theo better than you do," Kayleigh said. "Trust me. If you don't leave soon—right now, in fact—you will become the object of his next conquest."

"Any attempt of that sort will prove unsuccessful," Val said.

"Don't be so sure," Kayleigh said. "If you think a simple 'no' will deter him, you haven't met Theo Cox." She paused, her half-smile fading. "So, perhaps you are in danger, Miss Dawes."

"I can take care of myself."

Kayleigh threw her arms wide in frustration, her voice low and tense. "And then what happens? If he tries to seduce you and fails?" She took a step forward, her eyes wild and teary. "He...takes it out on me, Miss Dawes. And I've had enough of it."

Sammy's head popped into Val's peripheral vision, sitting at the kitchen counter with a bowl of cereal. She wondered how much he'd overheard, and how much explaining she'd need to do on the drive to Clayton.

"Message received," Val said. "Thank you, Mrs. Cox."

Kayleigh nodded, pulled open the door, and left.

"Sammy," Val said, "eat fast. Then pack your things. Time to leave."

"Okay." Sammy scooped cereal into his mouth. He chewed and swallowed, then set down his spoon. "Val," he said, his voice sad, "thank you for bringing me on this way cool vacation. Even if it was really short."

"You're welcome, Sammy. We'll do it again sometime, okay?"

Val wished she shared his warm feelings for their stay in Greenville. But she didn't. Not with Shelby still missing and the dire warning Kayleigh had just delivered.

***

Connor hated being grounded, and hated being confined to his room even more. At least if he could go outside, he could explore a bit. Look at birds or other animals through his binoculars, or find cool rocks.

He especially hated being grounded for not doing anything wrong. Mom had just told him to go to his room and stay there until she said he could come out.

Most of all, he hated that Mom grounded him instead of Dad. Mom never grounded him. Lots of times, in fact, she'd sneak in after Dad punished him and brought him snacks and told him it was okay, that he was a good boy anyway.

Not today.

"You're not going outside today," Mom had said. "Not after yesterday." That was all she said, other than, "Stay in your room and think about what you did."

What did he do? Played with his new friend. He even said "Sorry" to Sammy, even though Sammy's the one who hit him with a rock. Went exploring—

Oh, that's it. Sneaking into Dad's gun-storage place.

So what? They didn't *touch* anything. Just looked. Looking didn't count as doing something bad.

Connor heard a noise in the house. He hoped it was Mom bringing him breakfast. Pancakes or French toast with lots of syrup. Yum!

It didn't sound like anyone cooking in the kitchen, though. Instead, it sounded like someone dragging something heavy across the floor downstairs, then opening the door and slamming it shut.

He jumped off of his bed and gazed out the window. Down below, Miss Embley shuffled away from the house with a suitcase-type thing rolling on the ground behind her. She walked to her car, put the bag in, and gazed back at the house. Her face looked sad. She kind of waved, then got in the car and drove to the front gate. It opened, and she drove away.

Connor's heart sank. He knew what that meant. Like for Miss Thompson a year before, and Miss McEwan a few months before that, Miss Embley was leaving for good—like the others, without saying goodbye.

A moment later, the garage door opened, and his mom's car backed out onto the driveway. She, too, drove through the front gate, turning left instead of right.

He remembered his dad saying he needed to go to a meeting that morning. So that meant there were no grown-ups at home.

Nobody would know if he stayed in his room or not.

Connor tiptoed across the room and eased open the bedroom door, listening. No sound anywhere in the house. He was free.

Still, he needed to be careful. He took his time, creeping along the hallway, his stocking feet sliding across the hardwood floor. He listened again. Still no sound, even all the way down the stairs.

He stopped outside Miss Embley's office—well, not hers anymore, so what else should he call it?—and peeked inside. Her screens were dark, but the light on the computer box glowed green, so it was still on. His heart pounding, he slid over to the keyboard and struck the "Enter" key.

The screens all lit up, each showing an old photo of Connor with his mom and dad, from Connor's sixth birthday. In the center of the main screen, a little box asked for a password.

Would it be the same one his dad used on his laptop? He tried it: "C0nn0r2011." His name with zeroes instead of O's and his birth year.

The password box disappeared, and the screens came to life, showing pictures of The Grounds. The horse stables, his uncle's cottage, the greenhouse, the gun shed, and more. Each of the three screens showed four different parts of the property. Some of them changed when something moved—a bird or squirrel or the horses or Mr. Dupree. All very peaceful.

Except one. One screen showed something terrible. Something he didn't want to believe was real.

It had to be real, though. It was right there on the computer.

His uncle's words from the day before, when they'd been spying on Val and Sammy, came back to him. "If you see something bad, tell someone." Or something like that.

Connor was seeing something bad. Who should he tell? Both of his parents were gone, as was Miss Embley. His dad said to never trust Uncle Ambrose, and Uncle Am said never trust Ms. Dawes, and his parents said he can't ever see Sammy again. So who did that leave? Mr. Dupree, but the old man scared him to death.

Maybe he didn't have to "tell" anyone—in words. Maybe

he needed to show the world and God what he knew, in his own special way, and then hope the right person saw it and did something.

But how?

Connor thought and thought. And an idea came to him. As an explorer and scientist, he could use his discoveries to tell what he saw. If the right person came along—someone who also understood the language of science and discovery—they'd understand, and do something.

To do that, he'd have to go outside.

Chapter Twenty-Four

Val arrived in Clayton around 10:00 a.m. Tuesday morning amidst a steady, frigid drizzle that doused the sky in a sleepy grayness. She stopped once for coffee, unable to shake the weariness and worry that weighed her down and made her eyelids droop. Traffic seemed light for a Monday, and she wondered if the pandemic was responsible. Which reminded her of Gil, and that only redoubled her worry and sense of powerlessness.

Meanwhile, Sammy appeared oblivious to it all. He spent the first half-hour playing on his tablet in the back seat, then dozed the rest of the trip. He woke up when Val pulled into her father's driveway, parking behind his Ford SUV. The aging car, the shabby appearance of the house, and it proximity to the neighbors on each side made her dad's home look like one of the Cox's gardening sheds by comparison.

Nevertheless, so much more welcoming.

"Okay, let's get you inside," Val said to Sammy. "Grandpa made big plans for the two of you today."

"Really?" Sammy rubbed the sand out of his eyes. "The dinosaur park?"

"I can't tell you," Val said. "It's a surprise." To her as well—she had no idea what Dad had planned for them, and he probably didn't either.

Dad met them at the door in high spirits and, to her relief, agreed without protest to make the hour-plus drive to Rocky Hill's theme park. Sammy hugged Val goodbye and murmured into her ear, "Would you give this to Connor? It's a present." He pulled a shiny stone out of his pocket, flat and smooth and spotted with brilliant splashes of red, green, and white.

"It's my best rock," Sammy said. "It's big like a potato, except flat like a skipper. And long like a see-gar!" He held it up for Val's father to see.

"That is a very cool rock," Dad said. "Are you sure you want to part with it?"

Sammy nodded. "Connor's my friend," he said. "I want him to remember me."

To Val's surprise, her throat tightened over this. Sammy could be sweet when he wanted to. She wished she'd paid closer attention to him over the weekend—gotten to know him better, instead of having to treat their time together as an obstacle to finding Shelby.

She hurried her goodbyes and got right back on the road, worried that she might already be late for her appointment with the lawyer her brother, hopefully, found for her. They'd arranged to meet at his firm's Clayton satellite office across from the courthouse, close to police headquarters. Chad met her in the lobby of the four-story brick building, a grim expression on his face.

"Am I late?" Val said. "Didn't we say eleven?" Her phone said 10:52 a.m.

"You're not late," he said. "How's Gil doing? Hey, let me buy you a cup of coffee." Chad waved her over to a pop-up kiosk in the lobby.

"Aren't we meeting in your office?" Chad's joviality, rare for him, seemed forced. Suspicious, Val followed him to the kiosk. "Don't they have coffee up there?"

He ignored her, greeting the barista by name and ordering their drinks, remembering her preferences for a change.

"Chad? What's up here?"

Chad held up one finger, mouthing "Wait," and spoke in a low voice into his phone until their drinks came. He carried them to a small metal table near the wall, out of earshot of anyone else. He took a sip and fixed her with a sad gaze.

"I don't know how to sugar-coat this," Chad said, "so I'll give it to you straight. The partners in my firm declined to take your case. They said it's 'too far outside of our realm of expertise.' Which translates to 'too hot to handle' in lawyer-talk."

A heavy weight settled in Val's stomach, and she no longer had any desire to drink her otherwise-delicious cinnamon mocha cappuccino. "So, you're saying I don't have a lawyer for my hearing tomorrow?"

"Not yet," he said. "I'm still working on it. If necessary, I'll represent you myself."

"I love and appreciate your commitment to helping me, but you're a contracts attorney," she said. "Have you ever once stepped foot in a police disciplinary hearing? Shouldn't I retain someone who knows about Human Resources or police work?"

"I'm talking worst-case scenario. I won't let you walk in there unrepresented. But I've only had since last night."

"And I only have today to prepare," Val said, her voice growing heated. She inhaled a calming breath. "Sorry. I know you're trying to help. Do you have time to do this, with your existing caseload?"

Chad cast her a half-smile, sadness in his eyes. "I do now."

A long moment passed. "How—"

"When they told me of their decision, I told them they'd have to find another intellectual property attorney."

Val's jaw dropped. "You quit? Seriously? Is your wife okay with this?"

Chad's half-smile disappeared. "Kendra won't be pleased. Val, I can't stay with a firm that won't help my family. And—no, hear me out. Kendra and I have been talking about moving back to Clayton for some time now. This just accelerates the process."

Val sat back, stunned. "Last year they promised to

make you a junior partner. Are you sure you can walk away from that?"

"They weren't acting on that promise. So, I was going to, anyway. I've been in touch with some Clayton-area firms about prospects. In fact, those are the firms I've reached out to this morning. If you're up for it, our first appointment is in a half-hour. Stephanie Morgan at Lawson, Steiner, and Meyer. I went to law school with her."

Val took a sip of her coffee, now finding its sweetness cloying. They'd overdone the chocolate, gone too light on the cinnamon. Or something. Or maybe the unpleasant taste in her mouth came from having to swallow Chad's bad news. "I was hoping to get back to Greenville tonight. Shelby's still missing, and—"

"Aren't you staying the night? Your hearing is at 10:00 a.m. tomorrow."

"Yeah...about that." Val took another sip of coffee, then pushed it away. She recalled Gil's suggestion and pursued it. "Once we've secured counsel, is it possible to push the hearing back a day or two?"

Chad shrugged. "This is where having an expert would help. I don't even know who to talk to about that."

"Let me make a few calls," Val said.

He nodded. "Fire away. I'll wait."

Val pondered a moment over who could best help her inside the department. Grimes, her partner, was still on leave to deal with his son's illness. Petroni, as her boss, was management—technically neutral, but she always bent over backward to stay out of situations like these. Gil, a virtual Boy Scout, had never been the subject of an internal affairs investigation, and after last night's tense conversation, she didn't trust where that would lead.

That left one person—a former partner and mentor.

"Val, I'm so glad you called," Shannon O'Reilly said moments later. "Any word on Shelby?"

"No," Val said. "What I'm—"

"Crap," Shannon said. "Well, things are getting worse. Someone ransacked her apartment last night. Major B&E," she said, cop-talk for breaking and entering. "Simpson suspects Sanjit, and he's been grilling him off and on since late last night, but he's not talking without a lawyer present."

"Sanjit has a key to her apartment," Val said. "He wouldn't need to break in. And why would he toss the place? He practically lives there. He knows where everything is."

"Might it be her brother, then?" Shannon asked. "I ran his rap sheet. He's got a few A&Bs." Assaults and batteries. "And a drug charge. Maybe he's looking for money."

"Or he's looking for Shelby," Val said. "Austin called me yesterday from Greenville. He's definitely in the area. What did the scene suggest? A search, a robbery, what?"

"A search, and a thorough one," Shannon said. "Every drawer, cupboard, and tissue box emptied onto the floor. Somebody was looking for something specific. God knows what."

"Damn, that sounds like a pro job." Like, for instance, a private eye...or a cop.

Chad glared at her from across the table, tapped his watch, his meaning clear: *Hurry!*

"Listen, Shannon, sorry to change the subject, but I need to ask you something," Val said. "My suspension hearing is tomorrow, and I still haven't retained a lawyer–"

"Jesus, Val, what are you waiting for? Isn't your brother helping you?"

"He is," Val said, avoiding Chad's glare. "We're not quite there yet. Is there any way to get those things delayed? My attorney's going to need time to prepare, and—"

"No idea," Shannon said. "This late in the game, I'd guess no. However, I've got a friend in legal. I'll nose around a bit and get back to you after lunch. Sound good?"

"Thanks." Val hung up and faced her agitated brother,

his empty coffee cup crunched into a ball in his fist. "She said, uh, maybe."

"Let's hope Stephanie knows more." He stood. "Let's go. It wouldn't hurt to be early."

Val followed him out the door, her mind reeling from the one-two punch of news that morning. Her suspension situation careening toward disaster, and Shelby seemed in greater danger than ever. Who would toss her apartment while she was still missing?

She couldn't help but suspect Tackle Box Simpson. Probably, she admitted to herself, because she just didn't trust him.

***

The meeting with Chad's law school friend went as well as Val could have expected. Stephanie Morgan, a thirtyish, short-haired, no-nonsense brunette in oversized, thick-framed glasses, agreed to take her case and had some relevant experience in law enforcement Human Resources disputes. "I've represented both sides," she said, "though not in Clayton. Still, I've played this game."

"What are my chances, do you think?" Val fiddled with her mask, uncomfortable with how it restricted her breathing and chafed her skin. Stephanie, Chad, and everyone else at the firm seemed much more comfortable wearing them, so she didn't complain.

Stephanie pondered that for a moment. "Hard to say until I review discovery and their witness list. First things first. How soon can you get me a copy of the complaint?"

Val held up an open palm, her mind reeling. "Whoa, slow down. I understood less than half of what you just said. Can you translate into plain English?"

Stephanie smiled, chuckling a little. "Sorry. I figured, as a cop with a lawyer in the family, this would all be old hat to you."

"She means," Chad said, "we need to see what they've got first, starting with the charges. Can you send a copy of everything?"

"Of course."

"Perfect," Stephanie said. "Then we need to interview any witnesses who can help rebut the charges."

"I'll draw up a list of names right now." Val grabbed a pen and pad of paper.

"Excellent," Stephanie said. "In the meantime, I'll work on pushing back the hearing. It means you'll remain on unpaid leave for a while longer, though."

Val nodded. "That's a tradeoff I'll make any day. Thanks." A few minutes later, sequestered in a tiny conference room at the firm, she tore off her mask and listed all of her colleagues who'd attended the celebration at the Blue Line Tavern. Once completed, she realized what her list lacked: her strongest supporter and champion. That required making an overdue phone call she dreaded, given how rocky things had gone lately.

Still.

She speed dialed her favorite number. Gil picked up on the second ring.

"Darling," he croaked out, his voice as shabby as the night before. "Any good news?"

"I've hired a lawyer," she said. "Friend of Chad's. I'm at her Clayton office now, putting together some info for her. People who can testify on my behalf about what happened...and I wondered if there's a way you could...?"

He sighed. "I'm still under quarantine. Maybe I can submit something in writing? Or get deposed on some sort of online recording? A lot of people are trying that—a program called Zoom, I think."

"I'll ask. Thank you." Val paused. "Although I'd much rather see you in person."

"Me, too. How can I help? What can I say that would assist your case?" His voice faded to a whisper, and he covered the phone to muffle the sound of a nasty coughing fit.

"Anything about why I'd never sexually attack Ben Peterson," she said. "About me, or about him. I'll ask Stephanie to email you her questions."

"Who's Stephanie?"

"The lawyer. She's young, but seems smart and organized. And she's done this before."

"Good. Now, when you say 'anything,' does that include the, um, Milt incident?"

Val let the silence hang while she pondered the question. "You can tell them about my rape. Although I should tell Stephanie about it first."

"Are you sure?" Gil's voice softened more. "I mean, they might twist that around to say you're getting revenge or something. Or—and don't get mad at me for imagining this, please—they could claim you have a 'victim mentality' or some such."

Val's insides lurched, nausea boiling in her gut. She couldn't imagine someone trying a horrible tactic like that. "If they do, I'll—"

"Sit quietly, I hope," Gil said. "Any angry reaction would only validate that sort of bullshit claim. And Val...you need to be ready for it."

She took in a few deep breaths, let them out slowly, calming herself. "You're right. Thanks."

"Anyone at the Academy you can call?" Gil said.

"I'm thinking Jalen Marshall."

"Nobody better," Gil said. "As Ben's training officer in Hartford, he'll give you the straight dope on what he was like there. Although if I recall correctly, Peterson got bounced for ineptitude, not harassment."

"So you're saying I'm the only one he goes after? I can't believe that."

"I'm *not* saying that—only that there may not be a record of it in Hartford. Jalen would know, if anyone does."

Stephanie Morgan looked in through the glass wall, a questioning look on her face.

"I need to wrap this up," Val said. "Gil, thank you. I'm sorry you're still sick. I hope you can get over this and I can see you soon."

"Me, too," he said. "But I don't want to get your hopes up. Apparently I'm pretty contagious."

"How would you know? You've been quarantined the whole time, haven't you?"

Gil didn't answer.

"Gil? Who've you been in contact with since you came down with this?"

A loud rush of air filled her earpiece. "The doctor suspects I caught the virus in Clayton before I came. So, maybe you—though you don't seem to show any symptoms."

"Right. So, not me. Who else?"

Another pause. Then, in a low voice, "Possibly Jessica, when I first got here. I maybe even gave it to her dad, or she did after I gave it to her."

Val caught her breath. Ouch. "And...he died of COVID?"

"More or less."

"That sucks. From one short exposure...this disease is horrible, isn't it?"

Another long pause. "Well...not exactly. I mean, I haven't seen her in a few days, but it was more than one quick hello, I guess. Full disclosure here—before I tested positive and the hospital shut down all visitation, I sat with her for a bit, and we ate dinner together one night. That's all, though. Nothing, um, romantic."

Val's heart fell to her toes and her head grew dizzy. "Gil, you gave me the distinct impression that you'd barely seen Jessica on this trip. Now I learn you two have been hanging out—"

"We haven't been 'hanging out.' Not like you and Ben Peterson."

Val's anger flashed. "That's not fair. Ben saved me from

drowning and got me back to my cabin—"

"And stayed long enough to overhear your end of our private conversation."

Val, at a loss for words, sputtered for a moment. "Do you seriously think that Ben and I—"

"No, I do *not*. I just…" Gil's voice trailed off, then his tone softened. "I hope I can expect the same level of trust from you, Val. That's all."

Val started to object, then cut herself off. He had a point. Kind of. But she was still too upset to cut him any slack.

"I'd better call Jalen," she said after a long pause.

"I'll get going, prepare my testimony," he said in a soft voice.

That caught her off guard, and it took her several seconds to respond. "Still? After all this?"

Gil sighed. "Val, I know this feels bad right now. We're being tested, and it sucks. I've been through stuff like this before. In the grand scheme of things, this is a blip. It'll blow over and we'll be right back where we were a week ago. You'll see."

"Uh, huh." Val didn't know what to think. She *hadn't* been through this before, because Gil was her first serious relationship. And it *did* feel bad. Ominous, even.

"Val." He paused. "I love you."

She choked up. She should've have expected that, but she didn't. "I…I love you too, Gil."

They said goodbyes and, after hanging up, Val brought up Jalen's number and paused before calling him. The entire conversation with Gil confused her. She hoped he was right and that her confusion was a product of her rough couple of days while being away from him.

What if it wasn't, though? What if this ongoing tension between them signaled something far more serious in their relationship?

She didn't want to face that.

Chapter Twenty-Five

Val's call to Jalen Marshall went straight to voicemail. She left a brief message, saying only that she wanted to follow up with him about Ben Peterson, but didn't have high hopes of hearing from him. Jalen maintained a distant relationship at best with voicemail. Gil once quoted him saying it was "the devil's spawn," a sentiment she understood but didn't share.

To her surprise, he texted right back to her:

Let's talk. Claytown Cafe, 30 mins?

She replied:

Sure! What are you doing in Clayton?

He didn't respond. Probably driving. She looked around for her brother and her attorney, found neither, and sent them each a quick message that she needed to step out. Then she jumped in her car and drove to the Liberty Heights area, not far from Gil's house, and parked outside the café.

The Claytown Café, a small neighborhood coffee shop and lunch counter, was one of her favorite spots for meeting friends in her first year on the force. She and Beth once shared an apartment a few blocks away, and she'd loved stopping in for a quick breakfast-to-go on her walk to work at the Liberty Heights precinct. All that changed when she transferred to the WAVE Squad and moved in with Gil. She hadn't been back in months.

From the looks of things, neither had anyone else. The place was almost empty.

"Val-pal!"

The greeting came from a tall, slender woman in her early twenties with shaggy pink hair streaked with black, standing behind the service counter. She wore a sleeveless pink shirt that revealed delicate arms, which served as a tattoo artist's canvas. A parade of piercings across her eyebrows seemed to button her face together. She flung her arms wide and, even behind her mask, Val could see the grin poking through. "It's been furrr-evrrr, girlie-girl!"

Val returned the grin, her sour mood disappearing in light of Pinkie's unbridled positivity. She donned a mask and pushed her way through the café's array of tiny tables, packed close together with too many chairs at each one. Once she reached the bar, she claimed a vacant stool and smiled at her barista friend. "Great to see you, Pinkie," she said. "Life treating you well?"

Pinkie gestured with her arms at the empty café. "COVID sucks, but otherwise, yeah," she said. "I think your friend is in the restroom."

Val noticed a black, leather-sleeved jacket draping the back of a chair in the rear of the room, its Hartford Police Department insignia visible on the left breast. "Thanks. Got any specials today?"

"Tons-o-rama, girlfriend. Tell me what you want and I'll whip up something awesome for you."

A tall, mid-thirties African American man with a receding hairline and a bald crown emerged from the restroom. He gestured to Val to join him at the table with the police jacket. Jalen appeared to have lost 20 pounds from his hefty frame over the last year. His wide smile showed no loss of affection for her, and he proved it by crushing her hand in a tight handshake when she approached the table. Like Val, Jalen didn't do hugs—at least with women other than his very jealous wife.

"Dawes, you good-looking animal, how could you have fallen for that old dog, Gil Kryzinski?" Jalen said, pulling on a mask and taking his seat. "How's my boy doing, anyway?"

"Uh...he's fine," Val said, sitting across from him. "Except for catching the coronavirus, that is."

"Oh, that sucks. Hope it's not serious?" Jalen's expression turned grim.

Val shrugged. "He's still breathing. That's more than a lot of people can say."

"Well said. Hey, Pinkie? Coffee, please, black. Val? What's your poison?"

"Cinnamon mochaccino and an Americano, coming right up," Pinkie answered before Val could. The espresso machine whirred to life moments later.

"So, you've got questions about Ben Peterson," Jalen said. "I can't believe that Simpson idiot hired him after the kid flamed out in Hartford. I wouldn't put him on night watch at a strip mall. Or a strip club, for that matter."

Val lowered her voice and leaned closer. "That's what I wanted to talk to you about. Simpson and Peterson conspired to get me suspended over a bullshit assault and sexual harassment charge, and—"

"Wait. They accused *you* of harassing *him*?" Even behind his mask, it was clear that Jalen's jaw dropped.

Val nodded. "Unfortunately, nobody witnessed him groping me and slathering his grotesque mouth all over my face—only me kicking the crap out of him in response. And the only person who 'saw' that was Old Tackle Box. So, I'm curious. Did Ben ever get in trouble over stuff like this in Hartford? Or was it pure incompetence that got him booted out the door?"

Jalen's eyes grew large, and he sat back, making room for Pinkie to deliver their coffees. "Any nosh for you two heroes in blue?" she asked.

"Burger, fries, and keep the coffee coming," Jalen said. "Val?"

"Chicken Caesar salad, light on the dressing. Thanks,

Pinkie."

"Any time-zees." Pinkie strolled away, gazing out the glass front of the café, as if trying to lure in new customers with her friendly face.

Jalen tapped his finger on the table, pulled off his mask, and sipped his coffee. "Dawes, as much as I'd like to help you out on this, I...I can't."

Val cocked her head, catching something guarded in his tone. "Can't? What does that mean?"

"It means..." Jalen blew air out between his lips. "After Peterson's six-month probationary period ended, I recommended letting him go. I was his training officer, you might recall."

Val nodded. "I take it the Hartford PD disagreed?"

Jalen shrugged. "The kid couldn't tie his own shoelaces without a YouTube video. He complained I was 'biased' against him and somehow squeezed the department to give him another six months with a different TO. Five and a half months later, he 'resigned' his commission under a sealed agreement with HR. Meaning, none of the circumstances around his dismissal can be made public."

"Jeez. That doesn't sound suspicious at all." Val removed her mask and tried the coffee. Delicious. Much better than the crap at the kiosk.

"Which is why *I* can't help you." His eyes narrowed. "In any *official* capacity."

"I see." Val sipped again. "What about unofficially?"

He glanced around and leaned in. "What I might suggest, as a friend, is contacting a certain reporter who makes their living by exposing shady police practices." He jotted something onto his napkin, folded it, and slid it toward her.

"Wait. You aren't suggesting the Copwatch guy? Paul Peterson, Ben's own freaking cousin?"

"What? No, *hell* no." Jalen's expression turned to disgust. "This young lady's been investigating favoritism in police hiring practices in the Hartford area. Your situation might convince her to consider Clayton part of that area. And she might be willing to share what she knows about Ben's…extracurricular activities."

Val started. "He has a record? For what?"

"I didn't say that." His eyes crinkled into a smile. "Let's just say, sealed records sometimes find a way of getting unsealed…particularly when the woman at the other end of things doesn't like how things got resolved."

"A woman?" Val's heart rate picked up. "As in, a harassment victim?"

"Officially, I can't say," Jalen said. "Off the record…well, ask Pinkie here how many unwelcome hands grab *her* cute little derriere here in the café and how many guys won't take 'no' for an answer. Then you'll get an idea of what the settlement entailed."

"I don't need to ask Pinkie," Val said. "I'm on the receiving end of that bullshit myself." She opened the napkin, glanced at the name and number—neither of which she recognized—and slipped it into her purse. "Thanks, Jalen."

"For my man Gil's girl—any time." He toasted her with his coffee. "Speaking of which, did he share any news about Hank Swan?"

Val blinked. "You know Jessica's father?"

Jalen chuckled. "Every cop in Connecticut over the age of thirty knows Hank Swan. And every kid who ever passed through the juvie system."

Val stared at him, mouth open. "You were a juvenile–"

"Delinquent, like your boyfriend. At the same time, in fact."

Val choked on her coffee, coughing for a full thirty seconds before regaining control. "What did you say?"

Jalen's brows furrowed again, and a puzzled expression lined his face. "Are you trying to convince me that Gil never told you this?"

"No!"

Jalen sat back in his chair, twirling his empty cup on the table. "Wow. You two've got some talking to do."

"I'll say. For now, please—give me the nickel tour."

"Well...if he didn't want you to know—"

"Then he's in deeper trouble with me than either of you can imagine. Come on, Jalen. Spill."

Jalen sighed and thought for a moment. "Okay, I'll tell you my side of this story," he said. "When I was fifteen, I got nicked for stealing a car. Grand theft auto. It was more of a prank than an actual theft. By that I mean, I never intended on keeping the damned thing, I just wanted to take it for a joyride. The juvenile court judge taught me a lesson and sent me to what Gil and I lovingly call 'JD camp.' Basically a country vacation where they work you hard and fill your brain with wholesome American values like not stealing and staying off drugs and shit."

"Gil was there too?"

Jalen nodded. "That's where we met."

"Gil said you met at police academy."

Jalen laughed. "That's where he met Jalen 2.0. At camp, volunteers took us under their wing and mentored us. Taught us useful crap like how to build shit, knife sharpening, starting a campfire—sort of an intensive Boy Scout camp for troubled teens."

"Why was Gil there?"

His answer needed to wait, as Pinkie arrived with their food, refilled Jalen's coffee, and promised Val a second cinnamon mochaccino.

"He should tell you that—"

"He will. So will you."

Jalen laughed again. "You're worse than my wife." He took a deep breath. "Okay." Another pregnant pause. "Gil...beat the shit out of a kid who tried to get his high school girlfriend hooked on fentanyl at a party. He refused to testify about that last part, because he wanted to protect her reputation. So the judge sent him to camp, too."

"How does this all relate to Hank Swan?" Val asked, her mind whirling.

"Hank was our volunteer mentor—and a lieutenant in the New Haven Police Department. His recommendation got me into the academy, and I imagine he did the same for Gil, too. I owe that man my life, and I think Gil feels the same way."

Val leaned back in her seat, the weight of Jalen's revelations washing over her. "He never told me any of that. Only that Hank was like a father to him."

"To me, too."

"So Gil met Jessica through Hank? Not the other way around?"

Jalen nodded. "Jessica also volunteered at the camp. They hit it off right away." He took a bite of his burger. "Hey, sorry to change the subject, but Hank wasn't doing well last time I heard. Any word on his condition?"

Val's face fell, her heart heavy. "Sorry to say...Hank didn't make it. He died this weekend."

Jalen's eyes watered and he looked away, hiding his mouth with his hand. "Well, that sucks," he said, his voice hoarse. "When's the funeral?"

Val shrugged. "Not sure now. COVID has kind of messed that up."

"Jesus. Why didn't Gil tell me? I'll strangle that SOB when I see him."

"Get in line." Val took her first bite of salad. The chicken had gone cold—her fault for letting it sit there.

"Dawes," Jalen said, "if you tell Gil that I told you this, I'll deny every word. You've got to talk to him."

"Sure. I'll casually ask, 'Hey, remember that time you went to JD camp?' That will break the ice on our next date night."

"I don't care how you do it. Just don't rat me out." He stuffed a handful of fries in his mouth. "Same goes for the

Peterson shit. Got that?"

Val nodded, nibbling on her salad. It tasted bland all of a sudden.

For a moment she panicked: the press had reported that losing one's sense of taste was a symptom of COVID. She took another bite and confirmed, though, that it wasn't the salad's fault, or COVID's. The entire world felt gray and confusing.

On the one hand, she understood Gil's motivation to go to New Haven better. It wasn't to be there for Jessica—it was to be there for Hank, his mentor. That gave her a bit of emotional relief.

On the other hand, he'd kept this bombshell of a secret from her for almost two years, a full year of which they'd been together as a couple. Why?

It rocked her to the core. She didn't know what to do about it. Or what to do about Shelby. Or her situation at work, with the suspension hearing looming, and her being so unprepared. She didn't know who she could lean on, who to trust. And it felt like she was running out of options—and time.

***

The Redeemer woke up in a strange bed, and in a strange body, not his own. Pain and fatigue made it hard to move. Every muscle ached and he must have gained 100 pounds overnight. He sucked in a breath, and got almost no air, as if someone had packed his throat and lungs with cotton.

A blue light blinked, reflecting off the white walls, the only light in the room. It took him a moment to realize what it was: the digital clock on the nightstand. He'd lost power in his safe space, long enough for the clock to lose its settings. He raised himself up onto one elbow and nearly vomited, the hot bile reminding him of the tasteless dinner he'd forced down the night before.

Dammit! He hadn't been sick in over a decade. Living

apart from humanity protected him for so long. However, lately, he'd made contact with people from the outside world. Shelby, for instance. Dinker. That Larkin weirdo. And the others.

He glanced at the blinking clock. Its digits read 11:45. The faint grind of a motor hummed behind the thick concrete walls. That meant he'd been on generator power for almost twelve hours.

Christ. How long had he slept?

He checked his phone, plugged in on the nightstand. 1:25 p.m. He'd collapsed into bed well before 9:00 the night before. Yow. Over fifteen hours! He'd never slept that long in his life. Even as a baby, if he could believe his mother's stories.

It took a few minutes to wrestle his body from the bed, sleepwalk to the tiny bathroom, and relieve himself. He couldn't stand to look at his gray pallor in the mirror, the bloodshot eyes rimmed with black circles. He tried to brush his teeth, but the chalky, flavorless toothpaste made him gag.

He trudged to the bedroom door, gazed out into the dimly lit main room. Shelby lay unconscious on the cold concrete floor, blood still seeping from its genital wounds, red-stained gauze on the floor, soaked to saturation. So, he*'d* completed the penectomy and orchiectomy. Even half-ass sewed the kid back up. Which is more than he'd done for the other two pervs.

Then again, they'd caved and confessed to their obscenity right away. Shelby still refused.

He'd give Shelby one more chance at redemption. One last time to save its wretched soul.

And then, redeemed or not, penitent or proud, the creature must die.

A tiny blue light in the corner of the room by the ceiling caught his eye. He blinked it into focus. The security camera. Crap! It must've turned itself back on when the power clicked over to the generator. Which meant all of this was being recorded. Anyone with access could view it.

He sat at the laptop and logged in to the system. Fortunately, few people had access, and only people he trusted.

And in a few moments, there would be nothing to see.

PART THREE

UNLIKELY HERO

Chapter Twenty-Six

Val drove back to Stephanie Morgan's law office and parked in a paid city lot a block from Clayton PD headquarters. While limping past her place of employment, her ankle throbbing from her fall the day before, a familiar voice called out to her.

"Dawes! I was hoping I'd see you today." Her boss, Sergeant Brenda Petroni, waved and padded down the concrete stairway leading up to the police station's double glass doors. With a light rain falling, Petroni took her time on the slippery steps.

"Hey, Sarge," Val said. "No time to talk right now. I've got a meeting—"

"I don't have much time, either." Petroni stopped a few steps up from Val. "I wanted to remind you that the deadline for applying for detective is 5:00 p.m. today. How close are you to completing your exam?"

Val slapped her forehead. "Dammit! I haven't started. I've been so focused on my hearing and looking for Shelby, I forgot all about it." She paused. A thought occurred to her. "Wait, can I apply while suspended?"

"I'm not a hundred percent sure," Petroni said, "but you won't be eligible if you don't try. Besides." She glanced around, as if making sure nobody was overhearing them, and lowered her voice. "I, ah, pulled a little bureaucratic fast one on Simpson. Instead of suspending you, I put you on paid admin leave. That means you're still active—and thus, in my book, eligible."

"Thank you," Val said, overcome for a moment with gratitude. Petroni could be tough and irritable, yet generous and protective in her better moments. "The question is, can I even get the damned application done in…" She checked the time on her phone. "Three and a half hours?"

"I hope so. You can file online. Head to the library and use one of their public access computers if your laptop isn't handy."

"Good idea, thank you. And…if it isn't too much to ask…can you share any tips?"

Petroni smiled and rested a gentle hand on Val's shoulder. "Yeah. Don't be modest. That was my mistake, which is why I never made detective. Talk about all the collars you've nabbed in your first eighteen months. I, ah, took the liberty of emailing some data to you from our arrest records so you won't forget any."

"Sergeant, I don't know how to thank you."

"I do." Petroni grinned. "Ace that damned thing." She climbed up the stairs and disappeared inside the large glass doors without glancing back.

So much for trying to see a doctor about her ankle.

Val limped on to the law office, where Chad and Stephanie still had no update on their motion to delay her hearing.

"We'll know by 5:00 tonight," Stephanie said. "Can you hang around that long?"

"Of course. Ah…might I borrow a computer while I'm waiting? There's this thing I need to do…"

"I'll show her the way," Chad said, and escorted Val down the marble-tiled hallway. "Stephanie set me up in a temporary office, and the desk across from me is empty. I'll set you up with all the passwords and stuff."

"Sounds like you're fitting right in here, getting comfortable," Val said. "Have you discussed your own opportunities with them yet?"

"We've started the conversation," Chad said. "It doesn't hurt that I've already brought them a client." He smiled at her.

"Right. Ah, speaking of which, how much will this cost me?"

"All taken care of," Chad said. "Don't worry about that."

"Chad, you have a family to take care of—"

"It's not me," he said.

"Then who?"

"Someone who loves you. Let's leave it at that, okay?" Chad refused to tell her anything more, and his stubbornness proved greater than hers. The face he made when she guessed Gil, though, gave it away.

That bothered her a little. Val could pay her own damned bills. She didn't need a man to cover for her.

Val set those feelings aside, though, as she had work to do and limited mental bandwidth to get it done. She logged in to the police department's "Open Opportunities" site and dove into the application with a determined fervor.

As Petroni had hinted, much of the exam focused on her experience, and the time she'd spent on the WAVE Squad served her well. Petroni's email provided names, dates, and details of the offenders she'd arrested, and in many cases, information about their convictions. The examiners would love that, she guessed. Solid detective work helped seal those guilty verdicts, and much of it was hers.

A few, like her capture of serial rapist Richard Harkins, and the arrest of her own mother and Mom's rapist husband—Sammy's father—brought back uneasy memories. Those cases spoke more to her courage and intuition than her investigative talents. Another—taking down the mayor's husband for kidnapping, mutilating, and killing five teenage girls—made her pause. Would including such a politically charged case help her chances or harm them? She couldn't leave it out, though.

Halfway through, she hit "Save Draft" and glanced at the time. Almost 3:00. Chad had excused himself an hour before to attend a meeting. It gratified her that this could turn into a real opportunity for him. Still, it killed her not to know her hearing's status. She texted Chad: *Any word?*

Soon, I hope, came his instant reply.

The next section of the exam dealt with her skills and knowledge of investigative practices. Val approached it with some trepidation, but once she got into it, she realized she knew more than she expected. She lacked forensics experience, so she hoped her academic qualifications would get her by. She'd taken some courses in college, paid attention in Police Academy, and brushed up her skills since by taking every available seminar the department offered—all on her own time, of course. That, she realized, had put some pressure on her now-strained relationship with Gil. Despite his encouragement, the effort took time away from them being together—on top of her crazy-long work hours.

No wonder he'd run off to New Haven at the drop of a hat—

Val scolded herself for that snarky thought. He'd gone to see his mentor, not his ex. He and Jessica rarely spoke and he almost never mentioned her. Gil was being dutiful, not duplicitous.

She wished she believed it as much as she wanted to.

Val finished the application a few minutes after 4:00, surprised that it took so little time. She checked it over, top to bottom, fixed a few typos and awkward wordings, then held her breath.

She hit "Send."

A "Thank you" screen confirmed that her submission had been accepted. The top scorers would be called for follow-up interviews for open positions. Val heaved a sigh of relief. Good or bad, the damned thing was done and out of her hands now.

Chad popped his head in a few minutes later. "Good news," he said. "We got the delay. Only twenty-four hours, though. Thursday at 10:00 a.m. Meet us here at 9:00 and we'll all walk over together, okay?"

"Thank you!" She wrapped him in a huge hug. "I owe you, big bro. Please extend my thanks to Stephanie, too."

"Will do."

Buoyed with fresh energy, Val hustled—as well as she could on the sore ankle—down the stairs of the law building and up the street to the parking lot. She avoided all eye contact with anyone coming or going at police headquarters and reached her car moments after the sprinkling rain turned into a downpour. She fumbled with her keys, unlocked the car, and still got soaking wet, head to toe.

Who cares? Nothing could dampen her mood. Things were turning her way. Uncle Val, an avid neighborhood poker player, always said that was the time to push in all the chips. Val didn't have a lot of chips to push into the pot, but she had a few.

She had to get to Greenville. With the hotels all closing and her cabin off-limits, though, her lodging options were limited. She might end up boondocking in the state park. Or, worst case, sleep in her car.

Either way, she needed to take a moment to prepare.

Val made it to Gil's house before the evening rush hour got too crazy and raided his garage. She filled her Honda Civic's hatchback with a sturdy tent, two sleeping bags, a cook stove, some food, a rechargeable flashlight, and a heavy raincoat. She gathered clean, warm clothing from her dresser, enough for a few days. Just in case.

Val inspected her load, considered what she might've forgotten. Something Gil would do in that moment: one last reality check.

Thinking of him made her sad. She'd much rather go on a camping trip with him than alone, would love to have his steady hand at her side, his good humor, his powerful body.

She didn't, though, and she couldn't let that stop her.

***

Val arrived back in Greenville around 6:30, famished and without a plan. She needed dinner and a place to sleep. But downtown looked like a ghost town, with "Closed due to COVID" signs hanging on every restaurant, pub, and motel on the main drag. She considered parking off the strip and knocking on doors. Although the rain stopped, the pain in her ankle flared up, and walking more than a block or two seemed unfathomable.

Driving a second lap down the main drag, she found one place still open, to her surprise: Step Out, the gay bar where she'd spotted Ambrose Cox a few nights before. She donned a mask and pushed through the door. Once again, the bar was almost empty. Two men huddled close together in a booth in back, and another man sat alone at a high-top near the front, sipping a milky-white cocktail in a tall glass. A Tom Collins, she guessed—one of Beth's favorite drinks in college.

The bartender, the same short, stocky brunette who'd helped her before, waved her over to the bar. Like Val, she wore a light-blue medical mask over her nose and mouth. "Welcome back," Angie said. "And Happy St. Patty's Day."

"Is it? I didn't notice any decorations or anything," Val said.

"Fucking COVID shut all that down." Angie grabbed a seven-ounce glass. "Light beer again? I got yellow or green."

"Red wine, and a food menu," Val said. "And a recommendation for a place to stay, if you have one."

Angie shook her head and showed Val two bottles of red—a Merlot and a red blend. Val, recalling Gil's advice to always go with the varietal, chose the Merlot. Angie filled her glass to the rim, a generous pour, and said in a glum tone, "Afraid I won't be any help with lodging. Not much with food, for that matter. The cook's out sick, so I can only offer cold sandwiches and salty snacks. I recommend the giant pretzel with stone-ground mustard. My mom says I so suck at cooking, I even make lousy PB&Js."

Val winced. Pretzels didn't pair well with Merlot. "Can you put some of that mustard and a slice of turkey on wheat bread?"

"Your funeral." Angie set Val's wine glass on a beer-soaked coaster. "Any luck finding your friend yet?"

Val frowned. "Greenville PD is looking for her, too, but after 48 hours and with everything closed, it doesn't look good. Any help would be welcome."

"If you want help, I'd steer clear of the cops in this town. Worse than useless when it comes to sticking up for queer folks. They're more likely to be responsible for her going missing in the first place. They haven't even come around to ask about her."

Val rubbed her temples. She'd expected Torres, at least, to put some effort into it.

"This other guy did, though, a day or two ago," Angie said. "Big guy, dark hair. Said he was her brother."

Val's gaze shot up to meet Angie's. "Did he give a name?"

"Dallas or some such. I remember thinking he didn't sound Texan."

"Austin?"

"That's it. He said Shelby was a dude, though. Didn't you say they were a girl?"

"What did you tell him?" Val asked.

"Same as I told you: nope. He got pissed and stormed out. Hey, I'd better go put your sandwich together. We could get shut down any minute." Angie disappeared behind a swinging door into the kitchen.

Val sipped her wine—not bad, not good—and let the television catch her eye. The news was winding down, and a perky blonde in a bright blue knee-length dress forecast a chilly night and rainy morning. Then a "local interest" story appeared on screen, part of an "ongoing segment" on police corruption. Even with the sound off, Val got the gist of it: Clayton PD had hired a Hartford officer with a record of sexual harassment. They didn't name names or show faces, but Val knew to whom they'd referenced.

How—?

Then she remembered Jalen mentioning an investigative reporter looking into allegations of Ben Peterson's misbehavior in Hartford, and the pieces all fell together. Val's gut tightened and her mind raced as to how this might play out, with her hearing coming up. Would it help her case? Or make things worse?

She opened a search window on her phone and brought up Clayton CopWatch. It was worse than she expected.

Clayton PD Leaks Smear Sex Harassment Victim

Retaliation is the Name of the Game

by Paul Peterson

If you're an experienced cop looking for a new start, don't come to Clayton. And if you do, don't blow the whistle on one of its rising stars…unless you're prepared to have your character assassinated and your career destroyed.

Clayton PD's newest transfer to the force found himself the victim of sexual assault and aggravated battery before he even clocked his first hour of duty. Yet it is he who now faces allegations of past misconduct—of the type he was victimized by less than a week ago.

Even though this new officer has no record of misconduct, and was recruited for his exemplary service and innovation while serving on the Hartford force.

Sound trumped up to you, too? And oh-so-convenient?

Why does Clayton PD continue to foster corruption by protecting its own? Particularly when, as we have often documented in this publication, the ranks of the department are rife with crooked incompetents?

Val nearly choked on her wine. Exemplary service?

Innovation? She allowed herself a snarky thought: Maybe the story wasn't about Ben, after all.

Then her phone chimed with a familiar number, and her sense of humor about it vanished.

"What the fuck?" Ben screamed at her before she could say hello. "Who the hell do you think you are, Dawes? And for Christ's sake, *how* did you even pull this off?"

"If you're talking about what your cousin is claiming–"

"Never mind Paul," Ben shot back. "It's all over the news—TV, online, everywhere. Out of nowhere, a rehashing of baseless accusations, proven false a hundred ways from Sunday, supposedly sealed. But the moment you get into a little trouble, wham! It's character assassination time. What'd you do, Dawes? Call up your old buddy Jalen, bat your eyelashes, and promise him a BJ if he comes up with some dirt? Don't worry, he'll get his, too, goddammit. You*'ll* burn for this, Dawes. Every one of you!"

"Ben, I had nothing to—"

"This is how you thank me for saving your life, huh? Well, fuck you. Next time I'll let you drown."

Val's anger spiked. "For you to accuse me of leaking this story is pure hubris on your part, Peterson. I just found out about it myself, probably after you did. For God's sake, Ben, how would I know what you did in Hartford? For you to insinuate something between Jalen Marshall and me is absolute garbage. It's beneath even you, *Benny*."

Val paused, surprised that he'd let her go on that long...and then realized he'd already hung up. Because her phone was ringing again.

"Hello?"

"Dawes? Simpson. How fucking dare you!"

Val rolled her eyes, then realized she'd wasted that expression on an unsuspecting Angie, delivering her turkey sandwich with a side of kettle chips.

"Anything else I can get you?" Angie said in a low voice.

Val shook her head. "Thank you," she mouthed. Then,

to Simpson, in a calm, polite tone: "How dare I what, Detective?"

"You know goddamn well what," Simpson said. "Even for you, Dawes, leaking confidential HR files to the press is a new low."

"I assure you I did no such thing."

"Bullshit," Simpson said. "I've got proof that you did, and I'm going to use it. Your career as a Clayton police officer is over. Hear me? *Over.* I'm going to add this to the charges against you and there's nothing you can do about it. You're going down, Dawes, and I don't mean on me."

Val ignored the crude innuendo. "Listen, Tackle Box–"

"Don't call me—"

"*Tackle Box.*" She punched it, her irritation growing. "You *don't* have proof because there isn't any. It's a fucking lie. In fact, if I were to guess, I'd finger you as the person who leaked this in order to frame me."

"Speaking of no proof!" Simpson tried to continue, but Val talked right over him.

"It doesn't matter," she said, then calmed her voice again. "Include whatever you want on Thursday. I'll be there and I'll kick your ass with whatever you want to talk about." Her voice rose when he tried to interrupt again. "You think you've got me pinned? Forget it, asshole. *You're* going down. I've got *you* and you know what? It feels good."

Val hung up, her hands shaking so hard she couldn't even pick up her sandwich. She had nothing evidence-wise on Simpson, of course. Still, it made sense to her, even though the idea came to her only in that moment. She'd find evidence to support it if she put her mind and energy behind it.

But she couldn't. She had only one thing on her agenda: find Shelby, before it was too late.

Chapter Twenty-Seven

Val choked down her sandwich, somehow every bit as disappointing as Angie promised, and washed it down with a long gulp of wine. Angie had disappeared again, so Val left enough cash to cover the bill and a 30 percent tip. Too much, maybe, but she liked the barkeep and Angie at least tried to help.

Before leaving, Val used the bar's WiFi to Google and call every motel, hotel, and bed-and-breakfast in town. None would accommodate her, all citing COVID as the reason. She'd have to sleep in her car or camp in the state park—if she slept at all. Worst case, she could drive back to Clayton and return in the morning.

The bigger problem was she had no plan, no real leads, and only about a half-hour of twilight to work with. She'd hoped she could team up with Peterson, but that option had vanished.

She would have to wing it.

Val drove to the cabin and found it empty. Just for kicks, she tried the lockbox, but someone had changed the combination already. Dammit—she hated when people didn't trust her. Even when they had good reason.

She fished the pocket-sized flashlight out of the supplies she borrowed from Gil. It flickered on, shedding a dim glow on the route to the creek. It wouldn't last more than an hour or two. With a light mist falling, she limped down the path, taking care with each step to avoid twisting her sore ankle further. She headed straight to the spot where Sammy found the brooch—also, she recalled with a grimace, where she'd fallen in the creek. There she intensified her search, hoping to find something, anything, that would show where Shelby had gone from there. She looked for footsteps in the mud, crushed underbrush, broken branches, and other dropped belongings of Shelby's.

Nothing.

After a half-hour's hunt, her ankle pain got too great, and she needed to rest. Sitting on a downed log, she concluded that this part of the search wouldn't yield anything new. She returned to the trail and continued upstream, with the rain progressing from light mist to a steady drizzle. She scanned the sides of the muddy path with the flashlight as she walked, and found nothing that would lead her to Shelby.

Until, a minute or two later, she reached the tree whose branches stretched over the wall of The Grounds. At the base of the tree, she spotted a white clamshell, its convex side facing up. In the center of the shell, someone had written a crude capital "B" on it, in what looked like a black Sharpie pen.

Shell-B. Almost matching the sticker on the back of Shelby's phone case.

Someone left her a clue! Someone who knew that she'd discovered the hole in Theo Cox's tight security. But who?

Val didn't care. All she knew was, she needed to get inside those walls.

She considered the tree trunk, a little over two feet wide at the base. Burrs and stubs of chopped-off branches jutted out every few feet up the sides. If her ankle held out, she could make the ten-foot climb.

Val flicked off the flashlight and shoved it into her coat pocket. Then she grabbed hold of one branch stub a foot over her head, and a burr on the other side. Placed her right foot on the tree's broad base, then her tender left foot against the side of the trunk, putting no weight on it. She lifted her body up a foot or so until she reached another stub, and rested all of her weight on her healthy foot, pushing herself up again. She rested her left foot on a branch, with minimal weight. Over and over, yanking her body up the tree trunk, using her arms and right leg, putting only enough pressure on her left to maintain balance.

About a foot from the top, though, the branch under her right foot snapped, and her weight fell entirely onto her arms. Instinctively, she found purchase with her left foot— and pain shot up her leg and back, nearly paralyzing her. It was all she could do not to cry out, dangling from the tree branches by her arms, her feet hanging loose in the breeze.

Val was stuck. She couldn't find an anchor spot for her healthy foot, and her left was useless. Nor could she jump down. If she landed on her left leg, she might not be able to stand. If she landed full-weight on her right leg, she might injure that one, too.

Her palms grew sweaty, and she lost her grip on the wet branch—

Val swung her body toward the tree, reached out with her legs, and wrapped them around the trunk. That took some pressure off her arms. She pulled herself up, grimacing in pain again—a burr dug into her stomach, scraping her skin through her jacket and shirt. She pushed herself up a few inches, and the burr snagged on the waistband of her jeans, halting her upward progress. Bowing her back out from the tree to clear the snag, she shimmied up, squeezing the trunk with her thighs, and grabbed hold of a branch stub on the right side. She rested for a moment, panting, hopefully not so loud as to alert anyone who might be strolling the grounds at night.

After a few moments' rest, she continued the climb until she reached the sturdy branch that extended over the wall. She sat on the branch and tested its weight. It would hold. She scooted out on her butt, inches at a time, the branch sagging lower as she went. Her feet brushed the tips of barbed metal spikes that seemed to grow like weeds out of the top of the wall. Val hadn't noticed those before. She yanked her foot upward over the spikes—too fast, throwing her off-balance. Her body tilted backward, with nothing to grab to stop her fall, and her body hurtled down toward the sharp spikes—

Val righted herself by gripping the branch on either side of her legs and realized she'd barely slipped at all, maybe a few inches. Her heart pounded and her breathing grew labored. She leaned forward to steady herself, a bit too fast, and something solid tumbled to the ground on the outside the wall.

She checked her jacket pocket. Empty. Which meant the "something solid" was her flashlight. Crap. No way was she climbing down and back up that tree. She'd have to proceed without it. Which was okay—less chance of being spotted. Worst case, she'd use the light on her smartphone. Not great, but enough.

Val's next challenge: getting down. No more tree trunk to shimmy down. The ground sloped upward from the wall, though, and the branch sagged more and more as she progressed away from the trunk of the tree. By the time she slid out as far as the branch would hold her, the limb bent enough, and the hill sloped up enough, so that the distance from the branch to the ground was only about eight feet.

Val bent her body at the waist over the branch, grabbed ahold with each hand, and eased herself down until she hung from the tree. She glanced down at her feet, kicking air a foot and a half from the forest floor. She edged her body farther out from the trunk, hand over hand, and the branch sank lower and lower until her feet dangled inches from the dirt. Then she let go, landing on her right foot.

Breathing hard, she assessed her new situation. Had she still been on duty as a cop, she'd be guilty of entering and investigating without a warrant. As a private citizen, she was trespassing. A misdemeanor.

Anyway, she wasn't here to arrest anyone, just to find Shelby.

Val's eyes adjusted to the dark, and lights appeared through the trees, more or less toward the Cox mansion, or their outbuildings. That gave her some general bearings.

The trouble was, she didn't know where she should be looking.

The companion tree they'd used to climb out of The Grounds wasn't far, and she found it by following along the wall. From there she located the path down which she'd chased Sammy. That would take her by the greenhouse. Might as well start there.

Val crept through the darkness alongside the path rather than down its center, figuring that movement along open spaces would more likely trigger some sort of alarm, or at least, a security camera. That meant slow going, and more than once she snapped twigs or rustled leaves louder than she wanted. She wondered if sounds, too, triggered the security system. If so, she was toast.

No person appeared, no alarm sounded, no lights went on to indicate she'd been spotted. She trudged on, her ankle aching more with every step.

As she approached the greenhouse, the aroma of tobacco smoke tickled her nostrils, and moments later she spotted puffs of blue swirling in the air among the trees. She ducked down and peered between the branches of some shrubs in front of her.

Then she heard an unexpected sound—a cackling laugh mixed with a raspy cough. Then a voice.

"Goddamn, girl, you think you can hide behind a shrub?" More hoarse laughter, then footsteps crunching through the leaves, followed by the imposing figure of Clay Dupree. He pointed the glowing embers of his fat cigar at her. "For fuck's sake, girlio, it's not like you made yourself invisible. But I'll give you credit. That was quite a feat, climbing over that wall like that."

Val's face burned with humiliation and she stood, facing the old gardener. "You've been watching me this whole time?"

Dupree shook his head, wiping mud from his hands onto his overalls. "Not the *whole* time. Enough." He puffed on the cigar, removed it from his mouth, and tapped the ashes off the end with his finger. "What the fuck you doing, sneaking into this place in the dark? You're liable to get yourself shot."

"I thought I was being discreet. Uh…you're not armed, are you?"

"Heh." Dupree produced a sidearm out of nowhere, an old-fashioned revolver with a six-inch barrel. "Course I'm armed. You should be too, if you think you're going any farther on this property."

Val cursed her idiocy, thinking she could get away with this. "Are you going to turn me in?"

"The fuck for?" He laughed again and took a deep drag on the stogie. "Cox don't pay me to guard the place. Just to keep it pretty. I get rid of you, the place gets a whole lot less pretty all at once."

Val allowed herself a coy smile. Unlike Theo's, Clay Dupree's flirtations seemed harmless. "Uh, thanks." A chill breeze picked up, rustling some leaves between them. "So, where do we go from here, then?"

Dupree took another long, lazy puff of the cigar, tilted his head back, and blew the smoke skyward. "A storm is coming," he said, àpropos of nothing.

"Beg pardon?" She recalled the forecast—a little rain, nothing serious.

"You might want to find shelter."

"It's on my to-do list. Among other things." Val started to walk past him, but he held out his hand to stop her.

"You still looking for that friend of yours?" Dupree put out his cigar against the heel of his shoe.

"I have no other reason to be here."

"Gotcha. Well, I got no quarrel with that."

Val breathed a sigh of relief, growing more aware of the tension bunching up in her neck and shoulders. "Great. But I'm confused...why the warning about having a gun, then?"

Dupree shot her a puzzled stare. "Girlie, it ain't me you need to be a-scared of."

"Right." Val cleared her throat. "So, who, then?"

Dupree glared at her, then shook his head. "If you don't know, you ought not to be here."

Val nodded. "Yet, here I am. So...?"

"So, be the hunter, not the hunted." He widened his eyes and gave her an exaggerated up-and-down leer. "Some men don't get enough to *eat* at home. And I ain't talking about his wife's *cooking*." He glanced over his shoulder, toward the Cox mansion.

Val shivered. She didn't need to ask who or what he meant. Theo gave her the creeps every time she encountered him.

Dupree turned and stared off into the distance, tapping his chin with a long, crooked finger, then pointed it in the general direction of the horse stables. "You reckon rocks can walk?"

"Rocks? Of course not." What a weird question.

"Or pile themselves up in an organized fashion?"

"Are you saying such things happen on The Grounds?" Val asked, puzzled.

"Something like that. Except we know they didn't organize themselves, now, did they?"

"Right. So?"

"Somebody did. I'm the groundskeeper, and I didn't do it. So doesn't that strike you as odd?"

It did strike Val as odd. Oddly coincidental, in fact.

An idea dawned. "What kind of rocks?"

Dupree laughed, this time extra hard, holding his belly with both hands. "Do I look like a fucking geologist to you?

Rocks. Flat ones, round ones, some that are kind of pretty. Does it matter?"

"It might," Val said, excitement growing. First the shell, now the rocks. "Where?"

"Thataway," Dupree said, again pointing toward the horse stables. "Go down the path. When you pass the gun shed, you'll see them." He turned and winked at her. "Don't you go getting any crazy ideas about arming yourself. No sir, I would *not* recommend you do that a-*tall.*"

With that, Dupree plunged into the woods, and disappeared into the darkness.

Chapter Twenty-Eight

Val took a moment to collect her thoughts and settle her nerves after the strange encounter with Dupree. The gardener's odd manner unnerved her almost as much as his oblique warnings about needing a gun and finding shelter from a supposed storm. He seemed like such a plain-talking man, yet he spoke in riddles. Why? Where was the danger coming from?

She shook it off. She didn't have time to solve his word puzzles. Shelby had been missing for over two days. If she'd gotten hurt, or taken by someone, her time would be running short—at best. Val needed to find her sooner rather than later.

She limped on through the trees, parallel to the path, the density of the foliage growing thinner. When she drew closer to the Cox mansion, the path curved in, and she glimpsed the dark lawn through the trunks of the trees. The mansion peeked through on one side and a clump of outbuildings appeared on the other. Val recognized the small armory and recalled the position of a security camera facing its front door. She rued her lack of a sidearm and recalled Dupree's suggestion. Did he seriously think she should break in to secure a weapon? Stealing from his own employer?

No. Not possible. Besides, the security camera would alert the Coxes to her presence. Even if they weren't hostile to her personally, all that security suggested they feared intruders. The armory suggested they wouldn't be shy about engaging in an armed response.

Still: Dupree. Shelby. Time running short. And her

injury limited her ability to use her martial arts skills in hand-to-hand combat, should the need arise.

She should at least check out the opportunity.

But how would she avoid detection?

Val considered the layout of the buildings ahead of her. The path ran along the wooded area, passing the armory and continuing on toward the stables. She recalled the positioning of the cameras—all seemed to point at the buildings containing valuables: the armory, the tool shed, and others whose purpose she hadn't identified. Surely there were gaps in their coverage.

She focused on the armory. No windows, only the door in front for access. Which meant they probably hadn't positioned cameras at the rear of the small building. She moved through the trees in that direction.

Something rustled the leaves and brush a few feet away. Val's heart stopped, and she nearly screamed—

A squirrel scrambled from the base of a tree onto the lawn and raced along the path, around the armory, and into the shadows.

She exhaled a slow breath, her pulse racing. Jesus!

Then she realized: no lights had come on, not even the tiny little LED that indicated activation of the camera. What stopped it? Was the squirrel too low to the ground, or too minor a disturbance? She peered closer at the camera through the steady drizzle and noticed something unusual, something she didn't notice before.

Mud covered the lens and the small motion sensor mounted below it.

Dupree! *That's* why his hands were muddy. She'd assumed he'd gotten them dirty working in the greenhouse.

Still, she shouldn't take foolish chances...or at least, she should only risk the less-foolish ones. She continued through the trees until she'd reached a point well behind the armory, then dropped to all fours and crab-crawled behind the building.

No lights. No alarms.

Val circled around into the dark shadows between the armory and the cluster of adjacent buildings and pressed her body against the wall. She slid toward the front of the building and peeked around.

Still nothing from the camera, or anything else suggesting she'd been spotted.

She heaved a deep breath and stepped around to the front door. She pressed the "Enter" button on the keypad. The numbers lit up, pale green, startlingly bright in the darkness. Daring her: break my code, if you can.

Val recalled Peterson's easy decoding of the cabin's lockbox and wondered if the same combination—Kayleigh's birthday—would work on this door. Kayleigh had reset that code, and Theo intended to change this one after Connor and Sammy's prank. Did he?

She pressed the combination: 3-1-8-7. After each digit, the numbers darkened and relit. After the fourth digit, the keypad remained lit, with no sign yet of success or failure.

Holding her breath, she pressed "Enter."

The lights flashed several times, then went dark. She tugged on the door. It wouldn't budge. Crap.

Val pondered a moment more. Connor figured out the code. Maybe she'd tried the wrong birthday. She recalled Connor's from her online research about the Coxes and punched in the digits: 2-9-1-0-Enter.

The keypad flashed again. This time it produced an audible *click*, and the pad shone a brighter green. Val turned the handle and gave it a yank—

The door yawned open.

Val hurried inside and pulled the door closed behind her. The pitch-dark room smelled musty, with a hint of gunpowder. She pulled out her cell phone and flicked on its flashlight, shining it on the cabinets and drawers occupying three of the tiny room's four walls. Wood-framed glass doors fronted each of the cabinets, with small keyed letterbox-style locks. Not the most secure option. Val guessed that Theo, or his father or grandfather, figured that the door lock would keep most thieves out—and no cabinet lock would stop someone who'd gotten that far.

Thieves. Val realized that taking one of these weapons made her a thief, too. At least until she returned it.

She shrugged it off and assessed the inventory. The cabinets contained revolvers, rifles, and old-time muskets. Most appeared to be antiques, perhaps centuries old, but in good condition. Someone spent hours and hours keeping them clean and, Val guessed, in perfect working order.

On the far side of the room, one cabinet contained a display of a dozen or so handguns, a mix of old and new. One drew her attention, a 9mm Beretta semiautomatic. She'd trained on one of those at the Academy. A nice weapon—smooth handling, accurate, reliable. Perfect, if she located some ammo. Probably in the drawers below.

Val jiggled the handle of the top drawer beneath the cabinet. Locked, by an even cruder cam lock. She could destroy it with ease, if necessary.

However, there was no need. She flashed her cell phone around the room and spotted a ring of keys sitting atop a shelf, out of reach for the two boys, thank God.

With a minimum of fuss, she found the right key and pulled the drawer open. Sure enough, a box of 9mm rounds sat near the front, already open. Another key unlocked the cabinet. She checked to ensure the Beretta's firing pin hadn't been removed, then loaded the 15-round magazine and engaged the safety. Satisfied, she stuffed the weapon's 5-inch barrel into the waistband of her jeans along her back and covered it with her jacket.

Armed and ready. Where to next?

***

The gaming tablet blinked a warning that it needed charging and the unit would shut down, please close all apps, blah, blah. Connor raced to complete the game, hoping Mario would reach the finish line before the battery flamed out, but no. The stupid screen went black. Game over.

Frustrated, he closed the cover and slammed the tablet down on the bed. Sometimes that would wake the battery up. He waited, counting to fifteen, opened the cover, and clicked the "On" button. Nope. Nothing.

Connor's stomach growled. He hadn't eaten since breakfast. He hadn't seen or heard from Mom since she poured him a bowl of cereal and didn't even scold him for adding a second scoop of sugar on top. She said she felt sick and wanted to take a nap. Would Connor stay in his room until she came and got him? And no sign of Dad all day. Miss Embley hadn't returned since driving off the day before, all teary-eyed. So, nobody brought him lunch or even a snack, and no lessons or TV, either.

He got out of bed for the first time in hours, since going to the bathroom around noon, and realized he should pee again, too. He washed his hands like Mom always said to do afterward and crept down the stairs.

No sound of anything, anywhere.

Connor tiptoed past Miss Embley's office and glanced in. Both computer screens showed a pretty pattern of colorful lines swirling around like fairy wands, meaning nobody had used them in a long time. If he entered the secret code, though, he could watch the security cameras to see where Mom and Dad were, and one of them might make him some dinner. Hopefully Mom. Dad's cooking sucked.

He got the code right, as always, and each screen showed four different places on the property. The left screen showed indoor shots and the right screen, outdoor. The indoor ones showed the living room, his bedroom, the kitchen, and the TV-slash-playroom. After about ten seconds they changed to show the stairs and main hallway, the dining room, the front sitting room, and his parents' wine cellar. No people in any of them. No cameras for Mom's studio or Dad's office, or their bedroom. Nuts.

The outdoor ones also changed from one place to another every ten or fifteen seconds. Most of the time, everything was dark. Then one of them showed an indoor place, a room Connor had never seen in person. He'd seen it the last time he'd sneaked a peek at these screens a week before. This time, though, it showed that Shelby lady in there, all bloody around her privates, wearing only a T-shirt that didn't hide her big titties. He stared at her almost-naked body for several seconds, not knowing why, but he couldn't look away. Even though she was hurt and he should feel bad for her.

A strange robot-type voice said something to her. Even though he couldn't make out the words, it sounded scary, and Shelby opened her eyes and cried a little. Then the image changed to show an outdoor part of The Grounds again, near the gun shed. The screen was blurry, like someone had covered the camera with a thin cloth, but then some of the blurriness kind of melted away, like someone had sprayed water on it. Thunder boomed outside, and raindrops pelted the windows out in the hallway, and Connor figured it out: the camera had gotten dirty, and the rain was washing the dirt off.

Darn it. He missed out on his chance to sneak into the gun shed again without getting caught this time.

Then something weird happened. The door to the gun shed opened. A bright light came on, and the door closed again, fast.

"What are you doing?"

The woman's voice startled Connor, and he whirled around to see Miss Embley facing him, unbuttoning a wet raincoat. She flipped the hood back to show her pretty blonde hair, also damp in front from the rain.

"N-nothing."

Miss Embley strode toward him and pressed a key on

the keyboard, darkening the screens. "You aren't allowed in here. This is private."

"Y-yes, ma'am. I just...I was hungry, and—"

"There's nothing to eat in here and you know it. Go on, get out." She grabbed him by the collar and dragged him down the hall to the kitchen, shoving him toward a stool at the counter. "I need to check on your mother," Miss Embley said. "After that, I'll come back and make you something."

"Thank you." Connor gazed down at his lap, his hands folded. Her footsteps click-clacked across the tile floor, and he remained there until she returned a few forever-minutes later.

"Your mom is still feeling ill," Miss Embley said. "I'll make us each a sandwich. Tuna fish okay?"

"With pickles," he said, still gazing at his lap.

Miss Embley made the usual noises that someone makes when they do kitchen stuff. After a moment, he asked, "Is my mom going to be okay?"

Miss Embley stood across the counter from him, pushing a plate toward him containing a sandwich and two pickles. He wanted to tell her, the pickles go *inside* the sandwich. Oh, well. Beggars can't be choosers.

"She has COVID, I think," Miss Embley said. "That's why I came back. To help take care of her, and you."

Connor nodded and glanced up at her. "I...I'm glad you're back."

"Me, too, Connor." She took a bite of her sandwich. Connor let his sit. After a long moment, she asked, "Is something wrong? Besides your mom being sick, I mean."

He thought about what he'd seen on the screen, with Shelby all bloody and almost naked. If he told her, surely Miss Embley would help Shelby out.

He tried, but he couldn't find the right words. "Can I show you?" he said.

"Okay."

Connor slid off the stool and ran back to Miss Embley's

office. He entered the password before she followed him in.

"What is it?" she asked. "No, Connor, I told you—"

He held up a finger, the Wait signal. After a few moments, Shelby came on the screen again.

Then the image of a man, from behind, tall and lean, with light-colored hair, walking toward her.

"What in the world—?" Miss Embley held a hand over her mouth. "Where is this?"

"It's a secret place," Connor said. "I've never been inside. But I can show you where it is."

"No," Miss Embley said. "Connor, I want you to go back into the kitchen and eat your sandwich. I'll get help."

"The police?"

Miss Embley shook her head. "I know who to call. Promise me you'll stay indoors until I come get you, okay?"

Connor nodded. He didn't want to go outside in the rain anyway. "Where are you going?"

"Don't you worry," she said, taking his hand and leading him toward the kitchen. "It'll all be fine."

The worried expression on her face told him that not everything was fine. And maybe it wouldn't be, even with Miss Embley's help.

Chapter Twenty-Nine

The Redeemer returned to his laboratory, as he'd nicknamed the storm cellar's main room since beginning work on reconstructing Shelby's body to an unperverted state, in a grumpy mood. The security system's frequent false alarms made him regret restoring it to full functionality that morning. Twice now he'd been forced to stop, disable the camera filming his work, and destroy the stored footage. He would not tolerate a third malfunction.

He slid a chair into the corner under the camera mounted on the ceiling. He stood on the chair and nearly fell. Stupid illness destroyed his sense of balance and made him want to vomit all the time. Steadying himself, he grabbed the camera, twisting it 180 degrees, so it pointed at the wall. For good measure, he covered the lens with three layers of electrical tape. It took all of his limited patience not to tear the damned thing off its mount and smash it underfoot.

Then he resumed his work, tapping dialog into the laptop for translation into its robotic voice.

"Have you endured enough yet?" he typed. "Are you prepared to make a statement?" He eyed the coil of rope he'd placed on the counter, begging to be tightened around Shelby's neck.

Patience. Patience!

Shelby replied in a groggy voice, "You're going to kill me anyway. Why should I agree to anything you say?"

"Consider how much pain you would prefer to endure in your last few hours," the man typed. Then he laughed and added: "Or minutes."

"And why bother with that stupid machine?" Shelby said. "There's no need to disguise your voice anymore."

"Never mind my reasons or your foolish questions," he typed, his fingers shaking with rising anger. "Repent or suffer. Those are your choices." Heat rushed to his face, and another coughing spasm overtook him.

"Huh. Sounds like you might die before I do," Shelby said. "You got the 'rona?"

The man seethed. He hated stupid, irreverent slang for such serious matters as fatal infections. "Never mind me," he typed. He walked to the sink, filled a pitcher with water, and fetched the still-damp towel from their last go at this. Careful not to slip on the wet floor, he returned to Shelby's side and yanked its head back by the hair. He draped the towel across its face and returned to the laptop, typing in the question he'd asked a hundred times that day:

"Are you a man or a woman?"

Shelby laughed, spitting into the towel. "I am, and always have been, a woman."

He picked up the pitcher, strode across the room, held Shelby's nose, and raised it over Shelby's face.

***

When the outdoor lights flashed on, Val yanked the door to the armory closed, her heart pounding, fingers shaking. Somehow the security sensor's functionality had returned—the rain, no doubt, washed enough of the mud away. She had no way out of the shed without triggering it.

She couldn't stay inside, though.

Val took deep, calming breaths. The building had no windows and only one exit. She'd have to risk it.

She eased the door open a crack. The light had shut off in the time she'd taken to calm herself and didn't come back on in response to the door's slight movement. She waited a few seconds and inched it outward again. Paused, then pushed it out another half-inch. No response from the system.

Maybe...

Val repeated her operation—wait, inch the door out a bit, wait some more—until it was ajar enough for her slender body to fit through. Then she turned sideways, her face away from the camera, and slipped out. She darted around the corner of the building, the pain in her ankle spiking from the sudden exertion. The light splashed on, no doubt recording her backside for a moment.

She hoped nobody was watching. If they were, she'd find out soon enough.

The rain intensified, pelting her with thick, icy droplets, soaking her hair in seconds. She fished a pair of bobby pins out of her pocket and clipped her bangs back out of her face, then wiped raindrops away with her shirt. What a mess.

Dupree's suggestions came to mind again: she needed shelter from the storm. Val recalled steps leading down to what looked like a storm cellar, a short trek up the path from where she stood. Worst case, she could take cover from the rain in the covered doorway. Assuming it wasn't under camera surveillance.

Val slid along the wall to the rear of the armory shed, hunched low, and crept away from the building, parallel to the path. The defunct well appeared toward the wooded area, then the storm cellar entrance loomed into view. She hurried to the stairs and prepared to hustle down when something caught her eye.

A pile of rocks, as Dupree described.

No, not a pile. An *arrangement* of rocks. All different types. Ones that Sammy and Connor would categorize as skippers, potatoes, "see-gars," and "girl rocks." All arranged in what struck Val as a peculiar pattern at first.

Some stones formed a rectangle, a frame of sorts: potatoes and "girl rocks" on the sides, skippers in a row across the top and bottom. Inside that frame, a second arrangement was more representational. An oval rock on top, like a head, with long "see-gar" stones that suggested arms and legs and torso. Two cone-shaped rocks leaned against the "torso" in a manner suggestive of a woman's breasts. Cartoonish, out-of-proportion breasts, in the way a young boy like Connor might draw a busty woman.

Like Shelby.

And the woman-shaped arrangement sat not in the center of the frame, but toward the bottom, as if lying on the floor. An inch above the top of the frame, the artist had arranged tufts of grass and a layer of dirt.

The frame resembled an underground room—a basement.

The storm cellar?

Security lights flickered on overhead, and it took a moment to find the security camera, pointing right at her face.

***

After emptying several pitchers of water on the pathetic creature's face, the man returned to the laptop. "Were you or were you not born a man, with a penis and testicles and—?"

"Fuck you. I'm a woman," Shelby said, gasping for breath through the towel.

Enough. Time to get serious.

He opened the cabinet and retrieved the large dry-cell battery, one capable of delivering a charge of 20 amps and 120 volts of power. He hauled it to the counter, his lungs burning with exertion, and he rested for a moment. Then he attached the cables onto the exposed nodes and returned to Shelby, removing the towel, and clamped the negative node to the flesh of Shelby's arm.

Back to the computer. "You're soaking wet," he typed, "and grounded to the floor. If I attach the other cable to your skin, it will deliver an electrical charge that, while not fatal, will cause you serious pain. You will become disoriented, experience muscle spasms, and suffer burns to your skin."

"So don't do it," Shelby said.

"There is one way to avoid this pain," he typed, his breathing returning to normal. "Admit that you are a man and repent of your perversions."

"And if I don't?"

He snickered and typed: "You will die a slow and painful death, instead of a quick and painless one."

A long moment passed. Shelby seemed to consider his offer.

Then, something outside made a noise, as if colliding with the door itself.

He rushed to the bedroom-slash-office, where monitors displayed live footage of the stairway leading to his storm cellar.

That fucking meddling cop, Dawes, stood huddled in his doorway.

No, not huddling. Doing something with...her bra?

The Redeemer seethed. He hadn't wanted to include her in his plans. He'd tried to throw her off his path, get her out of there. Now he had no choice.

Dawes, too, must die.

Just in case, he returned to Shelby, removed the battery and wires, and stuffed them into the cabinet.

Back in the bedroom, he opened the door to what any unsuspecting casual observer would swear was a closet, stepped into the tunnel dug decades before by C.T. Cox, and closed the door behind him.

***

The bright lights spurred Val into action. She scrambled down the steps as fast as her sore ankle would allow, out of breath by the time she reached the tiny covered area at the bottom. The pain in her ankle flared when she pushed off the final step and she stumbled into the metal door, using her forearms to break her noisy fall.

Not the most elegant of escapes.

Of course, the door was locked. Not with a combination, either: with a standard keyed deadbolt. One that would take time and effort to pick, even if she'd brought her lock-picking tools with her.

Which she hadn't. But she wore two bobby pins in her hair, which she could use to manipulate the lock's tumblers. All she needed was something to apply torque once the pins were engaged.

Her former partner, Shannon, once told her she'd used the underwire of her bra for that purpose. Val hated the idea of destroying a $50 piece of lingerie, but...

Val removed her jacket and hiked her shirt halfway up her back. She reached behind her, unclipped the brassiere, and slithered it off. She took one last look at the bra, a light blue padded number Gil always enjoyed seeing her in, and tore at the fabric with her teeth. It took some doing, but after a few minutes she separated the cup from the strap and forced the thick, white wire to poke through. Wrapping the end around her index finger, she yanked the wire free.

Overhead, someone coughed. Startled, she dropped the wire and bobby pins on the dark ground. She backed away from the door, poised to run if necessary.

Bright security lights flashed on again above her, and before she could turn to look, a man's voice said, "Freeze."

Chapter Thirty

Hands up," the male voice said. "Turn slowly to face me."

Val did as she was told and gazed up the steps. A man stood on the top step, his arms extended, pistol aimed at her. Even with his face in shadow, some features stood out: tall, slender but athletic build, a baseball cap over short brown hair. The fringes of a trim beard showed around the edges of a light blue mask that covered his nose and mouth. Raindrops dripped off his hat and windbreaker.

"Ambrose," Val said. "Put the gun down. I'm not here to hurt anyone."

"You're trespassing," Ambrose said, coughing again, "and hiding in a stairwell. Pretty suspicious, in my book."

"I agree, it looks bad," Val said. "But I promise you, I come in peace. I'm concerned for the safety of my friend."

"You think she's in the storm cellar?" Ambrose laughed. "Nobody's used that place in years. Decades, even. The only thing you'd find down there are spiders and expired canned goods."

Val considered that. Anyone with something to hide would say that. She placed one foot on the lowest step. "How about I come up there and we talk—"

"Stay put." Ambrose sneered and shook the weapon at her. "I notice you haven't flashed a badge at me, Miss Policewoman."

"I'm not on duty. I told you, I'm here to find my friend. That's all."

"What makes you think she's down there?"

Val almost volunteered her discovery of the arranged rocks, then thought better of it. That might set him off and put Connor in danger as well. "A...hunch."

"A hunch." Ambrose cocked the gun back, its nose pointing skyward, and his left hand released its supporting hold on his right. He reached into his pocket and pulled out a set of keys. "Tell you what, Miss Dawes. I'll show you what's inside. I'm sure you'll be disappointed." He tossed the keys down to her feet. "See the large brass key on that ring? It'll open that door and most others on this property."

Val lowered her arms and bent over.

"Slowly," he said, pointing the gun back at her.

"Of course." She picked up the keys and inserted the one he'd indicated into the lock. The deadbolt slid with an easy click. The same key enabled the door handle to turn.

"Before you go in there..." He held out his left hand again.

"Yes?" Val braced herself for the warning—something awful, no doubt. She turned to face him again, her hand hovering near the weapon in her waistband.

Ambrose expressed a loud breath of impatience. "My keys?"

Val sighed in relief. "Of course." She tossed them back up to him. Almost. They landed two steps down. "Sorry."

He chuckled, a nasty little laugh. "I thought you were an athlete. Go on in, I'll wait here."

"You're not going to join me?"

"Pfft. Nah. Place gives me the creeps." He waved the gun at her. "Come on, I'm getting wet."

Val opened the heavy metal door and stepped inside. The door groaned shut behind her and enclosed the room in darkness. It took a moment for her eyes to adjust. She stood in a small foyer, where people might remove their muddy shoes and hang coats on hooks. The aroma hitting her nose surprised her—more of a sweaty dampness than the mustiness of a basement or dustiness of an unused shelter.

She pulled out her cell phone and shined it into the room. She found a light switch and flicked it on.

Val was not prepared for the horror.

Shelby sat on the floor, dressed only in a soaking wet T-shirt, her midsection covered in bloody gauze. Her hair and face were also wet, as was the floor around her. Her head lolled to one side, but she glanced at Val and smiled.

"I knew you'd come," she said.

Val rushed to her side. "Shelby, what's happened to you?"

"I got a little unwanted medical attention." Shelby nodded toward her bloody bandages and glanced around. "Is Sanjit with you?"

Val fought her frustration with Sanjit at that moment. "I...wish I knew where he is."

Shelby's body sagged. "Can you untie me?"

"Of course." Val helped Shelby slide away from the wall so she could access her hands. "Crap. Zip-ties. I'm going to need to find something to cut those with."

Shelby nodded, leaned against the wall, and closed her eyes.

Val spotted a counter on the opposite wall, on which sat a laptop, a coil of rope, an empty pitcher, and some flat, shiny objects. When she drew closer, she identified one of them. A scalpel, of all things.

She used a small dry towel to pick up the scalpel so as not to leave or smudge fingerprints. "Did...he..."

Shelby opened her eyes and glanced at the knife, then nodded. "The fucking butcher neutered me. And yes, it still hurts. A lot." She closed her eyes again. Tears crept down her cheeks.

Val cursed and sliced the zip-tie from Shelby's wrists. The binding fell away to the floor, and Shelby heaved a sigh of relief.

"Let's get you out of here. I'll call an amb—"

"First…please. I'm so thirsty."

Val patted her hand and jumped up. A small fridge contained some juice boxes and a few other things Val didn't recognize. She popped the tiny red straw into the box and brought it to Shelby, who drank it dry in seconds.

"Another?"

Shelby nodded. Val started toward the fridge again.

A loud *thump* in the next room stopped Val in her tracks. It sounded like a door closing. She waited, listening. No more sounds came.

"Let's get you outside, *then* I'll call an ambulance." Val's pulse raced. Ambrose would be in there any moment. She'd have to carry Shelby, firefighter-style. She'd need both hands to open the door, so she rushed over to it—

The deadbolt was locked. With no thumb turn to unlock it from the inside—only a keyed cylinder case. With no key. They were locked in.

Except that, as somebody—probably Ambrose—had just proved, there was another way in and out, through the adjacent bedroom.

Val drew the weapon out of her waistband and returned to Shelby. She needed to lift her, which meant using her right arm—her gun hand. No way could she support her with her left. She reached around her back—

"Stop right there," said a man's voice.

Not Ambrose.

***

Val's first instinct was to turn and fire her weapon on the man. However, with her right arm supporting Shelby's near-dead weight, that wasn't possible. Not before the man—if armed—fired on them first. It also meant dropping Shelby onto the floor, which might make her bleeding worse.

Instead she grunted, loud, and kept the gun hidden from his view. "I…need to…put her down," she said, huffing and puffing a bit more than necessary.

"Slowly," the man said.

Val lowered Shelby into a sitting position against the wall. She eased the pistol to the floor, or rather onto the wet towel, behind Shelby's naked butt without it making noise—at least not as loud as the noises she was making. She turned toward the intruder.

Sure enough, the man pointed a pistol at her, standing at a can't-miss distance away near the door to the bedroom.

At first, all she saw was the gun, its black barrel seeming to span a diameter wider than her head. She'd had guns aimed at her before, but never this close.

Then she took in the man's face, and sure enough, it matched the voice she remembered.

"Theo," she said, her voice shaking. "What in the hell are you doing?"

"Put your hands on top of your head, fingers interlocked, and face the wall."

"Are you going to execute me?" Anger rose in Val's voice. "You can't bear to look me in the eye when you kill me?" If only she felt as confident as she sounded.

"Oh, I plan on looking you in the eye," Theo said. "I want to see your expression when you realize how your misguided passion for helping perverts led you to your demise. However, Miss Dawes, I don't trust you. I've done my research. You're quite the little athlete, trained in martial arts, and fearless. That's a bad combination. Now, do as I say, or this will end far faster than either of us planned." He shook the gun at her. "Three. Two—"

"Okay, okay." Val rested her hands on her head and shuffled around to face the wall, putting too much weight on her injured left ankle. She winced in pain, sucking air in between her teeth with an audible gasp.

"A bum leg, too? Well, isn't that a delightful break for me." Theo chuckled, a mirthless laugh. "Now remove your clothes—not so fast. Arms out to your side, at an angle...that's right. Now let the jacket fall to the floor."

She did. A rustling noise told her he'd snatched the coat away.

"Thanks for putting your phone in your jacket pocket. That saves me a step. Now, take off your shoes."

Val kicked off her right shoe, then bent over to untie her left. He planted his foot on her butt and pushed her. She fell hard, landing next to Shelby, her back to the wall.

"Kick it off, like the other one."

"I can't," Val said. "I sprained it a couple of days ago. It hurts like hell."

"I don't care. Do it."

Val pushed against the heel of her shoe with her right toes and cried out in pain. "I...I can't. Listen, I'm willing to do what you say, but it hurts. Can't you pull it off for me?"

"Do you think I'm stupid?" Theo kicked her foot, and pain shot up Val's leg and back. Val cried out, and her leg landed across Shelby's lap. Theo pointed the gun at Shelby. "Clearwater. Help her."

Shelby blinked up at Val, unmoving.

Theo rushed forward, slapped Val's face with the barrel of the pistol, and retreated before Val could react.

Val wiped blood from her cheek, which stung a lot more than she'd have expected. She'd develop a good-sized bruise in no time.

"Shelby," Theo said, his voice calm. "How much of a beating do you want Miss Dawes to suffer because of your intransigence?"

Tears slid down Shelby's face. Val shrugged and extended her foot to within her friend's reach. Shelby removed her shoe and set it on the floor without moving.

Val smiled at her. Good. Keep hiding the gun, Shelby.

Shelby heaved a deep breath and met Val's gaze. So much sadness there.

Something else, too, though. A fierceness, a determination that seemed to say: We're not dead yet. Somehow, we'll get out of this.

Val's spirit lifted. If Shelby could endure all this torture, Val would find a way.

"Now the pants," Theo said.

"My pants? You want a strip show?" Val sneered at him. "Who's the pervert now, Theo?"

"There's nothing perverse about a woman getting naked for a man. Remember the Garden of Eden? Everyone was naked. Now strip or I'll smack you again."

Val noted his choice of punishment: hitting rather than shooting. Interesting.

She also realized something. While in the stairwell, she'd heard noises from inside the shelter. Which meant it wasn't soundproof. Anyone outside—Ambrose, for instance—would hear any gunshots fired.

Theo would know that, too. So shooting them would be his last resort. Theo couldn't have expected her, so he probably had no real plan. Yet.

She could buy time by playing along.

"I guess I have no choice, then," Val said.

Theo nodded, his eye glued to her pubic area, his eyes gleaming.

Val stood, shot another baleful glance up at him, and unsnapped the waistband of her jeans. His focus remained riveted on her privates, but he kept the gun pointed at her chest.

Val tugged the zipper down an inch and paused.

"Stop with the delay tactics." Theo waved the weapon at her. "Unless you want me to cut the damned things off with you in them."

Val exhaled and unzipped her pants the rest of the way, put her hands on the waist as if to tug them down, and stopped.

"Yes, keep going, slowly," Theo said again. "I want to appreciate the show."

"Sicko." She pulled them down to her thighs.

"Well, look at that," Theo said. "We've got ourselves

another, ah, natural woman, eh? S'matter, don't girls believe in shaving their pubes anymore?"

Val glanced down at her underwear, too sheer to hide anything from Theo's leering gaze.

"Let me help you out with that," Theo said. "I'll get you all cleaned up. Come on, pants all the way off."

Val obeyed, and her blood went cold. Theo intended to shave her pubes before killing her. Like the sicko who killed Isaiah Dinker and Jason Larkin.

She needed to force him to make a mistake. She had only one idea: piss him off. Not a strong plan, but at the moment, it was all she had.

"What is it with you and the prepubescent look on your victims?" Val said. "A little pedophilia obsession, Mr. Perv?"

Theo's eyes widened, and he took a step, his gun arm swinging toward her. She looked for an opening to counterattack—

A loud crash from the bedroom stopped his advance. The sound of a door being smashed off its hinges.

Chapter Thirty-One

The loud crash from the next room distracted Val for one unfortunate moment.

She glanced away from Theo's advancing form, over his shoulder to what she hoped would be her salvation. Instead, she found only an empty doorway, and by the time she returned her focus to Theo, he'd slid around behind Val. He wrapped his arm around her throat and pressed her against his body with his right elbow. The cold metal pressure against her temple, the unmistakable sensation of a gun barrel, convinced her to remain still.

Moments later, a man crouched in the doorway, gun drawn. Ben Peterson, in full Clayton PD uniform.

"Drop your weapon!" Ben commanded from his crouch.

"You drop yours," Theo said in a calm voice, "or I'll blow her brains out—and then yours."

Val fought hard to keep her body from shaking. She glanced down at Ben, who glared at them over the barrel of his sidearm. *Take the shot*, she mouthed. *Do it!* She prepared to allow her weight to sag onto Theo's arm, betting that he wouldn't be able to support her or get a round off before Ben did.

After a long few seconds, Ben lowered his weapon to the floor. "Sorry, Dawes," he said. "I'm not a good enough marksman to take that shot."

Her heart sank, although she also couldn't disagree. Ben had barely passed his marksmanship tests at the Academy, while she placed second in their class.

"Push the weapon toward me," Theo said. "Easy, now."

Ben nudged the sidearm with his toe, and it slid away

from him at an angle, away from everyone. Not exactly as instructed, but it seemed to satisfy Theo.

"Hands on your head and turn around."

Ben did as ordered.

"Take three steps backward, toward me."

Ben hesitated.

"Do it!" Theo dug his pistol into Val's temple, and she yelped in pain.

Ben took a step back, stopped.

"Two more. Don't pause again or I'll kill you both."

Ben took another step back. Theo extended his arm, aimed his pistol toward Ben, and his finger twitched on the trigger—

Val shoved her body back against Theo's, bumping his gun arm to the side. She stomped her healthy ankle into his instep, and Theo cried out in pain.

Ben, taking Val's signal, dropped into a clumsy backward roll toward them. He rolled into Val's shins, and Theo's weapon fired. Dust and debris fell on them from the ceiling.

Theo shoved Val to the side, still gripping her with one hand, and clocked Ben on the skull with his pistol. Ben sprawled onto his back on the floor, spread-eagle, and his eyes fluttered shut.

Theo pushed Val down, and she landed hard on Ben's ribs. She could have sworn she heard one of them break. Ben, out cold from the blow to the head, didn't react.

Theo retreated a step and pointed the gun at Val. "I wanted to do this a different way, Dawes. Give you a chance to renounce your pervert-loving ways before you die. But time runs short." He took careful aim.

"I don't understand." Val slid off of Ben's body toward Theo. "What do I need to renounce, exactly, in order to survive this?"

"There is no surviving this." Theo lowered the pistol from his eyes an inch. "It's a matter of how you want to leave this life. On the side of the good and the righteous, or in the camp of the strange and perverted."

"What makes you think I'm either of those?" Val caught Shelby's eye. Cocked her head a bit toward her hand, which she formed into a finger-gun, hidden from Theo's view by Val's body.

Shelby, sitting behind Theo, leaned to one side and reached around her back.

"It's not up to me to determine if you're normal or perverted," Theo said. "That choice is a hundred percent yours."

"What do you want to hear?" Val said. "Tell me what I need to say."

"Tell me the truth," Theo said. "And make that decision right now. I won't put up with any more delays. You have three seconds."

"I am a heterosexual woman—"

"Two."

"And I prefer men—"

Shelby screamed, and Theo whirled toward her. At the same moment, Shelby tossed the Beretta she'd been hiding to Val, who caught it in the air by the barrel and leaped to her feet. Theo spun back around and aimed his gun at Val. Val smashed the grip of the Beretta onto Theo's wrist, knocking the weapon out of his hand. He howled, cursed, and started toward her.

"Hands up," Val said, pointing the Beretta at him. "It's over, Theo."

Theo stopped and glared at her, still rubbing his gun hand. Then he straightened and did something Val never expected.

He laughed.

"I recognize that gun," he said. "That custom silver strip along the top of the barrel gives it away. You stole it from the Armory, right?"

Val, surprised by his calm demeanor, steadied herself,

gripping the weapon two-handed. With a quick glance, she confirmed the presence of the silver stripe. "Serves you right for not securing it. What if the boys had gotten hold of these weapons?"

Theo chuckled. "Oh, they're plenty secure. Try it. Go ahead, pull the trigger. I'll wait."

Val aimed at his shoulder, a non-lethal shot. Took a breath.

Squeezed the trigger.

Nothing happened.

Actually, something happened. Theo grabbed the gun out of her hand and tossed it into the corner of the room with a noisy clatter. "You see, Miss Dawes," he said, "my son is not the first Cox boy to break into that shed." He stepped sideways, toward Ben's weapon.

Val stepped sideways too, to cut off Theo's path to Peterson's gun, and made eye contact with Shelby. Shelby glanced back, puzzled: *What now?*

Then Val realized her mistake—for the second time, she'd taken her eye off Theo. While she'd glanced away, Theo doubled back and scrambled over toward his own weapon. He reached it before Val could catch up, and he pushed her away. Landing hard on her injured left foot, Val's ankle gave out, and she crashed to her butt on the floor.

Theo pointed the pistol at her. "These are your final moments, Miss Dawes. However, I can't let you die without knowing something important about me. Do you think I'd go to such lengths to protect my son against the dangers of your perverted friends and the wild animals you set free on legal technicalities—then keep a loaded arsenal full of functioning weapons within his reach? Are you kidding me?" He shook his head. "Every one of those weapons is disabled. Completely non-functional. Collector's items, all for show." He smiled. "Have been since my father caught my brother and me in there three decades ago."

"I checked it. The firing pin was intact."

"Not intact. Present, yes—it has to be, to preserve its value. But filed down enough to prevent the weapon from firing."

"So you want me to die knowing that you're a man of principle? How noble."

His smile disappeared, replaced by an ugly snarl. He extended his arms, one hand holding the pistol, the other supporting it, and took careful aim—

His body convulsed, he screamed in pain, and he slumped to the floor, blood seeping from a wound in his back, where a scalpel lay buried to the hilt. Behind him stood Shelby, wearing only a T-shirt and bleeding from the groin, breathing hard.

"I hope that's what you wanted," Shelby said, and she fainted.

***

Val performed a quick check on Shelby's pulse and breathing, then Peterson's. Both showed strong vital signs, though Shelby was bleeding again. Theo showed no pulse, no sign of breathing. She found more clean towels and covered Shelby's seeping wounds. She caught a glimpse of Theo's hack surgery on Shelby and nearly vomited. Somehow, she held it together, and, using Peterson's radio, contacted Dispatch, who promised a rapid response.

Noticing the room's damp chill, she put her pants, jacket, and shoes back on. She found blankets, laid one on Peterson and Shelby, and again replaced Shelby's bloody towels with clean ones. Val was still tending to Shelby when a noise startled her. She turned—

Theo loomed over her, his arm raised high, blood seeping from his fist, which held the scalpel and arced down toward her. Val swung her arm to fend off the blow and rolled to the side of Theo's free hand. She got up onto all fours, but he grabbed her hair from behind and yanked, hard. A moment later he landed on top of her, slamming her body to the floor. She bucked like a mustang, and he fell on his back next to her, still gripping the bloody scalpel. With a maniacal look in his eye, he flailed at her with the knife. Again she deflected his weak attempt.

Then he slapped her with his free hand and slammed her head into the wall, dazing her. In a moment he was on his knees in front of her, choking her, pressing her face sideways against the wall. The knife's metal gleamed and slashed toward her—

A shot rang out. Red liquid splashed the wall, Val's face, and her clothes. Theo's body jolted, stiffened, and slid to the floor.

Val turned, expecting to see Peterson holding a weapon behind Theo, but Peterson remained inert on the floor. Shelby lay to her other side, a few feet away.

In the foyer, next to the open metal entry door, still in a shooter's stance, stood the last man she would ever have imagined seeing.

Chapter Thirty-Two

G il!"

Val clambered over Theo's inert form and stumbled toward the door. Gil met her partway and lifted her into his arms, smothering her in a tight hug.

"Are you all right?" he asked over and over, no matter how many times she said yes.

After what seemed like two seconds but probably lasted several minutes, Val stood back a half-step and took in the beautiful image of his face. Even with the light blue mask covering his mouth, she could tell he was smiling. "How did you find me?" she asked.

Gil chuckled. "I tried calling you all afternoon, and got no answer—"

"Dammit!" Val grabbed her phone and checked it. Sure enough, she'd missed almost a dozen calls, most of them from Gil. She'd turned on "Do Not Disturb" while filling out her detective application and never shut it back off.

"So I used the Family Tracker app to locate your cell. When I got to the cellar door, I found these." He held up Val's bobby pins and underwire. "What I'm guessing is the Val Dawes improvised lock-picking kit, all ready for me to put to good use."

Val hugged him again, hard. "You're brilliant. And you seem healthier. Are you over the COVID?"

He smiled. "Feeling a little better. But you're inhaling all of my infectiousness."

"I don't care," she said. "It's worth it right now."

Someone coughed nearby. Fearing Theo had somehow revived, Val freed herself enough from their hug to identify the source: Peterson.

"Company," Gil said, glancing around. "Lots of it, it seems. You okay, Peterson?"

Peterson rubbed the gash on his scalp and winced. His hand came away smeared in blood. He sat up and winced again. "I feel like I got hit by a truck."

"You may have a cracked rib or two," Val said. "How did you get in here, anyway?"

"A woman named Cedar Embley called Greenville Police," Ben said, his voice slow and slurred. "I was monitoring their band on my radio and was in the area—looking for you," he added with an embarrassed dip of his head. "The young Cox boy, I forget his name..."

"Connor."

"Yes, Connor. He told me how to access this place through the tunnels."

"He's a resourceful little guy." Val stepped over to Theo's body, bleeding out on the floor, and checked his pulse and breathing.

"Is he going to make it?" Gil asked.

Val shook her head. "I'm no medic, but it doesn't look good." She returned to Gil's side, recalling the turmoil she'd experienced when she shot a suspect in her rookie year on the force. "Are *you* going to be okay?"

Gil grimaced, then nodded, but wouldn't meet Val's gaze.

She knew that feeling. No matter how bad a perp was, ending their life was always a traumatic experience.

"Cox would've killed us all, Kryzinski," Peterson said. "I'll testify." He held his head in both hands, as if holding it upright. "I'm so dizzy."

"He hit you pretty hard," Val said. "Try to stay awake until the medics arrive, okay?"

Gil erupted into a coughing fit, startling her. He held up one hand to keep Val away until he got control of it, then leaned against the wall for support. "I should probably wait outside. I don't want to infect everybody."

Val nodded, and Gil trudged out the door.

"Point me toward this tunnel you used," Val said to Ben.

He pointed into the bedroom. "The door's still off the hinges. It leads into the basement of the Cox residence. Careful, it's pretty dark."

Val stopped in the bedroom near a desktop computer with dual screens. One monitor showed security camera footage of Gil sitting on the top step of the stairs leading to the storm cellar. Another showed, among other things, some folders marked *Fīat iūstitia.* "Let there be justice," she recalled from her Philosophy of Criminology class. The Latin term implied that the system had failed and vigilante justice was justified.

Double-clicking on the folder produced a list of files—including one labeled "Isaiah" and another, "Jason." Dinker and Larkin? She recognized other filenames from past sex predator cases.

Val opened the Isaiah file. Sure enough, it contained details on Dinker's arrest record, a printout of the news story about his release, a headshot, and information on his friends, family, and places he frequented. The Jason file produced similar intelligence on Larkin.

A thrill of confirmation and discovery tingled her scalp, and a chill ran down Val's back. Her would-be killer victimized a string of people who'd escaped punishment for pedophilia, sexual abuse, and related crimes. Theo, she realized, viewed himself as a brave purveyor of retribution against those who slipped through the legal system. He was, in his own mind, exacting his own justice on those whose freedom seemed, to him, unjust. Somehow he'd lumped Shelby into that same group. How?

Val spied another folder labeled *imminems periculum*—"imminent danger" in Latin, she half-remembered, half-guessed—and clicked it open. Sure enough, Shelby's picture and information showed up near the top of the file. And a comment: "Renter—keep her away from C!"

From Connor, it meant. He viewed Shelby as a threat to his son.

In response, he became a threat to Val's friend—and the community.

***

Val used her phone to light the tunnel, a musty, narrow pathway long ago blasted through stone and dirt, supported by pillars and large crossbeams, smelling of mold and clay. It disappeared into darkness after about forty feet, then curved toward a doorway. The door sat ajar, and she pushed through it to find a dank cellar containing shelves of canned fruits and vegetables, dried meats, bottled water, and a wine rack that held at least 200 expensive-looking bottles. Theo Cox had planned to live well during any storm or other threat that might have come his way.

She found a stairway up to the main floor, capped by an unlocked door opening up to the foyer where she'd first met Theo and Kayleigh Cox. Outside, sirens wailed in the distance, drawing closer.

Ambrose emerged from the adjacent sitting room. The surprise on his face could not have been more palpable.

He retreated a step and patted his jacket pocket as if searching for a weapon. "Where did you come from?" he said.

"The basement you locked me into." Val kept her voice level. "Where, by the way, I found Shelby. Alive, no thanks to you."

Ambrose's jaw dropped open. "Oh...my...God..."

Val's frustration gave way to surprise. "You're saying you didn't know?"

Ambrose shook his head. His mouth moved, but no words emerged.

"What the hell are you doing here, anyway?" Val asked.

"In the house, I mean. Theo didn't exactly invite you over to dinner every Sunday."

Ambrose heaved a loud breath. "Connor saw me outside and begged me to come in. He said something horrible was happening. I...had no idea." He paused. "How...how bad was it?"

"Torture, mutilation, attempted murder...she's lucky to be alive. As am I."

His head drooped. "My apologies for not believing you— or helping you. I feel horrible about it."

"Why the *hell* did you lock me down there, anyway?" Val said, her anger rising.

"I...I panicked, I guess," Ambrose said in a low voice. "I caught you looking in the window the other day, and I thought you'd out me to my family. My father would've disowned me—and he probably still will. Anyway, I just wanted to gain some leverage over you and buy some time. It was stupid."

"Something tells me your brother's secret is a little more humiliating to the family than yours," Val said. "Not that he'll live to tell it."

Ambrose's brows rose. "What secret?"

"At least two murders, probably more," Val said.

Ambrose staggered back a step, his eyes going wide. "What? Who?"

"Some sex offenders who went free."

Ambrose's body sagged. "Good Lord." He buried his face in his palms, his fingers pressing his eyelids shut. After a moment, he wrenched his hands free and took a deep, calming breath. "I've always wondered..."

"Wondered what?" Val's suspicions grew.

Ambrose wrapped his arms across his chest, gripping his shoulders as if for comfort. "Just...the way Theo treated me, how he talked about queer and trans people...he went on and on at times about how criminals got off on technicalities and deserved harsh justice. I didn't know he...took it this far."

"It never occurred to you to *tell* anyone?" Val asked, exasperated. How clueless could this guy be?

A heavy silence lingered for several moments. Then Ambrose shrugged. "Suspicions aren't evidence. And he was family."

Connor and Cedar Embley appeared at the top of a wide marble staircase that led to the upper floors. "Evidence of what we saw on tape, you mean?" Cedar said. "Don't worry, Officer Dawes. We have ample video footage of what Theo did." She dried the tears spilling down her cheeks with a tissue and held Connor close. "I can't believe I ever..."

"Is my dad going to prison?" Connor said.

Val took a deep, slow breath and exhaled. "I'm afraid you won't be seeing your father again," she said.

Connor hid his face in Cedar's abdomen. She tugged him back down the hall for a few steps. Then Connor tore himself away, popped his head over the rail, and called down to them.

"Auntie Val," he said. "Did...did you get my message...my secret spy code?"

Val smiled. "The pretty rocks?"

"And the skippers and potatoes...and the rest."

"I did. Thank you."

"And the shell with the B on it?"

Val couldn't help but grin. "I did."

Connor paused, glanced up at Cedar, then back at Val. He lowered his voice to a hoarse whisper, as if passing a state secret. "Did it help?"

"It did, Connor," Val said, her heart ready to burst. "Because of you, Shelby's going to be okay." A stretch, of course—Shelby was mutilated and in serious trouble. But she was alive, at least, because of Connor.

"I'm glad. She's nice. Like you." Connor saluted her and marched down the hall ahead of Cedar, disappearing from view.

"How bad is she?" Ambrose said. "I mean, from Miss Embley's description of what she saw—"

A voice rasped over a speaker in the wall. "This is Greenville Emergency Rescue," a woman's voice said. Detective Torres, Val realized. "Can someone please open the gates?"

Ambrose pushed a button next to the speaker. Moments later, a convoy of ambulances, police cars, and a fire truck filled the circle at the end of the driveway in front of the mansion.

"Don't go anywhere," Val instructed Ambrose. "They'll want a statement from you."

Then she opened the door and did what she knew best: perform the role of police officer.

***

Val wanted to spend every waking moment with Gil, but the ongoing crisis and investigation at The Grounds demanded their attention. Gil's health seemed to deteriorate with each question asked of him by the Greenville police's incident response team. Because of social distancing, he stayed six feet from his interviewers, shouting his answers in a raspy voice, and he broke into coughing fits every few minutes. Greenville PD sent several batches of officers to interview him, either to make sure he kept his story straight, or because each team feared catching COVID if they stayed too long.

Meanwhile, Val coordinated the team's efforts, even though she was both out of her district and on leave from Clayton PD. Detective Torres deferred to Val, perhaps out of respect for what she'd gone through, and because Val knew the lay of the land better. Whatever the reason, it kept Val busy She directed medics to the storm cellar to tend to Shelby and Peterson, provided key details to Martina Torres and her forensics team, consoled Kayleigh and Ambrose Cox, and even escorted the coroner to Theo's body. She kept so busy, she lost track of time—until, to her unwelcome surprise, light crept over the eastern horizon. Only then did she realize she hadn't slept—nor eaten since lunch the day before.

"Where's Gil?" Val asked Torres around 6:30 a.m. "I haven't seen him in hours."

"He fell asleep during his last debriefing with my team," Torres said. "One of our folks drove him back to Clayton a few hours ago. Poor guy, he's got the 'rona pretty bad."

Val gritted her teeth. No one thought to inform her? "You look like you have this under control here. Mind if I call it a night?"

"Sure thing," Torres said. "You've earned it. I'll call you tomorrow to follow up."

Val fought to keep her eyes open on the drive home, stopping twice for coffee and to use the bathroom. She debated whether to go to Gil's, but Gil needed his sleep and had repeated a dozen times she should stay away because of how contagious he was. And emotionally, she wasn't ready for the conversation they needed to have.

Instead, she opted for her dad's place. Neither Dad nor Sammy had gotten out of bed yet. She left Dad a note, warning him to stay away from her COVID-exposed body. Then she crept into her old sleep space in the garage, her bed still made from the last time she'd slept there, months ago. She woke up a few hours later, groggy and still dressed, her shirt covered in Theo's dried blood. What a way to start the day.

Val showered, changed, and checked her phone for messages from Gil. None. She texted him:

Feeling better?

Five minutes went by. Ten. Thirty. Finally, he responded:

I wish. Going back to bed. Maybe see you tomorrow?

At her hearing, she hoped.
Until then, she waited.

Chapter Thirty-Three

Val was never good at killing time, especially when situations she cared about remained outside her control. She cleaned her father's kitchen, which had needed a good scrubbing for months, then one of the two bathrooms. That put her over the limit of her patience with housework, so she logged in to her work email account, only to discover the department had removed her access from all her assigned casework. Through it all, Shelby's situation stayed top of mind, and it drove her crazy every time she checked her phone to find no new messages waiting.

Around late morning, she realized nobody had any reason to contact her about Shelby's condition, other than Shelby herself, who probably couldn't. She'd need to take this bull by the horns and put her detective skills to good use.

First, she called Sanjit.

"I am sorry," he said. "I don't know much. Since I am not family, the hospital would not tell me anything, other than she is still alive."

Relief washed over Val at that news. "Where've you been these past few days, anyway?" she asked. "I could've used your help up in Greenville."

"Ask your racist colleague, Detective Simpson." Uncharacteristic anger edged Sanjit's voice.

"Simpson? Why?"

"He brought me in for questioning on Monday. His goons pulled me right out of my office while I was dealing with a work crisis—and accused me of ransacking Shelby's apartment," Sanjit said. "So stupid! I practically live there."

"I told them that," Val said, chagrined. "I guess they didn't listen."

"Well, he kept me in jail, without filing charges, until late last night," Sanjit said. "Two full days! I haven't slept since I left Greenville on Sunday."

Val gritted her teeth. That explained his sudden radio silence. In light of his news, she stopped herself from lashing out at him for not returning to Greenville immediately upon hearing of Shelby's disappearance on Sunday. If only to keep communication lines open.

"I'm going to try the hospital myself," Val said. "Let's keep each other posted." She hung up without waiting for a reply.

The scene at Mercy Hospital chilled her when she arrived. A semi-truck, parked outside the emergency room entrance, sported a makeshift sign—"Mobile Morgue"— with hazmat symbols posted all over the side. Gowned, masked medical workers pushed a gurney up the ramp, and she could tell it held a body. A half-dozen gurneys, also laden with corpses, waited their turns nearby, and a team of slumped staff in scrubs puffed out clouds of steam from their masks, waiting their turn. The truck's refrigerators hummed and the entire area smelled of formaldehyde. Gil had told her of scenes like that on the news, but seeing it in person made the pandemic hit home.

Val had no better luck getting inside the hospital than Sanjit. Armed sentries posted outside the doors—also wearing masks, surgical hoods, and police-like uniforms— halted her before she got within ten feet.

"Patients and staff only," one of them said, a male of about thirty with a Hispanic accent. "Masks are required. Are you showing symptoms?"

Val flashed her police badge and ID. "I need to interview a crime victim—"

"Not here, you're not," the sentry said. "Nobody goes in

or out unless they're giving or receiving treatment. Life-or-death cases only. Which you are not."

Val heaved a deep, frustrated sigh. "I'm investigating a crime. If I don't get a statement from her—"

"No one in here is in any condition to issue any statements to the police," the other sentry said, a woman in her twenties. "They're either intubated, unconscious, or on the operating table."

"But—"

"Trust me, you don't want to go in there," the woman said. "You may not come out alive."

Val held up both hands in surrender. "Thank you for what you're doing here," she said. "You have an impossible job."

"You, too, Officer," the Hispanic man said. "Thanks for understanding."

Val slumped away, hands thrust in her pockets. The chilly air gave way to a slight mist of rain, and she shivered from the cold. She tucked her chin into her too-thin jacket and hurried toward her car.

"Miss Dawes?"

The familiar male voice came from at least ten feet away, behind her. Val spun around and spotted a dark-haired man about five-foot-ten walking toward her. The man bore a strong resemblance to Shelby in his facial features: high cheekbones, dark eyes, light copper skin, and thick brows. His build, too, resembled hers—short, broad-shouldered, his torso tapering to a slender waist. "I'm Austin Clearwater."

"Keep your distance," Val said. "Neither of us is wearing a mask. What are you doing here?"

Austin frowned and stopped about six feet away. "I might ask you the same thing, but I bet our answers are the same. I'm here to see…my sister."

Val nearly fell over in surprise. "You're acknowledging her transition now, then?"

Austin shrugged. "What choice do I have? Thanks to that animal Theo Cox, he—she—doesn't have...the parts any more to be my brother."

"How big of you to acknowledge that," Val muttered.

Austin's eyes narrowed, but his voice remained calm. "I'd like to talk."

Val drew away from him, wary. "I have nothing to say to you."

"But I have news of Shelby," he said.

Her senses reached full alert. "What news?"

"Of her condition. And...I have questions of you."

Val considered that, peering closer at his face. Desperation showed in his eyes, and she would put up with a lot to gain information—something her detective training reinforced in her. Plus, she needed some exercise, so... "How about we walk, then?"

Austin opened a compact umbrella and invited her underneath with a sweep of his hand.

"I'm fine," Val said, keeping her distance. She didn't want him any closer. She'd rather get wet than...whatever he might do.

Austin shrugged and closed the umbrella. "Fine. I don't suppose either of us will melt." He stepped closer, and Val tensed—

He walked right by her, taking slow, measured steps, making it easy for her to catch up and walk beside him, and still keep a comfortable distance. A minute later they turned on a wide, empty sidewalk that encircled the hospital grounds.

They strolled in silence to the end of the block, where he paused. "Your city," he said. "You lead."

Val took a silent right turn, continuing around the hospital, and quickened her pace. Austin kept up with ease.

"I spoke with Shelby's surgeon," he said after another minute. "That Cox guy sure did a number on hi—uh, her."

"That he did," Val said.

"The doctor expressed confidence that she'll recover," Austin said. "There was a significant amount of infection—Theo didn't concern himself with sanitizing anything. I guess because he was going to kill him, anyway."

"*Her.*" Val glared at him.

"Her. Sorry." Austin turned toward Val, still keeping up with her brisk pace. "Cut me some slack, okay? I'm a little behind the times on all this gay-trans-queer-LGBT-whatever stuff."

"Is that what you call it? 'Behind the times?' Or just altogether opposed?" Val shook her head. Too many of her fellow officers used similar excuses as cover for hating on people she loved. Officers like Simpson, for example.

Austin slowed his pace, squinting into the distance. "Okay, I admit, I struggle with it. And Shelby..." He exhaled a sharp breath. "Shelby's *family*. I love him—uh, her. Even if I don't always show it so well. And what this Cox guy did to her...nobody deserves that."

Val eyed him for a moment. He looked and sounded sincere. "I know it's hard. Still, you're taking this better than I anticipated. To be honest, I'm impressed."

Austin laughed. "Shelby must've painted a pretty ugly picture of me. No wonder you did a double take when you first saw me. You probably expected green horns and giant warts."

"I did not," Val said, but she couldn't say for sure *what* she'd expected, and she couldn't suppress a wry smile. She resumed her brisk pace, and he hustled to keep up.

"I would have, in your place," he said. "Shelby and I haven't spoken in years, and the last time we saw each other...I said some horrible things." He paused and shook his head. "That was a long time ago. Things have changed since then. *I've* changed."

"Glad to hear." Val halted and turned toward him, noticing Austin's heavy breathing and flushed face.

"Enough to accept her identity as a woman? I mean, not just accept reality, but *really* support her?"

Austin grimaced and glanced away. "I'm trying. The reason I came here was to reconcile with...*her*, before all this happened. I didn't expect all this..." He took a breath and scraped the toe of his walking shoe on the sidewalk. "That brings me to what I need to ask you."

Val crossed her arms. "I'm listening."

"There's a chance that reconstructive surgery can...give her functioning woman-parts, sometime in the future," he said. "How they do that, I can't even imagine. However, given the choice, that's what he—*she*—wants to do."

"And you support that too?"

"What I support is Shelby making the choice instead of me or my parents—who, by the way, will *never* come around on this," he said. "But I don't know if it can even happen."

"What do you mean? Why not?"

"It's ridiculously expensive, and...well, the city's health insurance will cover her care to recover from the attack, but it considers the reconstructive surgery 'elective.' Which means that part will be on her. And it's a lot."

"That's absurd!" Val said. "How could she go forward without it? It makes no sense."

"It's considered 'elective.' If Shelby wanted a prosthetic penis, *that* they'd pay for."

"Screw that," Val said, her anger flaring. "The city's going to pay. I'll see to it."

"That's what I was hoping to ask you about," Austin said, relief evident in his voice. "And I hope it's not out of line to say this...I read in the papers that you've been suspended. How can you—"

"Don't worry about that," Val said, her mind racing. "I've hired a lawyer who knows a thing or two about suing the city over HR matters. My hearing is tomorrow, and once it's done, I'll see if her firm will take this on. There's no way the city can shy away from this responsibility."

Austi smiled, and something—tears or raindrops, Val couldn't tell—ran down his cheeks. "I hope your lawyer's a good one," he said, "for your sake, and for Shelby's."

Val let that sink in, and it weighed on her shoulders like a boulder on every step of her walk back to her car.

***

The spacious meeting room in police headquarters the Internal Affairs suspension review panel chose for Val's hearing Thursday morning could have housed a Taylor Swift concert. That, Val guessed, was driven by COVID social distancing guidelines, because fewer than a dozen people occupied its chairs, spread ten or twelve feet apart. Her nervous footsteps echoed in the room's poor acoustics before she and her attorney, Stephanie Morgan, took their places at a long table. They faced a three-person panel, also spaced out across a table that could seat twenty. All wore masks, including the handful of others present: Inspectors Blanchard and Finley, Brenda Petroni, Shannon O'Reilly, Ben Peterson, and Ed Simpson.

She was relieved that Petroni and O'Reilly showed up. She hoped they'd testify on her behalf.

No sign of Gil.

Val glanced at Peterson, who glanced away when he noticed her. He fidgeted in his seat, tugged at his tie, removed his suit jacket and put it back on, his skin glistening with sweat. By contrast, Simpson appeared relaxed, a smug smile on his face, anger smoldering in his eyes.

Shannon approached Val, ignoring the six-foot social distancing rule, and rested a reassuring hand on Val's shoulder. "You got this," she whispered. Petroni sent Val a thumbs-up from a safe distance.

Again, she wished Gil were there.

The chair of the panel, Captain Reardon, a silver-haired, white male captain with leathery skin and the build of a bowling ball, opened the hearing by introducing himself and his fellow panel members. On his left sat Lieutenant Small, a balding white man who looked like he should have retired a decade before. On his right, a sleepy-eyed Black female lieutenant named Casey reminded Val of her high school biology teacher. Neither said a word, instead nodding grim-faced when Reardon introduced them.

"Officer Dawes, please stand," Reardon said.

Val did as she was told. Stephanie Morgan stood as well.

"I see you brought representation," Reardon said in a monotone. "Will Officer Dawes's counsel please identify yourself?"

"Stephanie Morgan, Captain Reardon. Attorney with Lawson, Steiner, and Meyer."

"Be seated." Reardon cleared his throat. "Miss Dawes is accused of assault, conduct unbecoming an officer, and several violations of the Clayton PD code of conduct, pertaining to events occurring on Friday, March 13, at the Blue Line Tavern. Ordinarily, we would begin the proceedings with a statement from the lead complainant, in this case Detective Simpson. However," he said, interrupting Simpson's rise out of his seat, "co-complainant Officer Benjamin Peterson requested the opportunity to address the panel first. Mister Peterson?"

Simpson jumped to his feet. "Captain, may I take a moment to consult with my colleague before—"

"I'd like to go ahead without that," Peterson said, "if it pleases the court."

"We're not a court," Reardon said with a hint of a smile, "but nothing would please me more. Sit down, Detective."

Simpson's mouth kept working, as if forming words, but no sound emerged. He slumped into his seat, his gaze fixed on Peterson, his eyes wide with wonder.

"Officer Peterson," Reardon said, "you submitted a

sworn, written statement detailing the events of the night in question. I understand you intend to amend that testimony?"

"Not exactly, Captain." Peterson folded his hands in front of his stomach, kneading his fingers until his knuckles turned white. He dropped his gaze and cleared his throat. A low murmur of voices rose and fell in the meeting room.

"I'm confused." Reardon's curled eyebrows illustrated his puzzlement with almost comical clarity. "If not that, then what?"

"I...would like to recant my entire original statement," Peterson said, his words flying out in a rush. "Officer Dawes never assaulted me, never made sexual advances, nor flirted, and in fact, never so much as spoke to me until I approached her."

Val's body filled with elation. She couldn't believe her ears.

"Officer Dawes didn't try to kiss you, grab you, or proposition you, as you claimed in your sworn statement?" Reardon asked.

"No, sir."

"I object!" Simpson flew out of his chair. The others in the room stared at each other in amazement, some mumbling surprised expressions such as "Wow!" and "Oh, my God!"

Val, breathless, couldn't manage a single word.

Reardon banged a gavel on the desk. "Detective, please refrain from interrupting," he said. "If it happens again, we will remove you from the proceedings. That goes for the rest of you as well. Are we clear?"

Simpson sank back into his chair, his face and balding head as red as hot coals. Val gave silent thanks for the social distancing rules. He might have killed someone sitting too close.

"Now, Officer Peterson," Reardon said, "since you've

withdrawn your original testimony, would you mind informing the panel as to what *did* happen?"

Peterson coughed and gathered his thoughts for a moment. "About two weeks ago, I interviewed for an open position in Clayton PD. Detective Simpson served on the interview panel. He called later the next day and said he could revive my career—which was in the toilet. He offered me the job...on one condition." Peterson shut his eyes tight and rubbed them, as if forcing back tears.

"And that condition was?" Reardon prompted.

Peterson opened his eyes and continued, his voice breaking. "That I would help him, quote, 'Get rid of that bitch Dawes,' end quote. Excuse my language, Captain."

Reardon waved it off. "How so, Officer Peterson?"

Heat rose in Val's gut and she wanted to interrupt Peterson as much as Simpson did, though for different reasons. She wanted to strangle them both.

Ben exhaled a shaky breath and straightened up, meeting Reardon's gaze. "Detective Simpson knew Dawes and I had history, dating back to the academy. I was to somehow 'set her up,' as he put it. Draw her into doing something rash, or, failing that, frame her."

"I never—" Simpson said, then stopped, withering under Reardon's angry glare.

"You agreed to this? Just for the sake of getting an entry-level job in Clayton?" Reardon said.

"If that was all, I never would've agreed to it," Peterson said. "However, he also held leverage over me. And he used it."

"Leverage, how?" Reardon asked.

Peterson sighed. "Simpson somehow knew about the terms of my termination from Hartford PD," he said. "That I'd agreed to resign in exchange for sealing those details. That I'd been...accused of sexual harassment myself." He reddened and shifted his stance. "He threatened to release it all to the press if I didn't cooperate."

"This is utter bullshit!" Simpson said. "Complete fabrication. One hundred percent false. Lies, lies, lies!"

Reardon slammed his gavel down and waved two uniformed officers forward who'd taken up positions by the door, unnoticed by Val up to this point.

"Remove Detective Simpson from this proceeding," Reardon said.

The officers each grabbed one of Simpson's arms. He shook them off and, after a series of fiery glances at Reardon, Peterson, and Val, strode out of the room.

"Is there anything else you'd like to add?" Reardon asked Peterson.

"Yes, sir." Peterson took a more confident stance, feet set at shoulder width, hands folded behind his back, head raised. "Valorie Dawes is a good cop. No, a great one. What I saw her do in Greenville reversed my opinion of her one hundred percent. Dawes is smart, brave, tough, and honest. She'll make an outstanding detective someday. Clayton should be proud to have her."

Val's jaw dropped. Stephanie Morgan smiled and gave her a thumbs-up.

"You realize," Reardon said, "your statement here today exposes you to charges of perjury and likely termination of your employment with us?"

Peterson swallowed hard, hung his head, and nodded.

"In that case," Reardon said, "and I assume my colleagues on the panel agree—this hearing is over." Both of his fellow panel members nodded. "Officer Dawes, I will direct Human Resources to reinstate you at once to full active duty. Case dismissed." He banged the gavel a final time and stood, gathering a stack of papers in front of him.

Petroni and Shannon greeted Val out in the lobby a few moments later. "Congratulations!" Petroni said. "I can't wait to have you back on the squad."

"We were all set to testify that Peterson and Simpson were lying," Shannon said, sending her an air hug from six feet away. "But Ben did it for us."

Peterson appeared beside Shannon, his expression downcast. "Dawes," he said, "I wanted to apologize for all of this. I wish I'd never agreed to any of it."

"Apology accepted," Val said, although deep down she didn't feel it. "Why did you recant, though? Why not see it through?"

"You saved my life, Valorie. I figured I owed you."

"And then some," Shannon said with an edge to her voice. "Idiot."

"Gil's the one who saved us both," Val said.

"I owe him, too," Ben said. "All the more reason to help the woman he loves."

An awkward moment of silence passed.

"I don't get one thing," Val said. "If you knew Simpson leaked the story about you, why did you accuse me of it?"

"At the time, I didn't know he leaked it," he said. "He promised to keep it quiet if I went along. But the dumb son of a bitch double-crossed me."

"No, he didn't." The booming voice of Jalen Marshall intruded from behind Val. She turned to see him approaching, hand extended for a shake. He gripped her hand tight and cast Ben a disparaging look. "The reporter I mentioned the other day called me about an hour before the story broke. Apparently she checked back with Simpson to confirm some details. Instead, he threatened her, wanting her to sit on it a little longer. She said the hell with him and went to print." Jalen shrugged. "I guess it all amounts to the same thing."

"Dawes," Ben said, "I meant what I said in there, about you being a great cop. And one more thing." He cleared his throat and glanced around, then looked Val in the eye. "You're a hell of a human being, too. Gil Kryzinski's a lucky man."

"Before you go putting wings on her," Petroni said, "remember, she tends to treat rules as merely interesting facts."

Val laughed, then glanced at Peterson. His downcast eyes and slumped posture conveyed sadness and vulnerability. He'd conspired against her, but when it counted, he did the right thing. At the creek, he saved her life. In the hearing, he saved her career…and likely destroyed his own.

"Ben?" She offered a handshake.

Peterson hesitated, then accepted it.

"Thank you," she said. "For everything. And, for what it's worth, good luck to you—in whatever you do next."

"Thanks, Dawes."

"Ben? Do me a favor?"

He cocked his head, uncertainty spreading across his face.

"Call me Val," she said. "All my friends do."

Peterson gazed at her for a long moment, then smiled. "Thanks, Val." Then he turned and walked straight out the front door of the building.

"All right then," Jalen said. "What say we all celebrate?"

Chapter Thirty-Four

Friday morning, Val sat in her car, engine off, parked behind the blue Ford Explorer in Gil's driveway. He'd texted that he felt a little better, okay for a quick visit. She'd driven straight over, then sat there for over ten minutes, enough to allow the day's cool, light mist to blanket the windshield. So many mixed emotions swirled through her mind, so many ways this conversation could go.

How did she *want* it to go?

On the one hand, Gil deserted her in Val's moment of need. Granted, neither of them knew that before he left. They did soon after, though, and how did he respond? He stayed away, comforting his ex-fiancée during *her* moment of crisis.

Every time her mind landed there, she scolded herself for it. Gil didn't stay in New Haven for Jessica. If she believed him—and he'd always been honest to a fault, so why not?—they'd barely interacted after his first day there. He stayed because he'd caught COVID, and because *he* needed to see his mentor before he died, and honor him afterward.

Then, he returned in the nick of time and saved her life. Despite being deathly ill and knowing Val was pissed at him, he put his own life on the line for her.

So, did she want to vent at him for screwing up, or thank him for stepping up when it mattered most? Stay or run?

Or both? She couldn't decide.

A knock on her window startled her out of her internal

debate. Gil waved at her and smiled, his short, dark hair glistening with tiny drops of rain, his two-day stubble peeking out from behind his mask. Val lowered the window.

"Hey there, beautiful," he said. "May I buy you a cup of coffee? I hear it's great here, if you can stand the surly waiter."

She laughed, the tension easing out of her. "I'd love one. You're not too infectious?"

"I promise to stay six feet away from you."

She raised the window and stepped out of the car. He held the front door of the house open for her and waved her inside.

Val sat on the sofa and noticed he'd already placed a steaming mug of coffee—with cream, as she liked it—on the low table in front of her. He perched in a recliner, leaning forward, less than six feet away. Oh, well.

"Before you lay into me," he said, "I need to say two things. One is that I'm feeling much better than yesterday. And two, I know I have a lot of explaining to do."

Val nodded and sipped the coffee. Delicious, of course. "Glad to hear it. Both things." She paused a moment. "But first, I want to thank you. One, for saving my life, and second, for covering my legal fees. I'll pay you back—"

Gil held up an open palm. "I didn't pay your legal fees."

Val sat back with a jolt, nearly spilling her coffee. "Well, Chad said he didn't, and that it was someone who loves me. So who, then?"

Gil smiled. "Lots of people love you. Have you asked your father?"

Val shook her head. Duh. "You're right. I didn't even consider that." She should have. Dad was the only other person in her life with the means to do something like this. She'd need to make a point of thanking him when she saw him next. Which might coincide with her asking for her old room again if this conversation didn't go well.

Gil sat back and took a deep breath. "I understand why

my going to New Haven upset you," he said. "Although I didn't see it at the time, you had every right to be jealous."

"Thank you." She sipped the coffee again. "The jealousy wasn't the worst part, Gil. I needed you here...and you were there." Her hands shook, and she set the mug back down on the coaster.

"I'm sorry." Gil ducked his head, stared at the floor, and gripped his hands together on his lap. "The whole bit with Shelby disappearing, your suspension...I didn't see any of it coming. And when you told me, I didn't do a good job of connecting with what you were saying. I got so wrapped up in my own crap, I failed to give you the priority attention you deserved."

"Don't forget the fact that Ben Peterson sexually assaulted me and accused me instead."

Gil stared at her for a few seconds, mouth open, then nodded, again ducking his head. "Yeah. And that."

Val let the silence hang for a few seconds. Did he somehow forget about that? "Gil...you remember me telling you about that, right?"

He met her gaze, worked his mouth for a moment, then shrugged. "Vaguely. I mean, yeah, the basics of it. Sorry, I should've mentioned that, too."

A sense of alarm rose inside her. "Are you saying you *don't* remember the details about that?"

Gil cocked his head, as if considering the question. "If you needed me to repeat them back to you...I couldn't, no."

Val's heart rate doubled. "Gil. Those were some pretty important details."

"The old, pre-COVID me never would have forgotten," Gil said. "So...I guess now is the time to fill you in on how sick I got."

"I'm listening." Val picked up her mug and sipped her coffee again, mostly to keep herself occupied while he gathered his thoughts.

"Doctors say that COVID not only clogs up your lungs

and drains you of energy," he said. "In many cases, like mine apparently, it also affects the brain."

"How so?" Val's concern blossomed into all-out worry.

"I wasn't thinking straight these last several days," he said. "I forget things. Not just the details around the Peterson assault. Bigger things. I woke up each morning not knowing where I was. Monday I was convinced I needed to go visit Hank before he died."

"He died two days before," Val said. "Which you told me on Sunday."

"Exactly. I almost drove off the road on Monday going to visit him, and all I can say is, I lost track of what I was doing. I told myself it's because I wasn't sleeping right, but...I don't know."

"But you had the clarity of mind to find those articles about Simpson interfering with his niece."

"A *moment* of clarity," he said. "It comes and goes. Or came and went, I guess."

Val pondered that for a moment. "So when you said you couldn't drive back when I asked you to, you weren't blowing smoke."

Gil shot her a puzzled glance. "When did you ask me to do that?"

She sighed. "Sunday night. You don't remember?"

He gave her a long stare and shook his head. "I kept thinking I was going to die, that I wouldn't be able to take another breath, that someone would come break into my hotel room and strangle me. All kinds of weird thoughts," he said. "And, I know you don't want to hear her name, but Jessica called to check in on me on Monday and I about tore her head off. I mean, I *was* pretty fed up with her by then, but even so, I overreacted. Bad."

"Fed up how?" Val said. "I thought you barely saw her."

"That's what makes it even worse. I believed in my heart that she'd been pestering me all weekend, texting and calling and making demands on my time. In reality, we hadn't spoken in two days." He held up his phone. "I checked. No calls, no texts. Yet on Monday, the sound of her voice made my skin crawl."

Val finished her coffee and set her mug down. "That's not like you, Gil. Even people you hate, you put up with them far better than anyone else I know."

Gil shrugged. "None of this excuses my behavior, but I hope it helps you understand. Hell, I hope it helps *me* understand."

"It helps, Gil. Though it still hurts."

He nodded again, hung his head.

"And then you came to my rescue," she said. "How did that happen?"

"Two things," he said. "First, on Tuesday morning, Hank's brother called me. He said Hank left me a big inheritance in his will...on one condition." He blew out a noisy breath. "I needed to...reconcile with Jessica."

"Reconcile?" Val folded her hands to stop them from shaking. "As in, what? Get back together?"

Gil nodded. "And..."

The blood drained from Val's face. "Marry her?"

He nodded again. "Even in my addled state, I didn't want that. The entire conversation shook me to my core."

"So you told him no?"

"In so many words," Gil said. "Then, Jalen read me the riot act for not keeping him posted about Hank. I told him about the will, and he advised me to run for the hills—and made me realize I'd been behaving like an idiot. Especially toward you."

Val's insides grew all warm and squishy. "I like Jalen."

"Yeah, me too," Gil said, grinning.

"So," Val said, "I can't imagine what the second thing was."

"The second thing," he said, "was your brother Chad calling to tell me you'd disappeared, too. He said you'd left his law office Tuesday afternoon without saying goodbye and he wasn't able to reach you. That worried me. I tracked you to Greenville and started driving."

"Sounds like you got a lot more alert and clear-headed," Val said.

Gil leaned forward. "Val, thinking about you in danger cleared my head like no drug ever could. I confess, my imagination went pretty wild about what kind of trouble you might be in, though not as wild as you actually were."

Val chuckled. "If you'd known—"

"Wild horses," he said, "couldn't have kept me away."

She glanced around. "Well…I don't see any horses here."

He grinned. "Yeah, well, you don't want to catch this. Hell, you're probably too close—"

Val stood, stepped over the coffee table, and sat in his lap. She pulled off her mask, then his, gazed into his eyes, and planted a hungry kiss on his lips. After a moment, he responded, his arms wrapped tight around her, their tongues intertwined with lustful abandon.

"If you get sick—"

"You'll rescue me," she said, and kissed him again.

***

Val returned to work the following Monday, while Gil remained home. Though he'd recovered from COVID, Theo's shooting sent him straight to administrative leave, pending the mandatory Internal Affairs investigation.

Val did receive some good news: Grimes returned to work the same day, and they busied themselves following leads on new and cold cases that piled up in their absence.

On Wednesday, an email popped up in Val's inbox. From Human Resources. Subject: *Detective Exam Results.*

She hovered the mouse over the link to open the message, her fingers twitching with nervousness.

"Come on, open it," Grimes said over her shoulder.

"When did you get there?" she asked, grateful for a moment's distraction.

"Just read the damned thing," he said. "You're killing me."

"Wait for me!" Shannon said, and she stood behind Val's other shoulder.

Val held her breath and double-clicked on the message.

Congratulations! Your score on the exam is 92 *out of* 100 *possible points.*
Your rank is 2 *out of* 19 *applicants.*

"Holy smokes!" Grimes said. "Congratulations!"

"That's wonderful, Val," Shannon said. "You're a shoo-in to get a promotion as soon as a second slot opens up."

"That might take years," Val said, groaning.

"Maybe not," Petroni said, appearing out of nowhere. "Didn't you hear? Simpson got fired. And not Ben-Peterson-resign-or-else, either. He's terminated, with prejudice."

"Good riddance to bad rubbish," Shannon said.

Petroni's desk phone rang. "Hold that thought," she said. "I might know who's calling."

Val froze in her chair, too excited to move. Then she spotted Damari Price scowling at his computer screen. She caught Shannon's and Grimes's attention, and the three of them slid over to Damari's desk.

Price glanced up at them, then back to his screen. "Yeah, congrats, Dawes," he said, disappointment dragging on his voice. "You'll be a great detective. It'll suck to lose you from the team."

That hit Val like a punch in the gut. She hadn't connected making detective and leaving WAVE, although of course that made sense. She'd start at the bottom of the pecking order again and work her way up to a plum assignment like this one.

"How'd you do on the exam, D?" Grimes said. "Are you the one that beat out Dawes here?"

Price shook his head. "Fourteenth. Nowhere near the

hiring bubble."

"That's ridiculous," Val said. "You'd make a hell of a detective. Maybe they reversed our scores somehow."

Price shot her a sour smile and chuckled. "Nice of you to say, Val," he said. "I'm sure they got it right. At least in your case."

Petroni emerged from her office, beaming. "That was the Chief," she said, "with not just good news. *Great* news."

"Twelve more detectives hit the lottery and are retiring?" Grimes said with a grin.

"Not quite *that* good," Petroni said, "but close. Since the folks upstairs had assigned Simpson to WAVE, that means that his open slot is ours, too." Still beaming, she turned to Val. "Officer Dawes, I'm pleased to offer you the now-open detective position on the WAVE Squad."

Val gasped. "Just like that? No interview or anything?"

"According to HR rules," Petroni said, "I can choose any of the top three scorers on the exam with no further process. So, how'd you like to become the youngest person ever to make detective in Clayton PD history?"

Val's heart swelled. "Sergeant," she said, "I'd be delighted."

"Drinks are on Dawes!" Grimes announced, laughing. "Five o'clock at the Blue Line?"

Val held up one hand. "Drinks on me, sure," she said. "But not there. Anywhere but there."

From The Author

Thank you for reading *The Injustice of Valor.* I hope you enjoyed reading it as much as I enjoyed writing it.

If you would like to help out an independent author and your loved ones at the same time, please let others know by providing some feedback.

Email me at gary@garycorbinwriting.com, or maybe jot down a few notes on your favorite retail site, Goodreads, Storygraph, or social media.

Here are some ideas to prompt your review:

What first attracted you to this book?

What was your favorite part of the story?

What was your least favorite part?

What drew you in and made you keep reading?

What did you like or dislike about the main character? Or the villain?

What other books or authors does one this remind you of?

I would / would not recommend this book to a friend because...

And please, tell your friends!

ACKNOWLEDGMENTS

A common misconception is that authors are loners, locking themselves away from the world while they try to pound keyboards into elegant words and ideas onto pages. But the truth is, it takes a community to bring a novel to fruition. It's a project, and much of the time, the author is more of a project manager than an artist.

When I first started this series, my mom and dad helped in an infinite number of ways. Not least was my father, who pitched the original idea to me for what became the first book of this series, *A Woman of Valor*—and actually helped me write it. They read the first, very rough draft, and I think Mom still has it. They both drove me around Hartford on one of my infrequent visits home so I could revisit their old haunts. That exploration led to the creation of Clayton, Connecticut, and the neighborhoods in which the action of this novel occurs. From my earliest days, they awakened in me a love of books and reading, and always encouraged my writing.

My sister, Patsy Silk, helped me finish all nine of my first novels, volunteering to proofread the final copy and giving me suggestions for improvement. Unfortunately we lost Patsy to cancer in 2023. I miss her in so many ways, especially as I tried to bring this book to completion. If you caught mistakes in the text, it's because I'm not as good at catching them as my dear departed sis.

Several members of the Hartford Police Department assisted me in my background research for this book, and helped ground this fictional story in reality. In particular, Detective Buyak and Officers Mulroy, Kent, and King gave generously of their time, expertise, and personal perspectives, and I thank you all. The Valorie Dawes novels would not have happened without you.

Special thanks go out to my critique group partners—Erick Mertz, Laura Mahaffey, and Carol Burrows—whose scene-by-scene critiques improved this story word by word.

Thanks also to my Beta Readers—Danielle Faucheux, Erick Mertz, Lorelei Kennedy, and Sarah Coates—who gave me invaluable late-in-the-game feedback. In particular, Danielle's perspective as a young woman of Val's demographic helps me keep her real, and her literary insights are second to none.

No writer can survive without a great editor. The keen eyes of Laura Lee Bennett caught many errors long after my own eyes glazed over. Any errors that remain are 100% my fault.

I can never give kudos enough to Steven Novak, whose creativity and patience with me once again yielded an amazing cover design.

But most of all, thanks to Renée, the love of my life. I've lost count of how many times she's endured—and answered— my random questions about "What if I did X in my next book?" Always, her answers give me insight on what strategy to follow. But most important, Renée's kindness, patience, humor, and beauty light up the darkest night and brighten the sunniest day. After 16 years together, we tied the knot in 2024, but every day feels fresh and new. Renée, your support makes all of this possible. Without you, I'd be lost. I love you.

Book Group Discussion Questions

Characters

1. What do you think of Valorie? What terms would you use to describe her?

2. Do you think you would like Val if you met her in person?

3. Which of the other police officers did you like? Which did you dislike? In each case, why?

4. What do you think happens to Val and Gil and their relationship after the end of the story?

5. Do you think that the author—a middle-aged white male—portrayed Val, a young woman who struggles with her memories of abuse by older men—authentically and sympathetically?

Scenes and plot

6. Which scene or scenes stood out to you? Why?

7. Were you satisfied with the conclusion of the story? How would you describe the state of Val's personal development at the end of the book?

Personal connection

8. For the most part, what emotion(s) did the story evoke in you as a reader?

9. Did you identify with Valorie? Any other character? How did that affect your enjoyment of the book?

Writing

10. *The Injustice of Valor* crosses genres, blending elements of literary fiction and romance with the plot-driven aspects of police procedurals and crime novels. Did this work for you, as a reader?

11. If you could change something about the book, what would it be and why?

12. Describe what you liked or disliked about the writing style.

General

13. Name your favorite thing overall about the book, and your least favorite.

14. At what point in the book did you decide if you liked it or not? What helped make this decision?

15. If someone asks you what this book is about, how would you answer them?

About The Author

Gary Corbin is a novelist and playwright in Camas, WA, a suburb of Portland, OR. In addition to eleven published novels, his creative and journalistic work has been published in *BrainstormNW*, the *Portland Tribune*, The *Oregonian*, and *Global Envision*, among others. His plays have enjoyed critical acclaim and have been produced on many Portland-area stages.

Gary is a member of the Willamette Writers Group, Nine Bridges Writers, the Northwest Editors Guild, PDX Playwrights, and the Bar Noir Writers Workshop. He also participates in workshops and conferences in the Portland and Oregon North Coast areas.

A homebrewer and home coffee roaster, Gary is a member of the Oregon Brew Crew and a BJCP National Beer Judge. He loves to ski, cook, and root for his beloved Patriots, LSU Bengal Tigers, and Red Sox. And when that's not enough, he escapes to the Oregon coast with his sweetheart.

Connect with Gary Corbin

Keep up to date with the latest at
http://www.garycorbinwriting.com

Follow me on BlueSky:

@portermaker.bluesky.social

Follow me on Facebook:
https://www.facebook.com/garycorbinwriting

Follow my Amazon Author Page (and review this book!)
http://smarturl.it/GaryCorbinAuthor

Favorite me at Smashwords:
https://www.smashwords.com/profile/view/GaryCorbin

Also by Gary Corbin

Valorie Dawes Thrillers

A Woman of Valor

The book that started the Valorie Dawes Thrillers series!

In this exciting, character-driven police procedural, rookie policewoman Valorie Dawes has a mission: take serial child molesters like Richard Harkins off the streets of her small hometown of Clayton, CT—for good.

But Valorie's past includes childhood abuse trauma of her own, and her battle with this cunning, vicious criminal awakens memories and emotions she'd rather forget.

Battling sexism within the department and vilification in the media as a reckless incompetent, Val finds few allies in the pursuit of this elusive, cruel criminal, even as he continues to victimize women and girls in the community.

In Search of Valor

*The action-packed prequel to **A Woman of Valor***

Valorie Dawes fights an international kidnapping syndicate on behalf of a new college friend—and harbors serious doubts about her future as a police officer.

Anxious to prove herself worthy as a cop and a friend, Val puts her own life on the line, and discovers the kidnappers will stop at nothing to get rid of obstacles like her.

A Better Part of Valor

While jogging off duty along the riverfront, Val discovers the dead body of a teenage girl—and ignites a manhunt for a serial killer.

The Shoeless Schoolgirl Slayer has remained a step ahead of the Clayton, CT police for months. All of his victims drowned. All were found barefoot. And all bear the same strange, fresh tattoo.

Following her intuition, Val discovers clues that convince her she's closing in. But is she? Or is the clever and elusive Slayer laying a trap to make Val the next victim?

Mother of Valor

Val must stop an imminent violent attack by a ruthless, cunning extremist group. Standing in her way is the sudden return of a person she barely knows: her mother.

Val uncovers a national sex trafficking ring operating out of Clayton, one with ties to a violent shadowy right-wing splinter group. Her investigation reveals the group is planning a violent attack in a matter of days.

Then her estranged mother, who left without a trace a decade before, reappears on the scene, with a nine-year-old brother Val never knew she had.

As the violence draws near, Val tries to safeguard her family, leading to shocking discoveries about why her mother returned—and why she left in the first place.

Under the Banner of Valor

When a fanatical sniper takes aim at women entering family planning clinics, Val risks everything to protect her closest friend.

Valorie Dawes and the WAVE Squad get called into action after Clayton's family planning clinics receive ominous threats: Close the clinics, or else.

Val takes this threat personally, as her closest friend since childhood, Beth, discloses that she's pregnant and is considering an abortion.

Can Val support her friend and keep her safe from the armed madman? Or will Beth's stubborn recklessness thrust her into harm's way?

Valorie Dawes Thrillers are available in hardcover, paperback, audiobook, and eBook formats at garycorbinwriting.com, and at your favorite local retailers.

Lying Injustice Thrillers

Lying in Judgment

A man serves on the jury trying a man for the murder that he committed!

Peter Robertson, 33, discovers his wife is cheating on him. Following her suspected boyfriend one night, he erupts into a rage, beats him and leaves him to die...or so he thought. Soon he discovers that he has killed the wrong man—a perfect stranger.

Six months later, impaneled on a jury, he realizes that the murder being tried is the one he committed.

Lying in Vengeance

Peter's worst nightmare comes to fruition: Christine, his beautiful and charming fellow juror, knows his dark secret and uses it to blackmail him.

The price of her secrecy: Peter must kill again, this time to stop Kyle, the man who torments Christine and threatens her very existence.

Lying Injustice Thrillers *are available in hardcover, paperback, audiobook, and eBook formats at garycorbinwriting.com, and at your favorite local retailers.*

The Mountain Man Mysteries

The Mountain Man's Dog

In the small town of Clarkesville, in the heart of the Oregon Cascade Mountains, Lehigh Carter, a humble forester, stumbles into the complex world of crooked cops and power-hungry politicians...all because he rescues a stray, injured dog on the highway.

The Mountain Man's Bride

In this thrilling sequel to *The Mountain Man's Dog*, Lehigh's wedding plans get put on hold when the authorities arrest Stacy for the murder of popular acting Sheriff Jared Barkley. Mounting evidence of a secret affair causes Lehigh to wonder how innocent Stacy really is.

The Mountain Man's Badge

Appointed to fill out the unexpired term of disgraced sheriff Buck Summers, Lehigh battles the mistrust of the community's powerful elected elites, the sheriff's department he leads, and his own wife—until he finds shocking evidence of who really killed Everett Downey.

*All **Mountain Man Mysteries** are available in hardcover, paperback, and eBook formats at garycorbinwriting.com, and at your favorite local retailers.*